PRAISE FOR *TUNNEL VISION*
AND SARA PARETSKY'S
V. I. WARSHAWSKI

"EXCEPTIONAL . . . Paretsky's writing is as strong as ever."   —*Detroit Free Press*

"COMPLEX, SATISFYING . . . Paretsky's V.I. is a rare literary entity, a woman quick to anger and action, yet sympathetic and credible."   —*Publishers Weekly*

"V. I. Warshawski remains an appealing character, a soft-boiled detective who ages with time, who bruises when punched and who still misses her mother . . . best of all, she gets mad when pushed around or patronized, and goes to work determined to get even." —*The New York Times*

"ARTICULATE AND INDEPENDENT . . . Warshawski never wears thin."   —*San Francisco Chronicle*

Please turn the page for more extraordinary acclaim. . . .

Also by Sara Paretsky

TUNNEL VISION

□

SARA PARETSKY

A DELL BOOK

Published by
Dell Publishing
a division of
Bantam Doubleday Dell Publishing Group, Inc.
1540 Broadway
New York, New York 10036

ISBN: 0-440-21752-0

Reprinted by arrangement with Delacorte Press

Printed in the United States of America

Published simultaneously in Canada

June 1995

18   17   16   15   14   13   12   11

OPM

ACKNOWLEDGMENTS

As always, my work benefitted from the advice of experts. Egidio Berni first suggested the germ of what became this book by describing the events in Chapter Thirty-nine. Dave Sullivan and Bill Boardman were most helpful in providing information about great and small details of the contracting business in Chicago, including Wage and Hour Reports. Allan Fenske told me how to circumvent a phone-linked alarm system.

Although I try to do careful research, especially for physical sites that actually exist, I was never allowed access to the location described in Chapters Forty-two and Forty-three. Those scenes therefore are based partly on photographs—provided by Mary Lynn Dietsche—but chiefly on my own imagination.

Jeri Linas, the director of Rainbow House, was most generous in letting me tour this Chicago shelter for battered women. Anne Parry, on the Rainbow House staff, sought me out to offer me information, and made the necessary connections. Arcadia House is totally fictitious, and does not resemble Rainbow House in any way, except as it is a battered women's shelter.

Some people keep coming back with more help: Sue

Riter provided advice on the treatment of Jessie Hawkings; Marilyn Martin on what happens to people declared not guilty by reason of insanity; Jay Topkis again provided technical assistance. The Mad Go Player gave me tips on hacking. Professor Wright and Dr. Cardhu gave their usual —but extraordinary—support.

I owe a special thanks to the men and women who created a most wonderful space for me to work in. The Bauer-Latoza Studio provided the design. Firehouse Construction worked on it as carefully as though it had been their own home. Thanks to: Al, Bill and Bill, Bob, Carlos, Carm, Daniel, Dave, Doug, Fausto, Gerardo, Gino, Greg, Hannah, Joanne, John and John, and Paula. Thanks also to the Withers, Charlie, senior, Charlie, junior, and John. Gerardo, may light eternal shine upon you.

V. I. is a character who ages with time and who is located in historical time. The books detailing her adventures usually take place in the year I write them. For specific historical reasons, which will become clear in the course of the story, *Tunnel Vision* is set in April of 1992.

Except for the historical events described, this is a work of fiction, and no attempt should be made to connect any character in this novel with any real people, whether living or dead. Illinois has no Republican senators. For that reason Alec Gantner, the United States senator in this story, was made a Republican. This should not be construed as a belief that Republicans are more venal than Democrats—or vice versa.

Finally, as Cervantes—more or less—said: Idle reader, you can believe without any oath of mine that I wish this book, as the child of my brain, to be the most beautiful, the liveliest and the cleverest imaginable. But I have been unable to transgress the order of nature, by which like gives birth to like. It may happen that a mother has an ill-favored child, and that her love for it so blinds her eyes that she cannot see its faults, but takes them rather for talents and beauties. But I, though V. I. Warshawski's mother, will not drift with the current of custom, nor implore you, almost with tears in my eyes, dearest reader, to pardon or ignore the faults you see in this child of mine.

CONTENTS

□ 1
Power Failure

When the power went I was finishing a ten-page report. My office turned black; the computer groaned to a halt. Helpless, I watched my words fade to a ghostly outline that glowed on the screen before vanishing, like the mocking grin of a Cheshire cat.

I cursed myself and the building owners impartially. If I'd stuck with my mother's old Olivetti instead of going electronic I could have finished my work by candlelight and left. But if the Culpepper brothers weren't scuttling the Pulteney Building the power wouldn't have gone off.

I'd had my office there for ten years, so long I'd come to overlook its litany of ills. Decades of grime obscured the bas-reliefs on the brass doors and filled in missing chips in the lobby's marble floor; great chunks of plaster were missing from the cornices in the upper floors; three ladies' rooms served the whole building, and the toilets backed up more often than they worked. For that matter, I'd just about memorized the design on the elevator panels during the hours I'd been stuck in it.

All these evils were made palatable by the Pulteney's low rents. I should have realized long since that the Culpepper boys were waiting for the wave of Loop redevelopment to wash this far south, waiting for the day when the building would be worth more dead than alive. The dickering we did every fall, in which I walked away triumphant without a rent hike and they left without agreeing to put in new plumbing or wiring, should have been a warning to a detective like me who specializes in fraud, arson, and commercial misbehavior. But as with many of my clients, cash flow was too insistent a problem for me to look beyond relief from my immediate woes.

The building had already been one-third empty when the Culpeppers handed out their notice at New Year's. They tried first to bribe, then to force, the rest of us into leaving. Some did, but tenants who could take the Pulteney couldn't easily afford new space. Hard times were pushing everyone who operates in the margins right off the page. As a private eye in a solo practice, I felt the pinch as much as anyone. Along with a hatmaker, a dealer in oriental health and beauty aids, someone who might have been a bookie, an addressing firm, and a few others, I was sticking it out to the bitter end.

I picked up my flashlight and moved with the speed of much practice through the dark hall to the stairwell. The report I'd been writing had to be in Darraugh Graham's hands by eight tomorrow. If I could find a faulty wire or blown fuse fast enough, I could pull in enough material from my data files to reconstruct the essentials. Otherwise I'd have to start from the beginning on the Olivetti.

I undid the locks on the stairwell door but left them open against my return. With Tom Czarnik gone I'd put padlocks on the doors that all worked to the same key. Czarnik, who'd been the super—alleged super—during my tenure in the building, had done nothing for the last two years but deliver angry tirades against the tenants, so it was no hardship to manage without him. In fact it had dawned on me lately that the Culpeppers probably paid him to speed the Pulteney's disintegration.

The brothers were certainly doing what they could to drive our feeble group out ahead of schedule. They'd halted any pretense of maintenance immediately. Next they tried turning off the utilities; a court order restored electricity and water. Now it was just their negligence and sabotage against our wits—mostly, it must be confessed, mine. While the other tenants had signed on to the emergency petition to restore power, none of them ever came below stairs with me to mess with the wiring and plumbing.

Today overconfidence did me in. I was so used to the basement stairs that I didn't shine a light on my feet. I tripped on a loose piece of plaster. As I flailed to regain my balance I dropped the flash. I could hear the glass shatter as it bounced off the steps.

I took a breath. Was Darraugh Graham's wrath worth worrying about at this point? Wouldn't it make sense to go home, get a new flash, and deal with the power in the morning? Besides, I wanted to get to a meeting of the board I sit on for a battered women's shelter.

Trouble was, Darraugh's fee was going toward my deposit for a new office. If I didn't deliver on time, there was nothing to keep him coming back to me—he worked with a number of investigative firms, most of them twenty times my size.

I moved crablike down the stairs. I had a work light and a toolbox stowed by the electrical box on the far wall. If I could get there without breaking my neck on the intervening rubble I'd be okay. My real fear was the rats: they knew the place belonged to them now. When I shone my flash on them they would saunter slowly from the circle of light, flipping their tails with oily insolence, but making no effort to silence their scrabbling while I worked.

I was fumbling in the dark for an outlet, trying not to feel whiskers in every piece of dangling wire, when I realized a sound I was hearing came from human, not rodent, lips. I froze. The hair stood up on my arms. Had the Culpeppers hired thugs to frighten me into leaving? Or were these thieves, thinking the building vacant, come to strip copper and other valuables from the walls?

I knelt slowly in the dark and shifted to my right, where a packing case filled with wood scraps would give me cover. I strained to listen. There was more than one person in the room. One of them sounded on the verge of an asthmatic attack. They were as scared as I was. That didn't cheer me: a frightened burglar may behave more violently than one who feels he's in charge of the situation.

I moved farther to my right, where some discarded pipes might provide a weapon. One of the intruders whimpered and was instantly silenced. The noise startled me into banging into the stack of pipes; they clattered around me like a steel band. It didn't matter: that brief cry had come from a small child. I backtracked to my work light, found the plug, and switched on the bulb.

Even after my eyes had adjusted to the light it took some time to find the source of the cry. I poked cautiously among crates and old office furniture. I peered into the elevator shaft and looked underneath the stairwell. I was beginning to wonder if I'd imagined it when the muffled cry came again.

A woman was crouched behind the boiler. Three children huddled next to her. The youngest was shaking almost soundlessly, its face buried in her leg, an occasional squeak emerging when it shuddered too violently. The biggest, who couldn't have been more than nine or ten, was letting out asthmatic whoops, in earnest now that their terrors had come true: discovery by someone with power.

If it hadn't been for the asthma and the whimpering I could have passed them a dozen times in the dim light without noticing them. They were dressed in layers of sweaters and jackets that turned their emaciated bodies into heaps of rags.

"This damp air down here can't be too good for your son." It was so feeble a comment, I felt a fool as soon as the words were out.

The woman stared at me dumbly. In the dim light I couldn't tell what part of the soup of anger and fear was boiling closer to the surface.

"Ain't a boy." The middle child spoke, in such a soft

gabble I could barely make out the words. "That Jessie. She a girl. I the only boy."

"Well, maybe we should get Jessie up where she can breathe some dry air. What's your name, honey?"

"Don't talk to her. Ain't I told you, don't talk to no one unless you hear me *say* 'talk'?" The woman shook the boy hard and he subsided against her with a thin halfhearted wail.

The shadows cast by the boiler turned her face and hair gray. She couldn't have been very old, maybe not even thirty, but if I'd passed her on the street without her children I would have taken her for seventy.

"How long have you been living down here?"

She gave me a hard stare but said nothing. She could have watched me come and go a dozen times; she'd know I was on my own, that not too much could threaten her down here.

"They're tearing the place down in six weeks," I said. "You know that?"

She stared at me fiercely but didn't move her head.

"Look. It's not my business if you want to camp out down here. But you know it's bad for your kids. Bad for their eyes, their lungs, their morale. If you want to take Jessie to a doctor for her asthma, I know one who'll look at her for nothing."

I waited a long pause but still got no answer. "I've got to work on the wiring right now, and then I'm going back to my office. Four-oh-seven. If you change your mind about the doctor, come up there and I'll take you. Any time."

I moved back to the electrical panel. The Culpeppers sometimes deliberately sliced wires or drained the hot water system to hasten me on my way. I was learning a lot about electricity in my spare time, but today's job was pretty simple: a board had come loose from the ceiling, bringing a bunch of wires with it and breaking some of them. I took a hammer out of my belt loop, scrounged among the packing cases for some old nails, and got up on a wooden box to pound the board back in place. Repairing the wires took more patience than know-how—stripping the coat away from the frail copper threads, braiding the loose ends around each other, then taping them together.

It was unnerving to work with my dumb audience behind me. Jessie's wheezing had subsided when she realized I wasn't going to hurt the family, and the baby had stopped whimpering. Their silent observation made the hairs around the base of my skull prickle, but I tried to take my time, to do the job well enough that it would last six weeks.

As I stripped and taped and tacked I kept wondering what I should do about the kids. If I called anyone in the welfare system they'd come bounding in with cops and bureaucrats and put the children into foster care. But how could they survive down here with the rats?

When I finished my repairs I went back to the boiler. The four of them shrank inside their layers of rags.

"Look here. There are a ton of empty rooms upstairs, and a couple of toilets, even though they don't work too well. I can let you into a vacant office. Wouldn't that be better for all of you than hanging on down here?"

She didn't answer. How could she trust me? I tried proving it to her, but got so urgent in my words that she flinched as though battered. I shut up and thought for a hard while. Finally I took one of the duplicates for the padlocks off my key ring. If I didn't trust her, why should she trust me?

"This will open all the stairwell doors, including the one here to the basement. I keep the basement locked to protect my tools, so if you decide to go up, please lock the door behind you. Meanwhile I'll leave my work light on—that'll help with the rats. Okay?"

She still wouldn't speak, wouldn't even hold out a hand for the proffered key. Jessie whispered, "Do it, Mama." The boy nodded hopefully, but the woman still wouldn't take the key from me. I laid it on a ledge by the boiler and turned away.

I picked my way back across the room, retrieved my flashlight from where it had landed, and started up the basement stairs. Even though I knew the family were more frightened of me than I of them—and with far better reason —I couldn't stop the unreasoning part of my body from sweating clammily as I went. When the woman spoke below me, I jumped and bit back a cry.

"These children ain't starving, young lady. This may not seem like much to you, but I can look after them. I'm looking after them all right."

□2

Gift Horse

I slid into a seat, breathless, in the middle of Sonja Malek's report on plans for the spring benefit. Marilyn Lieberman, Arcadia House's executive director, waved a hand at me, and Lotty Herschel lifted a questioning eyebrow, but no one interrupted the speaker. Arcadia House, like most nonprofits, survives on a shoestring of grants and donations; the board's main job is raising money.

Most of us have worked together for years, through different incarnations of women's activism. I've known Lotty the longest, going back to my student days when she showed women in an underground group how to perform abortions.

"I saved the most exciting news for last," Sonja said, her plump cheeks pink with triumph. "Gateway Bank has written us a check for twenty-five thousand."

"Hey, great!" I joined the excited chorus. "How'd you swing that?"

"Praise where praise is due." Marilyn Lieberman patted the shoulder of the woman on her left. "Deirdre's got inside connections."

Deirdre Messenger ducked her head. Her straight, fair hair fell forward, hiding her flushed cheeks.

"Been screwing Gateway's chairman in a good cause, Deirdre?" someone said.

When the women around her laughed, Deirdre gave a short, mirthless bark. "It just feels that way. It's really Fabian. He's done some legal work for them. . . ."

Her voice trailed off, leaving us feeling as though we'd said something improper. Unlike most of us, Deirdre didn't have a special expertise but tapped her husband's wealthy contacts to fund the projects on whose boards she sat.

Sal Barthele, chair of Arcadia's board, pulled the meeting back together. "Vic, you want to talk about security now? Or do you need time to catch your breath?"

"No, that's okay." Because Arcadia House is a battered women's shelter, people think we must spend a lot of energy fighting off abusive men. Truth is, most of these guys are cowards who don't want outsiders to know what they do in private. We've only had three try to storm the place in the seven years we've been open.

Still, we want Arcadia to be absolutely safe for women and their children. Two weeks ago someone had managed to climb over the wall, swing an ax through the wooden play equipment, and run off before the woman on night duty had been able to call the cops. Marilyn Lieberman hired a temporary security guard, but I was asked to suggest some permanent solutions. None of them was cheap: take down the brick wall and put up iron—but would that make residents feel they were in jail; a system of light sensors around the perimeter; a permanent nighttime security force.

My own preference was for replacing the wall. Although the current one was six feet high—the maximum the city code allows—it was easy to scale. And being brick it blocked a view of the street from inside the house. We did have a TV monitor on it, but it was child's play to evade that. Near-term, though, a new wall was the most expensive solution. The discussion continued, passionately, until Sonja Malek looked at her watch, gasped something about her sitter, and swept her papers into her briefcase. Everyone else started packing up.

Sal pounded the table. "You ladies ready to vote on this? No? Why doesn't that surprise me? We put the same energy into deciding what kind of toilet paper to buy as we do deciding whether we want the kids tested for AIDS. You ladies want to learn how to rank your passions or you'll be worn out before you're fifty. You be ready to vote next month, or Marilyn and I are going to make the decision for you."

"Yes, *ma'am*!" Someone saluted Sal smartly as people started straggling to the door.

Deirdre Messenger came over to me. "So where were you until eight-thirty, Vic?"

She spoke with a jocularity that grated on me. It implied an intimacy that didn't exist. I'd known her only vaguely when I was in law school with her husband—she used to join us for lunch in the law building's common room. She'd been beautiful, then, in a dreamy, fairy style. Twenty years later her cornsilk hair had darkened only slightly, but her dreaminess had disappeared into a taut bitterness.

I didn't snub her now; she didn't recover easily from slights. "Just the usual curse of the computer, made more exciting by my decaying office. I lost a whole report and had to re-create it from scratch. Fortunately I'd been scrupulous about updating my research files, so I could rough out a document in a hurry."

Marilyn Lieberman and Lotty had stopped to listen to my tale of woe. To them I added my encounter with the homeless woman and her children.

"Vic! You didn't leave them down there, did you?" Marilyn cried.

I flushed. "What should I have done?"

"Called the city," Lotty said crisply. "You have friends among the police, after all."

"And what would they have done? Arrested her for neglect and put the children into foster care."

Lotty's thick brows snapped together. "One child has

asthma, you say? And who knows what's going on in the others' lungs. You don't always use good judgment, Vic: in such a situation foster care might not be so cruel.'' Her Viennese accent became more pronounced, a sign with her of anger.

Marilyn shook her head dubiously. ''The problem is—there are shelters for women with children. Of course there are. But they aren't always safe places. And most of them are only open at night, so you have to figure out something to do during the day.''

''I thought of suggesting she come here,'' I said, ''but I know you don't—''

''We can't,'' Marilyn interrupted. ''We can't start blurring the line, when we need all the beds we have for domestic violence cases.''

''So what are you going to do?'' Deirdre had stood to one side as we spoke, as if she didn't feel part of the group and yet was loath to leave us.

I took a breath and looked at them challengingly. ''I suggested she move into one of the empty offices upstairs. The place is coming down in a few weeks, after all.''

Sal Barthele, who'd been talking to the head of the shelter's counseling staff, came in on the tail end of our discussion. ''You've lost your white liberal mind, Vic. What's Conrad say to this?'' Sal, who's black herself, takes an amused interest in my ups and downs with a black man.

''I just date the guy. I don't ask his advice every time I blow my nose.''

''I'm not asking about his male mind, sugar—doesn't worry me. What does his cop mind say?''

''I expect if I tell him he'll agree with Lotty. The city will come in, send the children to three separate homes, where at least one will be sexually molested. The mother will lose her remaining grip on reality and turn into one of those tormented creatures you see on Michigan Avenue, ranting to herself and looking ready to throttle any passerby who talks to her.''

I spoke more bitterly than I'd intended, and everyone

shifted uneasily. I hugged myself, trying to pull in, away from my anger. When Deirdre grunted aloud, as though she'd been kicked in the stomach, the sound seemed remote.

"Easy does it, Vic." Marilyn's voice—professional, calm, for distraught women or staff members—brought me back to the room. "Not all foster care ends so disastrously. In a case like this, don't you think you should give the system a chance? Surely it's better than leaving the kids underground without proper sanitation or food."

"Maybe I could try to talk to her," Deirdre offered tentatively, as though I might ridicule her ability.

"Good idea." Marilyn used her counselor's voice for people successfully resolving problems. "Deirdre does a lot of work for Home Free, you know—the housing advocates."

I hadn't known that. Home Free wasn't a name I recognized, but what energy I have for volunteer work goes to women's programs, so I don't know a lot of the work done in other equally needy arenas.

Deirdre was looking at me pugnaciously, as though challenging me and fearing me at the same time. Her expression pushed me back a step.

"If you can persuade her to get some help, more power to you. I wanted her to let me bring the asthmatic kid to Lotty—you would take a look at her, wouldn't you . . . ?"

"Vic, I would—I will—of course. But don't let your idealism carry you away. You know why we couldn't eradicate TB from the street fifteen years ago when we had the possibility? Because people won't take their medication unless you're there to oversee it. I can look—I do look—at a hundred sick, desperate people a month, but I can't make them be well."

I managed a grin. "Lotty, if I get the girl to your clinic I will stand over her with my Smith & Wesson until she takes all of whatever drugs you deem her to need."

"I like that," Marilyn said. "A progressive Dirty Harry. Make my day: don't take your antibiotics."

Even Lotty had to smile at that. Sal added a ribald cap to the joke and Marilyn gave a loud crack of laughter.

Under cover of their noise Deirdre muttered at me, "I know you don't think I can do it, but why don't you tell me where your office is."

My anxiety not to hurt her made me imbue her offer with more importance than I thought it was worth. "Sure. Let's give it a try. The Pulteney Building, southwest corner of Wabash and Monroe. Want to meet me around three tomorrow?"

"You're joining the hordes at my house Wednesday night. I'm spending tomorrow in the kitchen."

I flinched from the venom in her voice. She and Fabian were hosting a retirement party for my favorite law professor. I'd been surprised but much pleased to have been included in the guest list. Now, though, I was getting annoyed, with Deirdre for throwing me off balance, and with myself for trying to placate her, a combination that made me wave my hands wildly when I answered.

"I hope you're not sacrificing your day for me; I eat anything. Cold pizza, McDonald's, you name it."

She bared her teeth, trying for a smile. "I'm not doing it for you, Vic: I've got every damned high hat in the city coming to watch Fabian grin and shuffle in front of Manfred Yeo, hoping he can get the federal judgeship he's aching for. I'll be spending the day mincing vegetables and stuffing goddam little cream puffs so people will know what a proper gent Fabian is." She finished with a savage parody of an English accent.

I winced. "If it's that hideous a prospect, I'll stay away —give you one less cream puff to stuff."

"Don't do that, Vic: you'll be the one human in the house. Anyway, Manfred wanted you to come. Fabian asked if there were any of his old students he wanted to see, and he mentioned you especially. Of course, all the ones who've gone on to be judges and shit will be there, but you were one he knew Fabian wouldn't think of.'' Her voice and face softened, making her look fragile.

''How many people will you have?''

''Thirty-five. Senator Gantner's son is showing up. If I could, I'd hide in the basement of your office building. I'll come down to see you Friday afternoon.'' She pulled a coat over her hunched shoulders, waited a minute to see if any of the remaining group would leave with her, and walked out alone.

''There's something wrong with that woman,'' Sal pronounced when we'd heard the front door shut behind her. ''I get the feeling she'd be happier in one of the beds upstairs than around the table down here.''

''She's just shy,'' Marilyn said. ''She always does her homework for the board here, and I know she does a good job for Home Free. It's hard on her, not having a career when the rest of you do. What was she upset about now, Vic? Your homeless family?''

''Oh, she and Fabian are hosting a big do on Wednesday, but Deirdre's so bitchy about it that it's making me think I should come down with the flu. She's making all the food for thirty-five people. He makes a good living—why can't they cater it?''

''You going to Fabian Messenger's?'' Sal laughed. ''Doesn't he give highfalutin advice to Republican bigwigs? What do you two have in common?''

I laughed. ''Only the fact that we went to law school together in the golden days of student protest. He took names for the administration during the famous sit-in while I was inside helping organize the first women's union. Then he did three years as a Supreme Court clerk and returned to his alma mater in glory. Now he sits on the right hand of the right-handed while I hang out in a rat's nest downtown. Speaking of which, Sal, you got any leads on space for me? Because if I don't find something soon I'm going to move into your office at the Golden Glow.''

Sal put an arm around me. "Now, that's a potent threat, girlfriend. But I warned you at the outset that the Glow is a fluke: most of what I buy and sell is residential rehab in neighborhoods you don't want to work in. Maybe I could find a place like this, but times are slow. Don't hold your breath."

Sal had negotiated the purchase and reconstruction of Arcadia House, but it was in Logan Square, too far from the Loop businesses that make up the bulk of my work.

"That's what I need, Sal—a whole house. I could live on top and work downstairs."

My tone was sarcastic, but she cocked an interested eyebrow. "Not a bad idea, Vic. Don't laugh it off."

We walked out together. Marilyn and Lotty, who were discussing the pregnancy complications of one of the residents—she'd been kicked in the abdomen in her sixth month—trailed after us. I stayed near Lotty until Marilyn and Sal had driven off.

"Why are you angry with me about the woman in the Pulteney?" I asked.

"Am I angry? Maybe so. I sometimes think you're too arrogant with other people's lives."

"When a surgeon calls someone else arrogant, you know there's a problem." I tried to make it a joke, but it fell flat. "I don't want to be a god for this woman. I just don't know what to do to help her."

"Do nothing, then. Or do the smart thing: let the appropriate agencies look after her. I worry, Vic, when you decide to intervene in other people's lives. Someone usually suffers. It's often you, which is hard enough to watch, but last year it was me, which was even harder. Are you going to get these children badly hurt and then bring them to me to patch up?"

In the orange glow of the sodium lamps I could see the rigid lines in her expressive face. A year ago some thugs mistook Lotty for me and broke her arm. Her anger and my remorse had cut a channel between us that we rebridged only after months of hard work. Every now and then it gapes open again. I wasn't up to beating my breast tonight.

"I'll try not to—either hurt them or involve you." I slammed my car door shut.

□3
Prodigal Son

I dressed carefully for my meeting with Darraugh Graham, in black wool with a white silk shirt and my red Magli pumps. Close to, you can see where the leather has become frail with age. I tend them anxiously, with polish and waterproofing, new soles and heel tips: to replace them would take almost a month of rent money. They bring me luck, my red Magli pumps. Maybe some would get passed to my homeless woman if I wore them to her hideaway.

On my way out I pawed through my closet for old blankets and sweaters to take to her. I'd have some spare time at lunch to drop them off.

It was only seven-twenty when I clattered down the three flights of stairs, early enough that I wouldn't have to run the three blocks from the garage to Graham's office. I couldn't afford to arrive with my shirttails hanging out and hair in my eyes.

The two dogs I share with my downstairs neighbor recognized my gait and began an insistent barking. By the time the old man got to his door I was already out front. Calling over my shoulder that I'd run the dogs tonight, I jumped into my car and took off.

Meetings with Darraugh are usually dry to the point of making my mouth chalky. Efficient subordinates and disciplined senior staff, brought in as their expertise dictated, run through reports with the smoothness of a Rolls transmission.

Early-comers to the boardroom get coffee and rolls. That's where I hear about children's basketball practice or difficulties with the snowblower. At eight o'clock Darraugh sails in and all idle chat ceases. There have been occasions when I was sliding into my seat after him, earning a frosty stare and a pointed invitation to begin speaking while still disposing of my coat and papers. I don't do that anymore. I'm almost forty. I can't afford to get fired.

Today when Darraugh marched in he had an ill-kempt young man in tow. I blinked. IBM at the height of its glory never displayed the amount of starch and pinstripe in Darraugh's boardroom. Anyone who came to work with a three-day growth, shoulder-length hair, and a dirty sport jacket hanging over jeans would be instantly slung into a black hole. I wondered if this was some junior exec gone wrong whose expulsion from paradise we were all to witness.

Darraugh did not introduce him, but a couple of men near me greeted the youth with a cautious, "Hi, Ken, how's it going?" For the duration of the meeting Darraugh acted as though Ken were an empty chair. The young man added to the illusion by hunching over and staring motionless at his belt buckle.

At the end, after Darraugh had informed us of the group's consensus and his secretary had assured us we would have minutes by two, Ken pulled his head out of his lap and prepared to stand.

"Just a minute," Darraugh barked. "MacKenzie, Vic, will you stay behind? I'll catch up with you downstairs, Charlie, to go over the Netherlands proposal. And Luke, we have a three o'clock, don't we, to discuss the Bloomington plant."

The rest of the room meekly filed out. Ken slid back into his chair, his hands deep in his jeans pockets, and gave the sigh linguists around the world recognize as contempt for the entire adult race.

Darraugh put up a hand to straighten his tie knot. "This is MacKenzie Graham. My son. Victoria Warshawski."

"Your agent," Ken muttered to his chest.

Darraugh affected not to hear him. "MacKenzie is home from college. We hope temporarily."

"I can see why," I couldn't stop myself from saying.

My client scowled, but Ken looked up with a sudden glimmer of interest.

"From Harvard. Where our family has gone for two hundred years." Darraugh bit off the words.

"If I'd broken tradition and gone to Yale it would be the same story," Ken said.

"Am I supposed to play twenty questions over this? Would it have made a difference if he'd gone to Berkeley?"

"Yes, it would," Darraugh snapped. "If it had been Yale or Berkeley he wouldn't be on probation: he'd be out on his ass earning a living. As it is they're giving him a year off. He can go back next January if he keeps himself—"

"Clean in thought, word, and deed," his son finished for him. "I was caught hacking. Everyone does it, but they only punish the people who get caught."

"How true. For that and a thousand other felonies. Everyone embezzles, but only Ivan Boesky got caught."

Ken flushed and resumed his study of his belt buckle. "The point is," Darraugh continued, "he's on probation with the government as well. He broke into Department of Energy classified files. If it weren't for the people I know in Washington he'd be doing five-to-ten in Leavenworth."

"So all the money you've given Alec Gantner over the years has paid off. One of your best investments," Ken muttered.

"I'm glad you've had a happy outcome," I said as politely as I could manage. "I hope you finish your degree. Computer science, is it?"

"Russian literature. Computers are just my hobby."

"I'm not telling you my private business to invite sarcasm, Warshawski. I need your help. Ken has to do two hundred hours of community service. I'd like you to set something up.''

My jaw worked a couple of times. "Don't you sit on boards? Give money to the symphony and stuff? You must know dozens of charities who would take him for you.''

"My wife handled that kind of thing," Darraugh said stiffly, as if acknowledging a weakness. "And they won't accept the Art Institute as that kind of charity. I'd pay your usual fee, of course.''

Darraugh had been a widower for almost a decade. When his wife died he'd buried himself in work, and eventually that became a habit, something he couldn't stop doing.

"I wanted to lecture schoolchildren on how to hack without getting caught, but my probation officer didn't think that would fly." Ken looked at me slyly, as if his comment were an important test I was bound to fail.

"What an unimaginative person. The trouble is, Darraugh, I know a number of outfits that could use someone with computer skills, but a kid this lippy causes so much aggravation, no one wants his services.''

"This is really important to me, Vic." Darraugh put enough emphasis on the words that he didn't need to spell out a threat. "I want you two to go downstairs for coffee, get acquainted. See what you can fix up.''

"Aye, aye, Captain." Ken hoisted himself out of his chair. "Do we drink it black? Can I have two sugars?''

Darraugh stared at him bleakly, but had enough sense not to try to answer. "The probation office is getting impatient. We need to have something in place by next week.''

I wanted to echo Ken's salute, but Darraugh wasn't my father—he didn't have to keep paying my bills. The three of us left the boardroom in silence. Darraugh turned right, toward his office. Ken and I walked to the elevators, where we waited like zombies for a car to take us to the basement. One of the new coffee chains had an outlet there. At least I could get a cappuccino as a small reward for the task ahead.

"So let's get acquainted," Ken said, sprawling in the

corner. "How long have you known my old man? He's kept you awful quiet."

"How bad do you want to go back to school?" I asked. "I know you don't need to get a degree to earn a living—your father won't let you starve."

"You answer my question and I'll answer yours: that's how people get acquainted."

I drank some coffee. "The only groups I know where you could do legitimate community service help women and children. Domestic violence, abortion services, homeless shelters. I'm not going to refer you to a place like that if the first thing you assume about a professional woman is that she's your father's lover. Your outlook is simply too old-fashioned to make you able to fit in."

He smirked through the first half of my remarks, but the suggestion that he might be old-fashioned made his head jerk in wounded surprise. He couldn't possibly be—he was half my age.

"I don't like to be paraded around like a damaged tomato the old man is trying to get some housewife to buy."

"I can understand that. But you committed a crime. Let's not pretend it didn't happen. And you must know damned well that if you'd been poor or black you'd be in the pen right now. Your punishment is to be a tomato. If you behave well enough to earn early parole I'll try to upgrade you—maybe to an avocado or eggplant."

He smiled suddenly, with a genuine humor that made him seem younger, more vulnerable. In a second he was frowning again, looking at his hands.

"I don't know if I want to go back to Harvard. Everyone there knows, see. And I won't be able to graduate with my class."

"Then don't go back. There are a thousand other colleges in the country."

"But only one has a library wing named for the Graham family. Darraugh could visit me in jail easier than he could watch me graduate from a state university."

Indeed, the heartaches of the rich and famous are different from yours and mine. "I'll make a deal with you. You act like a happy camper at whatever place I find for you, and I'll persuade your dad not to stop you from transferring to the school of your choice."

I held up my hand to forestall his objection. "I'll persuade him it's a good idea. Plenty of schools would like a chance to add a Graham wing to their libraries. Deal?"

"Yeah, I guess." He finished his coffee. "We're still not acquainted. But I know you don't put sugar in your coffee. You one of those perpetual dieters?"

"Nope. I don't like the taste." I stood up. "Better give me a phone number so I don't have to reach you through your father."

"You're supposed to ask me why I use sugar," he said. "That's how we get to know each other. I'm living with Darraugh these days."

I smiled. "But I don't have his home number. So now you know: your papa and I aren't intimate. Feel better?"

He scribbled the number on a napkin and handed it to me. "You could just be smart."

I laughed. "But in your heart of hearts you know I'm not. I'll be in touch."

I stomped up the escalator, feeling the metal vibrate through the thin soles of my pumps. In the lobby Ken caught up with me. In a parody of chivalry he grabbed my left hand and planted a kiss in the palm. He dashed through the revolving doors before I could react.

□4

Contract Woes

It was past one now. That gave me ten minutes to stop in the Pulteney before an afternoon session with a venture capitalist. I should have had a cookie with my cappuccino: I wouldn't have time even for a sandwich now.

I ran down the three flights to the Pulteney's basement but found no sign of the woman or her children. No footprints, no scrap of food wrapper—they might never have existed. Leaving my bag of blankets behind the boiler with an envelope stuffed with what cash I could spare, I raced across the Loop to Phoebe Quirk's office.

Phoebe and I had known each other for years—since our undergraduate days when we'd worked for the abortion underground where I'd met Lotty. I liked her well enough at the time, but we'd never been close: she came from the rich suburbs where kids wore tattered jeans and joined undergrounds to thumb their noses at their parents. During winter breaks, when I was making a few bucks waitressing, she stopped thumbing her nose long enough to ski Mont Blanc with her family.

Her idealism was genuine, though: after a checkered career including both the Peace Corps and a stint teaching high school, she'd become a neurologist. For five years she'd butted her head on the unyielding wall of organized medicine. One day she drove into the Lake Point Hospital parking lot, stared at the stream of doctors and nurses leaving their cars, and turned around and headed home.

A few months later she'd joined a small venture-capital firm, Capital Concerns. They wanted Phoebe's medical contacts and know-how for the biotech start-ups they specialized in; her grandparents' trust fund didn't bother them any either. Phoebe liked the excitement of high-risk capital. She proved to have a knack for it, but Capital also appealed to her because of the social programs they funded.

Thanks to Phoebe, Capital had started coming to me for background research on some of their prospective partners. During the last year they'd become one of my most important accounts. Today's meeting was more about ventures than capital, though: Phoebe had agreed to help one of Conrad's four sisters, Camilla, fund a women's trade collective.

When I got to Phoebe's office Camilla was already there. She and Phoebe were sitting on the corner couches, laughing. Camilla, smart in a form-hugging black jersey, didn't look as though she ever lifted anything heavier than a nail file. Phoebe, who wore expensive suits as if they were the tattered blue jeans of her youth, was the one you'd pick for a hard hat and scaffolding. Today's costume was a navy blue Donna Karan with a button missing from the skirt and coffee stains down the shirtfront.

"Come on in, Vic. Camilla's just telling me about her introduction to sexual harassment back in the mills. They kept leaving rust-coated tampons in the bathroom sink when she was the only woman on the shift. Why do you think all successful women have a bathroom story as part of their initiation experience?"

I was about to say that must be proof I wasn't a success, when I thought of the toilets at the Pulteney, forever backing up, and never properly repaired in my ten years there. For the first time it struck me that the men's restrooms in the building, while not beautiful, had always been more or less functional. And there was one on every floor, besides.

"Builds character. Or at least muscle. My bathroom story is learning to be a plumber: I can carry a fully loaded toolbox up three flights of stairs without flinching. How's tricks, Camilla?"

"Can't complain, Vic. How's Conrad? I haven't talked to the boy since they put him on night shift."

Camilla, just a year younger than Conrad, was the closest to him of the family. To their widowed mother's chagrin she'd eschewed the pink-collar jobs she'd trained for in high school and become an apprentice welder at the old South Works. With the death of the steel industry she'd learned carpentry and gone to work for a small general contractor.

"Now I need a change, need a stretch," she'd told me last summer. "I've worked for some good guys and some assholes, with the assholes predominating. But none of them ever wants to go past their hiring quota when it comes to women. Some of us want to change that—start a woman-only company. Only where are we going to get the money?"

My first thought had been Sal, who did a lot of real estate and sometimes rehabbed it, but the recession was squeezing her too tight to allow her to take on new projects. I'd then put her in touch with Phoebe, who helped Camilla and five other women form a company. They'd named themselves Lamia, for an ancient Libyan goddess.

At Phoebe's prodding they'd come up with a project they all wanted to work on: low-cost housing for single mothers. They'd found an architect to design plans so they could apply for funding, building permits, zoning permits, and everything else you have to have before you can do good works, or even bad ones, in construction.

"We thought our zoning permit was cast-iron, but that's suddenly fallen through," Camilla explained, bringing me up-to-date. "Not only that, Century Bank, which we thought was going to underwrite a big chunk of the cost, has backed out."

"That's where you come in, Vic." Phoebe flashed me a gap-toothed smile, her patented signal of charm.

"No," I said flatly.

"What do you mean, 'no'?" Camilla demanded.

"I mean I'm not digging into the rat's nest at City Hall to find out who is squeaking into whose cheese hoard to kill your permit."

"But, Vic," Camilla began, when Phoebe cut her off.

"Vic, this is an important project in the women's community. We need to find out what's fueling the opposition —is it because Lamia is woman-owned? Or because it's low-income housing? Because, not to be crude, we can change the project."

When Camilla started to object that the project was too important to change, Phoebe overrode her. "I know everyone at Lamia is committed to low-cost housing for women. But we need to get you capital first, and a track record. When you have that, you can be pickier about your work."

"Phoebe, you know the people at Century Bank. They'll talk to you for nothing. Why pay my rates?"

Phoebe leaned forward. "If it's some kind of collusion between them and the power brokers at City Hall, or even the trade unions, they're not going to want to talk to me. That's the kind of stuff you can figure out. Anyway, I thought your time on the Lamia project was donated, like mine. We pay your expenses, of course."

"Think that one again. An investigation like this could take several weeks. I can't afford to donate that much time."

"I'll do your legwork," Camilla offered. "I can donate a couple of hours a day to my own cause."

I pulled Phoebe's desk chair over and sat down in front of them. "Look, you two. I've got six weeks to find a new office. If I was far enough ahead of the game to donate a hundred hours of work I wouldn't be in my current jam. But every project I take on for the next six months has to earn for me—or I'll be first in line for a unit when Camilla's project opens its doors."

"You have to have a baby first," Camilla objected. "It's single *mothers,* Vic, not out-of-work dicks."

"Capital pays you a pretty good retainer." Phoebe frowned, annoyed for the moment with both of us.

"You want to audit me, see where the money goes?"

She flushed, revealing a crust of freckles across her cheekbones. "I want you to be more responsive to an important client."

I could feel my chin jut out. "Phoebe, I know you're donating your energy on this one as a sign of your goodwill and your impeccable politics. But I bet if *I* audited *you* I'd find your goodwill was going to be recompensed down the road when the Lamia group gets going. I don't have a personal fortune to sink into this. You know the old saying: White-collar girls play with matches for fun, blue-collar girls get burned."

"I never heard that one," she snapped. "And if you think I haven't put my own butt on the line—"

"Listen here, ladies," Camilla said. "I don't want you two hot and bothered and destroying a good friendship over this. Vic, why don't you do—oh, say, ten hours of work on this and see how big a deal it really looks like. If it seems huge, then Phoebe can pay for more of your time."

"And what's your donation going to be to your own cause?" Phoebe demanded.

"If someone tries to shoot Vic I'll get Conrad there ahead of the 911 crew."

"For which we both thank you." Conrad's probable reaction if I stepped in front of a gun again would be to pick it up and finish my assailant's work. He and I had had a word or two about "unnecessary" risk-taking by private individuals.

Phoebe screwed her face up in a tight ball, not wanting to bend but knowing compromise was inevitable. "Give me fifteen, Vic, and we'll see."

"In writing, Phoebe, and it's a deal."

"Camilla's a witness here."

I shook my head. "Nonprofits eat you alive, and *pr*

bono work is the biggest devourer of all. In writing or not at all. I won't do like your legal staff—charge you a full hour for ten minutes' work. It'll be fifteen real-time hours.''

"Oh, damn you, anyway, Vic, for the stubborn bitch you've always been." Phoebe flicked her intercom and asked her secretary to type up the necessary agreement.

As I waited for Gemma to bring it in I took names of some of Phoebe's contacts at the bank, and of Camilla's in the ward office.

Neither Phoebe nor I was very happy when I got up to leave, but Camilla laughed and said, "This makes me think of a madam who used to live up the street from us. She'd gone out of that business and opened an employment agency, but she always counseled us girls in the neighborhood to make sure the customer paid. 'That way,' she'd say, 'you don't feel cheated and he doesn't feel obligated.' ''

"V.I. as a madam? I like it," Phoebe said, getting up. "I've got another meeting. You two'll have to excuse me."

Camilla rode down in the elevator with me. "Give my brother a big kiss when you see him again."

I grinned. "More than likely."

"I meant from me. See you, Vic."

On my way back to the Pulteney I picked up a bagel with Swiss cheese. I had meant to enlist Phoebe's help in finding a placement for Ken Graham, but annoyance with her demands had put his problem out of my head. I scowled at myself in the mirror over the deli counter. I was out of my head, pure and simple. Ten years ago, five even, I would have told Darraugh and Phoebe both to take a hike. Incipient middle age was making me risk-averse. I didn't like that in myself at all.

Back at the Pulteney I set up a file on the Lamia project, dutifully logging it in to the work-management section of my computer. I'd done a hundred jobs like this in the last ten years. I could almost do it in my sleep, but that didn't mean it would go any faster. Actually, my weariness with the routine slowed me down these days.

l frowned at the screen for some minutes, as if that would make a complete report spring into being on its glassy surface. With an aggrieved sigh I dialed up Lexis, the know-all legal data base, and got a list of Century Bank's directors and officers. While these printed I called on the Dow Jones News Service for information about Century. In the electronic age secretarial school would be a better training ground for a detective than my years in law school and the PD's office.

Century is a tiny bank in Uptown and doesn't make the news much. They were celebrating their centennial this year: they'd been founded in 1892 as part of the Century of Progress and now were primed for a second century. The *Sun-Times* had a photo of the anniversary festivities—if I felt like paying a small fee I could have it re-created on my printer. I took their word for it.

According to the *Herald-Star,* Century tried to be conscientious about the needs of its Uptown neighbors. A partial list of clients was attached to the end of the story, among them Home Free, the homeless advocates Deirdre helped. Dow Jones reported interest in buying the bank by the JAD Holdings Group. Nothing very earth-shattering, but I sent the stories to the printer just to have them.

Maybe there was some kind of conspiracy between City Hall and the bank, but it was probably over something too petty, too routine even to make the papers. Perhaps some alderman had an interest in the plot of land Lamia wanted to build on. He muscled his colleague into canceling Lamia's zoning and building permits. End of story.

Over the noise of the printer I hadn't heard the door open. When a hand shook my shoulder I jumped, hard enough to ram my knee into the desk leg. The wraith from the basement stood behind me.

"Jessie needs a doctor," she said. Her eyes were fierce and her chin jutted forward belligerently, but her hands, pressed into the sweaters swathing her bosom, trembled.

"Immediately? Is it an emergency?"

"She can't hardly breathe. She just keeps gasping and

heaving. I moved her upstairs, like you said, but it didn't help her none.''

''Where is she now?'' I was surprised she'd left the children alone, so fierce had been her hold on them last night.

''You show me how you help me, then I'll tell you.''

I looked at my watch. It was six-thirty now. Lotty might still be at her clinic, but the thought of her angry words made me squirm.

''I'll take you to the emergency room at . . .'' I paused, trying to imagine which area hospital might be the least inimical to such a family.

''You can't,'' she burst in. ''You can't take her to a hospital. You know what they do: they call the cops, the cops arrest me for neglect, and who look after the children then?''

''You don't have any relatives to care for them? What about their father?''

''What are you? The caseworker? Their old man beat on me, he beat me up plenty, but I could handle it. When he start hitting on Jessie, though, that's when I draw a line, say enough. You take her to a hospital, that's where they going to send her back, back to her old man because he can hold a job and he wants to look after her. I see the way he look *at* her, not after her, and she's not going back there. Get that straight. You said a doctor, someone who would treat her for free, not a hospital.''

''Okay. No hospital.''

I went back to my desk, my knee still smarting, and called Lotty's clinic. The answering machine referred me to the emergency room at Beth Israel. I hung up and started dialing Lotty's home number. I didn't know whether to be relieved or not when she answered. I told her I'd found the homeless family and they needed urgent medical care.

She didn't sound enthusiastic, but no one who works as hard as Lotty would welcome such a greeting. She wanted me to send them to Beth Israel, but when I explained that the woman adamantly refused hospital help she sighed in exhaustion and agreed to meet me at the clinic.

When she'd hung up I turned back to the woman. "Okay. A doctor—one of the best in Chicago. No hospital. No forms. Go get Jessie and meet me back here while I finish a few things."

"You're not calling the cops." It was a command, not a question.

"No. I need to tell a friend that I'm going to be late. And I need to shut down my computer for the night."

She stayed at my elbow while I spoke to Mr. Contreras, telling him something had come up and I wouldn't be able to run the dogs after all. When I shut down the system the woman went to fetch her children. While they waited in the lobby, Jessie gasping for air, I took a cab across the Loop for my car.

Found—and Lost Again

"These children need a week in the hospital to recover from dehydration and malnutrition, let alone whatever underlying lung problems they have." Lotty spoke uncompromisingly.

She had met us at the clinic, taken one look at Jessie, and —after giving her a jolt of epinephrine to control her wheezing—phoned Beth Israel to prepare for an emergency admission. She then told me to make myself useful by bathing the children while she examined them in turn. Stripped of their layers of swaddling and filth they had the gaunt boniness we usually see only on televised reports of remote famines.

While Lotty prodded joints and listened to chests I ran their clothes through her office washing machine. As I dumped the bundle in I found a yellow sweater that looked familiar, and realized with a shock that it was one of the pieces I had deposited behind the boiler. It already looked as filthy as the rest of their wrappings.

"The lady here promised me—" the mother began.

"Vic spoke from her heart but she's not a doctor. I would be an absolute criminal if I allowed you to take these children back to whatever cellar you want to hide them in."

The mother let out an anguished "no," but didn't add to

it. I summarized what she'd told me about the children's father.

"There must be someone who you could turn to, at least for an address," Lotty said. "I'm not asking you to give up your children to an abusive man, but you must see how bad it is for them, living the way you do."

"If there was someone, don't you think I'd be with that person?" The woman dashed angry tears away.

"Look," Lotty said. "There are some shelters for women with children. I'll do my best to get you space in one of them. And I promise you I won't turn you over to the police. We'll use Vic's address for you—you can be their aunt, my dear—that should be appropriate for you."

"Touché, doctor. Fine." I turned to the woman. "I'll be your children's auntie. But you must follow Dr. Herschel's advice. If your children die you will be bereft forever, you know, not just for the time they're in someone else's care."

The woman didn't like it, but she saw we weren't going to budge. Lotty even got her name out of her while we waited for the clothes to dry: Tamar Hawkings. While Hawkings watched, eyes bright with suspicion, Lotty called the best of the shelters for women with children and explained Tamar's plight. They were crowded past any hope of taking on another family, but promised to put the Hawkingses high on the waiting list.

"Vic will carry on tomorrow finding you a place to stay. But for now, off to the hospital with you."

The mother's face took on a bleached, hopeless look. When Lotty called Beth Israel again, going over the children's situation in detail with the attending emergency-room physician, Hawkings listened with painful attention, as if to make sure Lotty wasn't arranging instead to turn them all in to the state. Myself, I felt certain the hospital would call Family Services: no one could look at those distended stomachs and bowed legs without reporting child abuse. And after that? Would they be forcibly returned to their father?

Lotty started locking up. "Dr. Haroon is the attending

physician and he's promised to speak to the admitting
nurse. If you have any trouble, ask for Rosa Kim. I'll check
on the children in the morning. And where are we going to
put Ms. Hawkings tonight?''

I made a face. ''I guess she can come home with me.''

Tamar Hawkings shook her head vigorously. ''No, you
don't. You don't trick me like that, putting my children in
the hospital away from me. I know my rights; I know the
mother can stay by her children in the hospital room.''

She didn't speak again during the short drive to Beth
Israel. It had started to rain, a freezing rain mixed with sleet
that made driving treacherous. Behind me I could feel the
children's fright. Infected by their mother's terrors, they
didn't talk, but the tension in their small bodies made the
tendons in my neck ache.

Since Tamar Hawkings had neither a green card nor a
financial guarantor, our first few minutes in the emergency
room were chaotic. I finally found the admitting nurse,
Rosa Kim, who took over the situation with brisk if imper-
sonal authority. Beth Israel was the major health care provider in Uptown; Kim was used to uninsured emergencies
of all kinds. When she assured Tamar that she wouldn't call
DCFS unless some unexpected problem emerged, I thought
it was safe to leave.

I called Lotty from the building lobby to thank her.

''Vic, when you saw them yesterday, why didn't you get
them help? Those children are in shocking condition.''

''I offered her help and she didn't want it. The only thing
I could have done at that point was to call the cops, which
would have been a real violation. And anyway, she did a
good job scuttling out of there—I didn't see her again until
she chose to appear at my door.''

''Even so, calling the cops would have been the responsible act in this case. You know I'm not a friend of police
intervention in people's lives; but, Vic, you just can't continue to set your own judgment up as God's in these kinds
of situations.''

''Hey, Lotty, ease up. Over a two-day period Tamar saw

she could trust me, so she came to me of her own accord. The kids are getting the help they need now. I don't think that's acting like God; that's doing their mother the courtesy of thinking her judgment is as good as mine.''

''But last night you could have talked to Deirdre about getting them into one of the Home Free shelters. Now I don't think the hospital will release the children into Hawkings's care. Frankly, I wouldn't.''

I bit back a hot retort. Maybe Lotty was right. Maybe I was only fighting with her because I couldn't admit I'd made a mistake on Monday.

''I'll ask Deirdre at dinner tomorrow night. The evening sounds like a prelude to hell—maybe she can do something useful and salvage it.''

Lotty gave a dry laugh. ''In fact, you've thought of the perfect hostess present. I'll check on the children in the morning when I make rounds.''

On that more pacific note we hung up. The last twelve months had been filled with moments like this— hot exchanges, painful temporizings.

All the way home on the icy streets I kept wondering what I should have done when I first found Tamar and her children. The question haunted my dreams; I awoke feverish from interrupted sleep to a world encased in ice. It glazed the trees in front of the apartment so that every twig, each nascent bud, seemed dipped in crystal, but on the sidewalk below people skittered and fell. As I shivered at the window I saw two cars slither into each other at the intersection of Barry and Racine.

My first appointment today wasn't until ten. By the time I had to leave the roads might be more passable. I slipped on jeans and a sweater and went down to the lobby for my newspapers. Behind Mr. Contreras's door the two dogs, Peppy and Mitch, heard me and set up a hearty cry. The old man opened the door and the dogs bounded out, tails thrashing against me. I caught their forepaws as they leapt up on me and let them lick my face.

''I know, I know,'' I said to Mr. Contreras. ''They need a

run. But look at the street—we can't go out in this. It should warm up during the day—it's April, for pity's sake. I'll run them tonight. Scout's honor. No matter what eleventh-hour crisis flings itself at my door. . . . I'm making coffee. Want to come up for a cup?''

"I got some hot, doll. Why don't you come in and have some of mine?"

The old man's coffee tastes like tar laced with gasoline. Improvising desperately, I told him I'd left water on to boil upstairs and needed to get back to it. Ten minutes later he joined me in my kitchen, a plate of sticky buns in hand, the dogs circling his legs.

That was the last joy I had all day. At noon, between meetings, I tried to flagellate myself into an interest in Phoebe and Camilla's problem. I turned on the computer and tried to organize some questions, but my mind seemed to be a chalky waste. I watched a clerk sort papers in the building on the other side of the tracks. The unending flow of paper, out of the mail, into file folders, back into the mail, seemed like my own dreary routine. Lay out the questions, make appointments, survey Lexis, get the SEC reports. Another train passed. The pigeons flew up again, obscuring the clerk.

When the phone rang I welcomed the interruption—until Lotty gave me her bad news. "Your friend Ms. Hawkings disappeared. She took her children, along with some shoes belonging to other families in the ward."

For a moment my brain refused to absorb the information. When Lotty repeated it, sharply, I dully asked for particulars.

Apparently a social worker had come up around ten to interview Tamar and the children. She acceded to the mother's demand that the father not be informed, but said that until Tamar could prove she had a stable home for the children, even a shelter, they would have to go into foster care.

"Great," I said. "The magic words. When I left last night I thought I had a clear understanding with the staff that they couldn't use that as a threat. Tamar has gone to considerable lengths to keep her children with her. She's not going to give them up now.''

''It wasn't a threat, Vic. It was reality. They don't want to take her children from her, but she can't go on living in basements with them.''

''Unfortunately Tamar Hawkings doesn't agree.'' My shoulders felt as though someone had tied lead bricks to them. ''I'll see if she's come back here. And call the cops to start a missing persons search. But short of putting her in jail I don't know what we can do to keep her from taking off again. Unless we can find a place that will house her children and her together.''

''The Chinese have a proverb for this,'' Lotty said at her driest. '' 'If you rescue someone from drowning you're responsible for them forever.' ''

On that ominous note she hung up on me.

◻6

Touch of a Scumbag

The rest of the day turned into a blurred nightmare, culminating with its chef d'oeuvre, Deirdre's dinner party. Any hopes I had of solving Tamar Hawkings's problems there disappeared within minutes of seeing my hostess.

I got to her South Side mansion an hour past the invitation time, and I was lucky I wasn't later than that. After hanging up with Lotty I called Kevin Whiting, an officer I knew in Missing Persons. Of course, as he explained to me, Tamar didn't technically count as a missing person—she'd only been gone an hour. But he promised to notify the Loop foot patrols in case she came back to the Pulteney.

A few minutes later Whiting phoned back: there was already a bona fide missing persons search for Hawkings on file. Leon Hawkings, of an address on West Ninety-fifth Street, had notified them six months ago that his wife had disappeared, taking their three children with her. So if anyone on the beat found her, they would call her old man first.

"Oh, no, Kevin—you can't do that. She ran away in the first place because he was beating up on her and the kids." I assumed she was telling the truth about that—why else would she live as she was these days? "Can you check to see whether you guys responded to any calls at that address

—domestic violence, disturbing the peace, that kind of thing?''

"You gonna put me on your payroll, Warshawski? You know we're not automated. No way I can look that up here. You have to go out to the precinct and ask."

I chewed my lower lip. "Until I know for certain, can you call off the dogs? I don't want to add to her misery."

"They're still missing, ain't they? So why bother the husband now? You just trot your little heinie over to Chicago Lawn and ask at the precinct. If any Loop patrols see a likely-looking family I'll get you to look at them before we bring in her old man."

"Thanks, Kevin. You're a prince."

The truth was he was lazy. If he didn't have to notify a worried spouse, with all that implied for meetings, forms, and follow-up, he was just as happy. I called Chicago Lawn, but I didn't know anyone at that remote outpost and they weren't giving free tips away to private eyes that day. I thought about roping Conrad into the quest, but decided against it. Finding out Tamar Hawkings *hadn't* filed any complaints against her husband wouldn't prove anything. Not every woman who's been beaten up calls the cops. Most don't, as a matter of fact. They just keep checking themselves into emergency rooms with tales of falling down stairs or running into doors.

I called Marilyn Lieberman, the executive director at Arcadia House. "You remember my mentioning a homeless woman camping out in my basement?"

"Oh, yes. You wanted to try to palm her off on me and I told you no. The answer's still the same."

"What if I told you she was running away from an abusive husband?"

"Would that be the truth?" Marilyn demanded.

"She says. And we're in the business of believing women's stories, aren't we?"

Marilyn expelled a long breath. "Oh, Christ, Vic. We're full up right now, but if it's a choice between your basement and doubling up with someone else, I suppose . . .

although if the kids have been on the lam for six months they're going to be pretty wild. I just don't know. Bring her over and let me set up an interview with Eva.''

Eva Kuhn was Arcadia's therapist. ''There is one small problem,'' I confessed. ''She's disappeared for the time being.''

Marilyn listened to my Tamar saga with scant sympathy. ''She needs more help than we can give her, Vic. But *if* she shows up again, and *if* you can persuade her to go anyplace else with you, I'll get Eva to do a diagnostic intake. Talk to Deirdre, though: she's got contacts at the shelters.'' She hung up with a snap.

I took my second-best flashlight and went down to the basement. It was a forlorn hope. Even if Ms. Hawkings returned here she wasn't going to hang around for me to find her. I even swallowed my fear of the rats and went behind the boiler, where I'd spotted the family on Monday.

The boiler was a great cast-iron monster that dated to the twenties, when the Pulteney had gone up. The furnace had been converted first from coal to oil, and then, early in my tenure, to natural gas. At some point, long before I moved in, a false wall had been built between the boiler and the foundation. It allowed just enough room for an average-size person to move—or six rats to walk abreast.

After the third one sauntered past me I shone the flash over the wall in a perfunctory way. Maybe the Hawkings were hanging out behind the false inner wall—that seemed to be where the rats were nesting—but I couldn't see an opening. I retreated hastily and returned to my office. Even my dreary routine of reports and accounts was better than crawling around with rats behind the boiler.

I discovered that I'd done enough work in the last few weeks to generate some invoices. By three o'clock I'd gotten two thousand dollars' worth of statements printed and stuffed into envelopes. I could do some work for Phoebe Quirk before going home to change. I tracked down an acquaintance at City Hall who might snuffle around to get some information for me on why the city had canceled Lamia's permit.

When Cyrus Lavalle heard my voice he whispered theatrically that I should know better than to identify myself by name to his co-workers. And no, I couldn't possibly come to his office, but if I would show up at the Golden Glow at five he'd meet me there.

"Come on, Cyrus. You know me by now. I'm not going to threaten you in public with pictures of Andrew Jackson —I just want to ask you a couple of questions."

"No way, Warshawski," he whispered. "There's plenty of people around here who rate you down below the sewer system. It's worth my job to be seen with you."

In other words, he wanted a free drink and the possibility of driving a hard bargain for information on Camilla's building project. I gave in with bad grace and went back to work.

I actually had an outstanding paying project for Phoebe —a background check on the owners of a little drug company she was interested in. They had a single product, a T-cell enhancer for which they'd been seeking FDA approval to begin human testing. The company was actually called Cellular Enhancement Technology, but in my files I used Phoebe's nickname for them—Mr. T. Mr. T had been languishing for two years, but if they ever got approval they could make someone like Phoebe a lot of money.

The biology they were working with was way beyond me, but not the credentials of the biologists. I called the various universities where they claimed to have studied, verified their degrees, and logged in to a credit rating service to see whether their financial backgrounds were as good as their academic ones.

That seemed to be enough work for one day. I shut down the system and locked up. On my way out I took a last tour of the basement, but the rats still had the place to themselves. I didn't really expect to find Tamar Hawkings again: in her eyes I'd probably betrayed her to the social worker. She wouldn't return for more treachery.

The temperature had risen steadily all day, melting the glass shards from trees and cars, turning the streets to slush, and filling the air with a horrible stench. On the way across the Loop to the Golden Glow my socks turned into damp mats inside my Nikes.

Inside the small bar I found a table by the heat vent and stretched my legs out gratefully. The warmth of the Tiffany lamps gave me a moment's illusion of rest.

I was early, both for Cyrus Lavalle and the commuter drinking crowd. Sal Barthele, who works the place personally, came out from behind her famous bar with the Black Label bottle. She'd found the mahogany horseshoe in the old Regent's Hotel when it was torn down twelve years ago. Sal had stripped and polished it by hand, returning it to the high gloss it had when it left its English manufacturer in 1887. Sal won't keep a waiter who doesn't wipe up every drop of liquid the instant it touches the surface.

I waved off the Black Label. "Not tonight. I'm off to Deirdre's after I finish with Cyrus Lavalle."

"Girlfriend, you need a drink to get through an hour with Cyrus. You coming down with something?"

I faked a punch at her. "Yeah. It's called middle age. I have to run the dogs and change and drive and socialize. I'll never get through that routine if I have whisky now."

She sat chatting with me until Cyrus showed up—twenty minutes late. He was a sight for jaded eyes, in a crimson Nehru shirt and lavender silk trousers. He made a great show of pleasure at seeing me, seeing Sal, seeing all the people he met on his regular rounds at the bar. When I was able to halt his dramatic flourishes I drew a blank. It didn't surprise me—Camilla's tradeswomen wouldn't generate enough gossip to filter along to ward heelers like Cyrus. He promised to initiate some delicate inquiries.

"And for a hundred I'll share what I hear with you, Warshawski."

"Forget it, Cyrus. For a hundred I can buy the alderman and learn it direct."

He smirked. "Yeah, you *could*. But you won't. You don't

know how to bribe people without turning red and blowing your moves.''

I guessed that was a compliment, although in Chicago it's kind of shameful not to know how to buy an elected official. ''I don't have a similar problem with you, my friend. Fifty is my top offer. I don't care more than that.''

He bargained me up to sixty-five and left a happy man. I, on the contrary, jogged back through the slush to my car with my head pounding. Between Tamar Hawkings, Darraugh Graham, Phoebe and Camilla—it was too much. I'd become a private eye because I wanted to be my own boss. Lately all I seemed to do was jump through other people's hoops.

I turned the Trans Am's heating system on full power and tried to dry my feet during the slow trek home. The fog had thickened so much that traffic was stalled on both the Kennedy and Lake Shore Drive. I zigzagged through the side streets, but the trip still took half an hour.

I longed for a bath and the drink I'd turned down at Sal's, but once home I resumed my headlong dash through the day. Putting on sweats, I collected the dogs from Mr. Contreras and took them over to the lake in my car—the night air was too thick to risk running through the streets with them. We chased each other around the lagoon a few times, not a wonderful workout for any of us, but enough to tide the dogs over until morning.

By the time I'd showered and changed into wool crepe slacks and a silk evening shirt it was past seven, the scheduled start of Deirdre's party. I shrugged into my old winter coat and clattered back down the stairs. Once in the car my earlier pettishness returned. I thought of Deirdre's hunched shoulders, the lost soul laced with venom, and drove well within the speed limit all the way south.

□7
The Cocktail Party

When Fabian Messenger joined the University of Chicago law faculty, he bought a home in the old Kenwood neighborhood. A mile north of the university campus, Kenwood is filled with mansions—thirty-room houses on outsize lots, built in the last century and packed with all the wood paneling and stained glass that the Victorian imagination demanded. For a long time the neighborhood went downhill as people who could afford the houses let racial fears drive them away. Nowadays, though, the rehab contractors were having a field day as rich doctors or law professors like Fabian fed their egos on size, opulence, and proximity to Lake Michigan.

It was eight when I pulled up across from the Messenger home. Palace. I took a deep breath and went through the open iron gates. I'd been afraid I was so late I'd have to sidle to a table while everyone dropped their forks and stared. The roar of happy drinkers reassured me as I rang the doorbell. Deirdre apparently favored a long cocktail hour. No one heard me over the din, so I pushed open the door and joined the melee.

Women in cocktail dresses and men in evening clothes spilled out of a brightly lit room on my left into the hall. A few people glanced at me, but returned immediately to their chatter when they saw they didn't know me. I looked around for some place to dump my coat. The day had grown so warm after its icy start, I hadn't needed a coat outside, let alone in here.

An old oak wardrobe stood against one wall, more for decoration than use: two flowered straw hats hung from its hooks, but nothing else. I hesitated to hang my shabby old wool there. As I hovered uncertainly next to the wardrobe I saw an umbrella stand, also decorative: instead of umbrellas it housed an old baseball bat, hand-signed by Nellie Fox.

I was about to take the coat back to my car when a small boy sailed into the hall, his pale bangs the same cornsilk as Deirdre's when I first met her. He was handing round a tray of Deirdre's cream puffs, but was so wound up with the excitement of the party that he couldn't stop long enough for anyone to take them. I put a hand on his shoulder, stopping his gyrations so abruptly that he dropped the tray.

He gulped. The vivacity drained from his face and his lower lip started to quiver.

"Sorry, honey," I said. "My fault for startling you. How about if I pick them up—no one will ever know they've been on the floor—and you find someone to help me with my coat."

He stuffed his fist into his mouth, nodded nervously, and fled toward the back of the hall, calling "Emily! Emily!" through his fingers.

I knelt below the uproar and reassembled the tray, putting pastry caps back on lopsided blobs of mushrooms and bacon. Deirdre must have spent a day on these, if she'd made enough to feed thirty-five. They'd come out rubbery and a bit burned. Why had she bothered, with dozens of catering firms to choose from?

As I was dusting off the sides of the last few pastries the boy reappeared through the swinging door at the end of the hall. He was hand-in-hand with a young woman whom I took for his nanny—the Emily he'd gone crying for. She was wearing a dress cut from an expensive wool, but designed for a woman broader in the bust and smaller in the waist than she was. Presumably she wore Deirdre's castoffs without caring too much how they looked on her, since the rich pink didn't go with her brown suede shoes.

She moved awkwardly in front of me, muttering something I couldn't catch over the uproar. When she finally took the tray from me, her round, undefined wrists showed she was much younger than I'd thought at first, surely a teenager still.

"What should I do with my coat?" I bellowed through the din. "Upstairs?"

"Josh will take it. Be careful," she said as the child grabbed it. "Don't let it drag on the ground."

She watched him anxiously as he ran up the stairs, trailing the coat along the carpeting. She took a step toward him, then glanced at me as if expecting censure.

"It's old," I said lightly. "He can't make it grubbier than it already is."

She didn't smile back. Her expression was lackluster under her mass of ill-cut frizzy hair; I wondered if she might be retarded.

"Drinks are in there. Can I get you something?" Her voice was so soft I had to strain to hear her.

"That's okay, I'll serve myself. Is Mrs. Messenger in there?"

She shook her head speechlessly, then roused herself to say Deirdre was in the kitchen. I declined an offer to go back to see her—kitchen chaos moments before putting a big dinner on the table strains guest and hostess alike. Assembling what I hoped was a social smile I pushed into the living room.

Fabian Messenger was holding court near the fireplace, his left arm on the mantel, his right casually touching Manfred Yeo's shoulder. A half dozen men were laughing at something he was saying.

I fought through the crowd around the drinks. Two bartenders, the only black men in the room, were working flat out to keep up with the group's thirst. I asked for whisky and was offered Red Label or Jim Beam. I would never serve guests such thin, raw Scotch, and my income is probably a tenth of Fabian's. I took the Scotch, grumpily—my day had been too long for chardonnay to do me any good.

I moved over to the sidelines to drink. A waitress who'd taken over the tray of hors d'oeuvres offered them to me, but I passed—they looked like the ones I'd just finished picking off the floor. Josh reappeared, his gaiety restored, clutching a bowl of nuts. I took a handful and watched him pirouette through the room.

Fabian apparently was calling to him. I didn't hear it, but one of the women tapped Josh's shoulder and pointed him toward his father. He immediately stopped gyrating and walked over, looking like an altar boy summoned to the pope. Fabian put a hand on his head, seeming to pose a question. The group around him laughed and Fabian laughed as well, but Josh squirmed between their legs. He ran through the side door, the nuts still clutched to his stomach.

"Cute kid," a man next to me said.

"He looks a lot like Deirdre did when I first met her—he even has her dreamy air."

"Oh, you an old friend of hers? I've done a little work with Fabian, but I hardly know her."

We wended through the laborious party chat of strangers and made it to introductions. He was Donald Blakely, the president of Gateway Bank.

"I'm one of your happy beneficiaries," I said. "I sit with Deirdre on the board of Arcadia House—we're terrifically grateful for your generous check."

"Arcadia House?" Blakely looked blank.

"Domestic violence shelter in Logan Square. You—or your bank—just gave us twenty-five thousand dollars."

He smiled. "Oh, yes. Yes, indeed. We welcome the chance to help out important community service groups. Do you work for them, Ms. . . . uh?"

"Warshawski," I repeated. "No. I'm just on their board."

He looked around the room, hunting for more important

prey. When he didn't see it he turned back to me and asked what I did, with enough show of politeness that I sketched a description of my work. Who knows—Gateway might need an independent investigator.

"Actually, I seem to be spending an inordinate amount of time on nonpaying investigations these days. I'm wondering if you might be able to help me with one of them."

He took a step away from me. "Not me, Ms. . . . uh. The work I do for nonprofits is limited to writing the occasional check. Anyway, I never wanted to be Dick Tracy, running around town with a gun."

I laughed. "Not that kind of help. But I wondered if you knew anyone at Century Bank who might talk to me."

Again he scanned the room, then asked why I wanted an introduction. As I explained Camilla's problem he started to pay closer attention, but when I finished, he said he didn't know anyone at Century well enough to send me to them. He asked how I would proceed. I gave him a brief précis of my usual methods.

"You'd be that thorough on a *pro bono* project?" he demanded.

"I'm that thorough on everything I do. It's the only way I can compete with the big guys."

He looked around again, finally spotting someone who would release him from me. Briefly clasping my forearm, he wished me well and hurried to the other side of the room.

Emily reappeared, tripping on her scuffed pumps as she interrupted Fabian. Fabian smiled graciously and left the group at the fireplace to head to the hall. The others walked off as well, leaving Manfred Yeo alone for a moment. I took the opportunity to go over to him.

He recognized me at once. "Victoria! How wonderful to see you. How are you, my dear? We've graduated many distinguished jurists, and a lot of them are here tonight, but it brings me great pleasure to read about your work—jumping from bridges is much more exciting than filing writs of certiorari."

Yeo had taught my class in constitutional law my second year. I'd started law school young, through an option the university gave of finishing my last year in college at the same time. My father had begun to show signs of the illness that would kill him five years later, and I was desperate to find a career with some financial security. Yeo's wit and insight had made me feel the study of law could generate passion as well.

He'd liked something about me, too, and rescued me from summers of factory and clerical work with a couple of good internships. He still sent me hand-signed cards at Christmas, but I felt I'd let him down by leaving law to be a private eye, and a penurious one at that.

I said this, a bit awkwardly, and he put an arm around me. "My dear, I'm proud of you for not abandoning your principles. I'm ashamed of the law these days. It's not the work I signed on joyfully to do fifty years ago, and I'm ashamed of too many of our graduates for putting billable hours ahead of justice."

Unexpected tears stung my eyes. My dreary work load, even my fatigue, dwindled in the face of his praise. At the same time I felt a kind of ignominious triumph: Donald Blakely, the banker, was pointing me out to the group he was with. My stock had risen fast at a touch from Manfred's arm. The thought made me chuckle a little.

"Ah . . . the cause of the hubbub," Manfred said, releasing me. "We can go in to dinner now."

Fabian was coming back into the room with a man about my age, handsome in the too-perfect way that makes people love themselves more than they ever can someone else. He looked vaguely familiar; I wondered if I'd seen him in the movies.

"Alec Gantner," Manfred explained. "His father was one of my first students. Fabian brought young Alec to represent the family—I'd better greet him."

Of course. Alec senior, the Republican senator from Illinois, had the same chiseled good looks, turned distinguished with age. No wonder Fabian had waited dinner for the son. If Deirdre was right and he was pining for a federal judgeship, courting senators was the easiest way to go about it.

As Manfred went off to shake young Gantner's hand Emily moved among the guests. When she came to me she whispered her message: we could go into the dining room now.

□8

Of Riches, Drunks, and Rats

A long table dominated the center of the dining room. It was covered in linen so white I thought I might go snow-blind if I stared at it too long. Complete with silver, flowers, and candelabra, it might well have been labeled IMPORTANT GUESTS ONLY. Others were relegated to small tables at the sides.

We all hunted our name cards at the main table first, hoping to be among the chosen. Disappointment rippled through the room as people found themselves excluded. Even I felt let down that Manfred's warm greeting hadn't extended to a desire to sit next to me at dinner: I was decanted with the dregs to a table near the kitchen door. I had to laugh at myself—all my professional choices have consciously led me away from wealth and power. It was absurd to resent denial from their ranks.

Deirdre arrived suddenly through some swinging doors near my table. She stood stock-still in the center of the room, her head thrust back on her shoulders like a cobra's, her eyes glittering. As people surged past her they tried to greet her, but she said nothing, until someone asked her point-blank for help in finding his seat.

Deirdre pulled her lips back in a parody of a smile. "If you need help, check with my darling daughter; she did the table arrangements. Like that old Georgie Price cartoon: Yes, there's something you can do, put around the place cards—while the wife is up to her eyeballs in the kitchen.''

She spoke loudly enough that the people at the kitchen end of the room could hear. Most laughed, but Emily, who'd come in with a toddler in her arms, turned red and hung her head.

It dawned on me with dreadful certainty that she wasn't the nanny, but Deirdre's daughter. Her broad forehead and wide cheekbones might have been stamped from Fabian's face. The resemblance was so obvious that my failure to notice it when she'd stood next to him in the front room seemed unbelievable.

I tried to remember if I'd said anything that would make her realize my mistake. And at the same time I wondered how Deirdre could be so cruel as to put her into one of her own dresses. The pink wool not only fit the girl badly but was clearly designed for an older person, a matron, not a child. Dressing her to look like an adult only added to confusion about Emily's status, especially since she seemed consumed with child care.

The toddler, who looked about two, squirmed in her arms. Emily tried to distract him by pointing at the chandelier, a massive piece whose pendants cracked light into winking blues and yellows. The child refused to be placated. The late hour, the noise, the strangers, all turned him fractious. He whimpered and lunged in his sister's arms, but neither Deirdre nor Fabian paid any attention.

Finally the main table sorted itself out, with Fabian at one end and Manfred Yeo at the other. Donald Blakely, the Gateway Bank president, and Alec Gantner sat near Fabian. Women were sprinkled along the table like poppies among penguins. They, too, may have been distinguished jurists or business owners, but they looked as though they had been invited strictly as decoration.

Two small tables each seating six were tucked into the bays at the south end of the room. I dubbed their denizens the rising stars—young, well dressed, and self-assured, they gaily discussed the end of the skiing season and the start of sailing.

Joshua, perched on a couple of dictionaries, was sitting by an empty chair at the main table. I assumed his mother would move next to him, but as Fabian finished seating his dinner partner, Deirdre planted herself aggressively at my table. This could present a golden opportunity to discuss housing for Tamar Hawkings and her three children, but Deirdre didn't look up to discussing anything more major than another bottle of wine.

Emily had been hovering near me with the toddler while people found their places. As soon as Fabian got settled she brought the child over to him. Her father made an impatient gesture and pointed down the table at Manfred. Emily flushed and dragged the boy down to him. The professor showed the usual enthusiasm of dinner guests for small children; after a quick look at her father, who ignored her, Emily headed from the room.

Deirdre called her back and fiddled clumsily with the child's pajamas. "Yes, Nathan. Now that your daddy has proved to Manfred what a virile guy he is, coming up with a baby son at the age of forty, you can go to bed."

She spoke loudly enough for everyone at Fabian's end of the long table to overhear. There was a brief pause in the conversation, like a momentary drop in current. The woman on Fabian's right gave a little scream of laughter and everyone began talking feverishly. Fabian was laughing, too, but for a brief instant fury had carved terrifying lines around his eyes and mouth.

Emily stumbled from the room again. The two bartenders joined the waitress in handing out cold carrot soup. By the time Emily returned to take the empty chair next to Joshua the staff was serving the main course. The food was excellent—a surprise, given Deirdre's drunkenness and the rubbery hors d'oeuvres.

Deirdre's back was to the center table, close enough to Fabian and Gantner that she could hear much of their conversation. The two men talked across the women between them, with Donald Blakely chiming in. The women made a few attempts to join in, but were shut out so effectively that they had to lean across the table and speak to each other like small planes flying under jumbo jets.

Every time Fabian spoke, Deirdre twitched in her chair. She made no effort to talk to those around her, but toyed with her food while she continued to drink. The six of us with her went through the social pretense of pleasure in our awkward situation. I felt as though I were swimming up a waterfall.

The most pitiable was a young woman named Lina, who'd been stuck on Deirdre's left. She was married to one of Fabian's students—the editor of the *Law Review*—and confided that she had just turned twenty-one when she married Brian at Christmas. As her hostess divided her mind between wine and Fabian's remarks, Lina kept trying to talk to her—about the dinner, the house, Chicago's opera, anything to prove that Deirdre was fine, her angry twitches a passing nightmare.

I did my duty with Brian by asking him about his classes and his and Lina's Iowa home. A woman across from us who worked for Donald Blakely at Gateway Bank gamely joined in with a discussion of a client in Cedar Rapids. We were doing . . . not well, but enough to make it seem we were at a party, when Lina brought up Deirdre's children.

"You must be so proud of them," she said desperately. "Everyone tells me how smart they are. And your daughter seems wonderful with her little brothers."

Deirdre jerked her head up. "My darling daughter is a saint." Her voice was heavy with sarcasm. "I couldn't do without her and her daddy would die if he lost her."

Lina turned her head, furtively blinking back tears. The rest of us sat stunned for a moment. Finally I leaned across the man on my right to talk to her.

"Brian's been telling me about your riding. The only time I was ever on a horse was when my dad got a friend in the mounted patrol to let me ride around Grant Park in front of him. I was thrilled and terrified at once. How did you begin?''

Lina bit her lip but gallantly produced an answer. Eleanor Guziak, the banker, joined in, speaking in the exaggerated way people use when embarrassed. As Brian and one of the other men started talking I looked past Deirdre to Emily. The girl was poking at her food, turning it over and over with her fork, but making no pretense of eating.

"What do you do, Vic?" Lina asked. "Are you a lawyer too?"

"I went to law school with Fabian and worked on the Public Defender's Homicide Task Force for a while, but I've been a private investigator for ten years now." My tongue felt thick from mushing social drivel in the midst of the Messenger family's disarray.

"Oh, Vic is one of our most prominent do-gooders." Deirdre, apparently realizing that she'd alienated her guests, was striving for jocularity. "She didn't stop working for the poor and desperate when she left the PD's office. Why, she even puts up homeless families in her own office."

Lina turned wide blue eyes to me. "You do? That's so wonderful of you. I get upset every time I go downtown and see homeless people lining the sidewalks, but I feel so helpless—"

"I'm helpless too," I interrupted her. "The amount of misery is overwhelming and I'm not brave enough, smart enough, or rich enough to know what to do about it."

"But to put a family up in your office—" Lina began.

"I haven't. Deirdre's exaggerating."

"Come, come, Vic. You're much too modest," Deirdre lunged in. "You told us on Monday you helped a homeless family camp out there."

She was too drunk to pitch her voice properly. Conversation at the main table broke off as people began listening in.

"How do the rest of the tenants feel about your generosity?" Alec Gantner, the senator's son, had turned around in his chair to look at me.

I forced a smile. "Deirdre's blowing a small thing into a big one. I found a woman with three children hiding behind the boiler when I went down to work on the wiring Monday. My building is going under the wrecking ball May fifteenth; only a handful of tenants is left. I thought the woman could live in one of the vacant offices for six weeks, instead of down below with the rats—as you can imagine, the basement is full of them. But when we took her three kids to the hospital last night, she got scared they'd be taken from her and disappeared. End of story."

"You didn't think to consult the owners?" Donald Blakely, the Gateway banker, called over.

"That's why I was working in the basement: the owners haven't cared enough about the tenants to do routine maintenance. I certainly didn't care enough about them to tell them about this woman: all they would have done is called the cops and get her arrested for trespassing."

"They'd be within their rights," Gantner said.

"The real problem is liability," Eleanor Guziak said. "I think Donald's point is that if the woman gets hurt, or injures someone herself, the owners are still on the hook for damages, even if they've let the building run down."

I didn't think that was Donald's point at all, but Eleanor was following the first law of corporate advancement: make the boss look good at all times. Donald seconded her warmly, then demanded to know where the building was.

"So you can call the cops yourself? No, thanks. Anyway, the woman has disappeared. I don't know if she'll come back to my building because it's familiar, or stay away because she thinks she'll be arrested."

"Donald doesn't want to call the cops. He wants to help the woman out, don't you, Donald?" Deirdre said.

"Deirdre." Fabian's voice was heavy with warning.

"No, don't you 'Deirdre' me. I know what I'm talking about. Gateway Bank is the biggest booster of housing for the homeless in town. We studied them at Home Free." She lifted her glass to toast Blakely. "So Vic shouldn't feel shy about giving Donald her office address. It's the Pulteney Building, isn't it, Vic, down near Monroe.''

I was surprised that she could recall that chance-dropped fact, and furious that she had made my private problem public.

Blakely smiled blandly at Deirdre and looked at Fabian. "The real problem is the number of drunks and crazies who are wandering the streets.''

"Funny how we only got drunks and crazies in such large numbers in the last decade,'' I snapped.

Gantner and Blakely affected not to hear me. Gantner turned his back on me again and loudly reported on a conservative think-tank study that proved most homeless people roamed the streets by choice. I snapped my fork down on my plate so hard that a piece of salmon ricocheted from it and landed on my silk blouse. As I got up to ask one of the staff for a glass of club soda, I saw Emily looking anxiously from me to Deirdre.

I went over to her. "What's the problem, honey? Worried that I'm arguing with your folks?''

She pulled on the ends of her tangled hair. "Would the cops arrest the mother if they found her?''

I didn't think that was what was really bothering her, but I answered her seriously. "They might. Most people would say she was being a bad parent, letting her kids live down there.''

"But you don't?''

"I don't know enough of her story. I keep thinking she may be doing the best thing she can when she doesn't have very many choices.''

"What were they doing there?'' she muttered.

"You mean, how did they get there? I don't know—I've been wondering about that myself. I walked around the basement earlier today but couldn't see any openings into it.''

"But what do they live on?''

"I don't know that either. She does manage to find food for the children.''

"Aren't the rats dangerous?" Her gray eyes were painfully large in her anxiety.

"Rats won't bother them unless they have food," I said with more conviction than I felt. "I go down to that basement a lot to work on the wiring and they never come near me. I think the mother is too smart to let her children eat where there are rats."

Fabian was looking at us from the end of the table, his countenance darkening. Emily, focused on me, couldn't see him.

"What about the father, though? What was he doing?"

"I don't know. Maybe he lost his job and is ashamed that he can't support them." Emily seemed to carry too many loads to burden her with Tamar's tale of domestic violence.

"Emily!" Fabian's voice cut across the table talk. "Ms. Warshawski doesn't need you bothering her."

Emily flushed again, but the anxiety fled behind the mask of stupidity she donned so easily.

"She's not bothering me. I like talking to her."

I put a hand on the girl's shoulder to reassure her. Through the wool dress I could feel the tension at my touch, a forced immobility of the muscles. I removed my hand and saw a slight relaxation. What was she afraid of? Surely not that I was making a pass at her—but of Fabian's reaction to me.

"You don't need to worry about the Hawkings family," I said to Emily. "That's my job. Okay?"

"Okay, I guess."

She stared at me, wanting something, perhaps some assurance about her own family that I couldn't give her. After a long moment she looked at her brother, who was clutching her sleeve. She gently turned him around in his chair and started whispering tales of bravado, how if they found rats they would beat them with sticks, then look at them with such mean faces the rats would run away. The little boy laughed. I wished I could have given similar comfort to his sister.

□9

End of Revelry

Fabian beckoned me so imperiously that I was tempted to ignore him and return to my seat, but Emily's mute anguish made me accede to his summons.

"I couldn't help hearing your conversation with Emily just now."

"You were paying close enough attention it would have been strange if you'd missed it."

"I heard you tell her it was your job to look after this homeless woman. I'd rather you didn't make it Deirdre's job as well; she's got enough on her hands without taking on your stray charities."

My eyes opened wide at this incongruous remark, but before I could command a coherent response he continued.

"You should turn the matter over to Jasper Heccomb."

"Jasper Heccomb?" I echoed like a half-witted parrot.

"The head of Home Free," Fabian said impatiently.

"But . . . that isn't the same guy who led the antiwar movement on campus when we were students, is it?"

"Heccomb?" Blakely interjected. "I guess he was something of a radical in his youth, but he seems to have gotten that out of his system. Runs Home Free very effectively."

"Come on, Donald—if he'd gotten it out of his system

he'd be underwriting bond issues." That was Alec Gantner. "Do you know him, Ms. . . . uh . . ."

"Warshawski," I supplied. "He was a senior when I started school here in sixty-nine. So I didn't know him, but I tagged around after him. I never knew what happened to him. When did he go to Home Free?"

"He went to Home Free five years ago." Deirdre spoke behind me, her voice loud, each syllable carefully measured. "And he's been doing just the kind of job Alec and Donald approve of."

Donald turned in his chair and smiled at his hostess. "Thanks, Deirdre. I'm glad to know that. Home Free is one of the charities Gateway supports and in days of tight capital you like to believe your charities are well run."

Back in my chair I looked bitterly at Deirdre. Having stirred up me, her daughter, Gantner, and Blakely she was calmly finishing her salad. She was even speaking cheerfully to Lina, as though sobered by our anger. I didn't need to stay for any more of this charade. I'd come because—supposedly—Manfred had put in a special plea for my presence. I'd had my moment to bask in the great man's sunshine. My career certainly didn't depend on staying to butter up him, or Fabian, or even the son of my United States senator.

Before I could leave the room, Fabian tapped his wineglass with a spoon to quiet the crowd. He stood to speak.

"I know many of you have to get up early tomorrow to squeeze the most billable hours out of the day"—polite laughter—"so I want to thank you all now for coming. After you've eaten Deirdre's fabulous Grand Marnier soufflé you won't want to listen to my twaddle anyway."

He smiled easily, the perfect family man and host. They could have afforded a caterer, I realized, but that wouldn't have given Fabian as much to brag about as a wife who stayed at home to make perfect soufflés.

He moved into an adroit tribute to Manfred. As he started to speak the staff went around filling our glasses with Dom

Pérignon. The money he'd saved on whisky had gone to champagne, apparently.

"Our little gathering tonight is a tribute both to Manfred and to the rule of law," Fabian concluded. "He has taught trial lawyers and judges, prosecutors and defenders, and even somehow trained both liberals and conservatives. Some of us have contested mightily with one another, but, as Shakespeare said, we gather here to eat and drink as friends, and to do honor to the best friend both we and the law have ever known."

We all stood to salute Manfred with champagne. I looked at my watch. It was ten-thirty, but my hopes of sidling out the door were halted as Fabian began to speak again.

"Other people also want to make some remarks, but before they speak, the youngest person present wants to say something. He's not a lawyer, at least not yet, but he knows, as Daniel Webster noted, that 'there's always room at the top'—and with Manfred's departure we have, of course, a great gap at the top. Joshua?"

As the little boy climbed down from his chair, the dictionaries he'd perched on slid out from under him and landed on the floor. Those who could see what had happened laughed. Joshua turned red. Emily bit her lip and helped her brother move clear of the books. She then turned her chair so that he could see her face.

Putting his hands behind him, Joshua started to recite Prospero's farewell speech. He spoke fast, in a high, soft voice:

> "Our revels now are ended. These our actors,
>   As I foretold you, were all spirits and
>   Are melted into air, into thin air:
>   And, like the . . . the . . ."

"Baseless," Emily mouthed.

> "Baseless fabric of this vision,
>   The cloud-capp'd towers, the gorgeous palaces,

The solemn temples, the great globe itself,
Yea, all which . . . all which . . .''

"It inherit," his sister prompted again.

"It inherit," the little boy repeated. "It inherit."

" 'Yea, all which it inherit, shall dissolve,' " Emily whispered.

Joshua's face worked as he mouthed the words. "I can't," he burst out. "I don't remember. I can't do it."

He started to cry. Emily got up and put her arms around him, but kept her eyes on her father. Fabian was smiling, but from where I sat he seemed to have an ugly gleam in his eye.

"It's awfully late for such a small boy to be up and on public display," I heard myself saying. "I think we all know he learned the verse. Let's give him a hand and let him go to bed."

Fabian turned to me in surprise, as though one of the candlesticks had spoken, but the rest of the crowd took up my suggestion in relief. We clapped for the boy, who ran from the room, his sister close behind him. I glanced at Deirdre as they left. She was gloating openly. Because Fabian had been embarrassed, or her daughter, or both? My stomach turned and I quickly looked away.

Other people rose to put in their two cents for Manfred. The waiters served dessert and coffee and people began soft side conversations.

Eleanor Guziak leaned across the table toward me. "Good for you. Fabian loves to trot out his children's accomplishments—they're all brilliant—but what a terrible ordeal to put a little boy through."

Around eleven, when I thought I couldn't endure another moment in the room, Manfred got up to respond. After thanking Fabian and Deirdre for the beautiful evening—and why not? he hadn't been sitting near them—he surprised me by repeating what he'd said to me earlier in the living room.

"The practice of law has changed too much since I began its study a half century ago. People seem to take more pleasure in money than in justice. If I've taught any of you here to care for justice, then I leave my professional life content. We've heard a lot of high-minded poetry quoted tonight. I'd just like to remind you of the words of another Elizabethan, Francis Quarles. He wrote them almost four hundred years ago, but they're not so out-of-date that we can't profit by them:

> 'Use law and physic only in cases of necessity; they that use them otherwise abuse themselves into weak bodies and light purses; they are good remedies, bad recreations, but ruinous habits.' ''

He resumed his seat to stunned silence. I got up quickly and went over to him.

"People have praised you more memorably than I can tonight. I just want you to know that every time I hear you speak you say something important. Thanks for doing it again tonight."

"Good luck, Victoria. I'll have plenty of time to see friends now. Stop by for a cup of coffee some afternoon if you're ever beating up thugs on the South Side."

He grasped my hand briefly. Other old students had swarmed over. I fled the house without saying good-bye to my host and hostess. As I turned the Trans Am in a tight U to head back north I could see the rest of the guests begin to leave.

It wasn't until I was at McCormick Place, some three or four miles north of Kenwood, that I remembered my coat. I grunted aloud in annoyance. If I didn't go back now I'd have to call and arrange a time to fetch it. And I'd either have to be social with Deirdre, or decide to let her know just what I thought of her antics tonight. Neither choice was appetizing. I whipped over to the left-hand lane, exited at Twenty-third Street, and returned south.

Light still poked around the shutters in the front windows. I tried the door but it had been locked. I rang the bell, tapping my foot impatiently as a minute or more ticked by. I rang again.

One of the bartenders finally came to the door. "The party's over, miss—everyone's gone."

"Sorry. I forgot my coat. One of the kids took it upstairs —I'll just run up and get it and be on my way."

He looked me up and down. Apparently my frank, honest face persuaded him I was neither burglar nor murderer. He opened the door wide and waved me toward the stairs. Halfway up I realized I had no idea where to go when I got to the top. I called down to ask him, but he'd already disappeared into the back of the house.

Antique wall sconces lit the stairs and the upper hall, giving a rich glow to the gray flocked paper. Thick carpeting masked my footfalls.

At the top I hesitated, not wanting to open doors at random and wake sleeping children. Voices were coming from a room at the end of the long hall. Its door was open a crack, letting out a bar of light along with the sound. By the time I was halfway down the hall the sound had clearly resolved itself into Fabian's voice.

"How dare you?" he was yelling. "Humiliating me in front of my guests like that. I told you weeks ago what I wanted and you agreed to coach him. You assured me he was letter perfect. How long have you been plotting to show me up? When did you realize this would be an ideal way to embarrass me?"

I paused outside the door. Emily was answering him, muttering something unintelligible.

"Were *you* a party to this?" Fabian demanded, apparently of Deirdre, because she said, "No, I wasn't a party to it. I asked Emily this afternoon if she was sure Joshua could perform and she told me he could."

I had been about to push open the door, but the sheer shock of the conversation stayed my hand. They were browbeating *Emily* because they'd kept their son up past his bedtime to expose him to a crowd of strangers?

"And what were you doing, baiting Donald and Alec

with all that crap about the homeless? If Warshawski wants to waste her time and energy in the gutter instead of turning her legal training to good use, that's her business. But what are you doing signing on for it?''

''I'm not signing on for it.'' Deirdre was using loud, measured tones, but her voice had cracks around the edges. ''You might remember I serve on a board with her and also one for the homeless. *You* wanted me doing good works instead of holding a proper job. You thought it would make you look good.''

A loud smack, hand on flesh. ''I'm not talking about Home Free, Deirdre, but this crap you were spinning about homeless families living in Warshawski's office building. Why did you have to bring that up?''

''I brought it up because I'm going to try to work with the woman. I've talked to Vic about it and she thinks I might be able to help her.''

''You?'' Fabian gave a crack of angry laughter. ''You can't look after your own house and children. What are you going to do with someone else's? And don't you try to sidle out the door, young lady. I'm not through with you yet tonight.''

I knocked loudly on the door and pushed it open. Fabian stood in front of an empty fireplace, facing his wife and daughter like an old-fashioned schoolmaster with errant pupils. Emily, still in her absurd pink dress, was kneading her hands in its skirt. Deirdre's head was back, cobralike, but the stain of Fabian's hand showed on her left cheek. They were so involved in their fight that they showed no surprise at my arrival.

We were in the master bedroom—the bedroom for mastery. It was large enough to hold a desk and a chaise longue and still leave room for ballroom dancing. I could see my black wool coat on the king-size bed in the far corner.

''You guys could let up on Emily,'' I said. ''How old is she, anyway?''

Deirdre moved to stand next to Fabian. They stopped glaring at each other and joined to look at me in hate.

"What business is it of yours, Warshawski? Why don't you save your interference for men who *pay* you to peek through their wives' keyholes?" Fabian spat out.

"Gosh, Fabian, maybe because I took Manfred's words to heart and want to do a little *pro bono* work. I've spent a nauseating evening in your house, with Deirdre drunk and you preening like a cock on a dunghill. I'm fed up with both of you for making your daughter act like a nursemaid, and not even questioning the absurdity of the burdens or accusations you're laying on her."

"I don't remember asking you to stay." Fabian tried to look haughty. "If we're so nauseating, why don't you leave?"

I crossed to the bed and picked up my coat. "I'd like to, but I'm worried about what you'll do to Emily if I take off now."

"Don't worry about Emily," Deirdre said. "She's her daddy's darling; she won't come to any harm."

Emily had started to cry. She was trying to do so quietly, but at Deirdre's words she gave a racking sob and cried, "I hate you. I hate both of you! Why don't you shut up and leave me alone!" She ran from the room and slammed the door.

"Thanks, Warshawski," Fabian said sarcastically. "Thanks for upsetting my daughter and ruining my party for Manfred. Now why don't you go home."

My head was spinning from trying to follow his dizzying loops around logic. "Yeah, I'll leave. And Deirdre, you and I need to talk. Tomorrow, when your head is clearer."

"My head is perfectly clear, thank you," she started, but I couldn't take any more of either of them; I followed Emily out the door, slamming it hard behind me.

Back in the hall I tried to guess which room Emily might have fled to. None of them showed any light, so I stopped to listen at each keyhole—the peeping eye Fabian had denigrated—until I heard stifled sobs behind one.

I knocked gently on the panel. "It's V.I.—Vic Warshawski. Can I come in?"

When she didn't answer I opened the door and felt my way through the dark room to the bed. She was sprawled fully dressed across the spread, bucking with the force of her sobs.

"Hey, there, girl, take it easy. You're going to hurt yourself if you keep on like that."

"I wish I would," she gasped. "I wish I would kill myself."

I knelt next to the bed and put a hand on her heaving shoulder. "I don't think you can cry yourself to death, but you might break a rib. . . . Out of curiosity, how old are you?"

"Four . . . teen."

"Awful young to be doing what you're doing. How old are those brothers of yours?"

"Josh is six and Natie's two." Answering simple questions was slowing her sobs down.

I kept my hand on her shoulder and rubbed it gently while I tried to think of what I might do to help her. I had a fleeting memory of Lotty's words, that when I decide to intervene in other people's lives someone always gets badly hurt. My worry that Lotty might be right kept me from suggesting any bold action to Emily.

"In a few years you can leave to go to college. I know at your age eighteen must seem a long way off, but it's something you can hang on to, look forward to." It was such a feeble thing to say I didn't blame her for not leaping up in ecstasy.

"Your parents are very disturbed people," I added. "In fact they seem nuts to me. Do you think you could remember that, when the going gets too rugged—that they're two people with a huge problem, but you are not the problem?"

"How can you possibly know that?" she said angrily into the bedspread. "You never laid eyes on me before."

"Yeah, but I've known your folks going on twenty years. Look, Emily, I spent the evening watching you—watching the three of you. You were the only person trying to take adult responsibility for the scene around you, but you're just a kid. Perhaps this seems normal to you, because it's the only life you know, but believe me, it's not the way most people do act or should act. Okay?''

She didn't say anything, but her sobs trailed off. I fished in my purse and pulled out a business card. My eyes had adjusted to the dark and I could make out the shapes of furniture. I stretched out my right hand to something that was either a desk or a low-lying dresser.

''I'm going to leave my name and phone number here by your bed. If you need a friendly ear to talk to, give me a call. Or if you think you can't take life here anymore, maybe I can help you figure out some other choices. I don't know what they might be, but we could explore that together.''

She turned over onto her side so that she could speak directly to me. ''I can't. I can't abandon the boys. They need me.''

''You have a right to a life, too, Emily, only nobody here is going to help you get one. Think about it. . . . You want me to bring you a glass of water before I go?''

''I'm okay,'' she muttered.

I shut the door softly, trying to get it to catch without rousing her parents. At the far end of the hall Deirdre and Fabian were still raging. Even at this distance, with their door closed, I could make out her screams and his furies. Downstairs the staff had finished cleaning up and had turned out the lights. I undid the dead bolt in the massive front door and let myself out.

I looked at the house from the curb. The master bedroom overlooked the street. The light seeping around the curtains abruptly disappeared. After a few seconds a glow appeared from a room on the south side. Emily's room. She'd gotten up, or one of her parents had joined her. My stomach churning from my own impotence, I fled into the night.

It was one when I finally got back to my own home. As I hung up my party clothes I saw the salmon stain still disfiguring the front of my white silk shirt.

A Frightened Mole

In my sleep I heard Emily sobbing. I followed the sound down an ornate staircase. At first, elaborate wall sconces made it easy to see my descent. My left hand traced raised flowers in the red wallpaper and my feet sank in plush. At a bend in the stairwell the light suddenly vanished and I had to grope my way in the dark. The velvet changed to stone under my hand; the stairs narrowed and the carpeting disappeared. Emily's cries kept summoning me but I couldn't reach the bottom. As I stumbled dizzyingly downward the stairs collapsed. I fell, seemingly for hours, until I landed in a heap outside the room where the girl was weeping. I pulled myself to my feet and pushed open the door.

Lotty Herschel stood in front of me. "Don't try to touch her," she said. "You will only hurt her."

Her angry words jerked me awake. I lay still a long time, watching the gray light make ghostly waves on the ceiling. A spider had died in one of the corners. It hung on a wisp of web that swayed in the drafts rising from my badly sealed windows.

In four months I would be forty. The dreams I'd had at twenty—the twin yearnings for glory and altruism—seemed as ghostly and futile as the bit of dirty silk the spider had released in her death spasm.

What was I doing trying to patch the hulk of the Pulteney together when it would only fall down around me in a few weeks? It typified my whole approach to life: enormous energy sunk into mending lives or causes that could never be made whole. Behind every patch great leaks sprang anyway.

Even the bureau in front of me, bought at a flea market with the sincere intention of stripping and refinishing it— there's solid walnut under there, the friend who'd gone with me, an expert in these matters, said. Five years later the chipped brown paint had become part of the customary backdrop of my life.

I pulled the sheet over my head, blocking out the spider and the bureau. When the phone rang I let it drag out, hoping the caller would go away. Finally, my eyes hot with grit, I stuck my arm outside the sheet and picked up the receiver.

"Morning, beautiful. How were the rich and famous?"

It was Conrad Rawlings, who'd been working the owl shift lately. I sat up, feeling more lively. "They wore me out. I haven't gotten up yet. What was your haul last night?"

"Six gunshots, one fatal, a stabbing, a hit-and-run where the guy dragged the body halfway down Western Avenue before it came loose, and a baby in a garbage can. I got the hit-and-run and one of the gunshots. And you say *you're* worn out. Tell me the high-end lawyers carry on like that."

"Nah. Just guys roughing up the wife and kids, the women drunk and disorderly. The easy stuff." I spoke gruffly to cover the crack in my voice.

"Hey, Ms. W. Don't take it to heart. Want me to come over?"

I was tempted, but it was past ten. My first meeting was set for eleven. I was sick of pushing myself, but the old blue-collar work ethic wouldn't leave me alone. Or maybe it was just my dead mother's voice. Once when I was eight and had been in trouble at school I couldn't face going back the next day. In tears I pleaded a stomachache. My tenderhearted father wanted to tuck me in bed with a book and my teddy bear, but Gabriella dressed me by force. Speaking in her heavily accented English, rather than Italian—to make sure I knew it was important—she told me only cowards ran from their problems, especially ones they'd created themselves. At the end of the day, though, she'd been waiting for me in the school yard, with a bag of meringues—so I would know that bravery was rewarded.

I swung leaden legs over the side of the bed. "Oh, how I wish. When do you go back on a human schedule? Next week?"

"Tuesday. Hold that beautiful thought right where it is and don't let any of those fast-talking bankers or lawyers tempt you. I'd hate to have to spend my life in Joliet on account of you—my mama would never forgive me."

"If you got into trouble on my account I wouldn't be alive to worry about it," I said drily. Give her her due, Conrad's mother would probably hate any woman he went with, but my being white didn't help our relationship.

He laughed softly. "Speaking of which, you remember Sunday is Camilla's birthday? Think you can handle it?"

"You're talking to Wonder Woman. I wouldn't miss it. Matter of fact, I'm working on a project for her—trying to figure out why Alderman Lenarski canceled Lamia's zoning permit."

"You got time for that nonsense, Ms. W.? You're not taking it on because of me, are you—because if so, I'll be on the phone to Zu-Zu and tell her to lay off."

Zu-Zu was Camilla's pet name in the family. "No. Just my conscience, digging its teeth into my neck."

"Don't sound so dismal, babe. If the work's that bad it's time you took some time off. Can't you go away for a few days?"

"I've dug myself into too deep a financial hole. Of course, I could sell the Trans Am and drive something cheaper. That would save me five hundred a month. Or sell everything and go travel in Tuscany for a few months. I have some friends who did that—just toured Italy and

France until their money ran out, and then came back to Chicago to find work.''

''Damn!'' Conrad said in admiration. ''How do people get the guts to do that? Maybe when you've been raised like me, earning money for the family since you were hatched, you can never live like the lilies of the field.''

''Maybe so,'' I agreed. ''I'd better go see a man about a dog.''

''I'm going to call you tonight, girl. Make sure you get through the day in one piece. You hear?''

We hung up on that note. The conversation didn't exactly refresh me, but it gave me enough to go on with the day— the usual round of client meetings, research at the County Building, visits to Chicago Title, checking in with a pal at Motor Vehicles. The same stuff I do every day, like a gerbil on an everlasting treadmill.

At three I returned to the Pulteney to make phone calls and put my day's findings into the computer. Before going up to the fourth floor I checked the basement. There was no sign of Tamar Hawkings or her children, but when I got to my office and called my answering service I had a surprise. Kevin Whiting had called. I reached him at his desk just before he left for the day.

One of the Loop patrol officers had spotted a family that matched my description cadging money in front of the coffee shop at the corner. When he went over to talk to them they scuttled into the Pulteney. He'd followed them in but they'd disappeared—he'd assumed up the stairs. He'd gone up to the second floor before deciding he couldn't search the place on his own.

''You let us know if you spot them, okay, Vic? We can't let a family wander around a condemned building.''

''Right, Kevin. Thanks.'' As long as he didn't have to come over and hunt them himself he was ready to play the concerned, efficient cop by phone.

I wondered about undertaking my own detailed hunt through the building. Frankly, my enthusiasm for a floor-by-floor search wasn't any greater than Kevin's. I left a message for Lotty, telling her the family had resurfaced, and switched on my computer to stare at the log of my outstanding case files. I had a nice little custom data base that showed investigations by stage, with the last and most welcome labeled FINAL CHECK CLEARED and the date. Not enough of those lines had been filled in lately.

I opened the file for Lamia, Camilla's tradeswomen's group. The number of tasks completed was small: I'd dialed up Lexis for the Century Bank's board of directors, and I'd talked to Cyrus Lavalle at City Hall. I called Cyrus's office. When he answered the phone I spoke in a hoarse whisper.

"Found anything on the Lamia project?"

"Who is this?" he demanded. "What do you want?"

"I can't tell you my name over the phone. You'd get in trouble. Your bosses might find out you were collecting pictures of your favorite presidents without sharing, and you know they take a dim view of that."

"You'd better tell me your name or I'm going to call security."

"And tell them what?" I said in my natural voice. "That I've been augmenting your paycheck?"

"Oh, it's you, Warshawski. You're not as funny as you think you are."

"Then I guess I'd better not give up detection for the *Letterman* show. Have you heard anything about Lamia?"

"I don't know what you're talking about."

I looked at the backs of the pigeons huddled on my windowsill. One was checking himself for lice. The others were shrunk in the misery that shrouds cold birds. Cyrus must be afraid of being overheard.

"When will you be alone? I'll call you back."

"I won't be here."

"Cyrus, what's the problem?"

"The problem," he hissed very fast, "is that you're asking about something people don't want to talk about."

I could see him huddled over the receiver like the pigeons, as if he could become inaudible as well as invisible to his companions. "So you took my money yesterday under false pretenses. Someone offered you more not to talk to me. I'm not in a bidding war for your ideas, Cyrus."

"I'll give you your money back. I don't need it that bad." He hung up before I could say anything else.

Great. Something about the Lamia project was too hot to touch. I knew the whole investigation was trouble the minute Phoebe broached it Tuesday. I punched her number so forcefully, my index finger throbbed.

When her secretary answered with the bright news that Phoebe was in a meeting, I insisted she be interrupted. Yes, it was an emergency. I spelled my last name, just as I did every time I spoke to Gemma.

Phoebe came to the phone in some annoyance. "What is it, Vic? You took me away from something really important."

"I thought the work you wanted me to do for Camilla and the tradeswomen was really important," I said reproachfully.

Phoebe was quiet for a long second. "Oh. That." Her casualness sounded contrived. "I should have called you. We resolved matters with Century."

"Great. What happened?"

"They explained their situation to me. That they're overextended in the community. But they persuaded Home Free to give Lamia a crack at rehabbing one of their homeless shelters. You want to send me a bill for any time you've put in?"

"Not especially." I drew a circle on my notepad and peppered it with dots. "We agreed I would donate fifteen hours. You still have thirteen and a half coming."

"I'll bank them, then. Thanks for calling, Vic."

"Not so fast, Phoebe. My City Hall spout, who eats money like a broken vending machine, is too scared even to say the project name. Now you tell me, as though you were announcing the weather, that you had a meeting with Century. Two days ago you said you didn't know anyone there you could talk to. That changed mighty fast, didn't it? I called to chew on you for getting me involved in something hot, but you're making me want to dig in earnest."

Phoebe laughed. "You've been a detective too long, Vic: everything looks suspicious to you. I got a call at noon from Camilla saying they'd worked out a new deal with a different source. I've been tied up all afternoon and haven't had a chance to call you. No big deal."

I attacked my peppered circle with a series of sharp lines. Maybe she was right. Maybe I was just depressed by the ugliness around me—physical as well as spiritual. The rot of the dying Pulteney was seeping into my mind, withering me and turning me sour.

"Okay, Phoebe. I'm seeing Camilla on Sunday. She can tell me all about it."

"I'm sure she'll be happy to." We hung up on that line, but Phoebe had paused an instant too long before delivering it. I could almost hear the wheels turning in her brain, that she'd have to talk to Conrad's sister before I did to make sure they were telling the same story.

I typed the first entry in the Lamia file. "Cyrus is scared and Phoebe is lying."

□11
The Old College Tie

Camilla wasn't at work. The small contractor for whom she did carpentry said they hadn't had a job for her today. She wasn't at home either. I left urgent messages with her boss and her answering machine.

I'd never heard of Home Free until my Arcadia board meeting Monday night, and now it was cropping up all over, like the dandelions in Lincoln Park. It was strange that Jasper Heccomb had ended up as head of it. I'd had a crush on him when we were students, when he'd been an upper-classman who ran with the coolest crowd on campus. He'd once bought me a cup of coffee in Swift Hall after a meeting. I'd been ecstatic until I learned he'd been using me to make his girlfriend jealous. She'd been sitting at a corner table with another guy, but I'd only known that when my roommate pointed them out to deflate me.

Jasper hadn't paid attention to me after that, other than to get me to do girl-work, like typing and stuffing envelopes. Somehow I'd always thought he'd end up like Jerry Rubin, a Yippie turned yuppie, and not be content with a small advocacy group.

Wondering if he'd even remember me, I looked Home Free up in the phone book. They had an office in Edgewater, a mile or so north of Lotty's clinic. I picked up the phone to dial, then put it down again. If I called out of the blue to catechize Heccomb about Lamia I might sour a perfectly good deal for the tradeswomen.

"Remember me?" I could say. "I used to hang around the C-Shop hoping for a chance encounter. One of the legion of women who did grunt work for the peace movement while you guys got the headlines, in the hopes you'd honor us with a one-night stand. Now I need to know why you've become a savior for Lamia."

Of course, I could ask about housing for Tamar Hawkings, even though she'd disappeared again. I picked up the phone again and dialed. A woman answered. Naturally.

"Why do you want to talk to him?" She spoke gruffly, as if I were a phone solicitor to be cut off at the slightest provocation.

"To get some information about homeless shelters."

"We're not a direct provider. You need to call the city's emergency housing bureau."

"I still would like to talk to Jasper. I have some questions that he might be able to answer."

"Are you a reporter?" she demanded.

I was getting exasperated. "Is there a policy against taking messages in your office? Jasper knew me twenty years ago—he might actually be willing to talk to me."

As often happens with belligerent people she became apologetic under confrontation. "We get too many people calling up either to find shelter or because they want to do stories on us. He has to be careful not to take too many calls or he won't have time to work."

"Well, give it a try. Is he in? I'll hold while you ask."

"He's out. I'll take a message."

"Great. Why couldn't we just have started there?" I spelled my name, wondering if she would bother to tell him.

In the morning, since he hadn't phoned back, I swung over to Edgewater before going downtown. I promised the thin air I wouldn't say anything to ruin Camilla's project. I just wanted to get a feel for how Home Free operated, see whether it smelled legitimate to me.

The office occupied a storefront between a Korean novelty shop and an Arab bakery. An old-fashioned panel truck, the kind they used to use for bread deliveries, took up most of the parking spaces out front. I presumed it belonged to the bakery and wondered why they couldn't park in the alley—I had to leave my beloved Trans Am close to Leland where teenage boys might strip it in my absence.

It was cold, as it can be in early April. Wearing only a wool suit-jacket over my jeans, I shivered as I trotted past the novelty store.

Home Free didn't advertise themselves to the public. No name appeared above the discreetly stenciled street number on the door. Vertical blinds, pulled flat against the storefront windows, didn't allow passersby to peer in. Almost invisible against them were the white plastic circles of an alarm system. I checked the address against the number I'd scrawled in my notebook and pushed the door open.

A woman of about thirty sat at a desk near the entrance typing into a computer. She hunched over the keyboard like a bow, her shapeless print dress hanging on her skinny body like sacking. Her gold-brown hair stood away from her face in corrugated waves. When she looked up, her thick brows contracting into a frown, I saw she had two tiny braids almost buried in the hair around her ears, as if ashamed of a concession to fashion.

''What do you want?''

It was the same gruff voice that had welcomed me on the phone. ''I'm V.I. Warshawski. I called yesterday. I want to see Jasper.''

''You don't have an appointment. He can't see you—he's very busy.'' Her muddy skin darkened as she flushed.

The room was tiny, barely big enough to hold her desk and a couple of filing cabinets. The printer was wedged against the windows. I looked around for a second chair but didn't see one. A door between the filing cabinets along the back wall presumably led to Jasper's space. I debated crashing in on him, but all it would prove was that I was more muscular than the young woman, and I didn't need to barge through doors to demonstrate that.

"I'll wait. I only need a few minutes." If she had asked me, in a normal polite way, what my business was, I might have said some magic words, but her sullenness was getting under my skin.

She frowned more ferociously, trying to make up her mind how to handle me. The problem was suddenly solved when the back door opened. A beefy man in a sheepskin jacket came out, a deep scowl cutting chasms into his jowls. Home Free's campers were certainly not a happy lot.

"I'm warning you, Heccomb: you'd better not leave me high and dry," he said over his shoulder.

Jasper Heccomb appeared behind him, clapping a hand on his shoulder. "I thought you were going to subcontract the job, Gary."

I'd forgotten how deep and resonant his voice was—a timbre for rallying the troops when faint of heart. Gary didn't seem to feel very rallied. He started to snarl that whether he or one of his men did the job, he expected—when he saw me and cut himself off. Jasper came into the room behind him.

I can't say I would have known him anywhere—it had been twenty years since I'd seen or thought of him. But knowing to expect him I recognized him at once. The gold hair that used to hang around his shoulders like a pre-Raphaelite Jesus was still long, but pulled back in a ponytail. Some thinning at the temples only made his narrow, dreamy face look distinguished.

"Who's this?" he asked across me to the woman at the desk.

"V. I. Warshawski," I answered. "I called yesterday. Did you get my message?"

"Did we get her message, Tish?"

"She wouldn't tell me her business; I didn't think you'd want to be bothered," she muttered, twisting her hands.

The change in Tish's attitude, from hostility to gaucherie, seemed to prove women still worked for Jasper out of love.

"We used to do some work together down at the University of Chicago—when you were organizing sit-ins and I helped stuff envelopes," I said. "Now I'm a private investigator and a . . . friend . . . of Deirdre Messenger's. I thought you might be able to answer a few questions for me."

Gary's scowl deepened. "Deirdre Messenger? Heccomb —are you coming or going?"

"I'll handle this, Gary." Jasper put his hand back on the other man's shoulder. "Why don't you head on out. And don't worry so much. We've never let you down in the past, right, big guy?"

Gary started to speak, looked at me in frustration, and stomped out of the office. He climbed into the bakery truck and drove off with a furious clanking of gears.

"So you went from stuffing envelopes to working for Deirdre Messenger, huh? I *guess* that's a climb up the career ladder." His quick smile robbed the words of some of their sting.

"You could say the same about going from sit-ins to this storefront. The University of Chicago no doubt expects better of its alums."

He grinned. "Judging by the fund-raising solicitations, they expect a lot better."

Tish banged angrily in a desk drawer. I felt sorry for her, wondering if I, too, had once frowned so obviously when Jasper smiled at someone else.

"So what does Deirdre want you to do?"

"She hasn't hired me to do anything. Merely, she and Donald Blakely both mentioned your name to me."

"Donald Blakely?" His brows went up. "Tish—has Blakely called recently about . . . sorry, I know I should remember your name if we worked together, but there were so many . . ."

"Yes, indeed," I said as his voice trailed away. "V.I. You can call me Vic."

Tish put in, "I can phone Mr. Blakely if you'd like."

"No, don't bother—we can do that later. I'll just talk to her a minute, see if it's something we can sort out in a hurry. You'd better sit in, though, in case it's something you know more about than I." He smiled again. "I've only been with Home Free three years. Tish here kept it going before that, during its lean period."

It was a meager kind of praise, but the young woman flushed with pride. Her bowed shoulders even straightened a bit.

The back room had been created by the simple addition of a wall down the middle of the storefront, but it was a good quality wall, fully soundproofed. Without windows, it made me feel as though I'd stepped into a tomb, although a modern one: the rest of Home Free's electronics sat here— a fax machine, another computer, and the latest in Hewlett-Packard printing technology. Jasper gestured me to a folding chair in front of the desk. Tish edged into a battered wing chair wedged in the corner.

"What kind of detective are you, Vic?"

His tone was patronizing enough to make me feel snotty. "A good one. Thorough."

He smiled, with a genuine touch of humor. "I'm sure you are. But I need to know what kind of good, thorough detecting you're planning on doing on me."

"Blakely and Deirdre thought you were the person to talk to about a homeless woman I'd found camped in my office building."

Jasper turned to Tish. "You could have saved Vic a trip. Told her we didn't do direct placement."

"She did," I assured him. "They were the first words out of her mouth. But I thought that was Home Free's mission: housing for the homeless."

"We *build* it," Jasper said. "That's why we keep a low profile, and keep our door locked. Before, we'd have hordes of people lining up every evening trying to find a place to crash. And we do advocacy work—that's my main job, going to Springfield."

"So how do you come up with funding for your buildings?"

"I should have added fund-raising—it's obviously the main job of any not-for-profit."

"And most of your funds come from . . . ?"

"Guilty businessmen—and women—who avert their eyes from the derelicts they pass at the station every night on their way home to Lake Forest or Olympia Fields. Why do you want to know?"

He looked at his wrist in an ostentatious show of how tight his time was. I couldn't be sure from across the desk, but it looked like heavy gold—maybe Rolex or Patek.

"Just curious. You usually build new units, don't you? But you do some rehabbing?"

He smiled, but not quite as warmly. "Maybe being a detective gets in your blood the same way that organizing does—you can't stop asking questions that aren't any of your business."

"Maybe so." I smiled, too, to show an amiable disposition. "How do you decide whether to do a rehab job or start from scratch?"

"We factor in costs, availability of site, quality of building scheduled for rehab, all those things."

"And put the job out to bid?"

Jasper leaned forward across his desk. "Vic. What is it you really came here for? I don't have a lot of time this morning."

"I really came here to see what kind of work you were doing."

He leaned back in his chair again. "Good work. Thorough."

I laughed. "Could I look at one of your rehab jobs?"

Jasper raised his eyebrows. "You sound like a potential investor, Vic, but you don't look like one."

"Don't go by appearances. If I only went by your watch I'd say you couldn't possibly be head of a shoestring advocacy group."

He glanced again at his wrist. "Oh, that. It was a legacy

and I had a moment of self-pity, wishing I'd gone into medicine or investment banking, like so many of my old friends. We have a couple of projects that we could let you look at. Talk to Tish here—she'll schedule an appointment with the managers for you."

"Under construction?"

"There's nothing much in the works. And now, Vic, you'll have to let me go. We'll get together some time for a drink, catch up on the old days."

I wanted to ask him what he owed Century Bank, to let them pressure him into giving Lamia the rehab project. I wanted to ask him how he handled bids, since Lamia had been awarded the job so suddenly. But either of those questions would have exposed the group and I didn't have a good reason, except my annoyance with Phoebe, for doing that. I allowed him to shepherd me to the front office.

"Gary didn't seem very happy," I said as he turned to his own office. "He's not an investor who got stiffed, is he?"

Jasper's smile played around his mouth. "No, indeed. One of our contractors, and a born worrier. If you're trying to smell out our investments you should go downtown to look at our 990 filing: it's there in the State of Illinois building, just as it should be. Good to see you after all these years."

Tish smirked as she took my phone number, pleased to see Jasper put me down. She said she'd call me when they had a site I could look at. Somehow I didn't believe I'd ever hear from her again.

On my way back to my car I stopped to look in the window of the novelty shop. I decided that if I could choose any item in the store window for my very own, it would have to be the lamp whose base was in the shape of a baby, and whose shade read "Oh, Mama," over and over in different shades of crimson.

□ 12
Return of the Hostess

It was close to five when I got to my office. I'd divided the afternoon between the State of Illinois building and the city-county building, looking up records. Since I was in Helmut Jahn's glass cupcake anyway I'd looked up Home Free's 990 filing with the state. They did work on a bigger scope than I would have believed, judging by their tiny office, but since most of it was in contracting and downstate lobbying I guess that wasn't too surprising.

Grants and private donations had given them almost ten million in revenue last year. About a third had gone directly to construction, another third to maintenance of existing programs, and the rest to administrative overhead, maintenance of an office in Springfield, and establishment of a trust fund. It all looked very solid. At least Lamia didn't need to worry about their bills being paid. Still, Home Free must be doing gold-plated work on their job sites. I was curious to see some of them.

Their accounts were audited by Strong and Ardmore, a biggish CPA firm in town. And both Alec Gantner and Donald Blakely served as directors. Again no surprise.

I took the information back to my office along with the data I'd gathered on other jobs and started entering it all into appropriate categories on my machine. So absorbed was I in my work that when Deirdre Messenger spoke close to my shoulder I jumped and swore; I hadn't even heard the door open.

"So you're here, Vic. I wondered when you were going to show up. I've gotten tired of the coffee shop down the street."

I stared doggedly at the screen, waiting for my pulse to come back to my body. "We have an appointment, Deirdre?"

"I talked to you on Monday about trying to do some work with the woman who's living in your cellar. I thought we had a date for tonight. Or do I have the wrong day?" Her jocularity seemed more forced than usual.

"I didn't think we'd set a time. Anyway, after Wednesday night all bets are off."

She planted herself in one of my guest chairs. It had been so long since I'd allowed anyone into the office that it was black with soot from the el. "You can eat my food, but I can't visit your office?"

I turned to look at her squarely. "Let's not pretend Wednesday night didn't happen, Deirdre."

"What's that supposed to mean?" Her tone was belligerent, but her eyes shifted away from mine.

"I saw you and Fabian and Emily together. You did not strike me as someone with the strengths to take on a troubled family." When she didn't say anything I added, "You do remember my coming back for my coat after the party, don't you?"

"I remember you coming to my bedroom and getting Emily so upset that she yelled at her father and me. I didn't appreciate it much and neither did Fabian."

"We weren't in the same room, if that's what you recall. I don't pretend to know what goes on between you and your husband—who goads whom into doing what—do you drink because he's intolerable? Is he intolerable because you drink? Does he often hit you? Is your daughter the sacrifice you offer up to his anger? But I won't pretend I didn't see you jettison Emily all evening long."

The veins around her nose glowed red. "You're right about one thing, Vic: you don't know what goes on between Fabian and me. If you'd ever been married—"

"I was," I interrupted.

"Oh, that's right—you and Dick Yarborough. But you couldn't stick around to make it work out. Marriage entails sacrifices, you know."

I tried to keep my jaw from falling open. "You been studying Rush Limbaugh in your spare time? I never thought marriage meant sacrificing my humanity."

"Not everyone has such inflated ideas about their value as you do, Vic. I thought it was worth my while to give up my own career to help Fabian in his. But that doesn't mean I can't make an effective contribution as a volunteer. You know, I don't just work at Arcadia House. I do a lot for Home Free too. I've taken courses in social work. This woman might talk to me where she wouldn't talk to you, especially since I have children and have some common bond with her. Most people find me empathic."

I pressed my hands against my face, trying to pull my splintering emotions back together. Everything Deirdre said about herself seemed totally different from the character she'd exhibited two nights before. I couldn't believe she wasn't aware of it, that below the surface of her prattling about her children she must have had an image of her daughter struggling with the little boys, and of herself remote from them. It's a commonplace joke that mental health professionals have the most ruinous home lives, but I couldn't imagine Deirdre being effective with someone as needy as Tamar Hawkings.

"All you women who went on to have careers are the same," Deirdre exploded into my silence. "You don't think those of us who stayed home and put our children and husbands first are worth anything."

I let my hands fall to my sides, too exhausted to hold them up any longer. "Oh, Deirdre, do you even hear what you're saying?" I began, then broke off. "Maybe you're right. Maybe you can talk to this woman in a way I can't. If her story can be believed, she left her husband because he beat her up and was threatening her older daughter. You'd have some common ground there."

As soon as the words were out I regretted them. Deirdre flinched and seemed to shrink inside her coat. Her face became a mask. Stripped both of jocularity and belligerence she seemed to have no personality at all. Against my will I felt a stir of pity for her.

"Why did you come up here, Deirdre? What did you hope I could do?"

Her face remained stolid. I had done the unpardonable—not only spoken the taboo words about her husband, but done so with disdain. As too often happens when I'm nervous or ashamed I started talking too much. I explained how I'd taken Tamar Hawkings's children to the hospital Tuesday night only to have her run away Wednesday morning.

"And the cops say she's probably come back here—that a beat officer saw someone who's likely to be Hawkings disappear in here with the kids. But it would be a job to find them—she seems to have some escape hatch I can't discover. So unless you have enough people to mount a thorough search party, I'd give it up for today. She'd be gone before anyone laid eyes on her."

Deirdre nodded when I finished my speech. "Believe me, Vic, I know more about homeless women than you give me credit for. And whatever she does she's going to be trying to find a safe berth for the children."

"I went to see Jasper Heccomb this morning. You and Donald didn't—"

"Why did you go see him? I thought you were going to leave that to me."

I ground my teeth. "You're assuming we've had conversations and agreements that never took place. Anyway, since you do so much work for them, you must know that they don't do any direct placement of people, so they never were a good place to go to. I've tried Marilyn at Arcadia

House and Lotty called Fiona's Place. We've come up empty."

"Jasper knows me. He'll do things for me that he wouldn't do for you. It really upsets me that you'd go behind my back this way."

She spoke loudly, as she had the other night when she was trying to stand up to her husband. I was starting to get angry myself when I noticed that she was gripping her hands together so tightly that the knuckles showed white.

"Okay," I said lightly. "Be my guest. Use your powers to get Jasper to find a place for Tamar Hawkings to live."

Her face took on a secretive, almost triumphant look. I wondered if she and Jasper had been lovers all those years ago—or even recently. When she shed her angry, pinched look she was still beautiful.

While I stared at her speculatively she suddenly bounced to her feet and draped her coat across the chair back. "I'm going to scout around for Tamar. I'll be back in a few minutes."

"I'm not staying much longer. And because of my electronics I need to keep the office door locked." The only reason it had been open for Deirdre to barge in was my vague thought that Tamar Hawkings might seek me out again.

"I won't take long." Before I could protest further she had sped out to the hall.

I was still fulminating over her audacity when she poked her head around the door. "If anyone comes looking for me, tell them I'll be back in a few minutes."

At that I dashed after her. "Just one sweet minute, Deirdre. Did you set up a meeting in my office? Without consulting me?"

In the unlighted hall I couldn't make out her expression, but I could see the silhouette of her body. She looked the way she had Wednesday night at dinner, her head thrust cobra-style back on her neck.

"Don't get on your high horse, Vic. I didn't set up a

meeting in your precious hideaway. Merely, I let . . . people . . . know where I'd be.''

I sucked in air in an angry whistle. In other words, she'd had a fight with Fabian and had come down here as a mark of bravado. I'm going to Vic's office to prove what a heroine I really am, try and stop me, or words to that effect. All that garbage about what she knew about Tamar Hawkings and Jasper Heccomb had been just that: garbage. I turned on my heel and slammed my office door shut behind me.

Back at my desk I glared at my computer. My name flashed in blue across the screen every time I stopped working. The sight seemed to mock me. I hit the space bar and returned to the Lamia file.

Before Deirdre's arrival I'd put in the data from Home Free's 990 filing. My last task for the day was to enter the names of Century Bank's directors from the list Lexis had given me on Tuesday. That would conclude anything I'd do on the Lamia project.

The directors' names had come in alphabetical order. Near the top of the list was Eleanor Guziak. My jaw dropped slightly. She was the banker who'd sat across from me at Deirdre's party Wednesday night. Right-hand woman of Gateway Bank president Donald Blakely, who'd blandly told me he didn't know anyone at the Century Bank well. My, my. How little we know of our own subordinates.

Gateway was a big downtown bank. Not in the same league as the Ft. Dearborn Trust or First Chicago, but part of the little group that made policy—both private and public—in the city.

Century, on the other hand, was a small community bank whose only office lay in the Forty-eighth ward, where Camilla's group wanted to put up their experimental project. It wasn't unusual for the officer of a big bank to serve on the board of a small one. What was strange was Donald Blakely's unwillingness to acknowledge the relationship.

I whistled tunelessly through my front teeth. I could call Guziak, and get her voice mail or her secretary and hope for a return call.

"None of your business, Vic," a voice inside my brain warned me. "You aren't going to jeopardize Lamia's deal, are you?"

It was close to five-thirty. If I hurried, and if I guessed right, I could intercept Guziak on her way out of the Gateway building. Turning off the machine, I pulled my papers into my briefcase and switched off the desk lamp.

As I got up I saw Deirdre's coat. In my excitement over Eleanor Guziak I'd forgotten Deirdre. I was damned if I'd wait while she futzed around hoping to stir up Fabian. She could retrieve her coat from my doorknob if she ever condescended to return. I wasn't running a checkroom.

She arrived just as I was balancing it on the knob. "Oh. You leaving, Vic? I was hoping I could use your phone."

"Sorry. I've got an appointment across the Loop." I handed her coat to her. "Any luck?"

"I may have found where they were sleeping for a few nights. One of the offices on six. If you have a spare key I could put it through the mail slot on your door when I leave."

My astonishment at her sheer gall was so great that I found myself fumbling in the zip compartment of my briefcase for a spare key. I handed it to her wordlessly. If she forgot to put it through the mail slot it wouldn't matter; I was going to move my office home in the morning. This dying building was dragging me down with it.

"Is there a washroom on this floor?" she asked, pocketing the key.

"You have to go up to seven. Unless you're desperate, I'd wait till I got home: the lighting's bad and the hygiene is . . . well, sketchy. Or go to the coffee shop you used this afternoon—they're pretty accommodating."

She followed me down the hall. "I'll manage. With the hygiene, I mean. And I brought a flashlight."

"And I'd use the stairs," I added. "The elevator is temperamental. Although, if it stops, you can open the trapdoor and climb out over the top. That's what I do these days."

She looked startled, but she was determined to show me

that she was just as tough as I was. She hit the button and the elevator groaned into a semblance of life.

As I started down the stairs I called, "And make sure you don't leave my office unlocked. If I come back in the morning to find that computer missing I'm going to make sure you replace it."

Deirdre didn't say anything, but as I looked over my shoulder at her she touched her hair in a mock salute. I ran down the steps two at a time to keep from going back up to throttle her.

□ 13

An Unsightly Mess

Gateway Bank named themselves a century ago when Chicago was called the Gateway to the West. In a more recent fit of corporate adventurousness, they'd built one of the first skyscrapers when the Loop moved west of the Chicago River in the early eighties. Gateway's ads had been trumpeting their resurgent pioneer spirit ever since.

It was a quarter to six when I panted into their building. By this point in the evening the bulk of the work force was on its way home. I shared the lobby with a security guard and a few desultory late-stayers. There was a good chance that Guziak was already gone for the day, of course, but most senior officers stay late. Even if they have no real work to do, such devotion sets them apart from the rank and file.

The Gateway lobby was a marvel of red marble and brass, but it didn't offer much entertainment. The owners hadn't thought to fill the ground floor with shops; the only artwork was a photo display of bank employees grinning happily at customers. I studied smiling tellers handing cash to old women, laughing officers in hard hats on top of oil rigs, hearty officers in business suits at the controls of combines, until my own mouth ached vicariously.

At six-ten the guard ambled over to see if I needed help. I

smiled politely and said I was just waiting for a friend who had to work late. He let me borrow his *Sun-Times*. At six-thirty I'd gleaned what counsel the paper had to offer and decided I must have missed Guziak. I returned the guard's paper and left.

Some impulse made me look back into the building as I was boarding an east-bound bus. Eleanor Guziak was cross-ing the lobby, briefcase in hand, her head cocked deferen-tially as she absorbed wisdom from Donald Blakely. I stepped back off the bus. The driver swore at me and roared off.

When Eleanor and Donald walked to the elevator leading to the building's underground garage I bit my lip. There's no natural way to run into someone who's driving off in a car, unless you rear-end her, which doesn't make her recep-tive to your feigned rapturous surprise at the encounter.

The elevator came. Donald stepped in. Eleanor waved good-bye and joined me at the bus stop. I feigned surprised rapture.

"Eleanor Guziak, isn't it? I'm Vic Warshawski—we met Wednesday night at the Messengers'."

Of course she remembered me, what a pleasure to see me so soon, what a coincidence that I should be meeting with a client just across from her office.

Now that I had her I wasn't sure how to proceed. I asked her where she was headed, hoping it was someplace I could tag along naturally, not something like fetching her children from day-care. It proved to be the next worst thing—her health club.

"Time for a drink first?" I suggested hopefully, but El-eanor was adamant: she hadn't worked out all week.

Since I'd just dismissed a bus, we might with luck have fifteen minutes here at the stop. Not ideal as an interroga-tion site, but better than nothing. We talked about how hard it was to work full-time, overtime really, and stay in shape, but of course you function better mentally when you're fit physically, only it was such a drag in the winter to work out, so much easier in the summer when you could ride your bike along the lakefront.

"When do you find time for your other activities?" I asked. "Volunteer work, that kind of thing?"

She didn't have time for volunteer work, Eleanor confessed, shamefaced. We women always think that holding an important job full-time isn't enough justification for our existence. If we don't have pet causes, too, that we give another full-time stint to, we're embarrassed at our own sloth.

"But you sit on other boards, don't you? I was just talking to a friend who said you play a really active role at Century Bank. How are they doing, anyway? Uptown isn't the greatest location for mortgages."

"Oh, that's a sad case. They've got overextended with the paper they put out in the community. We don't know how or whether we'll be able to salvage them."

"Is that why you canceled the Lamia project? The papers had all been signed. I guess the tradeswomen were taken aback when the loan was withdrawn so suddenly."

She stiffened and drew away from me. "How did you hear about Lamia?"

"The way you always do—friends. Why, is it some big secret?" I tried to sound casual.

"Secret? Oh, no." She looked up the street. "Where's the damned bus? I think it'll be faster if I walk over to Wacker and flag a cab: you never get them west of the river this late at night. Good to see you, Vic."

A minute or two after she disappeared across the bridge a number twenty rolled to a stop in front of me. As we passed the corner of Wacker and Washington I saw her huddled in the portico of the opera house. She wasn't flagging a cab. She was talking into her portable phone. Maybe she'd suddenly remembered her mother's birthday, but somehow I didn't think so.

I rode the bus to Michigan Avenue, then raced to the underground garage for my car. If I ever got another financial breather I'd invest in my own portable phone. It had to be cheaper and easier than my current communications system: in my hurry to get home to a phone I was pulled over for doing seventy in the forty-five zone on North Lake Shore Drive. Sometimes I get lucky and run into a patrol cop who knew my dad, but as time passes most of those men have retired. This one was young, earnest, and implacable. And he took his own sweet time writing up the citation. It was seven-thirty before I got to my living room phone to dial Camilla.

"Hey, girl, I hear you've been trying to reach me," she said. "Funny thing, I wanted to talk to you too. You know how we met at Phoebe's office on Tuesday to talk about the bum deal we got on our permit and financing? Well, today we got—I wouldn't exactly call it a miracle. More like a reprieve. Not all of the sisters are a hundred percent."

"I heard Home Free might let you work on some of their stuff. Is that in concrete?"

"More like drywall. Oh, you mean do we have a cast-iron guarantee? I don't know. I think we get the job of rehabbing a twelve-unit place. Near the corner of Lawrence and California. We drove by to see it today. It doesn't look great, tell you the truth. The electrics and the plumbing are shot to hell and they get to use their own contractors on those."

I fished a Chicago street map from the papers by the phone and found the location. "That's almost a mile south of your original location. Right in the middle of drug alley. Is that what you want?"

"Hey, it's like Phoebe said the other day: we've got to get a track record. This is how we'll stick our foot in the door, show what we can do, maybe start building a capital base."

"And the sisters who aren't behind you?"

"They wanted a place we could build from scratch. And we have a certified electrician, so that's a shame. It's harder even for a woman to become an electrician than it is any of the other trades. Except plumbing, of course. That union is so tight—well, never mind."

I folded the map, trying to put my finger on what didn't sit quite right about the deal. "Who pulled these strings?"

"I guess Century did—the bank. Jasper Heccomb—he's head of Home Free—is one of their outside directors, and they went to him to see if he'd do us a good deed since they'd had to pull the rug out."

"Hey, Zu-Zu, I smell rotting alewives."

Camilla laughed. "Phoebe's right, Vic. You've been a detective too long. Why should that be fishy?"

"You don't need me to spell out chapter and verse on back-scratching in Chicago. Guys don't just pop out of the woodwork to do you favors. Especially not construction-related favors. And most especially not for women in trades."

Camilla treated me to a spirited defense of her banker, a really *good* man who merely had the misfortune to be caught in the middle when financing fell through. Maybe he'd cashed in some chips with Jasper Heccomb. Why couldn't I let people do a good deed once in a while without having to poke it with a pointed stick until it broke into bits?

Why, indeed, I had to ask myself. Especially since Camilla and Phoebe were letting me off the investigation into Lamia's problems. Somehow, though, instead of feeling good about getting the hook from a job I didn't want, I was getting angry. People were tossing bright-painted eggs in the air to keep me from looking at the juggler.

I started to tell Camilla about my strange encounter with Eleanor Guziak, then shut my lips on it. She wasn't in the humor to hear any criticism of the deal. And after all, it *is* hard for tradeswomen to get funding. The housing business in Chicago was as stagnant as in the rest of the country. At least the job would employ most of the Lamia team for a number of months.

"Now, listen, Vic," Camilla pushed into my silence. "I want some authentic hip-hip-hoorays from you, not all this antagonism. Phoebe and I agreed we didn't want you going any further with your investigation. Maybe someone did do a deal under the table for us. Why shouldn't we take it? Why shouldn't women get a slice of the pie after all these years? But if they sense you sniffing around they'll just cut us off.''

She was right. Absolutely right. I made some feeble congratulatory noises and hung up.

I drummed my fingers on the phone table. Oh, yes, I wanted to support women at work. But if someone was using them as a front for . . . something . . . I cast around for ideas but couldn't imagine what evil use Home Free might make of them. Still, Eleanor Guziak had raced off to use her phone when I mentioned Lamia. That must mean some problem underlay the deal. And if Lamia took the fall for a corrupt operation, that could kill their chances of ever getting capital.

There was the indisputable fact that Cyrus Lavalle had learned something at City Hall so hot that he wanted to give me back the bribe I'd paid him twenty-four hours earlier. I didn't know all the places Cyrus dropped cash—probably a thousand a month went to Oak Street's unisex boutiques—but he desperately wanted to live like a drug lord on a city clerk's pay. For him to send money back, or at least offer to, meant someone had scared him badly.

Monday morning I was going make some phone calls, no matter how much that upset Camilla and Phoebe. At least I'd push more aggressively on Tish at Home Free.

But on Saturday morning my questions got shifted willy-nilly to a new subject. When I went into my office with an armload of boxes, all ready to pack up and move out, I found an appalling sight: Deirdre Messenger's body sprawled across my desk. I felt a momentary spurt of anger, thinking she had gotten drunk and passed out there.

Almost at once I realized she was dead, dead beyond doubt, dead with an ugliness so extreme I had at first denied it. Someone had savagely beaten her. A pool of brain and blood had congealed around her head.

Gray inkblots floated in front of me and light stabbed at the edges of my retinas. I suddenly found myself on the floor, with my left hand sliding across a sticky mass. I managed to pull one of the packing cartons in front of me before throwing up.

With the loss of my breakfast my head cleared. Keeping my left hand well away from my body I stumbled to my feet. I backed out of the room and ran up the three flights to the women's bathroom. By some miracle water was running today, although this late in the Pulteney's life only the cold tap functioned. The bar of soap I'd put in here three days ago was gone, as were the paper towels. I held my hand under the tap until my fingers were red and swollen with cold, long after traces of blood and brain had disappeared down the rusty sinkhole. I wiped my fingers dry against my jeans.

The smell of sewer gas was strong in the bathroom. Together with stale urine the stench made my stomach start to heave again. I held my breath until I found an open office across the hall. I pushed on the window but it was painted shut. Using one of my shoes I pounded on the glass until it broke. I gulped down mouthfuls of the sharp April air, grateful even for the sooty smell of the el wires.

In the abandoned room, with its cracked walls and exposed ceiling wires, my mind finally began to work again. I had to call the police, and soon. My sick leave wouldn't delay their work unbearably, but the sooner they got started the better. The blood I'd landed in had been cold, with a thick crust, but not hard. Deirdre had been dead long enough that it wasn't likely I'd surprised her killer.

I shivered slightly at the thought that the murderer might be close by. My Smith & Wesson was locked in my closet at home—I'm no Philip Marlowe forever pulling guns out of armpits or glove compartments. Marlowe probably never fainted, either, from the sight of a dead woman's splintered skull.

My office door had been locked. Whoever killed Deirdre had taken my spare key. They could come back at any time, but I was fooling them—I was moving my operation home. Of course, maybe it was someone who didn't know me, who thought they were killing me by assaulting the woman at my desk. But no one had seemed angry enough with me lately to smash my head in.

The likeliest possibility was random slaughter by a street punk looking for money for drugs. The violence of the assault made the murder seem fueled more by rage than premeditation. Why had he bothered to hunt my key from Deirdre's pockets and lock up, though? That argued a coolness not in keeping with the ferocity of the assault. For that matter, why hadn't he walked off with my computer? That would have bought a few rocks or lines, depending on his taste. Perhaps Deirdre had been carrying a large wad. For any punk cash is better than carry. But if she'd turned over a hundred dollars, would he have been furious enough to bash her head in?

Tamar Hawkings had been in the building and Deirdre had prowled around after her. She might not have liked Deirdre's interference. Could someone so slight, so frail, have administered such savage blows? To defend her children . . .

Of course, Deirdre had dropped broad hints that she was expecting someone, presumably Fabian, to show up. And I'd seen Fabian boil over quick enough and hot enough to beat her.

I retied my shoe and walked the seven flights down to the lobby. To call the cops I had to use the coffee shop's phone so as not to blur possible prints on my own.

14

Wiping the Slate Clean

"Not your brightest performance, Vic." Terry Finchley was talking to me in one of the interrogation rooms at the First District.

Mary Louise Neely, who'd just passed the detective exam, was taking notes. As always, she held herself parade-ground stiff, her copper hair smooth and flat as though painted to her skull.

"I know a professional would never throw up on a crime scene, and I'm filled with abject remorse." Neely's pen didn't falter as she noted my response.

Finchley shook his head. "Save it for the lieutenant—he likes letting you get his goat. Your building's falling over. Why'd you leave an inexperienced woman like Messenger alone in it?"

This was our third time down that particular path. I was getting tired of it. "You've worn me down, Detective. I lured Deirdre into the building—for reasons I'll reserve so you get some surprises at my trial—and bashed her head in."

Finchley didn't smile or frown or, indeed, move in any way, but stared at me as though I were a laboratory specimen—and one he'd seen a million times already. Unblinking silence can be an effective police technique. You find yourself imagining what they're thinking, what evidence they may be sitting on, until the silence becomes terrifying and you start to babble. I settled back in my chair and began running through "Vissi d'arte" in my head.

I've known Terry Finchley for years, since he first joined Bobby Mallory's investigative team—the lieutenant who liked me to ride him, in Terry's tableau. Finchley and I used to have a pretty good rap. Since I started dating Conrad, though, his attitude toward me seemed to change.

Terry is Conrad's closest friend on the force—they went through the academy together, then supported each other through the tribulations that pioneers suffer: they were among the first black officers assigned to tactical units. Now Finchley thinks I'm on some white liberal trip and will dump Conrad when I get to the end of my journey. It's put frost in the smile he gives me. Today he wasn't smiling at all.

I kept my eyes away from his face, focusing on Officer Neely's left hand while strictly keeping my mind on Puccini. I had reached the tragic climax of the aria, where Tosca begs Heaven to tell her why her piety is so ill-repaid, when Finchley finally broke the silence.

"I'm harping on this point because with all your faults you usually aren't cruel. I'm trying to get a picture of why you left Ms. Messenger there, if not out of vindictiveness."

"That suggests I knew she was destined for an evil fate," I objected. "I work late in that building all the time, even now, when there are only five or six other tenants left. The south Loop is spooky at night, but it's about the safest part of town—you know that.

"Deirdre made a big point about staying in my office when I was packing up to go home. Her personality was hard to respond to—she could be both roughly aggressive and terribly hurt at the same time. Last night she played those two strings like Paganini. Anyway, she—and everyone who knows both of us—kept saying what an expert on homeless women she was. She was sure she'd know just how to persuade Tamar Hawkings into getting help."

It was hard for me to put into words how confused I had felt talking to Deirdre last night. I gave in to her demand for a key because she'd thrown me off balance; I'd wanted to get away from her. It troubled me that she'd unsettled me so much that I hadn't paid attention to her state of mind. Had she been frightened, excited, exultant? I couldn't say.

"I'd like to know who she expected to join her at the Pulteney," I added. "My feeling was she'd thrown down a gauntlet for her husband. He'd been pooh-poohing her effectiveness—if you want to see cruel, wait until you meet him—and she was going to prove she was both brave and competent."

Throughout the interrogation Mary Louise Neely had sat like a manikin with an automated left hand. At my last comment her face changed briefly. I thought she flinched in pain, but the expression was so fugitive I might have imagined it.

Finchley finally let go of my abominable desertion of Deirdre and turned to the trials of Tamar Hawkings. Of course, as soon as I'd explained why Deirdre wanted to stay at the Pulteney he'd detailed a search party for Tamar. If she hadn't bashed in Deirdre's head herself—furious, perhaps, at a rich know-it-all telling her what to do—she might have seen the killer.

A five-member crew had swarmed through the basement, he told me, before scouring the upper floors. Tamar had slipped away. I told Finchley about Deirdre's reporting she'd seen some sign of the homeless family on six. Whatever it was—assuming Deirdre hadn't made it up—Tamar had erased her presence.

I had to keep reminding myself that I'd seen Tamar Hawkings, spoken to her, not just imagined her. Even with three children in tow she moved like a bug skating on water —no trace of her journey remained behind her.

I was worried about her, worried about her sick, hungry children. Even so, I'd felt a secret surge of pleasure in her disappearance. Keep away from the cops, girl, I urged her wraith: it would be too easy for the state's attorney to pin Deirdre's death on a marginally stable homeless woman.

"Okay, Vic," Finchley said at length. "You can take off. You're lucky Neely and I got the call. Some stranger finds you with a dead woman in your office you wouldn't walk out of here without posting bond."

"Gosh, thanks, Terry. It's reassuring to know we live in a police state where who you know is all that gives you due-process protection. . . . Before I leave I have a question for you. How seriously are you guys taking Fabian Messenger as a suspect?"

Terry tightened his lips. "We don't need you telling us how to do the job, Vic. Everyone knows that the nearest and dearest are the first suspects. We'll send someone to talk to him—after we break the news about his wife's death."

I flashed a smile. "I know you'll be gentle and discreet. I just hope all the judges and senators and stuff that he knows don't blind you to evidence."

"Contrary to public opinion we do not discriminate based on wealth or influence," Finchley said stiffly. "Officer Neely will have something for you to sign later today, so if you would check back in?"

I said I would, although I didn't intend to: if they wanted me they could come looking for me.

"By the way," Finchley added, with the casualness they learn in police school as a dead giveaway that they've come to an important question. "We'd like to know where the missing evidence is. You had plenty of time to ditch it before you called us."

I smiled down at him. "Cheap trick, Terry. I don't have a clue what you're talking about. You push on that button again, though, and my first call won't be to my lawyer, but to some newspaper reporters. They're going to want my story anyway."

"Your files, Warshawski. We'd like to take a look at them, see what light they shed on the murder."

It was my turn to scowl. "You're going to have to get a warrant to look at any of my papers. And you'd better believe I'll fight that hard. You have no way of proving my work is connected to Deirdre Messenger's death.''

''Probable cause. When you erase your hard disk before the cops can take the machine away—''

''You took my machine? And this is how you tell me? That's my livelihood. And you're going to sprinkle dust all over it—I can't even imagine what that'll do to the keyboard—''

''Nothing worse than the woman's brains already did,'' Finchley interrupted. ''Anyway, we won't keep the machine. Since Forensics saw it had been wiped clean, there's no point to it. We'll return it Monday. I want to know where your backup files are.''

I stared at him blankly. Whoever killed Deirdre had wiped my disk clean. Nothing on it could possibly be of interest to anyone else. I hadn't done any incriminating work lately. Unless it was connected with Lamia's problems and whoever killed Deirdre was taking no chances. . . .

''My floppies?'' I finally asked Terry. ''Anything I've done lately would be on them.''

''No floppies in your office.''

I took a deep breath, hoping to steady my gyrating wits. Of course, I back up my current files every time I use the machine. Then I slip the floppy in my pocket. With the state the Pulteney was in I was more scrupulous than I might have been ordinarily. I squeezed my eyes shut, trying to remember what I'd done last night. Had I made a copy? Had I taken it with me or not? My anxiety to be shed of Deirdre was great enough I might have left without it.

''Well, Vic? Shall I get a warrant for your home? Or did you mail it to Dr. Herschel or your lawyer?''

I had never heard Finchley speak with such contempt. A fireball of anger swept through me. I jammed my hands into my jeans pockets to keep from leaping over the table to punch him. No one ever got anywhere hitting a cop.

''Try it, Detective. Try it and see how much cooperation

you ever get from me again.'' I was shaking so with fury
that my voice came out in a harsh tremolo.

On my way out I kicked a chair over and slammed the
door shut. I walked the mile to the Pulteney churning between Finchley's unspeakable attitude and the loss of my
files. Income taxes were due in eleven days, I suddenly
remembered. How could I possibly reconstruct my accounts
for the past year from the chaos in my office?

As I crossed Monroe Street my anger passed, leaving me
prey to a dull sinking, of stomach and spirits. My affair
with Conrad already had bristles to it. A major fight with
Terry Finchley would turn it into an actual porcupine.

I hoped Terry would get my machine back to me Monday
—electronic equipment has a strange tendency to evaporate
in the evidence room. I snorted derisively: good thing I'd
hung on to Gabriella's old Olivetti when I went electronic.
I'd taken it to my apartment, not wanting to discard one of
my mother's few tangible legacies.

I walked into the Pulteney with my chin out, ready to
take on any cops who might be on duty. After sweeping
through the building in search of Tamar they'd apparently
decided not to post a guard. The only trace of their presence
was a McDonald's bag one of them had stuffed in a corner
of the lobby. They'd padlocked the stairwells when they
left, but I had my keys. I walked up to four and broke the
police seal on my office door.

15

Senatorial Privilege

In my shock at finding Deirdre I hadn't noticed the condition of my office. Now, after a rough going-over by the forensic team, it was impossible to know how much of the chaos the murderer caused, and what the police had added to it. Of course, no one had cleaned up Deirdre's blood. Great clotted clumps of it stuck out on the desk and on my chair, and the mark of my hand when I'd fainted was still visible in the congealed remnants of her brain.

Papers seemed to lie everywhere. Someone had gone through ten years' worth of records with a winnowing hand, tossing the chaff so that it landed on chairs, the floor, even the window ledge. And on top of it all lay the thick dust of fingerprint powder. My servants and protectors, mine and Deirdre Messenger's, had sprinkled even my Nell Blaine poster.

I gave a convulsive sob. *"Ti calmi,"* I said aloud, using my mother's voice to push back an emotional storm. I took on Gabriella's fierce eyes and surveyed the wreckage. I might not have much time: I didn't know if the police would be returning.

Anyway, some atavistic fear made me want to run from the room where the newly slain had lain. The skin behind my ears tickled, as if Deirdre's ghost were breathing there. I scratched my ears and tiptoed to the far side of my desk.

Reaching across the filthy surface I rummaged in the drawer where I store my floppies. Finchley was right: they had vanished. I opened the other drawers in a futile hope that I might have misplaced them, but found nothing. Even my box of unformatted disks had disappeared.

Without my computer, what did I really need to set up shop at home? Certainly not the printer. And how could I sift my current accounting files from the wreckage on the floor? Only my Rolodex might prove helpful. I scooped that up, along with the phone, and took a last look. On my way out I lifted the Nell Blaine and Gabriella's engraving of the Uffizi from the walls.

Dumping everything into one of my packing boxes, I moved as fast as I could down the stairs to the lobby. I was prepared to plow through a police cordon and sprint for freedom, but the lobby was still empty. Even so, the Furies seemed to be on my heels. I ran all the way to the garage, the box bouncing against my abdomen, and flung myself into the Trans Am. I needed to bathe, to wash the dirt of the elevator shaft, the residue of Deirdre's brains, the soul-piercing filth of murder and pillage from my bones.

Mr. Contreras met me in the hallway as I entered the apartment. His faded brown eyes were bright with alarm.

"You okay, doll? I heard the news on the radio when I was eating lunch. What happened? Who was that lady? Why was she in your office?"

The dogs joined us. Mitch, a hundred pounds and still growing, jumped up and knocked me off balance. The box fell. Phone, Rolodex, and pictures crashed around me. The glass covering the Uffizi splintered. The wood frame split and fell away from the engraving. My father had made that frame for my mother one Christmas, out of walnut, sanding and staining the wood to a high gloss. Gabriella hung it over the piano, where she could watch it while listening to neighborhood children pick out "The Happy Farmer" or "The Flight of the Bumble Bee."

I pushed the dog down with a leaden hand. My stomach twisted in pain. I wanted nothing more than to go to bed and take refuge in the world of sleep, to find a place where I might lie a hundred years undisturbed.

Mr. Contreras seized my arm and impelled me into his apartment. "You sit down, doll. You're worn out and these animals ain't helping none. You just rest here in the armchair. I'm going to clean up your treasures, don't you worry, I won't hurt nothing. I'll get all that stuff tidied up and fix you some hot tea. You had any lunch? You want some fried eggs?"

"I want that picture frame." I sat on the lumpy cushion, shifting away from a broken spring. "Be careful how you pick it up. I want to see if I can fix it."

"Don't worry, doll; I see it's valuable to you. You just shut your eyes and leave it to me."

Nothing made the old man happier than to feel I needed him as caretaker. I leaned back in the chair. It smelled of must, as any chair that hasn't been cleaned in two decades will, but after the traumas of the morning I was too tired to mind. The smell even seemed soothing, like the embrace of the old man himself.

Mitch still hadn't fully expressed his delight at my arrival. He shoved his huge black head into my legs. When that didn't get a response he ran to the couch, picked up a knotted rope, and started tossing it and growling at it, hoping to entice me into playing tug-of-war. Peppy, his mother, barked at him once, trying to get him to mind. Sensing my mood she sat down next to the chair and began grooming my right hand, which dangled over the chair arm.

"It's okay, girl," I told her. "Just too much going on today. But I'm telling you, if your idiot son busted that picture frame beyond repair it's coming straight out of his hide. Why'd you produce such a hulking monster, huh? Why not someone sleek and well behaved, along your own lines?"

Peppy attacked my hand more vigorously, which I took for agreement.

"I just can't make sense of Deirdre's death. Not that murder ever makes sense, mind you, girl. But why kill her and erase my machine? If someone wanted to kill me because of my case files, they'd have known that wasn't me in the office. But if someone murdered her on purpose, I mean, because of who she was, there wasn't any reason to wipe out my files."

Peppy stopped licking me. She sat back on her haunches, eyes alert. I fondled one of her ears. Maybe it was someone who feared the progress I was making on an investigation and came to delete my files. They surprised Deirdre in the office and killed her to cover their tracks.

"Ludicrous," I told Peppy. "Even if that weren't straight out of *Cagney & Lacey,* I haven't been working on anything that's upsetting people. Except for asking questions about Century Bank, but I only started doing that yesterday. It's true Eleanor Guziak was upset by my questions, but I don't think she'd have hired a hit that fast." And of course it was ludicrous to think a bank officer would want to hire a hit.

"What's that, doll?" Mr. Contreras bustled into the room. "Oh, you're talking to the dog. Now, don't you worry about your picture frame. It's broke at the joints, so you can just glue it together, all but a couple of chips that came out. I know a guy'll fix it for you, a first-class carpenter. You say the word and I'll get right onto him."

I inspected the nicks in the dark wood. Yes, I'd let Mr. Contreras's friend repair it, but I knew I'd never look at it again without a sense of loss.

The old man bustled off to the kitchen to make tea. He returned with a sweet black cupful. While I drank it he fried up eggs and bacon. The rich greasy smell reminded me that it had been seven hours since my breakfast, a meal that hadn't stayed with me.

Mr. Contreras pulled a TV table up next to the armchair and fed me like an anxious stork with one chick. While I drank a second cup of tea I filled in the gaps left by the radio report, including Terry Finchley's threat to get a warrant for my apartment.

My neighbor was appropriately indignant. "He's got no call to be rude, doll, not any reason whatsoever. . . . You told Conrad yet?"

I squeezed the older man's hand. His normal jealousy of anyone I dated was augmented by his revulsion at the idea of me in the arms of a black man, but he was working hard to take our life in stride.

"I haven't had a minute to myself since finding Deirdre's body. It's time I went upstairs and phoned him." I waved aside my neighbor's offer of his own phone; I wanted to bathe. More than anything else, though, I craved some time alone. I kissed Mr. Contreras on the cheek and left him feeding the remains of my eggs to the dogs.

After my bath I wrapped myself in blankets and sat cross-legged in my armchair, staring at nothing. More and more the murders in Chicago—in America—make no sense at all. People are shot for not driving fast enough, for smiling when they should frown, for wearing green when they should wear yellow. Someone came into my office and bashed Deirdre's head in. And I wanted it to make sense.

As the day dwindled into evening my living room windows turned black and reflected me back to myself. A bedraggled caterpillar in an untidy cocoon. I switched on the table lamp and called Conrad.

He'd already heard about the murder from three different sources, but was waiting for me to feel like calling him myself. "And I already heard from the Finch that you two didn't part friends, so don't think you have to hide that from me, Ms. W. How you doing?"

"I've been better. Any news from Forensics? And did Terry say what happened when he spoke to Fabian Messenger?"

"He didn't tell me he suspected the husband. I thought he was trying to find that homeless woman you let hole up in the place."

"As a witness or a chief suspect?" I demanded.

"Whoa, there, Vic. Don't jump down my throat. It's not my case and I don't have any opinions about it. . . . I don't suppose I could persuade you to follow the same path."

I thought it over. "If Finchley talks to Fabian, *really* talks to him, and finds out whether he was down at the Pulteney last night, you might. Although I won't promise."

Conrad coughed, a sign of nervousness with him.

"What is it?" I asked.

"If I tell you, you're just going to start raving, and I can't handle that right before I go on shift."

I made a face and watched the window reflect it back as a distorted, streaky grimace. "I promise that any raving I do will be confined to my private thoughts."

"Alec Gantner's already been on the phone to the Finch."

"Papa or son?"

"The senator himself. How distressed he was at the death in the family of such a distinguished citizen and how he hopes the police will leave no stone unturned. The kind of thing that gets lots of resources assigned to your case but makes it a major nightmare. Terry's got to find that woman, Vic. He's not going to railroad her, but she's the only one who might have seen anything last night. If you know where she is, don't sit on her in the belief you're protecting her from police brutality."

I rubbed my forehead but didn't speak until Conrad's cough in my ear made me realize he thought I was fuming in my armchair. "I'm not raving, Conrad. Just staggered. Why would a U.S. senator . . . oh, I suppose because Fabian was angling for a federal judgeship. But I will swear to you, on my honor, I don't know where Tamar Hawkings is."

"I wish I could see you in person," he grumbled. "You know a dozen ways to slice the truth, but when I look at your face I can tell what you're doing to it."

That made me laugh, a feat I wouldn't have thought possible thirty minutes earlier. "This is the whole truth and nothing but—not that I don't know where she is at this precise moment, but I haven't a clue whether she's in the Loop or Uptown, or even back on the Southwest Side. . . . Oh, yes—I guess you guys don't know—tell Finchley her old man filed a missing persons on her some months ago. She says he was starting to molest the oldest kid.''

And then Terry would have a fit, thinking I'd held out on him on purpose. The cops never believe you may genuinely not remember something they think is vital.

When Conrad and I hung up, more or less in tune, I scrambled into my jeans and a knit cotton shirt. Alec Gantner might be able to force the city to tiptoe around Fabian Messenger, but he didn't have any clout to hit me with. I wasn't angling for a federal appointment.

□16
A Doting Father

Fabian opened the door to the mansion himself. "Oh, it's you, Warshawski. If you've come to see Deirdre, she's dead."

His greeting jolted me. "I know. I found her body when I went to my office this morning. It was quite horrible; I'm sure you must be shocked as well."

"If you knew she was dead, why did you come down here?" he demanded.

"To see you, Fabian. Shall we go inside?"

I'd been betting he'd slam the door on me. To my surprise he backed into the hallway, allowing me to follow him. Once inside he looked around uncertainly, as though the house were strange to him. I began to think his off-balance remarks might token genuine shock at Deirdre's death.

"Where are the children?" I asked.

"The children? Oh. They're upstairs with Emily. Did you want to see them?"

"Not especially. Although maybe I should talk to Emily. Her mother's death must be hitting her pretty hard."

"Do you think so?" Fabian looked at me in surprise. "She and Deirdre didn't seem to get on very well."

My own mother's death, when I was a year older than

Emily, had been the cataclysmic event of my life. In some ways I don't think I've ever recovered from it. But what if Gabriella had been like Deirdre—drunk, angry with the world, hostile to me personally? I tried to picture it. Death wouldn't have released me from her fury. On the contrary —it would have made the cataclysm more violent. My own wishes to be rid of her would torment me beyond the fact of her death itself.

"Doesn't she have a grandmother or an aunt she could stay with?" I asked Fabian. "This is no time for her to be alone here looking after your sons."

"Emily is good in a crisis. I won't have Deirdre's mother hovering uselessly around the place, and my own mother died years ago. I can't afford to do without Emily right now. Maybe after the funeral we can see."

I blinked a few times, hoping to keep reality in focus. "Bring in a nanny to look after the kids and give your daughter a break."

"Is that why you came down here? To lecture me on parenting? Of course, you don't have any children of your own—it's always people who've turned up their noses at parenthood who think they can lecture the rest of us poor slobs. For your saintly information, we have a housekeeper, but the boys don't like her because she can't speak English. They won't let her baby-sit them."

"Deirdre came to my office last night." Fabian was treating me to such a mix of arrogance and intimacy that I couldn't possibly approach my main questions with finesse. "She was expecting you to meet her there, wasn't she?"

"No. No, she wasn't, Warshawski. I had no idea she'd gone downtown. I only found out when I got in from work. After a late meeting I was expecting to find dinner waiting. Instead, she'd left me an insolent note. The last thing I wanted to do was chase after her. Now I see it would have been better—but at the time—anyway, I called Emily down."

"So Emily made you dinner. And then you went downtown to find Deirdre, to tell her just what you thought of her for going off in that irresponsible way. And she sneered at you and you lost your temper and started pounding on her. Then it got out of hand and before you knew it she was dead. So this morning you called your senator and got him to put some pressure on the cops for you.''

''What are you talking about? Are you trying to imply that I hurt Deirdre? I was here all night. It was Mrs. Sliwa's night off and Deirdre left me alone with the children. I couldn't go off. In fact I—''

He broke off abruptly. In fact he what?

''You called the cops? Or sat waiting by the door to beat her up when she might choose to walk in?'' I prodded him.

He looked furious but didn't answer, going instead to the foot of the stairs. ''Emily! Emily! Come down here. I want to talk to you!''

At first there was no sound, but when he called her name again, more sharply, I heard a faint shuffling on the upstairs carpet. His daughter came down the stairs, her frizzy blond hair matted to her head on one side and blooming like a giant bush on the other. She was wearing jeans and an ill-fitting yellow blouse that made her blotched skin look muddy. She stopped on the lower landing, five stairs above us. Behind her, like mice, I could see her little brothers huddle in the shadows.

''This is Miss Warshawski, Emily. She's come here with some impertinent questions that are none of her business, but we're going to answer them anyway, in the hopes she'll go away and leave us in peace to do our mourning for your mother.''

''Hi, Emily. I'm Vic. We met Wednesday night.'' I climbed up a step and stretched a hand out to her, but she didn't respond; her face had subsided into the dull mask that made her look retarded.

I moved up to the landing and sat on the stair behind her. ''Your mama came to my office last night. Did she tell you where she was going? Or did she just assume you would take charge?''

Emily looked at her father, who sharply adjured her to answer the question.

"She was gone when I got home from school." Her whisper was so soft I could barely hear her, even sitting four feet from her mouth.

"Did she leave you a note?"

Emily nodded fractionally. "Just that she was out, she didn't know when she'd be back, but we could have leftovers for dinner. There was a lot of food left over from the party."

"Do you still have the note? If I saw it maybe it would tell me something about her plans."

"We didn't keep it, Warshawski. Not being oracles, we didn't predict it would be needed as evidence twenty-four hours later." Fabian's voice cracked across us, making his daughter flinch.

I ignored him, hoping that if I kept Emily looking at me it would lessen Fabian's control of her. "She was expecting your dad to meet her at my office last night. Did he go out?"

Emily's mouth started to move but no words came out. Her shoulders began to heave under the weight of suppressed tears.

"Tell her, Emily," Fabian commanded. "Tell her whether I went out or was here last night."

She gulped convulsively, looked at Fabian, and started to cry.

"You don't have to lie for him," I said gently.

"Just tell her the truth, Emily," Fabian insisted. "Was I or was I not here last night?"

"Yes!" she screamed. "You were here! I know you were here!"

She stumbled back up the stairs, tripping on my left hand in passing. The mice detached themselves from the shadows when she passed. They clung to her shirttails as they all three scurried along the upper hallway.

"Satisfied, Warshawski?" Fabian was smiling triumphantly.

"I'm satisfied, yes, Messenger." I got slowly to my feet. "I'm satisfied that you have terrorized your daughter into lying for you. I'll pass that message along to the officer in charge of your wife's murder investigation."

"Pass this one on to him, too: that I won't tolerate your interference in my private affairs. I intend to take steps to see that you don't do so."

"With what? The same weapon you used on Deirdre? I'll write a note to alert them to the possibility."

"I don't know how you stay in business, Warshawski—I really don't. You seem to reason with your endocrines instead of your synapses."

I paused with my hand on the front doorknob. "Is that supposed to be an insult, Fabian? Is that how you started beating down Deirdre, telling her she only had feelings instead of the superior firepower of your masculine mind? And was she needy enough to listen to you? I've felt sorry for her for a long time, but what a sad epitaph: I gave up my mind to bolster my husband's failing ego."

"Yes, yes, that tired feminist cant. At least Deirdre was smart enough not to fall for it. You got what you came for —now go."

"Don't take your rage out on Emily after I leave. She's too young to know how to stand up to you."

At that his superior smile vanished and rage boiled over in him. "I want you staying away from my daughter. You're a terrible influence for a young girl, with the ramshackle way you live. I found out you sneaked into her room in the middle of the night after our party. If I learn you've come near her again without my permission, believe me, Miss Know-it-all, I'll be taking legal action so fast it'll make your head spin."

On an impulse so sudden I hadn't known it was in my head I ran up the stairs to Emily's room. Fabian remained in the hall for a moment, too taken aback even to call out to me.

I knocked sharply on Emily's door but didn't wait for a summons to open it. The three children were huddled together on the bed. It hadn't been made up and sheets and blankets were churned into a lumpy knot. The little boy, Nathan, was tucked under his sister's right arm, sucking his thumb. Joshua, the elder, leaned cross-legged against her other shoulder, reading a book aloud.

He stopped when he heard me. The three stared with frightened eyes like birds caught in an ill-made nest. I shoved aside a heap of books and papers to kneel next to the bed.

"Emily, I want to talk to you. I'm very worried by what may happen to you if I leave you here alone with Fabian—with your dad."

She had her idiot face on, but I was beginning to know that was a shield to cover strong feelings. Joshua had already learned to assume it, but the toddler started whimpering behind his thumb. Emily hugged him closer to herself.

"You don't have to stay here to be hurt," I said. "There are safe places for you. If you want to come with me—now or at any time—I can see that you get help."

Fabian suddenly erupted into the room behind me. "I told you to stay away from my daughter."

I stayed on my knees next to Emily. "Do you think your grandmother would let you and the boys come stay with her? If she's someone you trust, call her. Or call me. Or you can come with me now. I'll wait while you pack a toothbrush."

"You'll do no such thing," Fabian bellowed. "You'll leave my house at once. And as for you, young lady, if I catch you going near this woman again—"

"You'll what?" I snapped. "Prove what a he-man you are? . . . Emily, I'm parked out front in a red Trans Am. I'm going to wait there for a while in case you decide you want to come with me. And if you don't, I'm going to check in with you every day or so to make sure you're okay. Do you still have my card?"

"She certainly does not. I found it on her dresser yesterday and wormed out of her the news you'd been in here trying to seduce her. You don't need to give her another one.''

I got to my feet. ''Fabian, you're boring. You're utterly predictable. I would love to appear against you in court —it would be so much fun to watch you turn cartwheels. How did you ever get a professorship here? Influence peddling?''

I saw his hand go back. I put up a forearm in time to block his blow. I grabbed his arm and pulled down hard enough to make him wince.

''Don't get physical with me, Fabian—I learned to fight on the South Chicago streets. Nobody there knew the Marquess of Queensberry. . . . I'll be out front, Emily.''

When I left the room Fabian slammed the door on me. I lingered in the hall for several minutes to make sure he wasn't beating on her, but heard only a soft murmur of voices. Bending shamelessly to the keyhole, I could see him perched on the bed next to his children. I couldn't make out what he was doing, but the snatches of words I heard sounded sympathetic, even loving. I went out to my car scratching my head. I'd heard him strike his wife and bully his daughter, but his tenderness now almost made me doubt my own memory of the abuse.

I waited in front of the house for nearly an hour. No one emerged.

▫17

A Family Affair

"Listen, Vic, I'm not trying to tell you what to do. I'm just trying to lay out life as it is. You may think Fabian Messenger is a psych case—hell, from what you say, the guy needs a straitjacket and some good drugs. But he's got friends who wield a lot of power in this town. You saw him at six last night, right? And by nine Kajmowicz was talking to the Finch at home. Someone got up the ladder almighty fast."

Ted Kajmowicz was deputy superintendent of detectives. A call from him to a sergeant at home could be the chance of a lifetime—or career-ending. I could only imagine whether Finchley had been nervous or angry or embarrassed at the idea I'd put him on the spot with his most senior commander. I could only imagine because he hadn't felt able to talk to me about it—he'd gone to Conrad.

I was trying to explain why this upset me. "It's the idea that I'm your woman, not a professional whom he should talk to directly. I don't like being sent messages by my lover telling me to behave."

"Hey, girl, we know it's hard on both of us, trying to mix all the things we're mixing. Not just race, but you being ama—private—and me being public. If you're saying the Finch should have called you direct, yeah, he should have. He was afraid he'd be too angry to talk to you straight.''

''It's my perversity that I'd rather face someone's anger than be ignored.''

I turned my head to stare out the window at a trio of boys playing cops and drug lords. We were in Conrad's car in front of his mother's house, trying to clear the air between us before going in to face Mrs. Rawlings's heavy guns.

Conrad had called me this morning with the news that Fabian Messenger had sworn out a peace bond on me and that I had better never go near his daughter again. When I asked whether Finchley had interviewed Messenger as a serious suspect, Conrad told me he couldn't discuss the case with me. It had not made our drive south a happy one.

''Well, it's the cop in me that doesn't want a civilian mucking up a murder investigation,'' Conrad said. ''But it's the friend in me that doesn't want to see you burned by someone with Fabian Messenger's connections.''

He put a hand on my arm. ''Look, I know you're upset, but think about this: most of your clients want favors from the U.S. government. Your bread-and-butter, Darraugh Graham, gets three quarters of his business through federal contracts. On top of that he's probably a Republican who spends a good chunk of change on Alec Gantner. If the senator calls and tells him either to cool you down or stop doing business with you, don't you think he will?''

Before I could respond, one of Conrad's nieces danced down the walk to fetch us. She opened the passenger door and pulled on my hand.

''Come on, Vic. Auntie Zu-Zu won't open her presents until you're inside. What did you bring her?'' Jasmine, at six, was one of the pleasures of joining in Conrad's family life.

''It's a surprise. If I tell you it won't be a surprise anymore.''

I'd found a sterling collar pin of a crossed saw and hammer, which seemed suitable for a woman in the trades. I pulled the little box from my pocket and gave it to Jasmine.

She squeezed it and ran down the guest list for me while I fetched tortellini salad, my contribution to the potluck, from the backseat.

Jasmine hurled guesses about my gift at me as she shepherded us up the walk. At the door Conrad turned to me.

"You're not going to let this spoil Zu-Zu's birthday, are you?" he asked.

"Of course not, Conrad. I'm not a prima donna—but I am a professional. It's an uphill battle getting you boys in blue to believe it; but I'm not ready to concede defeat yet."

He grinned. "I was afraid you'd caught that slip."

Jasmine, tired of adult procrastination, got behind her uncle and tried shoving him into the house. We laughed a little and let her push us inside.

"I got them, Aunt Zu-Zu. I got them. Now won't you open your presents? Mommy got you the prettiest sc—"

"Jazzy," her older sister shrieked, cutting her off. "You spoil everything. Shut up!"

Jasmine, an irrepressible party lover, ignored the outcry. She took my offering over to Camilla, who got up from the floor to hug her brother and me.

The room was packed. The whole Rawlings clan had turned out, all except Conrad's youngest sister Janice, a neurology resident in Atlanta. In addition, old family friends, the tradeswomen who were working with Camilla to put together the Lamia cooperative, and all their children had arrived. Phoebe Quirk, as Lamia's main investor, had shown up. And Tessa Reynolds, a sculptor whom Conrad had dated for several years, had been sitting on the floor next to Camilla.

Mrs. Rawlings hoisted herself from the couch where she'd been talking to Elaine, her oldest daughter. She groaned audibly and rubbed her back to let us know how much the effort of courtesy to her son's girlfriend cost her. I stepped around the thicket of people on the floor to greet her and Elaine.

"Hi, baby," Mrs. Rawlings said to Conrad. "You've

been working too hard lately. We've missed you. Tessa came by; I know you'll want to talk to her.''

"Vic's here, Mama," Conrad said gently.

"I know she is; I can see. How are you, Vic?" She gave me her hand in a greeting as formal and distant as a queen's.

A thickset woman in her early sixties, she'd been left a widow with five children when Conrad was twelve. None of them had had an easy time of it; Mrs. Rawlings put in long hours at a bakery. The older ones did odd jobs while still in high school. Only Janice, the baby, had had the middle-class luxury of college, financed by her hard-working siblings.

As the one boy, Conrad had been drafted willy-nilly as man of the family. In that role he'd worked twenty or thirty hours a week all through high school. He'd still managed to be an honor-roll student—a fact that left him with no sympathy for the current crop of high school dropouts.

As Camilla had told me more than once, no woman would have been good enough for Mama's boy under those circumstances. The fact that I was white made me less desirable than many, but apparently Tessa, now Mrs. Rawlings's darling, used to get a greeting only marginally less frigid than mine.

Camilla thought Conrad would be living with his mother still if Vietnam hadn't sucked him up out of high school. "Conrad can't stand to hurt anyone," she'd explained. "Mama would weep and moan about her back any time he talked about moving out, so he'd stay—just a few more weeks until she feels better. And when would that have been? No. That war was a pisser, and Uncle Sam treated Conrad just as shitty as every other South Side black the army got their hands on. But I still gotta think Vietnam had a silver lining.''

I thought of that conversation now, as Mrs. Rawlings answered my conventional greeting by putting a hand on the small of her back. "I'm fine, Vic. These aches and pains are what you get when you're an old woman. Of course, I wouldn't have moved the sofa if I'd known for sure Conrad was coming, but now that he's seeing you his family doesn't—"

Her son put an arm around her and gently moved her to her seat on the couch. Whatever comment he made to her was swallowed in the shrieks of the children, but in a few minutes I saw her start to smile: a gentle, long-suffering smile—as if to say she was only enjoying herself as a favor to her beloved children—but a definite upturning of the lips nonetheless.

Mrs. Rawlings summoned Tessa Reynolds to the couch. When Conrad gave her his ironic smile and a hug I was surprised to feel a stab of jealousy. Since my divorce I've embarked on a number of affairs—relationships—what have you—but I'd never felt jealous of any of my partners' other loves before. The feeling so astonished me that I stared at Conrad and Tessa, trying to sort out why. I realized suddenly that Elaine was watching me with a sly smirk about her mouth. Kissing my fingers at her I sat down with the group around Camilla. The third sister, Clarissa, embraced me and slid over to make room for me.

Phoebe Quirk, looking about sixteen in baggy jeans and an embroidered peasant blouse, was in the middle of explaining financial details of Lamia's rehab project to two of the tradeswomen in the group. She eyed me warily, but continued her exposition until Jasmine plopped down briefly to describe the food.

"Vic brought some of her spaghettis," Jasmine informed us. "The short round ones that look like toffees."

"Tortellini, *bellissima*." I tweaked one of her pigtails.

"That means 'beautiful one,' " Jasmine told Camilla. "I can speak Italian, can't I, Vic?"

"*Molto bene, cara*," I agreed.

"*Grazie, Victoria*," Jasmine piped back, then darted off to share her erudition with her mother.

I turned to Phoebe. "You were starting to explain how this rehab project is being funded. Home Free has to raise the money to pay Lamia? Or do they already have it in hand?''

Phoebe raised sandy brows in a warning twitch. ''Century Bank, Vic. They feel bad about not being able to fund the original project, so they're floating a bridge loan.''

''My, my—a bank with human feelings. Who's signing? You? Lamia? Home Free?''

''We'll spread the risk, but Home Free has a good track record as a fund-raiser. I don't think we're going to be overextended.'' Her mouth tightened in anger as the other women—a carpenter named Agatha and a painter whose name I didn't know—started looking anxious.

''Why are you trying to get everyone so upset, Vic?'' Phoebe demanded.

''Less than two days after you told me City Hall was denying your permit, you get the rehab project. That's the part I don't get.''

''Suspicious. This girl is so suspicious for a living, she can't get it out of her system even at a party!'' Camilla said to the group. ''I get the sweetest birthday present you can imagine, tied up in a bow, and Vic wants me to send it back because she can't read the ingredients on the package.''

Clarissa, who worked for an accounting firm, spoke sharply to her sister. ''If there's a problem with the funding, you should find out, Camilla. Otherwise you could get squeezed halfway into the project. You know, if you lay out fifty grand on supplies and suddenly the line of credit dies, not only do you have to declare bankruptcy but your name is mud all over town.''

''My lawyers—Capital Concerns's lawyers—are going to make sure that doesn't happen,'' Phoebe said.

''You can write all kinds of guarantees into the contract, but you still spend months going before arbitrators if something goes wrong,'' Agatha, the carpenter, persisted. ''If Vic thinks there's a problem, I want to know about it.''

''It happened too fast, that's all,'' I said. ''On Tuesday Lamia was dead, for reasons so politically volatile that my usual City Hall source was scared to talk. Was it just a coincidence that twenty-four hours after I started asking questions Home Free came through for you with this rehab job?''

''Maybe you overestimate the power of your questions,'' Phoebe drawled. ''There is such a thing as coincidence, you know. Let it alone, Vic. This project is too important—not just for the six women in Lamia, but for all the tradeswomen in Chicago. If we can make it succeed it'll open so many opportunities for them. They'll find work they just can't get access to in the current environment.''

She was right. Why did I want to stir that pot? Between Deirdre's murder, Darraugh's son, the mess in my office, the upcoming income tax deadline, I had troubles enough to occupy me for some time to come. I held up my right hand, Girl Scout fashion, and promised to leave Lamia's affairs in peace.

Jasmine brought Camilla's presents over and stacked them around her on the floor. I joined in the excitement that gifts always arouse, talked to Tessa about her newest commission, and danced with Jasmine in a small space in the front hall.

At five-thirty Conrad asked if we could leave. ''I want to get you home in good time so that I don't have to race to make roll call.''

When we said our good-byes Mrs. Rawlings was desolate. Nothing Conrad said could persuade her I wasn't deliberately dragging him away early in order to wound her.

Police Review

When Conrad dropped me off I managed to slip inside and up the stairs without rousing my neighbor or the dogs. We'd had a run this morning, the dogs and I; I could leave them overnight with a clean conscience.

I pulled the bottle of Black Label from my small liquor cupboard and poured a drink. My unsettled life made me long for security right now: I took out one of my mother's red Venetian glasses, usually saved for special occasions, and tried to capture her fiery warmth in its refractions.

Conrad and I had kept the conversation light as he drove me north. The only reference to the disagreement between us came after he kissed me good-bye, when he warned me to take Fabian's peace bond seriously.

"It would be real stupid of you to get arrested under the new stalking law because you think his kid needs protection from him."

"She does need protection, Conrad. And—just so you don't think I'm going behind your back—I'm going to call Terry to ask for it."

Conrad played with my fingers. "I've been dreading this case. Not Deirdre Messenger's death specifically, but what would happen between you and me if you got involved in a police investigation again. You're so single-minded when you think you're right. You can't seem to compromise, and that makes you hard to live with.''

In my living room now I flushed as his words came back to me. But what kind of compromise? I had agreed to make one for Lamia. Let well enough alone for Emily too? I couldn't.

Looking into the ruby of the glass I could see my mother's fierce dark eyes. Gabriella had been like some wild bird, choosing a cage as a storm haven, out of bewilderment, then beating her wings so fiercely she broke herself against the walls. If that was what compromise brought, I didn't want it.

The red glass was bringing not comfort but agitation. I poured the whisky into a tumbler and sat down to call Terry Finchley. The conversation was not warm, but we didn't part irreconcilable foes. In fact, before we finished Terry even apologized for sending me messages through Conrad.

''Believe it or not, I didn't mean to insult you. I thought you'd listen to him where you wouldn't to me.''

''As a favor to you, I'm going to put the best spin possible on that one.'' In turn I apologized if my interview with Fabian had landed Finchley in hot water.

''I guess I owe you some thanks,'' he said sourly. ''Without you I might never have had a private conversation with the chief of detectives.''

''Out of curiosity, whom did Messenger call?''

''Oh, he went straight to the state's attorney. And when it's Fabian Messenger backed up by a U.S. senator, even a Republican one, Clive Landseer talks to him in person. He apparently told Fabian he could swear out a bond on you, Warshawski. Then Landseer called Kajmowicz to make sure I wasn't harassing an important citizen.''

Finchley gave a bark of bitter laughter. ''By the time I talked to Messenger this morning he'd calmed down some, but we had to walk on eggs to get him to let us speak to the daughter. Officer Neely handled the interrogation. Frankly, the girl didn't seem all there. She had the animation of a robot, just mumbling 'yes' every time Neely asked her about her old man.''

"He terrifies her," I said. "I've never seen him hit her, but I did come in on him just after he'd smacked Deirdre. With his daughter watching. Who knows how many times that happened? He didn't have to beat Emily for her to be afraid he'd treat her the same way he did her mother. And I have seen the . . . the psychological warfare he uses against her. He used it on his wife too. That's why I want to make sure he hasn't coerced Emily into giving him an alibi.''

"Just watch your step, Vic," he echoed Conrad. "If you go near the kid and he wants you arrested as a stalker or a molester we'll have to do it.''

"Oh, for Pete's sake, Terry. Don't come the heavy cop at me. If I have to leave Emily alone I want some assurance that you guys won't.''

He paused at that. "I'll check up on her at school Monday. Even though I don't share your belief that she's got a story to tell.''

"How can she know Fabian was home Friday night?" I asked, trying to sound sweetly reasonable, not aggressively hostile. "She couldn't possibly have stayed awake all night long. Which reminds me: Fabian said Deirdre left a note— 'an insolent note' was his expression—the night she was killed, saying she was going downtown. Did he tell you about it?''

"A note? No." Finchley was startled. "This is the first I've heard about it. I'll ask Neely, but . . . are you positive, Vic?''

"Yes. I don't make stuff up just to get the cops to pay attention to my suspicions.''

"Calm down. I'm not throwing that particular accusation at you. But why would Fabian tell *you* something like that and not me?''

I swallowed some of my whisky. "He doesn't know I date a cop, or even have occasional friendly talks with other cops. It might not occur to him that I'd have the wherewithal to ask. Speaking of questions, you find the murder weapon when you roared through my office?''

''No. Dr. Vishnikov says it was a blunt instrument, but a finished one. A mallet, a bar, a bat—not a raw piece of wood that left splinters in her brains. It wasn't done with your computer,'' he added in what he thought was a joke.

I tried to take it as such, reminding him that he was supposed to return my machine in the morning. He said he'd get a uniformed man to take it to the Pulteney first thing.

''You do know, Vic, our best bet is to find that homeless woman,'' Terry added. ''You say Deirdre had positive evidence she'd returned to your building. If that's the case, I'll bet anything you like she saw whoever killed Deirdre. Always assuming she didn't kill Deirdre herself.''

I took a breath to keep from howling into the phone. ''Terry, I know you're under unbelievable pressure on this, with Channel 2 giving the latest garish updates every half hour and Kajmowicz watching you. But you're an honest cop, an honest man. Don't let the pressure blind you to evidence.''

''Get me evidence and I will believe it—not reports of notes which may or may not have ever existed. And don't let your own biases blind you to the reality of street life, Vic. Tamar Hawkings wasn't too balanced when she ran away from home with her children. I checked up on her today. She started in a shelter, fought with one of the other residents, and had to leave. She's been on the streets for four months now. Even if she'd started out a model of mental health, that kind of life would rock her. And as you learned yourself she's not the most stable person in Chicago. She could have dived right off the deep end if she thought Ms. Messenger was from the hospital, coming to snatch her kids.''

''You're right, Terry. But I know Deirdre was expecting someone to join her Friday night. She was keyed up in a funny kind of way.'' I shut my eyes, trying to pull Deirdre back into focus. ''She thought she was showing someone up, and I have to assume it was Fabian. I thought she was using the search for Hawkings as a front. I'd appreciate it if you took my opinion as having some value. After all, you never talked to Deirdre Messenger.''

''True, Vic. It sounds like I missed a treat.''

We hung up then, while we could still laugh. I prowled restlessly around my apartment. The amount of food at Camilla's party had been staggering: platters of fried chicken, five kinds of potato salad, mounds of greens, acres of cakes. Even though I'd eaten sparingly, the thought of more food seemed nauseating. I finished my whisky and stared balefully at the papers piled on the living room table. If I wanted to work at home I'd have to sort through those and put them away.

I wondered what would happen if I tried to talk to Emily Messenger at school. Would Fabian have alerted the staff to have me arrested if I lurked about the Midway looking for her? What other approach would get me a credible account of Fabian's whereabouts Friday night? I could talk to the neighbors, but on a street where mansions float on outsize lots the mark of neighborliness is to pay no attention to anyone else.

I realized I couldn't bear an evening at home alone, churning thoughts of Conrad and Deirdre. Before I could second-guess myself I picked up the phone and called Lotty. She greeted me with a friendly concern that acted like a balm.

''I've been reading about Deirdre and wondering how you were feeling,'' she said. ''How's Conrad taking this?''

When I gave her the thumbnail version of what had happened, I got my first sympathetic hearing of the weekend. She had no trouble believing why I'd left Deirdre alone in my office. She had known Deirdre for years and understood the combination of neediness and arrogance that had made her so frustrating.

Finding her sympathetic, I poured out my worries over Deirdre's daughter. When I described my meetings with

Emily, at the dinner party and last night, Lotty clicked her tongue.

"So Sal Barthele was right about Deirdre. I don't see what you can do, though, Vic. Unless you want to try to find Deirdre's mother, see if she's the kind of person who might come to the girl's rescue."

That was good, if wearisome, advice. The *Herald-Star*'s obituary should include the names of surviving relatives. It shouldn't be impossible to track down Emily's grandmother. I thanked Lotty, bleakly, and paused, wondering how to end the conversation.

"Maybe you'd like to drop by this evening," Lotty suggested, brusquely, as though afraid of rebuff. "Or is Conrad entertaining you?"

"Conrad is on night duty. And yes. I'd like to come over. I'm not enjoying solitude tonight." As I locked my front door I felt closer to peace than I had for weeks.

□ 19

All My Pretty Chickens and Their Dam?

I spent Monday cleaning my apartment, preparing it for what I hoped would be a very brief stint as a home office. Weeks' worth of newspapers and magazines infested every surface of the living room. I bagged and carted them to a recycling stand, along with a collection of cans. Interspersed among the magazines, I found old bills, unanswered letters, paper of every description. Gritting my teeth, I paid the bills, wrote letters, polished wooden surfaces, washed plastic or metal ones, put away sheet music, laundered two baskets of clothes.

Once started I couldn't seem to stop: I scrubbed the bathroom, even the furry mold between the tub and the floor. On my way home from the recycler I bought lye and cleaned out the stove. When I woke up Tuesday morning, between clean sheets, I frowned at the ceiling, wondering what was amiss. The spider thread was gone, I finally realized. I was so used to seeing the shriveled body on her trail of tattered silk that its absence unsettled me.

I lay in bed awhile, basking in the pleasure of cleanliness. It felt like a return to childhood to lie in my perfectly clean, well-scrubbed nest. Darraugh Graham blasted into my calm a few minutes before eight.

"What progress have you made finding a placement for MacKenzie?" he demanded without preamble.

"None," I said baldly, startled into telling the truth. "A woman was murdered in my office Friday night. That's distracted me from providing outpatient therapy for your son."

"That's not what I'm asking you to do. Just find a charitable organization that needs some help. It can be anything. I'd be happy to see him scrubbing toilets. But I need to see it happening soon." He sounded like Mitch barking for attention.

"I'll do my best." I was annoyed that his top-executive mind could think only of his own problem: a murdered woman, after all, is a little more obstructive than cramps or a flat tire.

"I'd appreciate that, Vic. When you do your best you generally perform very well. But you have a tendency to be flippant and I'm not in the humor for that this morning."

"Just a minute there, Darraugh. Don't you ever read anything besides the financial pages? Deirdre Messenger was bashed to bits in my office Friday night."

"Oh." His bark subsided to a muted growl. "Fabian Messenger's wife? I saw the headlines but didn't read the story. I'll send Fabian a note. Not that I know him well, but we've met a few times. I'm sure it's put you off your stride, but try to make MacKenzie a priority. I want him back in college. He's getting on my nerves."

He'd get on mine, too, if I had to be around him very long, but Darraugh had hung up before I could commiserate. My calm destroyed, I got up to make coffee and do my exercises.

After a quick run with the dogs I called Marilyn Lieberman at Arcadia House to see if they had any use for a hacker on probation. She turned me down emphatically. Such expertise in programming as Arcadia required was provided by a board member.

"Frankly, Vic, I don't want a hacker looking at my system. It would be too easy for him to break into confidential files about our women."

I protested, but feebly: MacKenzie Graham hadn't impressed me as an icon of trustworthiness. I did try Lotty, for form's sake, but she didn't want the kid for the same reason: she wasn't going to entrust patient records to a hacker.

I pressed my lips together in frustration—with Darraugh for putting me onto a task better suited for Psyche, with myself for needing the money too badly to be able to tell him to take a hike. Before I left the building the mail arrived, compounding my woes: Lakeview had become such a trendy neighborhood my property taxes were being raised a hundred dollars a month. The bank that held my mortgage wrote in ecstatic terms, knowing how pleased I'd be with my valuable property investment.

Mr. Contreras, living on Social Security and a pension, was as sickened by the news as I was. He met me at the mailbox, talking distractedly of how he'd rather live in a car on underground Wacker than move in with his daughter, but where was he going to get another twelve hundred a year? With a heartiness I was far from feeling I clapped him on the shoulder and told him I'd think of something.

I went downtown to the Pulteney to make a concerted effort to pull my accounting files together. Using cold water from the seventh-floor bathroom I removed as much of Deirdre's remains as I could from my desk. The greasy fingerprint powder covered so much of my office I didn't even try brushing it away.

Terry had said they would return my machine yesterday morning. I called over to the station to find out where it was. Terry was out. I spoke with Mary Louise Neely.

After leaving me on hold for fifteen minutes she came back with more annoying news. "It's still in the evidence room. I'll get someone to bring it by later today. You're not in your office, are you? You know that's a crime scene: you shouldn't be disturbing it."

"And what are you wonder workers doing with it?" I snapped. "Are you going to pay my IRS penalties if I don't get my taxes filed on time?"

I called my accountant, who told me I could get a filing

extension—but only if I paid what I owed by the fifteenth. After three hours of sorting papers, trying to figure out what unmarked papers belonged to ninety-one, versus those that stretched back to the Mesozoic, I'd had enough. Too much. I'd hire a temporary accounting clerk to help me finish the mess later in the week.

Unfortunately, when I started calling agencies I found that everyone else in Chicago had a similar need in tax season: the soonest I could get someone would be next Saturday, and I'd have to pay double overtime. I thought of my property tax bill and decided to come back in the morning to finish the work myself.

After that I went to the public library to go through the newspapers in an effort to locate Deirdre's mother. The obituaries, while giving her name—Elizabeth Ragwood—didn't give her home. She wasn't listed in the city or suburban directories. I left messages with a couple of newspaper friends, asking for help, but didn't hear anything before I left for home.

I stopped at Mr. Contreras's before going up to my own place. "I'm running with the dogs: I need to clear my mind and straighten out my body. Then I'm going to get something nice for us for dinner—let's pretend we're plutocrats who can eat lobster and champagne when we feel like it."

"No, don't go adding any more to your debts, doll. Let's just have pizza or Chinese takeout or something."

I kissed him lightly. "Leave it to me."

On my way back from the park I stopped at the high-end grocer near Fullerton for scallops and a bottle of Taittinger. As I drove home I hummed the snatch of an old song of my mother's, about a fisherman who caught a whale and kept it in a bucket where it cried out of its blue eyes not to be eaten.

The song died on my lips when I pulled up across from the building. A police car, unmistakable with its bristling array of aerials, was parked in front. Terry Finchley opened the driver's door. Before he had his feet on the ground Fabian Messenger had bounded from the passenger side. I went on up the walk to the front door. If they had business with me let them come to me.

"Vic!" Fabian ran after me. "Vic, please—give me back my daughter."

His voice was cracking with grief. I stared at him dumbfounded. When Terry caught up with him he gave me a look of controlled fury that astounded me. Officer Neely, standing behind him, looked equally somber.

"What gives, Detective?" I asked. "Has Fabian here joined the force?"

Terry didn't smile. "We talked about this Sunday, that you needed to stay away from Emily Messenger. I thought you promised Conrad—"

Anger swept over me. Calling the dogs to heel, I wheeled around and stormed into the building. Mitch, less disciplined than his mother, stayed behind to sniff the newcomers. When he saw the door shut on him he gave an outraged yip. He jumped up, his forepaws on the outer door momentarily blocking Finchley and Fabian's entrance.

Mr. Contreras bustled into the hallway. Naturally he'd been watching the tableau unfold from his living room window. He hurried down the half-flight of stairs to the lobby door.

I cut off his "what's going on, doll" midstream. "I'm going upstairs and locking myself in my apartment. Will you wait until you hear my door shut to get Mitch? If Finchley wants to talk to me he needs a warrant."

I was halfway up the first flight by the time I finished speaking. Mr. Contreras followed, fretting with incomprehension, as someone began an energetic tattoo on the inner door. Mitch, furious at his exclusion, let out a thundering roll that drowned out Mr. Contreras's worried questions.

"Just give me thirty seconds," I shouted at the old man, pushing him away from me.

I ran up the stairs two at a time. Seconds after I'd secured the locks Terry pounded on my front door. I went to the bathroom to sponge off. I would have loved a shower—the dogs and I had run hard—but my sangfroid didn't extend to standing naked in the bath while cops surrounded me.

My front door has a steel panel in it. Terry would have to shoot out the locks to get in. He wasn't that kind of cop, but I still wanted to be fully dressed as soon as possible.

In jeans and a sweater, with a jacket in case I got hustled downtown too fast to grab a coat, I opened the door the length of the chain—the steel plate made it impossible to speak through it shut. The chain admitted a crack of air about a quarter inch wide, too narrow for a gun muzzle, say, but allowing conversation.

"What is it, Terry?"

"Open the door, Warshawski. You've pushed this past the joke stage. Way past. I have a warrant for your arrest, for violating the peace bond forbidding you from having any contact with Fabian Messenger's daughter."

"What happened? Did she intercept my thoughts?"

"I told you this has gone five miles beyond funny. If you think Conrad will protect you—"

"I haven't asked a man to protect me since my daddy walked me home past the thugs in seventh grade. If you can't tell me in a simple, civil way what the problem is, and ask me what I know about it, I guarantee I will make you a laughingstock in this town before the ten o'clock news goes on the air. And you can see what the chief of detectives will do about your career after that."

I couldn't see Fabian, but I could hear him pleading, almost in tears, for news of Emily. Terry turned his head from the door.

"I'm sorry, sir; I know you're upset, but can you be quiet for a moment?" When Fabian subsided, Finchley put his face back to the crack. "Don't make this uglier than it already is, Vic. I have a warrant for your arrest. If I have to break into your apartment to execute it, I will."

"Then you'll have to break in. I'm going to shut the door now. While you're shooting out the locks I'll be on the phone to the networks and my lawyer."

Through the crack I could make out the outline of

Terry's tightened lips. I thought we had reached an un-
avoidable showdown when Mary Louise Neely stretched a
hand past Fabian to tap Finchley's arm. The two retreated
from my line of sight, to be replaced by Fabian. He started
to offer me a bargain, voiding the warrant in exchange for
Emily's immediate release, but the bulk of his plea disappeared under the bellowing of the dogs.

Great. Mr. Contreras had decided it was time to come to
my rescue. I was tempted to walk out the back door and
disappear. Not just from my neighborhood, but the city, my
job, the whole stupid mess of my adult life. Instead I
opened the door and let the raging horde stream in.

When I'd quieted the dogs I turned to Finchley. "Before
you cuff me will you tell me what the hell this is about?"

His black eyes were hot coals. "Emily Messenger, Vic.
Where is she?"

"I'm not clairvoyant, Terry. Get yourself a medium if
you want someone who can answer a question like that out
of the blue."

"She's been missing since yesterday afternoon. Messenger here says you know where she is."

"Messenger here is pretty damned stupid." I was too
furious to try to help Terry out.

Officer Neely cleared her throat. "When did you last see
—talk to—Emily?"

"We could have started there and saved a lot of aggravation. I have had no contact with Emily Messenger since
Saturday night. I have not spoken to her, seen her, tele-
phoned her, written, faxed, telegraphed, or . . . or have I
left something out? If Fabian has misplaced her he needs to
generate some new ideas about where to find her."

"Vic, please!" Fabian cried. "Don't torture me. And
don't lie. You came to my house Saturday night and tried to
make Emily leave with you. Do you deny that?"

"No." I folded my arms across my chest. "And do you
remember why I did that? Because I'd seen you hit Deirdre
and verbally torment Emily. I thought she would be—"

"Oh!" An anguished howl burst from Fabian. "Detective, please—do I have to listen to this slander? My daughter's gone, and all Warshawski can do is make up lies about her.''

His voice was filled with genuine tragedy. Finchley frowned at me, demanding an answer. Mr. Contreras looked at me sternly. Even the dogs whimpered.

"Come on, guys," I protested. "Turn the melodrama down a notch. I have zero idea what's happened to Emily.''

Fabian's throat worked convulsively. "She started crying in school yesterday. When they asked her what the problem was she wouldn't talk. The only thing she did was ask to speak to you.''

I folded my arms and stared at him. "So far I haven't heard about a crime being committed.''

"The girl went home from school about two o'clock yesterday and hasn't been seen since," Finchley said tersely.

I sat limply in the armchair. "She's been gone twenty-four hours and you're wasting time howling at me? Get a grip on yourselves. Talk to her girlfriends, her teachers, search the parks, the lakefront—"

A pulse began to move in Finchley's forehead. "Don't goad me, Vic. She's a lonely girl. She doesn't do after-school activities. We spoke to the teacher in whose class she started crying. She says they went to a private room to talk things over, but all the girl would say was that she wanted to see you. But Mr. Messenger had already given the principal a call warning him—at any rate asking him—''

"You're damned right I did," Fabian cut in. "For all the good it did me.''

"So the staff knew they shouldn't call me. And they didn't. Then what? They sent her home?''

"When she broke down in earnest they tried to find Mr. Messenger and couldn't. They asked her whom else they could call; she would only give your name. They didn't have a record of other relatives besides the parents. There's a housekeeper at the Messengers', but she doesn't speak

English. The nurse escorted Emily home and left her with the housekeeper."

Finchley pulled out a notebook to check where the story went from there. "Oh, yes. We got a Polish translator for the housekeeper. She says the girl went up to her room without speaking. The toddler— -Nathan—heard her and demanded to go in with her. When the older boy came home half an hour later, Emily put them in their winter coats and took them out. She didn't say anything to the housekeeper, who assumed they were walking over to the park where Emily often takes them."

I shut my eyes. "I assume you've been to the park and asked the housekeeper for the names of any girls who ever came to see Emily."

"Of course," Finchley snapped. "We checked with the neighbors. We called her grandmother. We located two girls who sometimes worked on team projects with her. So we wondered if she'd come to you."

I opened my eyes and gave him a sardonic smile. "And naturally you swore out a warrant before talking to the neighbors: the new procedure when hunting a missing person. You check my office? The Pulteney's address is on the business card I left with her. If she was enterprising enough to start hunting for me that's where she'd go." I couldn't picture Emily being that definite, but I'd never seen her at her best.

Finchley made a gesture of annoyance. "We started there. And found you'd broken the seal on the door. That's a felony, in case you don't remember."

That didn't seem like an important enough issue to debate just now. "What do Emily's brothers say?"

"They're gone too," Fabian said. "You must know—"

"All your children have disappeared and you're wasting time screaming at me? You should be terrified. This is a big city. It's no place for three children to roam around on their own, especially if they have zero street skills. . . . Look, Terry. I'm just about mad enough to sue you for harassment, but we both need to put all this passion to one side and concentrate on the kids. I don't know where they are. If you decide to arrest me to keep Clive Landseer happy, not only will you regret it, but you'll be wasting precious time. Call in and get someone to void the damned warrant, and then go find the girl.''

"I agree, sir," Neely said, so softly I almost didn't hear her.

"We'll search the premises," Finchley announced. "Yours and the old man's. If we find any trace . . ."

He let the threat trail away. I didn't take him up: he was losing enough face as it was. He called Lieutenant Mallory, explained the situation, and asked if they'd send over a forensic crew to search both apartments.

"The lieutenant wants to speak to you," Terry said stiffly, after a few minutes of saying "No, sir" to Bobby.

"Hello, Vic. You screwing up my tac unit again?"

"Hi, Bobby. Good to talk to you too."

"So you don't know where Emily Messenger is."

"No, Bobby, I don't."

"You *really* don't know where she is? This isn't jesuitical hairsplitting, where you've parked her at Dr. Herschel's but don't know at this precise moment whether she's in the can or in front of the tube."

I had to laugh at that but said seriously, "Bobby, I swear by Gabriella's memory that Emily's disappearance from home comes as a complete shock to me. I knew nothing about it until Terry showed up just now with her demented father."

Bobby was willing to accept that. "I don't think we need to send a forensic unit over. I'll tell the Finch that, and I'll see to voiding the warrant. I didn't know Messenger had gotten them to issue one. Enterprising citizen, but we'll overlook it in a man worried about his kids."

Or a man able to summon the state's attorney to his side, I thought sourly, giving the phone back to Terry. Fabian insisted on talking to Bobby himself. He kept repeating his pleas that I be made to understand his grief. Finally, as a sop to his parental feelings, Finchley agreed to search my building.

I gave Neely my keys to the basement and asked Mr. Contreras if he'd let them go through his apartment as well. While they wasted time poking through closets and under furniture I stayed in my armchair, my anger dying into a shiver of fear for Emily. The world must have seemed a terrifying place when she woke up yesterday. Responsibility for little brothers left solely in her fourteen-year-old hands. No mother, however imperfect, to help deflect the father's rage. She was a lonely child indeed if I was the only person she thought could help her.

When Terry finally returned my keys his face was tight with mingled worry and anger. "The lieutenant assures me you're not lying—that you haven't given the girl to one of your friends to look after."

"That's correct. I'm not lying, Terry—I wouldn't put someone through this for my own vanity. What's the name of the girl's teacher—the one in whose classroom she broke down yesterday?"

"She doesn't know anything."

I gave the ghost of a smile. "None of us knows anything. I have to start somewhere."

"Alice Cottingham. Sophomore English at University High." The words came out on a whip end as he hurried out the door.

Mr. Contreras, overwhelmed by the emotions of the evening, didn't protest my extravagance in buying Taittinger's. He finished two helpings of pasta with broccoli and scallops, drained the bottle, had a grappa, and left me with the optimistic news that we'd find the girl and pay our taxes. Not that we had either money or ideas where to look, mind you, but champagne can create the illusion of prosperity and good luck.

□20
A Bat Out of Hell

The cold corridors of the high school seemed like a place remembered in a dream. Not that I'd attended this private hothouse: I'd gone to the public school a few blocks from my home. But the bright posters on drab walls, the high ceilings, the planters and bird feeders I spied through doorways provided the artificial cheer of all large institutions. I felt no rush of nostalgia, only a faint puzzlement that such a place had ever seemed familiar, let alone welcoming.

Ms. Cottingham's classroom, which I found after several false turns, looked out on a bleak courtyard. In the summer it might be pretty, but the ground now was a mass of churned mud, littered with the cigarette butts of the school's unregenerate smokers.

The room itself held tables and chairs, not the prim one-seat desks of my youth. While I waited for Ms. Cottingham I studied the slogans on the walls, which also contrasted with the conventional proverbs I remembered. "Our visions begin with our desires" (Audre Lorde); "Respect the beauty of singularity, the value of solitude" (Josephine Johnson); and, less earnestly, an unattributed "Elvis Lives."

Alice Cottingham swept in as I was flipping through a copy of the *Norton Anthology of Poetry* left behind on a tabletop. Her salt-and-pepper hair was cut close to her head; fine lines around her mouth and eyes gave an impression of latent humor.

"V. I. Warshawski? I wanted to meet you, despite Fabian Messenger's warnings, because I wondered what you'd done to inspire such trust in Emily."

I shook her hand. "I've only met her twice. Maybe the simple fact that I stood outside her family. Or perhaps my telling her she didn't have to stay to be abused. You know she's disappeared—I'm concerned about her. And I feel some responsibility. Perhaps she wouldn't have run off if I hadn't told her on Saturday that there were places of refuge for girls like her."

Cottingham raised her brows, sandy question marks in her narrow face. "Girls like her in what way?"

I repeated what I'd observed of Emily in the context of her family—her role as nursemaid, and Fabian's volatile temper.

Cottingham shook her head. "News to me. She's a very intense girl, withdrawn in some ways, more . . . I won't say idealistic—many of the kids here are idealistic—but more intense than most. She's creative; noticeably so, even in this school where we get a lot of bright adolescents. Her father has always seemed to me, oh, overprotective, not wanting her to take part in normal activities, but not cruel. And in this day and age who can blame a parent for being overly concerned?"

I remembered Emily's passivity when I first saw her. Her creativity was certainly muted at home.

"When you're a child you think what happens in your house is normal," I said. "If she doesn't have friends she may not know other kinds of households exist. She might not talk about it. But I've seen Fabian in action. Believe me: he's a wild man."

"Is he? I've never noticed that. Perhaps . . . well, autocratic. But we see a fair amount of that: the parents here often are in positions of considerable authority and are used to deference.'' The humorous lines around her mouth deepened, but whatever amusing memory had come to mind, she wasn't sharing it.

My lips tightened bitterly. Fabian exuding witty charm with his guests last Wednesday, displaying heartbreaking distress over his lost daughter last night—his public personality persuaded a shrewd cop like Terry Finchley. Why not a high school teacher as well? If I hadn't returned for my coat last week and seen him in action would I have believed he could be violent? Instead of trying to persuade Cottingham of Fabian's sadistic side I asked what had precipitated Emily's flight.

''She broke down reading her poem. That was Monday's assignment—to write a poem. I make them draw straws to read, since some are exhibitionists who will hog all the time and others are so shy they never volunteer. Emily's turn came fourth. She read a few lines and then started to cry. Pretty soon she was suffering a major emotional storm and I had to get her out of the classroom.''

''Was it about her mother?''

Cottingham grimaced. ''I hope not—it was quite a grim piece.''

''Do you remember it?'' I tried to curb a swell of excitement at the possibility of a direct lead on Emily's frame of mind.

''Oh, I've got it here. She left it on the table when we went down to the nurse's office.''

Cottingham's table, at the front of the room, was distinguished from the others by the stacks of paper on top. She fished in one pile and pulled out a sheet of pin-feed paper. She frowned more deeply as she looked it over.

''Certainly something is going on in her life. Kids usually cover standard subjects—the grandeur of nature, the pain of racism. This is just . . . well, pain.''

I took the sheet from her.

A Mouse Between Two Cats
by Emily Messenger

Quaker Mouse decked out in gray
Leaves her hole for work, not play.
Every sound makes her shudder—
She's too small for the fray.

Small nose twitches, whiskers flutter,
She seeks crumbs—not bread and butter.
What the gods refuse to eat
She knows must suit her.

Two cats are lords on this beat.
Their approach means her retreat.
One is fat, the other lean,
Cruelty their meat.

Late one night they move unseen
As Mousie nibbles on terrine
They trap poor Quaker and press her
Sharp claws between.

Lean cat sings, would caress her;
Mousie darts toward a dresser.
Fat cat snarls and holds her close—
As if to bless her.

Fat cat grins, You get to choose.
Lean cat sings, You are my Muse—
Stay with me and be my pet.
You can't refuse.

Fat cat grins. His lips are wet.
Go with him, you go to death.
Stay with me. You'll be my slave
And in my debt.

Slave or Muse, Mouse feels depraved.
Claws on neck can't make her brave.
Caught twixt grins and songs she faints.
Poor sport, cats rave.

Two cats howl their loud complaints
On her back red stripes one paints.
The other rakes out her nipple.
There's no restraint.

Quaker lives, badly crippled,
Creeps round her hole on tiptoe.
Cats grin and sing, hunt for sport.
Their muscles ripple.

I shivered. The furies raging in the Messenger home came to grotesque life on the page. I was surprised, too, by the care invested in the language. I wouldn't have suspected the Emily I'd seen, by turns tearful and withdrawn, to have such inner control.

"Do you have any idea when she wrote this?" I asked Cottingham. "You said it was Monday's assignment. Does that mean she wrote it over the weekend? After her mother's death?"

Cottingham pursed her lips, considering. "I made the assignment two weeks ago, when we'd been discussing poetry for a few sessions. Students usually wait until the last minute, so the probability is she wrote it on the weekend. It is strange, though, isn't it—if she knew her mother was dead. And also, how could she have the . . . well, the emotional energy to write anything within hours of her mother's murder. I'd guess she did it ahead of time. But then, why read it now?"

"Presumably Emily sees herself as the mouse. But maybe she's seeing her mother like that, and herself some guilty monster. I'd like to take the poem with me."

Cottingham shook her head. "Nope. It's a student's private paper. You don't know—"

"I don't know where she is. The longer it takes to find her the less likely she is to be in decent mental shape, or even alive. And she's got her two brothers with her. Anything that can help me learn enough about her to figure out where she may have gone is crucial."

"The police are looking—"

"And I wish them every success." I cut her off again. "But they're not studying *Emily*. They're focusing on the situation. Fabian is confusing the investigation by hauling in the state's attorney every time he wants action."

"And you have special skills?"

"I thought you knew. I'm a private investigator." Surely I had told her that last night on the phone. Or was I so rattled by events that I couldn't even identify myself anymore?

In the end Cottingham gave unenthusiastic assent to my making a copy of the document, as she called it. She stood next to me in the office while I used their copier. I even put a dime in the tray—the donation requested for personal use of the machine.

"And you'll call me if you think of anything—or hear anything—that might tell me where she's gone?" I said as she left me at the door.

She promised, but not with the air of someone placing great confidence in my abilities. As if to test her assessment I stopped at the Messenger house on my way north. The housekeeper opened the door a crack.

"No reporting." Her accent was thick, almost unintelligible.

"I'm a detective." I spoke slowly. "Is Mr. Messenger home?"

"No reporting," she repeated firmly, starting to shut the door.

Sticking my toe in the crack, I fished frantically in my brain for the few words of Polish I'd learned from my father's mother. Those didn't include private detective, of course, but since he'd been a policeman I'd heard her mention that. To palliate the lie I pulled out my wallet to show her the photostat of my investigator's license.

She frowned at it, reiterated "Policjant," and opened the door. When I asked again for Fabian she answered in Polish. Disappointed at my blank stare, she said, "No home," and turned on her heel.

Feeling guilty—at impersonating the police, at trespassing on Emily's privacy—I trotted up the stairs to her bedroom. Someone had sorted through it with an undiscriminating hand. The times I'd been here it had held the mild disarray of the average teenager, but today drawers stood open, trailing bits of sweatshirts and underwear, books lay haphazardly on the floor, and papers tilted drunkenly over the sides of the small desk. I couldn't believe Finchley or Neely had searched the place so carelessly. Either Fabian had vented his rage here, or Emily had been hunting something crucial before she fled.

I picked up the papers from the floor. They were all schoolwork—essays, geometry problems, class notes. The essays expressed what Ms. Cottingham had called "the standard subjects"—the intense yearning for love and death that catches you at adolescence.

I hoped for more poems, or a diary, but found nothing so personal. Only in the margins of the notes, between savagely etched doodles, were occasional remarks. "Why, oh why?" appeared, and stern adjurations to silence, in English and French. The hand itself, although still juvenile, was tiny, as though the writer were trying to efface her presence from the paper.

Stuck among the papers was a snapshot of Emily with Joshua and Nathan. She was cradling the baby, holding Joshua by the hand. The picture might have dated from the previous summer: she wore the muddy yellow shirt I'd seen her in last Saturday, but over shorts. Both she and Joshua stared at the camera with a painful solemnity. I tucked the picture into my notebook and continued hunting.

A letter from Emily's grandmother, in the round script taught in the thirties, thanked her for her card and described the coming of spring to Du Quoin, in downstate Illinois. The cat was catching sparrows in the garden instead of the mice in the kitchen. The college students were feeling their oats with the warm weather; Grandmother hoped Emily was behaving herself and taking advantage of her own educational opportunities. I copied down the address, wondering if someone who saw herself as a mouse would turn to a grandmother who wrote so prosaically about her own murderous cat.

I took a quick look through Emily's wardrobe. Girls today wear anything, from leggings and smocks to tattered jeans and granny dresses. Girls whose fathers earned Fabian's kind of money have drawers spilling out with teddies and other feathery lingerie. In Emily's closet the pink wool dress she'd worn to Manfred's dinner hung with some of Deirdre's other castoffs and two pleated skirts, last in fashion when I was in high school. I shut the door, embarrassed to have pried on such desolate ground.

After that I couldn't bring myself to go through her dresser, even in the hopes of finding a hidden diary. Where the plain cotton briefs stuck out I shoved them in and firmly closed the drawers.

I picked up a few of the books at random. The old standbys, *Charlotte's Web* and Laura Ingalls Wilder, were mixed with Marion Zimmer Bradley and Ursula K. LeGuin. A dreaming child, or perhaps one in retreat from the painful world she inhabited. I jotted some of the titles next to the grandmother's address, wondering what possible significance I could hope to find in them.

A fat book had been thrown in a corner, its edge just visible where it poked beyond the radiator. I lay down flat to pull it out. It was a copy of Churchill's *History of the English-Speaking Peoples*. In the dust jacket Fabian had written "To Emily, the Alpha and the Omega. Happy Birthday. Love, Father." The alpha and omega? Let alone that it was a strange thing to write to his daughter, Fabian had never seemed to me to treat her that way. Although there was his unexpected gentleness when I was leaving the house on Saturday.

Something else lay behind the radiator. Impelled by what curiosity I couldn't say, I stuck a hand in to pull it out. It was a baseball bat, signed by Nellie Fox. I'd noticed it, casually, last Wednesday night, in the hall umbrella stand. The head was covered with a dried, scabby mess. I looked at it, stupefied, knowing what it was but refusing to accept knowledge, then stuffed it back under the radiator and fled the house.

◻21
What's in a Poem?

I drove over to the lake. The ground was still brown, cut in ugly hillocks by the stones flung along it during last winter's storms. I walked out to the promontory jutting east at Fifty-fifth Street. The day was cool; the city to the north was shrouded by fog. The water, gunmetal-blue, slapped at my feet. An old man sat by a line, a bucket and net next to him. He didn't look up as I passed.

Emily could not possibly have killed Deirdre. I made myself repeat those words. The bat somehow had gotten into her room. Fabian put it there and threatened to turn her in for her mother's murder if she didn't give him an alibi for last Friday. The pressure proved too much for her, poor little mouse, and she ran away. I liked it. But would Terry Finchley?

In a second's unthinking revulsion I had thrust the bat back behind the radiator. I wanted to protect Emily and I didn't want anyone to know the weapon was there. But I would have to tell the police. Staring sightlessly into the mist, I saw it had been foolish to think otherwise. And my first impulse, to make an anonymous call, was also foolish: my prints were on the bat. At least I hadn't been so stupid as to wipe them clean. The surface might show Fabian's as well.

I realized my cheeks were wet. A thin rain had started to fall without my noticing. I walked back to my car, as slowly as though every muscle in my body had been flayed from the bone.

Going in the Eleventh Street entrance to the police station I was struck by an unexpected nostalgia. It's an old precinct, still with the high wood counter, narrow corridors, and dim lights I remember from the stations where my father used to serve. I longed for the sight of him at the counter, waiting to buy me an ice cream after school, or to listen to my tale of woe with a gentle smile my mother never wore. I longed for a comfort that life could not give me.

The desk sergeant sent me up to the detective area without even a smile, let alone an ice cream. Several of the crew I knew were at their desks. John McGonnigal, a sergeant I hadn't seen for a while, looked surprised, but called out a cheerful greeting. And Bobby Mallory, my father's oldest friend on the force, now a year from retirement, saw me from his office and came out.

"What's up, Vicki? Come to see how the worse half lives? Or do you have something on your chest after last night?" Bobby has moved from active dismay at my career to a grudging neutrality.

"They say confession is good for the soul. And I have a confession to make."

Bobby looked at me sourly, but called Terry to his office. Finchley's face showed a little gray at the edges. His normal poise had been worn raw by the stresses of dealing with the wake Fabian was churning up.

"Have you found the girl?" he demanded. "We've notified airlines, bus lines, circulated the CTA, the cab companies, and we're not hearing anything."

"Except round-the-clock from Clive Landseer, Super Kajmowicz, and the networks," Bobby interjected.

"No," I said baldly. "I'd much rather be here with Emily than what I do have: the murder weapon."

When I explained what I'd found and how, Bobby

snarled, but Terry smiled bleakly. "So the girl killed her mother?"

"Instead of Tamar Hawkings doing it, you mean?" I couldn't keep a nasty inflection out of my voice.

"Look, Vic, we do the best we can with what evidence we have. Now you've got the murder weapon in the girl's bedroom. How did it get there if she didn't put it there?"

"Fabian lives in that house too. He could have stuck it behind her radiator."

"And she left it there? Come on, Vicki, think what you're saying: Would she have slept three nights in the room with her mother's brains stowed behind her radiator?" Bobby was keeping close tabs on the case—he had the whole chronology in his head.

"And she would have slept if she'd put it there herself?" I demanded. "You're suggesting that if she murdered her mother she kept the weapon as a trophy, but shoved it out of sight. If Fabian put it there maybe she didn't know about it."

"Come on—why would a man try to frame his own daughter?" Bobby, who doted on all four of his own daughters and numerous grandchildren, couldn't imagine a home like Fabian's.

"Easier to believe the girl killed her mother?" I demanded.

Terry pressed his temples with one hand, as though trying to make sure his head stayed in one piece. "The important thing now is to send someone down to collect it. Not being a private citizen like Vic, I need a warrant. And you know how Fabian Messenger is going to react to learning you've been searching Emily's room behind his back."

"Come on, guys: I found the murder weapon for you. Don't act as though I hid it there myself."

"Come to that, I wouldn't put it past you." Bobby thought he was being funny. "The Finch has told me you've got a bee in your bonnet about Fabian Messenger. If you didn't think we were going after him hard enough to suit you, you could have put it there."

I smiled. "In that case I would have planted it in Fabian's room. I wish I'd thought of that—instead of taking evidence seriously. I did come here, even though I knew you guys would start haring after Emily. Just as you did Tamar Hawkings. Whom you've yet to find."

I swept from the station in a fine dudgeon. Back in my car, though, my worries about the girl returned full force. I couldn't swear she hadn't killed her mother. I didn't have any sense of what a teenager under the kinds of stresses Emily endured might do. I pulled her poem from my pocket and read it through again. What if she and Fabian were the cats and Deirdre the mouse whom they'd attacked together? I didn't like that idea at all. It implied a thralldom to Fabian of unbearable servility.

I put the car in gear and drove north to Arcadia House. Marilyn Lieberman came out of a meeting to talk to me.

"Any news about Deirdre?" she asked. "People keep calling me, wanting to know if her death had any connection to the shelter. And everyone on the board is worried. You found her . . . her body, didn't you?"

"Yeah. I feel like Lady Macbeth—in my house? Right now I'm more worried about the kids. You heard they vanished?"

Marilyn opened her eyes wide. "No. I tend not to watch the news. Life around here is too harrowing without thinking about war and famine. Where . . . ? Why . . . ?"

"I wish I had a clue. I'm worried that Fabian killed Deirdre and is coercing Emily—his daughter—into giving him an alibi. That she freaked from the pressure and took off. He's got too many important friends for the police to push very hard on him."

I couldn't tell Marilyn about the baseball bat before the police had recovered it. I did recount my evening at the Messengers', and what I'd seen of him since. Unlike Emily's teacher, Marilyn had no trouble believing me.

"In fact it probably explains why Deirdre did so much for us. Sal suggested she was an abused wife, but I didn't want to think about it. The trouble is, a job like this—

you're giving all day long. I want support from my board—so I turn a blind eye to the possibility that they have problems.''

''There's something I'd like you to look at.'' I pulled Emily's poem out of my bag. ''Does this tell you anything?''

Marilyn read it. ''This Deirdre's daughter? Sounds like one unhappy girl. 'A mouse between two cats.' Ugh. Let's get Eva to take a look at it.''

Eva Kuhn, Arcadia's therapist, was conducting a group therapy session, Marilyn's administrative assistant told us. She'd be free in half an hour. Marilyn took me to her office to wait.

It was a Spartan room, furnished with leftovers from some of Arcadia's corporate sponsors. Marilyn had done her best to humanize the space with plants. Artwork by the residents gave the room a jolt of eccentric color.

While we drank overboiled coffee women and children darted in for brief moments of recognition. Marilyn greeted each by name, with a personal question—had this child made a crown in artwork that morning? had that mother been to the jobs counselor yesterday?—then picked up the thread of our conversation without missing a nuance. No wonder she needed a board that supported rather than drained her.

''You find anything for that kid you're trying to help?'' she asked.

''Oh, Christ. My bread and butter. I'd forgotten him. And I have until five P.M. Friday. I feel like Gary Cooper in *High Noon*.'' Ken—MacKenzie—Graham and his blasted public service.

''You tried Home Free?'' Marilyn asked.

I looked at her approvingly. ''What a brilliant idea. Not just for the young Graham. But for Deirdre. She did a lot of work there. Maybe they know something about her we don't.''

''Something that'll lead you to Emily?'' Marilyn was skeptical.

"That'll give me a bead on Deirdre's killer, keep the cops from fingering either Emily or Tamar Hawkings. If Hawkings ever reemerges. Do you think a child of fourteen would have the capacity to pound her mother's head in?"

"Deirdre's daughter? You don't really think—" She cut her remark short with a shake of her head. "I can't give you some kind of cast-iron assurance about the character of a girl I never met. All I can tell you is I've seen people do unbelievable things.

"We had a woman here for a while, she's doing ten years now, who poured lye on her old man while he was asleep, then coated him with molasses. He burned to death—he couldn't wash the stuff off. She was four-foot-eleven. The courts didn't care that she only had one major limb the guy hadn't broken. And you've got to agree it was a hell of a way to die. So I'm not betting on what some girl on the brink might or might not do to her mother. Although I'm with you—I'd rather the husband got nailed."

"Only if he's guilty, of course," I murmured.

Eva came in on Marilyn's sardonic snort of laughter. "That's what we like: a cheerful heart among our happy workers. How's it going, Vic? You want an hour of therapy? I'm revved up and ready to take on you or anyone else your weight you want to name."

"Bad session, huh?" Marilyn said. "We want your diagnostic skills. Don't tell her who wrote it, Vic. Let her read it."

"And guess?" Eva watched while I cut a piece of masking tape to cover Emily's name. "In school they give you case studies where you're supposed to make a diagnosis and recommend treatment, but no one's ever given me a piece of paper and asked me to construct a case study."

She had played basketball, first for Tennessee and then professionally in Japan, before deciding on a career in social work. In jeans, with a white shirt rolled up to expose her muscular forearms, she still looked more like a ball-player than a therapist. I tag along after her in pickup games sometimes. She's ten years my junior and from a different planet in ability. I'd often wondered whether her fast-breaking physical style carried over to her counseling sessions. Still, I knew the Arcadia staff thought highly of her.

She read the poem carefully, her dark hair hiding her face as she bent over the paper. When she looked up again she was frowning. "You'd better tell me something about the writer. This a woman in trouble?"

"A child in trouble." I told her what I knew about Emily. "I'm clutching at straws. Is there anything in that poem that would suggest that Fabian had killed her mother? Or where Emily might go to hide?"

A faint smile crinkled Eva's dark eyes. "I'm a social worker, not a literary critic. If the kid's the mouse—and we can assume that's true: she's not going to write so despairingly about someone else, even her mother—she feels violated by both parents. *She's* the one who gets hurt in the poem—the two cats are on the prowl at the end."

"Then it doesn't make sense. She wanted to make a special point about the poem: it's likely that's why she went to school Monday. But if her mother was dead, would she think of her that way?"

Eva tapped the paper as if it were a ball she was trying to dribble. "It seems likely that she didn't know her mother was dead when she wrote it."

"Maybe she wrote it Friday night," Marilyn suggested, leaning forward in her chair. "Deirdre went out, leaving Emily holding the bag. If what you say about the family is true, Fabian could have blamed Emily for her mother's defection. Maybe the girl finally had enough. She can't confront her parents—they're out to lunch. She knows she needs help, but not at a conscious level: she can only ask it obliquely of her teachers."

"Could be." Eva nodded. "Deirdre's dead and she needs help more than ever. She goes ahead and reads the poem in class, then is overwhelmed—by having criticized her mother, who's dead. She might even be imagining her harsh words killed her mother."

"Then how—" I clipped the words off.

How did the bat get into her room? If Fabian was in all night—no. He was forcing Emily to say he was in all night. It seemed all too likely that one of them had killed Deirdre. I wanted it to be him, not his daughter, but I couldn't want it so badly I didn't think the situation through.

I took the paper back from Eva. "I was hoping it would give me some kind of hint—either about Fabian's guilt, or where she's fled to."

"The poem makes it clear that Fabian's guilty of something," Eva said. "But just what, you'd have to talk to the girl to find out. She sees herself as small and helpless. I don't know whether that means she'd flee to someone powerful, or find herself some kind of bolt hole. That's probably why she came to you, Vic. You seemed like a powerful outsider, big enough to stand up to the cats."

"And thanks to her wretched father I wasn't able to respond when she needed me," I said bitterly, getting up. "But it's possible she might have turned to one of her teachers instead, someone who's being quixotic in not turning her in. I'll go back to the school and dig some more. Thanks, Eva. See you at the next board meeting, Marilyn."

Hoping Emily might have gone there after all, I went first to my office, where I received a rude shock. A murder in the building had sapped the Culpepper brothers' remaining patience with their tenants. The Pulteney was boarded shut. A notice pasted to the window directed inquiries to a phone number printed in minute type.

Striking the Scent

I went to the coffee shop on the corner to phone and got the boarding company, not the Culpeppers' management office. They couldn't help me locate the contents of my office; they didn't know anything about that. Just that the building had been vacated by the end of the workday yesterday: they'd boarded the doors at ten this morning.

"You're sure no one was in the building?"

"Look, lady, we've been doing this for thirty years. Believe me, we've never nailed anyone prematurely into a coffin yet. You got any other problems, take them up with the building's owners."

His receiver slammed in my ear. In other words, they hadn't searched the building first. I wondered if Terry Finchley even knew the Pulteney was boarded shut. After all, there was still an active crime scene inside.

I didn't want to call back to the Central District, not after having just given them evidence they wanted to use against Emily, but I needed to know they'd done a thorough search of the building. Finchley was gone, presumably to the Messenger mansion; my call was shunted to Officer Neely.

She hadn't known the Culpeppers were closing the Pulteney, but assured me a police team had gone through it last night. After leaving my apartment Finchley had detailed a crew—a *good* crew—she emphasized, to make a floor-by-floor search both for Tamar Hawkings and Emily. They'd found the office Deirdre claimed to have seen, where Tamar had been nesting, but no signs that she or her children had been there within the last few days. And no trace of Emily.

"What about my office, now that the building's closed?" I asked.

"You have to take that up with the building's owners," she said, as stiff as ever.

"Is my computer sitting in it? Terry told me they were going to bring it over and I need it."

"Oh!" For once she was disconcerted. "I'm afraid we've been so chaotic, I forgot—it's still in the evidence room."

I sighed. "Then will you put through the paperwork so I can collect it myself?"

She apologized and said I could get it tomorrow. I was ready to hang up, but Neely seemed to be toying with saying something else. I waited, not speaking, and was finally rewarded.

"About the Messenger kids. We canvassed the street, of course. One of the waitresses in your corner coffee shop thought she might have seen the kids. But there's no way of knowing for sure. Even though you're at the tag end of the Loop, there's still plenty of foot traffic."

"You're sure they're not in the building?" If they'd been seen here, in the coffee shop where I was phoning, where else could they be?

"I hope not. If they somehow eluded us . . . I don't know. I'll see if Terry—if Detective Finchley—will let me open up the building and go through it one more time." For once Neely's stiff police mask slipped; she sounded worried, even a bit scared.

When she hung up I went over to the counter to find the woman who'd spotted Emily. The waitresses all know me by sight from the years I've been coming in, but we'd never gotten down to names. When I explained my errand, and showed them the snapshot of Emily with her brothers, they treated me with a friendly camaraderie. Business was slack; I was someone new to talk to. After a few minutes' whispered consultation a solidly built woman of about fifty came over to me. The plastic tag on her massive bosom identified her as Melba.

"That's the girl, all right, just like I told that girl from the police." In her slow, strong cadence she emphasized the first syllable, making the police seem much more ominous than usual. "It was about four P.M., just when I'm ready to go off shift, and she come in asking for the Pulteney.

" 'That's right next door,' I tell her. 'But ain't hardly anyone left in it now. What you want there?' I ask her. I wondered about her, see, since she had these two little boys in tow, and I'm thinking, Lord, they start in younger every day, because she wasn't more than nineteen, tops, and the bigger boy had to be six. And I'm wondering if she wants to hole up in there on account of she knows it's coming down. So I give her and the kids some tuna sandwiches and a bag of fries. But I couldn't honestly tell you if they went inside the Pulteney or not."

She pronounced the building name majestically, with the weight on the second syllable, evoking a brief image not of the derelict I'd rented all those years, but the stately home for which it was named.

"I'm wondering if there's a way into the Pulteney basement through yours. Another homeless woman has been living there, but we've always kept the only door down there locked."

Melba looked dubious. "I couldn't let you look, not without the manager's okay, and he isn't here right now. Won't be back, probably, until tomorrow morning."

I pulled a ten from my bag and held it casually. She took it with dignity, but indicated I ought to square the other two waitresses as well. Five apiece seemed ample to me for them. Melba led me through to the back, past the kitchen where two cooks were laughing over a game of twenty-one, to the basement door.

The stairs were old but clean. A giant cooler stood at the bottom, the only part of the basement they really used, Melba explained. She turned on the light by the cooler and let me borrow the flashlight hanging there to poke through the rooms behind it. The boiler and heating pipes sat in the first one, a system as old as the Pulteney's, installed when furnaces were built of cast iron and could handle a century of heating without a belch.

Beyond the boiler lay a series of storerooms, whose contents were a guide to the history of the building. The most recent layer held Formica tables and plastic booths that might have dated from the fifties, when the site was already in use as a diner. Beyond them, I found relics of a barber shop, antique shoe repair equipment, and what looked like the remains of a Linotype machine. I'd never known the old printing district had offshoots this far north.

I couldn't find any signs of recent use of the premises. And, although I poked and prodded long after Melba lost interest in my activities, I couldn't see any place where the basement connected to the Pulteney. When I finally gave up on the project it was past four. I put the flashlight back on its hook and went upstairs, coughing from the dust I'd been breathing. The cooks were still playing cards. Business hadn't improved in my absence.

Melba burst out laughing when she saw me. "You could use a week in a bathtub, that's for sure. Any luck?"

I shook my head. "Could you get me a BLT while I wash some of this off? And fries."

French fries are my weakness; I felt I'd earned a plateful after all that futile work. As I went into the bathroom I heard Melba order the grillman to fry up some fresh bacon: "The lady don't need that heap of grease you been saving all day."

In the tiny mirror over the sink I could see why Melba had laughed. Grime encased me in a layer so thick, my face and hair had turned gray. I scrubbed off what I could under the tap, but everything I had on would have to go to the cleaners.

When I came out I went back to the phone to call my landlords. I had a hard time running them to earth. I finally reached Freddie Culpepper on his car phone, much to his annoyance. He wasted valuable message units demanding to know how I'd gotten the number.

"Sources, Freddie. You locked me out of my office, and my rent is paid in full. I need you to let me into the building to collect my belongings."

"We notified tenants who were in place yesterday. We regard you as voluntarily abandoning the premises, which means your office and its contents now belong to us. And don't even think of trying to break and enter. We know your habits, Warshawski, how you used to break into the basement despite Tom Czarnik's repeated warnings to you, and we'll know who to go after if that boarding comes off."

"Or if one of your own computers disappears. Along with ten years of your records." I didn't have time to screw around getting a court order to retrieve my papers.

I hung up as he sputtered something about getting his lawyers if I was resorting to threats. Giving Melba another ten, I took the sandwich outside with me to eat in the car. That left me with three singles and a bit of change, and an unwelcome sense of alarm. It would be a close thing to get more cash out of my account this week.

As a vain hope I talked to the tender of the corner newsstand, an unshaven man with bloodshot eyes and a black hole where his teeth once had been. He glanced at the snapshot, but he hadn't noticed the children. He hadn't noticed anyone on the street since a boy beat him up after he'd noticed the boy shoplifting and fingered him to the cops. That had been in '83, or maybe '85, but whenever it was it had permanently broken him of the noticing habit.

Discouragement made me impatient with everything, including my own appetite. I gave the man my sandwich and fries and drove home.

□23
Cop's Night Out

Conrad had gone back to the day shift yesterday morning. We had agreed to meet for supper and dancing at the Cotton Club to celebrate, but I felt too overwhelmed by the events of the day to feel very celebratory. I called to see if I could beg off.

"I've had a tough day, too, Ms. W. I'm not asking you to drink champagne and cheer, just help me put some of the garbage behind. And maybe let me do the same for you."

Put like that I couldn't refuse. As I went off to bathe, I realized my reluctance to see him stemmed not from fatigue, but from his friendship with Finchley. Finchley, whom I'd always liked, who seemed like a good and fair cop, was beginning to act like an enemy.

I turned on the bath, pouring in a generous dollop of juniper oil—it's advertised as lifting the spirits. Conrad had been right last week to call Deirdre's death the case he'd been dreading. It was starting to feel like a lump of leaden porridge sitting in my stomach when we talked.

I climbed into the green water and inspected my legs. A circle of small broken veins near my left kneecap was an early sign of age. The dark marks on the right one seemed just to be a bruise.

Perhaps a delicate stomach is the luxury of a private

citizen. It's not so much that the police slice everything into dipoles—right/wrong, black/white—but that they rate themselves by how many people they arrest. The pressure to make an arrest means that age or situation doesn't count. Can't count. So you inevitably end up across a chasm from them: you for mercy, they for justice. You for justice, they for law. I scrubbed my legs so hard, my skin stung when I lay back in the water.

Over dinner at I Popoli, I eyed Conrad warily. He seemed withdrawn, speaking in half-sentences, not paying much attention to what he was saying. I was sure he and Terry had been discussing the Messenger case, as well as last night's fiasco at my apartment.

Some of Conrad's depression might have stemmed from his dinner. He'd been warned at his last physical to cut down drastically on fat; in an act of self-pity tonight he had ordered poached turbot without sauce. Now he picked at it morosely. After his third random remark I couldn't take the strain, and asked him point-blank if he had been talking to Finchley.

"He caught up with me this evening. Just before I set out to meet you."

"And told you how he tried to arrest me last night?"

"Sounds like an ugly scene all the way around. He says you impersonated a cop to go into the Messenger mansion today."

"Technically, no. I showed my PI license to the house-keeper, but I didn't know the Polish word for it. She thought I was a cop. I'm sorry in a way that I did it. As long as Terry didn't take Messenger seriously as a suspect he wasn't going to search the house, and that bat could have lain there for decades." I tried to keep my tone reasonable, conversational, not threatening.

"You're wrong about that, Vic: Terry has wondered about Fabian. But there didn't seem to be any evidence hard enough for the state's attorney to agree to a search warrant."

He took another bite of fish and held his breath while he

swallowed it. I scooped some of my calamari alla marinara onto a bread plate and handed it across to him.

"Eat some of this. It doesn't have any fat in it, and it's got some flavor. . . . But as far as evidence goes, no one wanted to pay serious attention to my saying that Deirdre was expecting someone to meet her at my office."

"It's not that, Ms. W. Everyone knew you were protecting that homeless woman, so no one knew whether to believe you or not."

I set my fork down with a bang. "Outrageous, Conrad. To think I would manufacture evidence in order to shield someone I believe in. Do you think I didn't want to take that baseball bat today and burn it? No one ever would have known. Except Emily or Fabian." Or Emily and Fabian, I silently amended.

"Cool your engines, babe: it's a tribute to your passion for people in trouble, not a swipe at your integrity."

I tried to ease the taut muscles in my face. "What happens now?"

"Now the Finch will talk to Fabian. To the kid if he can find her."

"And what if Fabian makes Finchley believe it's the kid when it's not, when it's really him?"

"Give Terry some credit, Vic." He took my right hand and massaged it between his own. "He can sort out the truth. Pressure won't make him believe a lie."

I held my fingers rigidly, unable to respond to his touch. "Four days ago both you and he told me Tamar Hawkings was the likeliest person to suspect, not Fabian. You even seemed to think I would have manufactured evidence to shield her."

"Take it easy, Vic. We go with what we have. Four days ago we—he—didn't know the murder weapon was in a missing teenager's bedroom. An unstable homeless woman was not an unlikely suspect. She was a likely suspect: the one person on the scene."

He hesitated, then spoke in a rush. "As a favor to Terry, I went out to interview her husband, Leon Hawkings.

There's a history of violence in that household, but I'm not sure who's beating on whom. The woman has a sister who tried to kill her own husband, alleging violence, but she stabbed him when he was asleep, not provoked, so she did five years at Dwight. Leon seemed to think—''

"That's a real problem for women in violent households," I interrupted. "They know if they fight back when the man's assaulting them they're going to be hurt really badly. So they withdraw—emotionally—from the scene. It's only later that they can feel the anger you or another man might experience at the moment of attack."

"You can't stab a guy while he's sleeping. Not and claim self-defense, anyway."

"But it's okay to hit her while she's wide awake?" I spoke bitterly.

His grip on my fingers tightened. "You know I don't believe that, Vic. Don't put that kind of twist on my words. . . . According to Hawkings, when Tamar's sister came out, her old man murdered her. Tamar went off the deep end, started accusing Leon of being an abuser, and went to a shelter. When she left the shelter she stayed home for a week and then split with the kids."

I pulled my hand away to cover my head. Whose story did I believe—the husband's or the wife's? Finchley's or mine? Emily's or Fabian's—assuming they had separate stories.

"You hiding under there, girl?" Conrad asked.

I attempted a smile and looked up. "So Finchley thinks Hawkings was demented, and might have killed Deirdre just because Deirdre frowned when she should have smiled? Or vice versa?"

"We'd just like a chance to talk to her. And now to the Messenger girl. Those are the only two people we know for sure were hovering around the crime scene Friday night."

"I'd like to talk to them, too, but maybe ask slightly different questions. . . . How many people are in Joliet who never committed the crime they were convicted of? One? Five? Five hundred?"

"All of them, if you ask them," Conrad said. "What's your point? That we sometimes get the wrong person? I agree. I don't like it, but I won't try to pretend it doesn't happen."

"But we execute people, including teenaged girls. We sometimes do it when we're not a hundred percent sure they're guilty. Maybe they've exhausted their appeals, or the evidence comes up in such a way it can't be used on appeal. We know it happens. So when I hear about evidence, even when I find evidence that I send the police to, I need a lot more. Story. Context. It's the only way to decide if someone's story is . . . I won't say true—but more consistent, more authentic. I'm afraid Terry's going to take this bat and, because he's under pressure from the state's attorney, bludgeon Emily with it."

Conrad frowned at his turbot, now cold and flaking into pieces, and pushed it to one side. With a glance at me, as if to see whether he could eat my food without reprisals, he finished the share of calamari I'd given him and stuck his fork across the table into my pasta. It was meant as a gesture of reconciliation, the sharing of food.

"Why do you think she ran away?" he asked. "Do you think it's impossible she killed her mother and is racked by guilt?"

"I don't think anything's impossible. What I want to believe and what I'm able to accept are two very different things. But can't you imagine a scenario, Conrad, where she's had to swallow an enormous amount of unpalatable stuff, and the last thing to go down is her father forcing her to give him an alibi? I can see where that could push her past the brink, as much as if she'd killed her mother herself."

Conrad coughed, his sign of distress, and started shredding a roll into tiny pieces. The waiter hove into view.

"Is everything to your liking, sir?"

"That fish wasn't too hot," Conrad said. "Reminded me of the overcooked mush I had to eat in the hospital when I was recovering from a knife in the abdomen."

The waiter blinked, as did I: Conrad usually didn't let things like restaurant meals bother him. The waiter offered to bring him another entree, his choice on the house.

Conrad coughed again. "I'd like some apple pie. With ice cream. And don't go telling me how much fat or cholesterol or what have you it's got in it, because I don't want to hear about it."

"Certainly not," the waiter said. "None of our desserts have any fat in them. For you, ma'am?"

Sweets have never been my weakness. I could have eaten a second plate of linguine, but that seemed unnecessarily piggish. I ordered a double espresso.

"You're at odds with two of the people I'm closest to," Conrad said. "If Zu-Zu and Jasmine didn't like you so much I'd start wondering about you. Or at least you and me. As it is, the pressure is hard to take some days."

"Conrad, really, I try to be polite to your mother, but she treats me so glacially that I start to feel like a frozen mammoth when I'm around her."

We stopped talking while the waiter delivered both his pie and an intrusive comment about its low-caloric, healthful properties. Conrad's remark about his stab wound seemed to have stimulated the waiter—he hovered within earshot, hoping for more juice.

"You gotta put Mama in context," Conrad said, shooting a dirty look at the waiter. "We lived in Hyde Park for a time after my dad died. Mama thought the schools would be better and that it would be a safer neighborhood for the girls, and it always has this rap as a liberal, integrated place. I was stopped and frisked on the street three different times, just walking back to the crib. Once when I was alone and twice with my buddies. I didn't want her to know: she was working two shifts, doing scut work, but they made her come pick me up from the precinct. It was just one more insult, and not the first she'd ever faced, but she started getting bitter. Life was too hard for her after my father died."

I swallowed some coffee. "After that history I'm surprised you even wanted to join the police."

He grinned, his gold front tooth glinting. "Maybe I wanted to even the score. No, things had changed. Some. When I got home from Vietnam I tried college, but I felt too old, too out-of-place. I had to do something and the options didn't look that great—drive a bus, be a busboy—so I took the test and went to the academy. The Finch was in my class. He was a college boy. University of Illinois criminal justice major. They thought he was too big for his britches. A couple of the guys jumped him one night when I happened to be passing by. After that we got to be buddies."

His beeper went off. "This had better not be some triple homicide calling me back to work."

He got up to find a phone but came back a minute later. "Speak of the devil. It's Terry, looking for you."

I went to the pay phone in the back of the restaurant. Terry was stiff, a bit formal, but straightforward. He wanted to share the lab results with me. The bat did have Deirdre's brains on it. Besides my own prints, the only ones they'd found were Emily's.

"Doesn't look good, Vic. I just wanted you to know."

"Isn't it strange, Terry? Wouldn't you think you'd find her brothers' or her parents' prints? Even visitors'? The thing sat in the hall where anyone could see it—I noticed it when I went to dinner down there. And a star like Nellie Fox—it makes you want to pick it up and hold his signed bat. I did it myself at the time."

"Maybe." Terry was dubious but polite: perhaps Conrad had been lecturing him too. "I'll put it to the lieutenant."

I thanked him for letting me know right away. On my way back to the table I felt curiously optimistic. Unlike some of the stories I try out in the hopes they'll work, I believed what I'd said to Terry. I didn't know where Emily was, or what the bat was doing under her radiator, but I felt sure she hadn't killed her mother.

Conrad and I finished the evening at the Cotton Club after all. While I leaned against his shoulder, lazily moving to the band, I wondered what part of my story he might have told Terry Finchley to make me seem more human.

24

In the (Electronic) Eye
of the Beholder

Before leaving my apartment I called Alice Cottingham at Emily's high school. It had occurred to me last night that the girl could have confided in some of her other teachers, and that Cottingham might be able to find that out. I caught her just as she was about to start a class, so she was curt. She didn't think her colleagues would shelter a student without telling the parents, but—to get me off the line—she agreed to get Emily's class schedule and see whether any of the teachers felt the girl had singled them out for special confidences.

This morning I found a meter available right in front of Home Free. When I went inside, Tish was at her desk, her thin body shrouded in a giant khaki sweater and shapeless granny skirt. Her heavy brows furrowed when she saw me. The usual warm Home Free welcome.

"Hi, Tish. V. I. Warshawski. I was in here last week."

"I remember." Nothing in her deep voice made it sound as though she'd been lying awake at night savoring the recollection.

"You were going to set up a tour of some of your projects for me so I could see what they look like. Remember that too?" Her churlishness made me speak brightly, as one does to a peevish toddler.

Tish gestured at the stacks of paper on the desk. "I've got all this work to do and no one to help me with it. I don't have time to respond to frivolous requests."

"Nothing frivolous in it. But I'll tell you what—I'll get you some first-class volunteer help if you'll take five minutes to answer a few questions."

"What kind of questions?"

"About Deirdre Messenger."

She looked away from me to the computer in front of her. She was working with some graphs. I couldn't make out the details. As we both watched, goldfish began to swim across the screen in a random pattern.

"I can't talk to you about Deirdre."

"Is she considered classified information, high-level, for your board only? Should I ask Jasper?"

"He doesn't want to be bothered right now." She glared at me.

"It's a choice between you or him, Tish. If you can't talk to me I don't mind it being him."

I started toward the rear of the room, where Jasper's door was. Tish moved out of her chair and across the small space between us so fast that she had her arms around me before I could touch the doorknob. I disengaged myself without much difficulty—not only was I stronger and used to fighting, but her own action startled her.

"What's he doing in there?" I asked mildly. "Holding an orgy?"

Her face flooded with color. "How can you say things like that?"

My pity at her gaucherie warred with impatience at it. "Come on, Tish. You're making such a big deal out of this that you're rousing my curiosity. I only wanted to ask some questions about Deirdre Messenger's role on your board. And see if in exchange you'd like a volunteer. You're acting as though I've stumbled onto the secret of the century."

She drew herself up straight. I was surprised to see she was taller than me—she took a good five inches from her height by hunching down into her clothes.

"If you don't leave these private premises I will call the police."

"Fine. I don't mind the police."

"Oh . . . oh . . . *fuck* you anyway."

When she stormed back to her desk I tried the door. It was locked. Tish picked up her phone and spoke into it. She tried to shield the mouthpiece with her hand, but the room was too small for secret conversation.

"I'm sorry, Jasper. I know you didn't want to be disturbed, but that detective who was here last week came in and she won't leave. I threatened to call the police. . . . Deirdre Messenger . . . Okay."

She hung up and turned back to her computer. A few seconds later Jasper came out of the inner room, shutting the door carefully behind him.

"Vic. Good to see you. Tish says you have some questions about Deirdre Messenger? She was murdered in your office, wasn't she? That must have been a shock. I hope the police don't suspect you." He smiled at me with a friendly sympathy.

"Until the police make an arrest they suspect everyone. I'm helping out by trying to learn who Deirdre met with that night."

"It wasn't me," Jasper said. "How about you, Tish?"

Her lips pressed together, she typed furiously, refusing to share in his banter.

"If that's all, Vic . . . I hate to be rude, but when you come by unannounced you can't expect people to meet with you." He looked at the heavy metal weighting his wrist.

"You guys don't have a good track record returning my calls. All I want to know is what Deirdre did for you. Who she worked with. I'm trying to generate some names of people to talk to—new leads, you might say. So I can find out whom she was meeting last Friday night."

Jasper looked reproachfully at his aide. "We can't dismiss questions like this, Tish. Not when one of our own volunteers has been murdered."

Tish sat rigidly in front of her machine, not looking at us.

"I'm sorry, Jasper. I shouldn't have lost my temper. It's just . . . I'm swamped."

"I know that, Tish. You work far too hard as it is. It's difficult balancing so many demands." His smile was still beguiling; I found myself feeling I'd been the source of unfair demands on Tish.

"I don't think Deirdre was close to anyone at Home Free," he continued, to me. "Of course, the day-to-day work she did for us Tish knows more about than I do. What's your afternoon like, Tish? Got any time later on?"

"I can make time. You tell me which is more important, talking to her or finishing this report."

He went over to her and put a hand on her shoulder. She sat still under his touch, like a timid rabbit, trying not to show the pleasure she found in it.

"Tish, darling, if you will make time to meet with Vic, and if you will be an absolute angel and stay late to finish the project, I will come back here after my afternoon meeting and whisk you off to the fleshpot of your choice."

She kept her eyes fixed on the computer screen. "All right, Jasper. If you want it bad enough to spring for dinner. You can come back at three-thirty," she added to me.

He squeezed her shoulder and let her go. "Atta girl. Tish makes this office work. If I had to pay her what she's worth, we'd need to double our revenues."

You're used to people working hard for love, I wanted to say, but couldn't be so cruel to Tish. Instead I grunted noncommittally and thanked both of them.

"There is one other thing, Jasper, which Tish tells me only you can decide but which could make a big difference in her horrendous work load. Do you know Darraugh Graham?"

"You mean the CEO? Don't tell me the cops suspect him of killing Deirdre."

I gave a thin smile. "He has a son who needs to do some community service work. How about letting him do it here?"

"Community service?" Jasper raised his brows. "What'd he get busted for? A few lines?"

"A few telephone lines. Into DOE files. He needs to put in about five weeks in a not-for-profit. I'm sure the judge would be extremely enthusiastic about Home Free."

Jasper narrowed his eyes at me. "A hacker, Vic? Do you think I was born yesterday? Or were you?"

"What's that supposed to mean? You'd rather have someone who might sell your electronics to support a drug habit than a computer whiz? He could get this office automated and straightened out in a week."

"Tish is a computer whiz too. And don't be naive, Vic. I don't want a hacker who can poke into my files. If that's a big letdown for Darraugh Graham, I'm sorry. We'll write him off as a donor. Tish will see you this afternoon. I've got to get back to my meeting." He stalked back to his office, for once forgetting to smile.

What was in his damned files that he had to protect— unreported income? I was consumed now with curiosity about who in that back room needed such careful sheltering. Once outside the office I looked around for a convenient place to watch the entrance. The vertical blinds still shut out any view of the inside. When I glanced up at the lintel I found an electronic eye watching me. An important precaution in a neighborhood like this? Or overly vigilant for a storefront operation?

I went back to the Korean novelty shop. The lamp I'd admired last week was still there. Dust was gathering on the baby's upper lip, but the shade still trumpeted "Oh, Mama" in bright red letters. If I went inside to look at it, though, I wouldn't be able to tell when the Home Free door opened.

For the benefit of the electronic eye I drove my car around the block and parked close to Leland. Picking up the towels that I kept in the backseat for the dogs, I crossed to the far side of the street and went into a Laundromat. It was about three doors south of Home Free, with big windows that afforded a good view of the street.

A couple of women in Azeri headscarves were chatting in one corner. Another young woman sat by herself reading a Korean newspaper. None of them paid any attention to me; I didn't really even need the verisimilitude of doing laundry, but it wouldn't hurt the towels to be clean once a year.

The water had just started roaring into the machine when the Home Free door opened. I squinted and then felt my jaw go slack in surprise. Phoebe Quirk came out, accompanied by young Alec Gantner, the senator's son whom I'd met at Deirdre's last week. The impulse to run outside and grab hold of her, to shake her until she told me what the two of them wanted together with Jasper Heccomb, was so strong my legs ached from the effort of standing still.

It wasn't surprising for Phoebe to meet with Heccomb: she was a backer of Lamia, and Lamia was rehabbing a building for them. It wasn't surprising for Alec Gantner to be there—he was a director of Home Free. Why, then, did Jasper and Tish feel they had to shroud the meeting in secrecy? Was there some conflict of interest—were Phoebe and Alec involved in some other deal that should have precluded the Lamia project? But what could that be?

I looked at the washing machine. It would take almost an hour for it to complete the cycle. I was coming back this afternoon to see Tish: if someone wanted to steal the towels in the interim, she was welcome to them. While Gantner and Phoebe climbed into her BMW I scuttled down the street for my Trans Am. By the time Phoebe got to her office I was sitting in the antechamber waiting for her.

25

The Old Girl Spiderweb

Phoebe was humming under her breath. She gave a cheery ''good morning'' to the receptionist before noticing me.

''Vic! What are you doing here? I thought—'' she broke off.

''I know. You thought Jasper had successfully booted me out the Home Free door and I'd taken off in my sporty roadster. The three of you sat in Jasper's little office watching me on the TV monitor and cheering. But I snuck back in time to see you and young Alec waltz away together.''

''So?''

''So why is your seeing the head of Home Free such a secret?''

She looked from me to the receptionist, suddenly aware of how public our conversation was. ''It's not a secret, Vic. And, as Jasper told you, when you drop in on people unannounced you can't expect them to find time for you. I have a meeting to get to.''

I stood up. ''I know, sweet pea. It's with me. We can have it out here in the foyer, in your office, or downstairs in the coffee shop, but we are going to talk.''

Her face bunched together in frustration. ''Oh, very well. We'll go to my office. Hold my calls, Laura.''

She walked down the hall at race-qualifying speed, ignoring greetings from co-workers and a frantic demand from one man that she respond to a Japanese fax immediately. In her office she sat at her desk, an imposing piece of ebony about a tennis court wide. Her desk chair built up her height; wing chairs in front put visitors a foot below her head. I opted for one of the corner couches behind the desk. She swiveled and glared, angry at losing her barricade.

"Okay, Vic. This had better be good."

I blinked. "You stole my line, Phoebe. I want to know what you and Alec Gantner are up to. With Heccomb thrown in for sauce."

"Private business. You're on retainer *for* me, in case you'd forgotten. Not to investigate me."

"We seem to keep having this conversation. You paid for my professional help. You did not buy me. In case you'd forgotten, last week you used that same line to coerce me into investigating why Century Bank had pulled the plug on Lamia. When, just two days later, Home Free agreed to give them a rehab job, you trotted out those very words to pull me off the investigation."

She started to say something, but I spoke through her. "In a minute. I want to spell this out clearly for you. I left the investigation most reluctantly. My main City Hall informant was so nervous about it that I knew I'd inadvertently walked in on something sensitive. Ordinarily I would not have dropped such an inquiry, but two things decided me: Camilla Rawlings's ardent pleading for Lamia, and Deirdre's murder. Her death, and the disappearance of her three children, pushed other less-important questions out of my mind. Also, I had inspected Home Free's 990 filing and their finances looked good enough to pay Lamia's bills."

"So why come around now?" Phoebe's fists were knotted in her lap. "Leave it alone for good, Vic."

I pressed my fingertips into my forehead. "You're not listening, Phoebe. I didn't drop the inquiry on your orders, but for the reasons I just outlined."

"What's made you change your mind?"

"Nothing. Until I saw you and Alec Gantner waltzing

out of Home Free this morning I had scrupulously avoided all mention of Lamia in my few sessions with Jasper Heccomb. Now—all bets are off.''

She pounded her right thigh in frustration. ''Then what were you doing there?''

''Looking for leads into Deirdre's murder. She was an active Home Free volunteer. I'm trying to find someone she talked to the night she died. Now you tell me what you were up to this morning.''

She swiveled around to commune with her desk. ''I was going over some details of the Lamia deal.''

''With Alec Gantner?''

''He *is* on the Home Free board, Vic,'' she shot over her shoulder. ''He has a legitimate interest in their projects.''

''I see.'' I walked to a sideboard against the far wall and opened its doors.

''What the hell are you doing?''

''Looking for a refrigerator. I thought you might have eggs. Which you'd be willing to show me how to suck.'' I shut the cupboard doors and leaned against the edge.

Phoebe frowned ferociously, her jaw jutting out far enough to cause permanent damage to her overbite. ''It's time for you to return Capital Concerns's retainer, Vic.''

''Great. I'll be happy to. I can't work for someone who's as secretive as you are about your actions. You keep me totally in the dark and then are outraged if I bump into a giant sofa you've stuck in the middle of the room.''

''Don't bring furniture into this, Vic. You promised me —Camilla and me—last Sunday you would leave Lamia's affairs alone. I can't have someone on my payroll who's so untrustworthy.''

''Pot calling the kettle, Quirk.'' It was an effort to keep my voice light. ''My accounting records are boarded up in the Pulteney. I'll send you a check as soon as I can get in to see how much of your retainer is owed you—I've done some work on Mr. T that I haven't billed you for yet.''

''Mr. T? What's he got to do with me? You're not just arrogant, you're insane.''

"Your little T-cell company. That's what you called it when you gave me the assignment. I don't remember its formal name offhand."

Her skin turned so pale that her freckles stood out like drops of blood against her skin. "I want you to drop that investigation at once. What have you found out?"

"I'll look it up this afternoon and send you a report and a bill." I spoke stiffly, uninterested in masking my own anger.

"I don't want you looking it up. I don't want you sending me a report. I'll write off the retainer in lieu of a fee for the work on that company." She got up. "And stay away from Home Free. Neither Camilla nor I want those waters muddied any further."

"Phoebe, you just fired me. You can't order me around. And anyway, you never have realized I'm not a blender to start and stop by throwing a switch. You need to remember I'm a professional with whom you *contracted*—not hired—to get work done. And that means I design the work plan. If I turn up startling material that changes the work plan, I make that decision."

"Professional?" She curled her lip. "With your accounts boarded up in an abandoned building? What a joke! I hired you out of pity for a struggling woman entrepreneur. But there are plenty of other firms around town who will do what I need with a lot less grief."

As I rode the elevator down to the ground I felt a sour taste in my mouth. There was too much truth in her criticism. Nothing about my life these days looked remotely successful, let alone professional.

I tried to find a quick place for lunch on my way up Dearborn. I'd have liked a bowl of old-fashioned barley or matzo ball soup, but the mom-and-pop delis have all disappeared—replaced by trendy cappuccino bars to gratify yuppified palates such as my own.

I found some ersatz minestrone and a lump of dough calling itself a bagel and went on up to the *Herald-Star*. Without my modem I had to revert to slogging the streets

like an old-fashioned gumshoe. Good thing I'd worn my
Nikes—I was dressed for the part.

I climbed the stairs to the second-floor news offices and
made my way through the labyrinth of cubicles to Murray
Ryerson's desk. My lucky day. Murray was in, hunched
over the phone. He looked up when I tapped his shoulder,
wound up his call, and stood to hug me. An outsize Viking
in a red beard, he tops my five-eight by a good nine inches.

"Nancy Drew in the flesh." His voice boomed around
the floor; a woman in the next cubicle poked her head
around to stare.

Murray, oblivious, fingered my hair. "You've got some
white in that curly mop of yours. It's been so long since
you've spoken to me, you've grown old."

I disengaged myself; the woman next door scooted back
to her desk. "Just showing the effects of working with you
all these years."

"*With* me?" he mocked. "When was it ever cooperative? I never got anything from you except with a crowbar,
and then only if you needed a favor back. Which makes me
wonder what you're doing here now."

Murray and I go back to my days in the PD's office when
he'd been a rookie reporter trying to find who was leaking
defense files to the state's attorney. He had interviewed me
for the story. Even though I'd suspected my assistant director, residual clannishness from growing up on the South
Side kept me from squealing. Murray eventually got the
information from a disgruntled secretary. I'd taken the heat
anyway at my next performance review and had always
wondered if Murray fingered me out of pique for not making his job easier.

Over the years, as he became one of the city's preemi-
nent investigative reporters, our relations remained colored
by that early experience: he came to me for stories; I held
on to information to protect clients or friends; he got angry;
I got burned. For a brief time we'd compounded the mess
by becoming lovers, and that interlude added to the ambiva-
lence we felt on seeing each other. Did we welcome a meet-

ing or recoil from it? Did we gain or get hurt by it? Neither of us could figure that out.

"Oh, well, since you know I've come to beg for help, I won't beat around the bush. I want to look up some stories on the news data bases." Murray had access to the *Times, Tribune,* and *Herald-Star* as well as the Dow Jones News Service.

"Whoa, there, Nancy. I'm not running the public library here."

"Okay. I'll go to the library. You know, the police impounded my computer after Deirdre Messenger died, on account of they think they can bully me into explaining why the murderer erased my hard disk. Or maybe Deirdre did it because she was in a bad mood. And the Culpeppers boarded my modem up in the Pulteney on Wednesday. Otherwise I'd do this myself. But the library's a good tip. Thanks."

I sauntered toward the door. Murray caught up with me at the elevator.

"Not so fast, Vic. This in connection with Messenger? I was in Washington last week—they've got me poring over Congressional finance records now. I forgot you were sitting in the front seat on this one. What's with Deirdre's kids? They've hogged the front page the last two days. Someone said Messenger beat his wife and killed her because she was having an affair."

"Could be." I pushed the button.

"Oh, *damn* you, Warshawski." He got down on one knee, with more agility than you might expect from a guy his size, and kissed my right hand. "O She-who-must-be-obeyed, I will dial up all data bases for you with my own fingers if you will only tell me about the murder, omitting no details however trivial they may seem to you, and tying them up with the computer search you are undertaking."

I laughed. "I'm not sure how what I want to know ties to Deirdre's death. I'm just fishing around. But I'll tell you something for nothing that the cops aren't interested in:

Deirdre had made an appointment to see someone in my office. I'm trying to find out who.''

Murray loved it. He danced me around the hall and told me he took back all the mean, ugly things he'd ever even thought about me, let alone said, adding that the white hairs looked sexy, and whisked me down to Lucy Moynihan's hamburger joint to talk. While he ate three burgers and I supplemented my soup with a basket of onion rings we discussed the pros and cons of Fabian as a suspect.

"I know he beat her: I heard him do it once," I said. "But who was she supposed to be sleeping with?"

He shook his head. "Idle talk—no one had any serious names to throw around. You know the odds-on suspect is the daughter. That's why she's supposed to have run away."

"I know. But I don't believe it. I think it was Fabian. And I think the only thing I can do to help the kid is find who Deirdre was meeting in my office last Friday. It might even have been Alec Gantner or Donald Blakely—she was making suggestive remarks to them at her dinner party last week. If they saw Fabian enter the building, maybe they're not squealing out of brotherly solidarity. I want a lever that will make them talk to me."

"And what's your pal Conrad saying while you show the police how to do their job?" Murray jeered. "Aren't he and the officer in charge good old boys together?"

"You want to do a story on my love life or on Deirdre's death?" I snapped.

Murray laughed. "I love to catch you off guard, Warshawski. It's good for you."

"Yeah, like castor oil."

I looked at my wrist. Even if I'd had an inheritance I wouldn't have spent it on a pimp watch like Jasper Heccomb's. My father's old steel watch, which I'd had fitted with a new band so it didn't fall off my wrist, told time just as well as a Rolex. Right now it told me I had two hours before I was due back at Home Free. I herded Murray back up to daylight and his computer.

▫26
Whirling Dervish

Endless stories had been filed on the Gantners. Alec senior was a U.S. senator and had been a secretary of agriculture. His wife served on the Symphony and Ravinia boards; their eldest daughter, Melanie, had flirted briefly with the Weather Underground before buying a farm in Oregon. She lived there in ostentatious simplicity, cultivating a hundred acres without modern chemistry or machinery, and writing well-publicized polemics against modern agribusiness.

Gantner family money derived from agriculture, the kind Melanie blasted—twenty-five-thousand-acre spreads kept going with tons of pesticides, herbicides, and diesel fuel. The endless miles of corn that bore Easterners as they zip through Illinois and Iowa on their way to California turn to gold in the right hands. Corn oil and syrup can be found in everything from coffee whiteners to plastic. And the Gantners had a kernel of every cob.

Young Alec, trying to set himself up independently from his powerful papa—without going to his sister's extremes —had turned to gasohol. He led the Illinois lobby for price supports for corn fuel production and distribution. He also dabbled in real estate and banking.

Young Alec's desire to prove himself hadn't led him to set up independent shop: Gantohol, as he called his subsidiary, had offices in the Gant-Ag headquarters near Morris. It was hard to picture the urban sophisticate in the middle of Illinois's corn fields.

By three I was growing dizzy from the information scrolling across the screen. I had to stop anyway to meet with Tish, but I couldn't have gone on reading the fuzzy type much longer. I asked Murray to queue the stories for overnight printing—I'd pick them up in the morning.

"You be sure to leave anything hot on my desk," he warned me in parting. "Big Alec always tiptoes on the edge of breaking scandals. He and the old gov did a lot of interesting state contracts together. Your ass is grass if you sit on something juicy about him, Warshawski. It's not easy to bag a U.S. senator. I could retire on that."

"You're so damned greedy, Ryerson," I grumped, packing up my bag. "One of these days you'll get indigestion."

Before going into Home Free I dashed into the Laundromat to check on my towels. The place was noisier than it had been in the morning, as mothers brought along children they'd picked up from school. Someone had put my wet laundry into a wire cart. Dumping the towels into a dryer, I went across the street.

Tish was still planted at her computer when I came in. She shot me a resentful glance but closed her file and folded her hands with the exaggerated patience of one who has little.

"It must be hard to work in here with the blinds shut so tightly," I commented.

"It doesn't bother me—I'm used to it."

"And worse for Jasper, in the back there without any windows at all. You at least could pull open a slat to look out. Of course, he can watch the street on his TV monitor, so no one could sneak up on him unawares."

She scowled. "This isn't a very safe neighborhood. We can't afford to have our computers ripped off. Do you want to talk about Deirdre or can I get back to work?"

Before we talked about Deirdre I prodded Tish to give me her own background. She disgorged information in

small, hostile pellets, but I finally learned she had been at
Home Free for five years, first as a summer intern while she
completed a masters in urban planning at IIT, and then full-
time as the office manager. Deirdre had started doing volunteer work for them a few months after Tish began her
internship. In those days they still did direct placement of
homeless people and they needed help in interviewing
them.

"When did you stop that?"

"When Jasper came," she said shortly. "He took over as
executive director three years ago. He saw at once we were
duplicating services the city and other charities provided.
He decided we'd be more effective building housing."

"Your board had no problem with that?"

She stared at her computer. "It took a while—almost a
year. We had to wait for some of the old people to leave."

"And for Alec Gantner and Donald Blakely to join?" I
suggested.

She shot me an angry glance. "Does this have anything
to do with Deirdre?"

"How did she feel about the change? Did it affect her as
a volunteer?" Was that what had lain behind her comments
to Gantner at her dinner party? Had she fought for Home
Free to remain a direct provider and resented the change?

"For a year or so she only was here for board meetings,
because our work load changed so much. But six months
ago we had to lay off our secretary, so Deirdre filled in
when she could get up here."

Pressed for specifics, Tish would only say Deirdre helped
keep their computer files up-to-date. Work logs from construction projects had to be entered, bills generated, key
money people kept happy.

"Didn't you think it was strange for a woman in her
position to do clerical work for you?"

"Not really. Jasper said she was at loose ends, to humor
her because her husband's friends could bring us a lot of
money. We'd lost some of our donors. People who couldn't

keep up with the times left over the placement issue. Jasper thought Deirdre could help bring them back.''

"Was she hard to get along with?" I pictured Deirdre and Tish in a scowling contest.

"She came to work, same as me."

"She have a crush on Jasper?"

Tish flushed. "She was married. I suppose she liked him to tease her. Sometimes she could be pretty childish . . ." Her voice trailed off.

"I had lunch today with a reporter who said there are rumors she and Jasper were having an affair."

Tish's flush turned to crimson. She picked at her sweater, shaking her head, but unable to speak. I let it drop and asked her to step me through some of Deirdre's work. "Just show me the stuff she did the last day she was here."

"Absolutely not. Our files are confidential. Jasper said to talk to you about Deirdre. He didn't say anything about showing you our books."

I raised my brows. "Won't they stand the scrutiny?"

She turned a darker red but was spared answering me by the phone. "Home Free, Tish speaking . . . Oh, hi, Gary . . . No, he's not in. . . . He told you not to worry about it, that he'd take care of it. . . ."

Gary, the beefy man in the sheepskin jacket who'd been here when I came last week. He apparently was still unhappy—I could hear him barking at Tish, but I couldn't make out the words.

"I can't tell you anything else, I've got someone in the office with me." She laughed suddenly, lightening her face and revealing its underlying beauty. "No, definitely not a friend . . . I'll let him know you called."

"But why am I not a friend?" I asked when she hung up. "Why are you so set against me?"

"Because you come snooping around into things that aren't any of your business. Like just now: that was a private phone call. Now I've got to get back to work."

"So you can be ready for dinner with Jasper when he comes back. I'm not competing with you for his attention, you know. Perhaps Deirdre did, but I'm not interested in spending the night with him.''

''That's good, because he wouldn't touch you with a ten-foot pole.'' Anger and jealousy made her voice quaver as she tossed off the childish insult.

I found myself patting the top of my head where my white hairs had appeared, but I only said, ''Mutual, Tish, mutual. He's too smooth for my taste. Now let's line up some construction sites for me to visit.''

''Construction *sites*? No way. You can see some of our finished projects, but we don't let anyone go on site unless they have official business there.''

''So you do have projects under construction? Jasper told me last week you didn't have much going on.''

Her jaw dropped, and she looked sickly, but she made a quick enough recovery, saying Jasper knew more about construction than she—that she was just speaking generally.

We argued it back and forth, but she was enjoying the chance to put me in my place. After that I couldn't get any information from her. Finally, not intending to, I brought up Lamia.

''How did they get the rehab project? Did you put it out to bid?''

''How do you know about them?'' she demanded.

''I'm connected to them professionally. Is there a problem with their bid?''

She looked impulsively at the phone, as if hoping Jasper might call to advise her. After a long pause she muttered that she didn't know anything about their bids, that Jasper did all that work.

''So if I told you they'd never submitted a bid, but that they got work on a publicly funded project, and that that's against the law, you wouldn't know anything about it.''

''I've told you,'' she shouted. ''I don't know anything about it. Are you happy now? Go away and let me get to work.''

As I slowly shut the door she was already punching a

number into the phone. I longed to be able to eavesdrop, but couldn't think of any discreet way to do so. Across the street I collected my dry laundry. My towels were in another wire basket, and some kind woman had folded them. The day hadn't been a total loss: I had clean towels now.

□27

Gentleman Caller

Mr. Contreras bounded from his apartment as soon as I had my key in the front door. "Hi, doll. You've got a visitor. I let him in after he'd been waiting an hour. I didn't think he was someone who'd hurt you."

The dogs joined him, greeting me as though we'd been separated for months instead of the ten hours since our run. Over their delighted yips and squeaks it was difficult to convey my annoyance with my neighbor for involving himself in my business.

Catching my mood if not my words, Mr. Contreras's brown eyes clouded reproachfully. "I'm just trying to help out, doll, not to interfere. There's no place for people to wait for you now that you're having to work in your home. What do you want me to do—leave potential customers wandering around in the rain, where they'll go off to one of those big suburban outfits you're always worrying about, just because I didn't think to offer them a cup of coffee and a place to sit? Now, that really would be cause for you to get upset."

I threw up my hands in resignation. "All right, all right. You did the best you could under the circumstances. Who is it and where is he?"

As if on rehearsed cue Ken Graham came to Mr. Contreras's doorway. I'd noticed an Alfa Spider, a car I love, when I came up the walk. It must belong to the hacker, who was still in jeans and a mangy sport coat. Still, he'd trimmed his hair and shaved.

"Great dogs," he greeted me.

"Thank you for coming by to inspect them." I hustled them inside before Mitch could make good on an escape attempt.

Ken grinned involuntarily, stripping some of the loutish cynicism from his face. "I went to your office and saw it was all boarded over. Your answering service didn't have a new office address for you, so I came here."

"Very enterprising. Was there some special reason?"

"Don't get so huffy. Dad is riding my butt pretty hard and I wanted to see if you'd turned up any leads for me. For community service, you know."

"I haven't forgotten. And your dad has been in touch as well. Riding my own butt pretty hard, you could say. As soon as I have anything I'll call you."

Mr. Contreras was listening with lively attention, but not asking questions: he didn't want a young sprout to think he wasn't fully in my confidence. He tried now to get Ken and me to join him back in his apartment, but I wanted to be alone. Or at least not with those two.

Young Ken already owned some of the confidence his father wore—that people would do what he wanted because he was a Graham and owned a large chunk of stock in a very big company. Now he tried to persuade me that he could do some work for me.

"Yes, I'm sure you could. But I'm not a charity. In any sense of the word."

"Who's to know? Dad says you do a lot of *pro bono* work. You could set me on some of those projects. I'm sure we could persuade my probation officer—"

"Maybe you could, but you can't persuade me. Thanks for going to all the trouble of stopping by. Give my regards to your father."

I started up the stairs. Ken followed in my wake. The

dogs, thinking any group of people offered more chance for fun than an evening in front of Mr. Contreras's TV, ran up ahead of us. Mr. Contreras brought up the rear. I couldn't imagine any other detective in the metropolitan area with such an entourage. Any other detective in the world.

"If I could tell Dad I was working with you, he would get off both our asses for a while. And it would help me get better acquainted with you. So far all I know is you don't like sugar in your cappuccino."

I started to undo the dead bolts in my steel-plated door. "Good night, MacKenzie. Good night, Mr. Contreras. If anyone else comes to visit, give them two aspirins and ask them to call in the morning."

I shut the door firmly on their protests. The dogs took it hardest. Even through the thick door I could hear sharply expressed barks. I opened the door again as the four were just beginning their downward trek.

"I'll borrow Peppy for the evening if that's okay with you."

"Sure, doll, sure. She's your dog as much as mine, you know that you don't have to ask. But with you gone so much . . ."

I went out to the landing and kissed his cheek. "Right, I know. You do it out of a keen sense of duty. And Peppy and I both appreciate it."

Pushing Mitch away, I ushered Peppy inside with me. She was delighted to be top dog again, wagging her tail and affecting not to hear Mitch's hurt cries from the other side of the door.

After brushing Peppy and playing a little fetch I phoned Camilla, hoping to reach her ahead of Phoebe or one of her partners. The sunny cheer of her greeting evaporated when I told her what I'd been doing this afternoon.

"I didn't mean to bring up Lamia's affairs. But the response I got from Heccomb's office manager unsettled me."

"What kind of detective are you if you spill all you know

every time you get rattled?'' Camilla asked, not unreasonably annoyed.

"I scrupulously avoided your name until this afternoon. But I'm getting more and more uneasy. There is something wrong—with that organization, or with Phoebe's connection to it."

I told her about Phoebe's reluctance to be seen at Home Free with Alec Gantner. "Jasper Heccomb is a smooth dancer but his office manager is tripping over her feet. I wanted to see if Lamia is the banana she's afraid she's going to slip on."

"And was it? Because if *we* trip on it thanks to you, Warshawski, my mama is not going to be the only member of this family who thinks you're dirt."

I massaged the back of my neck with my left hand. "Look, Camilla, I agreed on Sunday not to ask any more questions about Lamia. But Phoebe is sitting on something that she's not telling you. I would be a bad friend if I turned my back on an illegal situation that landed you and your friends in hot water. Think about it. Talk about it with your partners."

"We've thought about it and talked about it. We're happy. So you be happy, too, Vic. Because no one wants you stirring this pot." She hung up with a snap.

I thought about calling Conrad, but I couldn't rat on his sister to him. And I was damned if I was going to run to him for comfort just because people were annoyed with me. That was a fact of my business life: people were always more or less peeved with me for the questions I asked. It was only fatigue, or chronic financial stress, that made me care now.

"But what else can I do now?" I cried out loud to Peppy. "I'm almost forty. I don't have any other skills and it's been too long since I practiced law."

She looked at me in concern, hoping my anguish wasn't connected to her, and was relieved when I stopped howling to stomp into the kitchen.

It had been some time since I'd been to the store. My

lettuce was wilted, with black slime on the tips of the leaves. In fact, the only vegetables I had that weren't withered or rotted were onions and garlic. I sautéed them in my last tablespoon of olive oil while I cooked a pot of polenta. Stirring it all together with the case-hardened end of a piece of cheddar, I sat in front of the tube and watched the Cubs fumble through a game against St. Louis. At my feet Peppy cleaned out the cookpot.

At eight-thirty I couldn't take any more, either of the Cubs or my own suffocated mood. I went downstairs to knock on Mr. Contreras's door.

"I'm going out for a bit. I'm taking Peppy for company. Since it may be late when I get back I'll keep her overnight. Want me to take Mitch too?"

My neighbor complains a lot about my neglecting the dogs, but he's jealous of my relations with them. As I'd expected he hung on to Mitch.

"Maybe when you come back you'll be in a better mood. You act this way around Conrad, you're going to be on your own again before you know it."

"Yes, sir. I'll bear that in mind." Conrad said it was my orneriness that had initially attracted him, but I suppose like any repeated charm it might wear thin with time.

The Alfa Spider was still out front. In the dark it wasn't possible to see into its low-slung body, so I couldn't tell if Ken was inside, but as we went down the street I heard the engine start. What was the boy doing?

I bundled Peppy into the Trans Am and drove north to Belmont. The Spider was definitely behind us. It stayed there all the way across Belmont to Lake Shore Drive. I rode a mile south, then exited abruptly at Fullerton and waited at the entrance to the park. A few seconds later the Spider trundled along, saw me too late to stop behind me, and pulled over ten yards or so ahead. I ran up to it and yanked open the passenger door. Ken Graham sat at the wheel grinning as though he'd done something clever.

"What the hell do you think you're up to? Taking up

harassment to tide you over until you can start hacking again?''

''I've got you interested. That was my goal.''

''And what was the point of that? If you think you have to vamp me to keep me from marrying your father, you're insulting all three of us. Or at least your father and me. *You* could use a few insults, I expect.''

''Maybe I like you for your own sake.''

''Yeah, and maybe my mother was the pope. Get a grip on yourself, Graham. If you keep stalking me I'll tell Darraugh without mincing words why I refuse to help find a placement for you.''

''You sound like my old baby-sitter. Behave or I'll tell Papa. I had the hots for her too.''

''Then maybe it's time you grew up, kiddo. I'm not interested in boys whose diapers I have to change.''

I turned on my heel and walked back to the Trans Am. While I stood with my hand on the door handle he idled his engine for a bit, then gunned it and roared off with a great show of speed.

28

The Somewhat Lower Depths

I made a U in the Trans Am and continued south. A couple of times I thought Ken might still be following me, but it was hard to be sure. I wondered whether he really did believe I was dating his father and posed a threat to his trust fund, or if he was simply amusing himself. Presumably all his friends were off in school. Time must lie heavy on his hands. Proving to a middle-aged detective that he could track her and outwit her might seem like an agreeable game to him.

When I left the drive at Forty-seventh Street I went past the light at Lake Park and pulled over again. Two cars went on ahead of me; one even seemed to slow a bit, but I'd lost the Spider. I drove on over to Fabian's mansion and rang the bell.

When the housekeeper answered the door she remembered me and let me in. Whatever the police had said to her they hadn't persuaded her I was there under false pretenses: I held out a card but she ignored it, saying "Oh, polices" and turned back into the house, leaving me in the hall while she went upstairs. In a few minutes she returned with the command to follow her.

She led me on down the hall to a library built behind the massive stairwell. It was a room suitable for Fabian's professorial status—dark cherry shelves lined three walls, black leather chairs were stuck in alcoves, and an antique double-fronted desk, covered in leather, sailed on top of a suitably threadbare oriental rug. The room looked oppressive to me, but maybe if my income ever went into six figures I'd change my mind.

I lifted the edge of one of the crimson drapes on the far wall. Mullioned windows overlooked the backyard. I squinted in the dark to try to see the extent of the Messenger property, but could only make out an elaborate playset, as big as Arcadia House provided its children.

Turning back to the room I couldn't resist the temptation to open the desk drawers. Fabian claimed he'd been preparing to lecture Saturday morning. I didn't trust Terry to have checked his alibi. Presumably he had a diary or a lecture schedule or something. I started rustling through his papers.

I didn't see anything of interest, certainly not a diary, and was closing the drawer when Senator Gantner's name jumped out at me. He had written a letter stuck in a file labeled JAD HOLDINGS. I was starting to read it when I heard Fabian's footsteps outside the door. Feeling like a hundred kinds of fool I stuffed the letter into my jeans pocket and slammed the drawer shut.

He looked so ill I'm not sure he would have noticed my rifling the drawer in his presence. He was huddled inside a flannel dressing gown, his face tinged with yellow. He moved with something like a shuffle. It was hard to believe that he was the same man who had bounded up my walk two days ago, accusing me of kidnapping his daughter.

"Oh, it's you, Warshawski. They warned me, but Karin told me the police were here."

I blinked, taken aback by the greeting. "Who warned you? The cops?"

He stood next to one of the leather armchairs, looking around uncertainly as though he, not I, were the stranger to this room. "It doesn't matter. Did you come to tell me Emily killed her mother? I'd already figured that out."

"How handy for you. Are you sure of that? Or is Emily

turning into a handy scapegoat for you? First a surrogate mother for your children, now a surrogate murderer of your wife.''

''My family's private life is none of your business.'' He tried to speak with his usual hauteur, but the words came out in a fireless mumble. ''The police came around and found my Nellie Fox bat in her room. Which she'd clearly used to kill her mother.''

''Come on. You can't possibly believe that. Anyway, it had been wiped clean of prints. Didn't they tell you that?''

When I sat down in one of the padded chairs he stumbled into the room and sat as well, not behind his desk, but in a straight-backed chair near the door. He pulled his robe close around him as though it might protect him from me.

''Not of all prints, Warshawski—Emily's were on it.''

I took a breath. ''The popular theory seems to be she killed Deirdre. Let alone that she wouldn't have wiped everyone else's prints from the bat only to plant hers smack on it, why would she want to kill her mother?''

Fabian smiled with a flash of his usual smugness. ''I've consulted a psychiatrist on this one, Warshawski. It's totally plausible that she would want to be caught if she'd murdered Deirdre. Adolescent girls go through this stage. Rivalry with their mothers for their fathers' affections. She might have thought with her mother out of the way she could step into her place, and then been overcome with guilt and taken steps to ensure her arrest.''

''You must have found a senile Freudian, Fabian—a lot of people think those sexual ideas are way out-of-date. And anyway, Emily already had taken over her mother's job in a lot of ways, hadn't she? She might have been angry about it, but she sure didn't need to kill her to displace her.''

''What do you mean? What kind of ugly thing are you trying to insinuate now with your sewer mind, Warshawski?'' Despite the fierceness of his words he remained huddled in his chair, looking like a wounded animal.

''She already looked after your younger children. She seemed to be the main person in charge of the family at that dinner party. Deirdre was too drunk to be of much use, and you were too concerned with preening yourself in front of your guests. But a different question has to do with your alibi. You were very fierce with her last weekend, demanding she confirm you'd been here all night. How could she know that if she wasn't here to vouch for you?"

"Oh. Oh, I see. That's a good point." He subsided back into his robe and chewed on his lip.

"Maybe you were both gone," I suggested, thinking of the mouse between two cats. "Maybe you went downtown together to kill Deirdre and decided you'd better give each other an alibi."

"I thought I'd made it clear that I was here all night that night. I didn't go out."

"And Emily?"

"I don't know. I thought so, but she must have left after I went to bed. She was here in the morning, though: she got the children dressed and fed."

"How did she seem that morning?"

"Seem? What do you mean?" He blinked as if I'd asked him to explain the principles of general relativity.

"Was she upset? Did she act like a girl who might have spent the night killing her mother?"

"Oh." He chewed his lip some more. "I don't think I talked to her that morning; I was in here preparing my lecture. I think I might have called to her when I heard her go into the kitchen."

"What do you think you might have said?" I felt as though I were rowing a boat through molasses.

"Probably to make sure Joshua drank his milk. Something like that. She can be too lax in getting him to do things he should be doing—like letting him get away with not memorizing the poem for Manfred. Still, that's water over the dam. I may have told her not to leave until Mrs. Sliwa came, because we had to make sure someone was here with Nathan."

"That someone couldn't have been you?"

"I thought I told you I was preparing my lecture." His hauteur flashed through once again.

It sounded like a wonderful household: Papa the king, whose every act took precedence over the lives or even thoughts of his vassals. "You must have been quite annoyed that Deirdre stayed away all night. Or had she done that before?"

He flushed. "What are you trying to insinuate? That she had a lover? She was a faithful, loving wife. I won't have her memory maligned."

The picture of the two of them in the master bedroom after their dinner party came vividly to mind. What went through his mind? How did he reconcile his own brutality with the ideal of the loving spouse, faithful unto death?

"But weren't you upset when she didn't come home Friday night? Did you and Emily discuss that?"

"I came home from work and asked where her mother was. She said Deirdre had gone out, that she'd left a note saying she wouldn't be back for supper and we should have leftover salmon. I must say it was inconsiderate of her—but never mind that, she's dead now."

"And Saturday morning?" I prodded. "What did you and Emily say then?"

"I've told you twice already, Warshawski," he cried out. "We didn't talk."

"This symposium . . . Do you have some flyer announcing that? Or did the police already take it away with them?"

"Are you trying to imply I made up an important speaking engagement as a cover-up for my wife's death? I resent that more than your other filthy aspersions."

He sat up briefly, and his robe opened over his chest. He realized in a moment that he was exposing himself to me— a pale, hairless expanse—and pulled the robe shut, sinking back into his seat.

"So you were out at your symposium when the police came with the word that Deirdre was dead. That must have been difficult news for Emily to absorb on her own."

"Not if she'd killed Deirdre," he muttered from the depths of his chair.

I scratched my head, trying to think of a way to get a straight story out of him. "I'm really worried about Emily, Fabian. Aren't you? Where could she have gone?"

He moved his lips, as if rehearsing a point with himself, but wouldn't speak.

"If you have some idea that you don't want to share with the police, I'd be happy to check it out. At no charge, and without making it public. Do you have some colleague, or a minister, or anyone you wouldn't want people to know she'd run to?"

"She ran off to you. That detective, the one you're so friendly with—Finchley, is it?—told me she'd been spotted near your office building. You've got a hell of a nerve to come here demanding her, Warshawski. I'm seriously thinking of bringing charges against you for corrupting her. If not for you her mother would still be alive today and I wouldn't be going through this hell. Don't tell me you didn't entice Deirdre down to your office—what else was she doing there? And then encouraging Emily to run away to you. I could sue you for undue influence."

"You'd make a laughingstock of yourself, and Alec Gantner would never put you on the federal bench."

"Thanks to you and Deirdre that'll probably never happen anyway. Get out, Warshawski. I got out of bed to see you, but I've had enough. Go home."

With his yellow skin and glassy eyes he looked too ill for me to feel much besides an unwelcome twinge of pity. "You ought to see a doctor, Fabian. You might start feeling better if you had some proper medication." Like lithium, I thought, or Thorazine.

29

Not a Waggy Tail

Once or twice on the way home I thought someone was behind me, but when I pulled over to check the traffic no one else slowed down. At least I didn't see the Spider's headlights in my mirror.

I stopped in Grant Park to let Peppy stretch her legs. When I turned off the drive I again thought someone stayed with me, but no one else parked. I kept near the sidewalk along the inner drive, where the cops keep a regular patrol, and kept an eye cocked for shadows. Peppy, sensing my nervous state, didn't stray far. She'd bound off for a minute or two after a phantom rabbit, then return to press her nose into my hand.

Back on Racine I parked north of my building and across the street, surveying the entrance. I finally decided that concern over Emily was making me jumpy, and got out of the car. Still, I ordered Peppy to keep close to heel. I didn't put her on her leash, but wrapped it around my hand with the metal clip hanging free.

As we came up the walk Peppy suddenly stopped and growled. Her hackles rising, she looked intently at the curb. I knelt down next to her, wishing I had my gun, or was wearing a full suit of armor. Peppy gave a great yelp and tore away from me as a man rose from between two parked cars. I was about to plunge headlong after her when I realized it was MacKenzie Graham.

My heart was pounding so hard that my larynx vibrated. "I don't even want to know what you're doing, Graham. Go home and get your diapers changed."

I called to Peppy. She was wagging her tail at Ken to show there were no hard feelings, but she followed me to the door.

"Can't I at least say something?"

I gave a good imitation of Peppy's growl and told him to make it good.

"Could I come inside? I've been out here for ages and it's not that warm."

I pressed my lips together, but jerked my head toward the entrance. Inside the foyer I could hear Mitch whining and scratching from inside Mr. Contreras's apartment. That meant he—and Mr. Contreras—would soon be joining us. If I wanted any semblance of privacy I'd have to take Ken upstairs, instead of talking in the foyer as I had intended.

We were halfway up the stairs when Mitch caught up with us, followed by the old man. "Oh. It's you, doll. Mitch was making such a racket I thought maybe someone had broken in."

"Right you are. Your young pal Graham has something to say to me. If he's not back down in fifteen minutes call Conrad—one of us will be dead."

"Sure, doll, sure. I get you. You want privacy."

"No. I want to put a slug through this young pest. But the fact that you've seen us together will stop me."

Mr. Contreras called to Mitch, but Peppy, glad of a change in her routine, stayed with me. I let Ken go ahead with the dog. If he had some notion of adding to his cuteness by showing how easy it would be to jump me, I didn't want to make it simple.

When I'd ushered him into my living room I looked at my watch. "Okay. Give it to me in two minutes."

"Don't go imitating the pinstripes, Warshawski. I have some news for you."

"I'm all ears." I stayed on my feet.

"I wasn't the only person following you tonight."

I leaned against the piano, my arms folded. "Are you spinning a line to make yourself interesting, or did you really see someone?"

"I didn't shiver between those cars for over an hour just to play a game with you. Matter of fact I'm freezing. I could use some coffee."

"In a minute. Tell me what you saw."

"After you stopped me I made a circle through the park and got back on the drive at North Avenue." He gave me a sidelong glance to see how I'd react. "I didn't know if you were going downtown or not and thought I'd missed you at the Michigan exit. But I went on south just to see and caught sight of you at the second light in Grant Park. The dog was sticking her head out the window."

I nodded.

"I didn't want to get too close—I figured you'd be watching for me. So I hung about six cars back. And then I noticed someone else was after you. So I tagged along to see."

"Uh-huh. You kind of bored hanging around your old man, or what, Graham?"

He scowled. "I thought you'd be interested."

"Did you get a license plate or something to prove your point?" I kept my voice skeptical.

"No. It was too dark and I was trying to stay out of your mirror."

"So where did I go, Marlowe?"

"Why are you treating me this way? I hung around in the cold to give you a friendly warning that someone was after you, and you act like I'm two years old."

"You've been tagging around after me trying to prove how clever you are. This could be the relish on the hot-dog." I leaned back against the keyboard.

His face crumpled in frustration, but after a bit he pulled himself together. "You got off at Forty-seventh, right? I hung back so you wouldn't see me, but the other guy stayed right with you. I had bad luck with the light by the exit there—you and he got through on the yellow and I had to wait it out. By the time it changed you'd disappeared.''

''Assuming you're right, and someone was following me, why did you come back here? And by the way, where's your car? You can believe I was checking for it.''

''I parked around the corner. I thought if your tail spotted me watching him . . .'' His voice trailed away. ''I didn't know what else to do. If they were going to hurt you maybe they'd wait until you got home.''

''So you wanted to be a hero? But why? What are you getting out of tagging around behind me?''

''I like you. You're the only person who ever worked for Darraugh who didn't fall over and play dead whenever he frowned.''

''Give your father his due: he's never fired me for having an independent attitude.''

''Wish he'd give me the same break,'' Ken muttered.

''Flaws terrify parents: they know they can't look after you forever, so they lose all perspective when they see aberrations that may keep you from having a decent life on your own.'' I stood up. ''You still want coffee? I'm going to have whisky.''

He flashed a smile, grateful that I wasn't making fun of him anymore. ''Coffee for me. Drinking isn't one of my flaws.''

He followed me out to the kitchen. ''Don't you want to know what happened when you came home?''

''There's more?''

''Yeah. Someone came down Racine after you. They didn't stop, but I figured they were just making sure you'd gone home.''

I put beans in the grinder but paused before running it. ''I did see a car turn south after me, but there's no way of knowing if it had been behind me all the way from Kenwood. And if it was it doesn't matter, since neither of us saw the plate.''

He leaned against the sink, watching me fiddle with the

beans and the teakettle. "Well, if it *was* your tail, there were two of them in the car. I'm pretty sure they were both men. I didn't see the make, but it was a four-door. Dark— blue or green. Maybe brown."

"That narrows it down to a few hundred thousand, all right."

He laughed. "Why would someone be watching you?"

"Beats me, sonny—you should have the answer to that, not me." I took the coffee into the living room, stopping for the Black Label on my way.

While he was drinking coffee in the living room Mr. Contreras came up, fueled by a jealous curiosity. He decided he wanted coffee too. While the two of them sat talking I went into my bedroom to use the phone.

Fabian answered on the first ring, as though he were expecting a call. When he heard it was me his voice lost its eagerness.

"When you saw me tonight you said you'd been warned I would show up. Who warned you, Fabian?"

"I don't know what you're talking about, Warshawski." It was bluster, and hollow sounding at that.

"Don't screw around, Messenger: someone's following me. Who did you put on my tail?"

"No one. I repeat: I don't know what you're talking about."

"If you think you can execute end runs around me to find your daughter, think again."

He slammed the phone in my ear. I went back to the living room, where Mr. Contreras and Ken were in the thick of a conversation about military history. My neighbor had fought at Anzio. His own grandsons shared their mother's noninterest in his life, but Ken had studied something about that war and had a lively thirst for details. At midnight I finally shooed them away.

As soon as they'd left I turned out the lights and watched the street through a crack in the blinds. In a few minutes Ken's Spider roared past. No one pulled away from the curb to tag after him. I stayed by the window for twenty minutes.

If someone was watching me he was very skillful: I didn't see anyone on the street.

I was halfway convinced Fabian had sent my escort, thinking I'd lead him to his daughter. It did look like someone who wanted to keep track of me, rather than menace me: if it weren't for the fluke of Ken's coming after me I might not even have noticed they were behind me. And even suspecting it as I drove home I hadn't spotted them for sure.

Maybe it was in Ken's imagination. Still . . . I went to my closet and took the Smith & Wesson out of the safe. The clip was loaded. I inserted it into the gun and climbed into bed.

The best thing to do with a tracking tail is confront it. The second best is to lose it. Which meant driving something other than the Trans Am. I couldn't afford to rent anything, though, and I couldn't afford to risk any of my friends' safety by borrowing their cars.

I turned out the light and prowled through the apartment, checking all the windows as well as the back door. I'd installed an alarm system last year. I knew it would be hard for anyone to come in after me, but it didn't make it any easier for me to relax: I hate being under siege in my own home.

As I pulled my jeans off in my dark bedroom I heard paper rustling and remembered the letter from Senator Gantner I'd pulled from Fabian's desk. I turned on the bedside lamp to read it.

The senator thanked Fabian—"Professor Messenger"—for his advice on the Boland Amendment. And he asked if Fabian could recommend someone knowledgeable about tax law respecting loans from offshore banks.

Fabian would have leapt to respond to the wish of the man who could get him his judgeship. But the letter had nothing to do with his wife's death, or with Home Free's reluctance to talk to me, or Lamia, or any of the other questions I was trying to answer. In short, I had been not just nosy but stupid to take it. How on earth could I get it back to him?

It was past two before I fell into a light, restless sleep, filled with feverish dreams. I was chasing Emily but I had gone blind and had no idea how far ahead of me she was, or even where we were. The remote spectator who inhabits dreams showed me the action laid bare like a Dutch interior. I was following Emily down endless flights of stairs while Phoebe, Lotty, and my mother stood in doorways along the way mocking my blindness.

□30
Files for Thought

I staggered through work on Friday, punch-drunk from sleeplessness. After checking in with Alice Cottingham, who predictably had not found any teachers sheltering Emily, I drove down to the *Herald-Star*. I didn't make any effort to hide my route: my destination didn't have to be a secret, and it wasn't likely anyone would jump me downtown in broad daylight. Still, the back of my neck prickled all the way to the Loop.

The stories on Alec Gantner filled a large box. A piece of paper on top of Murray's desk showed an arrow to the box underneath, along with a message informing me that all material would be sent to the recycler if I wasn't there to claim it by day's end.

"P.S.," he had added. "I've looked through it but didn't see anything I didn't already know."

Murray was out somewhere putting some politician's feet to the fire—or perhaps a beer mug to his own lips. I helped myself to his desk and started to read. We hadn't been able to distinguish between Alec the senator and his son in the search; most of the material discussed the father.

Senator Gantner had spoken to the American Jewish Congress in November, assuring them of his respect for Israel's integrity. He'd spoken for an hour in the Senate on the importance of crop price supports, and sponsored a measure along with Jesse Helms to guarantee them. CORN LIKKER AND TOBACCY, an accompanying cartoon had lampooned the two men.

Gantner went to Carbondale for a town meeting, Peoria to help Caterpillar with an international contract, Chicago to welcome the president. He was heading the president's Illinois Reelection Committee.

I skimmed the articles faster. Gantner testified before a Senate Select Committee on Intelligence that Gant-Ag had not violated trade sanctions with Iraq in the fall of 1990. The senator's brother Craig was running Gant-Ag by then to free Big Alec for his senate work. No conflict of interest there, of course.

Young Alec came in for his own share of press, but on a more modest scale. He, too, had testified before the Senate on Gant-Ag's clean hands and pure heart—that had been in the *Wall Street Journal.* The *Sun-Times* had covered his joining the Home Free board. They hadn't done a story— just one of those "who's in the news" blurbs, announcing Gantner and Blakely agreeing to serve on the board shortly after Jasper Heccomb had started to head it.

My head felt like a plastic bubble someone had pumped full of helium. It floated remote above my body, making it hard for me to concentrate on what I was reading. I kept skimming the material, hoping for more mention of Heccomb or Blakely. A piece was missing, but what? I shut my eyes, which made the floating sensation worse.

What tied Gantner to Blakely? I presumed some of Gant-Ag's accounts were at Gateway—a huge corporation like that spreads them around. But Blakely and Gantner seemed more than just banking acquaintances. For that matter, what tied the two of them to Jasper Heccomb?

I used Murray's password to dial up Lexis on his computer and checked the Gateway board of directors. Young Alec was one of their outside directors. And so was Heccomb. I didn't feel like taking off my clothes to run down Wabash shouting "Eureka!" It wasn't unusual for heads of not-for-profits to sit on corporation boards. In fact, since the hue and cry over social responsibility in the seventies most companies have their token do-gooder. Neither was it surprising, if the three were pals, that they all sat at each other's tables.

Out of idle curiosity I dialed up Gant-Ag. Blakely served on that board. So did the chairs of the Ft. Dearborn Trust and Chicago's other giant banks. Heccomb wasn't listed, but that didn't prove anything—maybe young Alec hadn't been able to sell his uncle on the third musketeer as a Gant-Ag board member.

Nothing in the stack of print told me what drew Blakely and young Alec to Jasper Heccomb. I hadn't read everything, but what I'd sampled made me agree with Murray— nothing startling popped out. I fanned the remaining pages. I was so tired I saw the name without thinking and was about to drop the whole stack back into the box when it hit me.

Feverishly I went back through the printout a page at a time. The story had run inside the *Wall Street Journal* last year: Craig Gantner assured a Senate Select Committee on Banking and Narcotics that Gant-Ag had nothing to do with Century Bank or JAD Holdings.

The article didn't say why the Senate had been questioning their distinguished colleague's brother on a connection. And why did it matter? I propped the story on Murray's keyboard and studied it. When I did my search on Century Bank last week I had learned that the JAD Holdings Group had bought Century, but I hadn't bothered to find out what JAD was. Now . . . now I was clutching at straws just because they were mentioned in the same paragraph as the Gantner family. Still, the letter I'd taken from Fabian's home last night had been in a file labeled JAD. I asked Lexis for the JAD board, but was referred to a dummy managing agent.

Of course, there was one remaining question about Century Bank—besides their abrupt withdrawal from the Lamia project, that is. Why had Donald Blakely disclaimed all knowledge of Century, when his right-hand woman sat on their board?

I rubbed my forehead in frustration. If I got a good night's sleep maybe I could make better sense out of the paper thicket in the morning. I stacked all the paper in the box and hoisted it up. Paper weighs a ton: carrying it to the elevator and out of the building I could feel the veins bulging in my forearms.

"Now I know something else about you: you're strong as well as beautiful."

Bent forward with my load I hadn't seen MacKenzie Graham as I came out of the *Herald-Star* building. I looked up to see him grinning with the same imbecilic self-satisfaction he'd displayed last night when I stopped his car. I thought after our late-night session he would move away from proving what a prize jerk he could be.

"Why don't we see if you're as strong as you are smart . . . alecky." I dumped the box into his arms.

It gave me a small twitch of satisfaction to see him stagger as he assumed the load. It was only a slight twitch, though—it couldn't make up for my annoyance at not noticing him on my tail this morning. That's how you get killed in this business.

"You collecting scrap on the side?" Ken asked.

"Yep. That's how I picked you up." I opened the Trans Am's trunk for him to stow the box.

He gave me a sidelong glance. "I wanted to make sure you were okay."

"Umph. So you came back to my place early this morning and tagged along behind me. Not in the Spider, I take it?"

"Dad let me borrow the Lincoln. I told him I had a lead on a job. He was too excited to wonder why I couldn't drive my own car to it."

I chucked him under the chin. "I'm touched. I hate to think of you lying to your papa."

"You moral too?"

"In a manner of speaking. Tell you what—I might have a

job for you.'' When his face lit up I said, "Grunt work only. Whoever killed Deirdre Messenger in my office last week erased my hard disk. They also dumped my paper files all over the floor, so reconstructing my accounts is going to be a major job. Since taxes are due next week I have to get those files rewritten—by hand. You up to that kind of manual labor?''

"You didn't back up your hard disk?'' he demanded, like a dentist who can't believe you haven't flossed.

"Yeah, but the murderer stole all my floppies. . . . I know, I know, you should keep the copies off-site. They always give you these horror stories about fires and flood. They never say anything about brains on the disk drive.''

"You have Mirror installed?''

"Only over the bathroom sink.''

"It's a program. You use it for tracking files in times like this. Without it I don't think I can execute 'Undelete,' especially not after the machine's been down this long.''

I snapped my thumb against my car keys. "You know I don't understand a word you're saying. Can I get my files back or not?''

"We need to get you into the Nineties. Here's where you need *me,* not that cop of yours. Everything depends on how he wiped out the disk. Or she,'' he added with another of his sidelong glances. "If he reformatted it you'll never see the files again. But if he was in a hurry, didn't want to hang around to be caught while he executed a bunch of commands, he might've just deleted the files, you know, typed DEL star dot star. He could do that and go, in which case, if you haven't written over them, I might be able to reconstruct your accounts. It would be a huge job, but not impossible.''

"I couldn't pay you what your time would be worth in that case. I'll have to fling myself on the mercy of the IRS —a notoriously compassionate outfit.'' I moved around to my car door.

He came after me and grabbed my arm. "Hey—I have to

do community service. Convince my probation officer you're a 501-c(3) and we're in business.''

I had a feeling we'd never fly that kite: the court probably demanded to see some kind of tax return. But I'd worry about that problem later. If Ken really could reconstruct my accounts it would be such a big help I might bully one of my charitable friends into saying the work had been on their behalf.

Ken wanted to buy me lunch to celebrate our new pact before we stopped at Eleventh Street for my machine. I vetoed using his father's membership at the Athletic Club, but let him pick up the tab at the New Orleans Gumbo House on South Dearborn. Darraugh would probably pay that bill in the end, too, but it wasn't quite as obvious a poke in Papa's eye.

At police headquarters I was in luck: Officer Neely was at the desk she shared with three other cops. She'd prepared the paperwork for me—when we got to the evidence room it was a simple matter of filling out a few hundred forms. I showed my driver's license, she showed her badge, and the man behind the grille handed over my 386, along with the keyboard. Pushed, he dug up a box. I packed in the drive and monitor, balanced the keyboard on top, and handed the package to Ken. Manual labor would only build character in him.

Ken looked at the machine and grimaced. ''This thing is pretty dirty. I don't know if the drives could even survive that much crud in them. I'll do my best, though. When we're done maybe I should steal you a 486—I hate a slick detective like you working on an obsolete chip.''

He gave Neely his sidelong look to see if his comment would provoke her, but hassling by punks is all in a day's work for a cop—especially a female cop. Ignoring him, she asked if I'd heard anything about the Messenger children.

It was my turn to make a face. ''I talked to Fabian last night. He seems very disconnected—not the brave bully of the court- or bedroom. I got the feeling that someone had been putting the screws to him. Has Terry been questioning him seriously about Deirdre's death?''

She snorted. ''I wish! If he did beat her—if you were right, what you said on Saturday—then he could well have killed her. But it's his daughter's prints on the murder weapon. And he's a good friend of the state's attorney. . . .''

Her voice trailed away. She flushed and bit her lip, embarrassed at betraying herself. She didn't say anything further, but escorted us to the State Street exit at a clip that left Ken panting under the load of the computer.

□31
Corn off the Cob

The drive to Morris exhausted me. The suburbs west of town seem to replicate endlessly, here pushing up enormous fingers of pylons for new tollways, there churning out giant malls or new townships, all the while devouring farmland like an engorging dragon. Passing through this scarred landscape I felt like an antipioneer, traversing endless miles of concrete to find open country.

I was so mesmerized by the road that I almost missed the turnoff to Morris. I pulled into the gas station at the corner of the junction to feed my steed and get directions to Gant-Ag's headquarters. The attendant, a middle-aged man with stringy arms, interrupted a conversation with another man in overalls to direct me south along the highway.

"You can't miss 'em, ma'am. You go about fifteen miles and you'll see all the signs—they own most of the land down there."

"And up here," the man in overalls added. "The Lord knows they own me, that's for sure."

The two laughed together, more in shared misery than humor, ignoring my parting thanks. I climbed back into the Trans Am and turned south. Even though the highway was a secondary road it had four lanes, the concrete surface spanking new with its lane markers freshly painted. It was

Gantner's town—the U.S. Highway Commission was happy to help out. "Build me a senator and the roads will follow," I muttered.

I shared my drive with dozens of semis, many sporting the Gant-Ag logo—a tasseled ear of corn with the legend: CORN FOR AMERICA'S FUTURE. The Trans Am felt like a tiny tug rocking in the wake of giant steamships.

Behind well-tended fences new crops covered the fields with a faint green glaze. Every so often I'd see a small metal sign fixed to the fencing. Finally I pulled onto the shoulder and climbed across the drainage ditch to read one. It was scarcely worth the bother—beneath the logo lay an announcement that this was a Gant-Ag experimental cornfield. I bent down to look at the lacy plants. To my city eyes they didn't look very different from any other corn. As a matter of fact to my city eyes they could just as well have been wheat or barley.

As I started back to my car a helicopter appeared on the horizon. I stood, one hand on the door, and watched. It sailed purposefully over the field toward me, hovered above the Trans Am for a moment, and then receded. I waved and smiled in a parody of tourist friendliness, but the episode startled me. Somewhere along the roadside a camera was watching me. I looked around but couldn't see it. I had nothing to hide but I still didn't like it.

When I got back on the road I deliberately moved into the slipstream of a giant truck. The cameras were probably built into the fence posts, where they could see me from the side, but the semi gave me the illusion of cover. I followed it to a turnoff signposted by the familiar corn tassel.

A quarter mile down the road we came to a security booth with crossing rails lowered in front of it. The semi driver leaned out and spoke to the guard, who raised the rail for him to pass. It came down smartly in front of me. The guard demanded my business by mike, staying inside his cage—no doubt the windows were lined with bullet-proof glass.

"I'm here to see Alec Gantner. Gantohol Alec, not Senator Alec," I yelled back.

"What's your name?" the tinny voice asked.

"Come, come," I called. "Your helicopter scouted me: you've had time to run my license plate through the DMV. Just see if the guy'll talk to me."

He wasn't amused. After a further exchange I blinked first, pulling a business card from my wallet and handing it up. I half expected a metal arm to snatch it from me so the guard wouldn't risk exposing his flesh to the air, but he slid back a glass panel and took it himself.

After a few minutes on the phone he grunted at me to go in. "Follow the right-hand fork to the office block and park in one of the visitor slots. Someone will meet you at the entrance."

Six or seven trucks had lined up behind me by the time we finished these formalities. Figuring the guard would be busy for a few minutes I took the left-hand fork when the road divided. It led me past warehouses where trucks were busy and ended at a small but active airstrip: two helicopters, some crop dusters, and a baby jet were parked on the tarmac. As I watched, another helicopter landed—perhaps the guys who'd been spying on me. Just in case I waved at them before turning around and heading back to the right-hand fork in the road.

The office block was a no-frills modern building with a short front. Smoked windows were the only concession to design—although they were probably utilitarian given the glare of the prairie sun. Carved into concrete around the portal was the ubiquitous CORN FOR AMERICA'S FUTURE. Crossing the threshold I felt as though I were entering a concentration camp—the Nazis went in for those cheery, chatty slogans too.

A young man in shirtsleeves and suspenders was waiting just inside the door. He gave me a firm handshake but wanted to know what had taken me so long. He had the nasal twang of the prairies, an accent that always makes the speaker seem ingenuous, unlikely to engage in skulduggery. When I said I'd gone the wrong way he eyed me narrowly but didn't challenge me, turning instead to lead me down a corridor on the north end of the building. The place was bigger than it seemed on the outside: the short front had long wings tucked behind it.

"You don't mind stairs, do you?" my guide asked at the end of the corridor. "It's only two flights and it's faster than waiting on the elevator."

I responded amiably and trotted up after him. At the top we came to a suite of rooms behind a door whose lettering proclaimed GANTOHOL—FOR AMERICA'S FUTURE. Come to think of it, that had been Alec senior's political slogan—Gantner for America's Future. Or maybe it had just been Illinois's.

The young man left me in an antechamber with a stack of *Fortunes* and *Business Weeks* and a twangy "Just a minute now," and disappeared behind a closed redwood door. Before I had time to read an impassioned defense of the North American Free Trade Agreement my guide reappeared and led me inside.

Like the building itself, the office suite was bigger on the inside than I expected. Behind the redwood door lay a short hall with offices stacked on either side. A woman fielded calls at a console at the head of the corridor; inside the rooms people sat two at a desk working on computers or telephones.

My guide took me to a corner room overlooking the airstrip. Young Alec got up from behind a cluttered desk to shake my hand.

"Thanks, Bart. Welcome to Gant-Ag, Ms. Warshawski. We didn't really get a chance to chat last week at Fabian's. Sad news about Deirdre. I understand they think his daughter may have had a brainstorm and then run away. What can I do for you?"

His pleasant bass moved quickly between pleasure, muted condolence, and brisk business with the skill of a Samuel Ramey. I shook his well-groomed hand, conscious of the rough skin on my fingers: I did too much heavy work without using hand lotion. Gantner sat back in the leather swivel chair behind his desk and gestured me to an upholstered wing chair facing it.

"It was good of you to see me without an appointment. Did Jasper tell you I might be calling?"

Gantner gave an easy, boyish laugh that showed his perfect teeth. "Suppose you tell me what you want—then we won't have to be second-guessing each other."

I leaned back, the woman at ease. "My concerns are the same as yours: Deirdre Messenger's death and her daughter's disappearance. But I'm looking at the two events a little differently. The police would certainly like to find Emily Messenger. Chicago's streets are no place for a teenager, let alone one who's got young children with her. But the cops have by no means made up their minds that she's a murder suspect. There are a lot of unanswered questions about the night Deirdre was murdered."

"Such as?" Gantner laced his fingertips together.

Even with the smoky windows the setting sun behind him made it difficult to see his face. I moved the wing chair to the side of his desk. He raised his brows, then nodded appreciatively at my initiative.

"Such as who she was meeting in my office the night she was murdered. We know she had an appointment with someone—that's who I'm trying to track down."

He nodded again, this time frowning a bit. "We hadn't heard that. But if it's true, surely the police are better equipped than you to find out?"

I ignored his question. "Is 'we' you and Jasper, you and Donald, or you and your dad?"

For the first time his practiced mannerisms slipped and he spoke sharply. "All of us are concerned about Fabian Messenger. Which means all of us are following his wife's murder investigation. Does that matter?"

"Since the four of you, or at least you and Donald Blakely, can get the state's attorney to pay serious attention to your questions, maybe even your directives, your interest matters more than that of ordinary concerned citizens."

"And are you one of those? My information is that Fabian does not relish your involvement in his affairs."

His tone was of one closing off argument, but I shook my head. "Deirdre's death isn't his private business. Even at the rate Americans are falling in action these days, murder is still a crime, not something he or even your distinguished father can declare private business.

"I'm trying to get a lead on who Deirdre met with the night she died. That person may have seen her murderer— without knowing it was someone committing murder, of course. So I'm talking to people in the organizations where she volunteered. Home Free and Arcadia House. Since you sit on the Home Free board I'm hoping you can give me names of people who worked closely with her."

He was sitting straight up in his chair now. "Absolutely not. That's Jasper's decision, and if I'm not mistaken he chose not to expose our board to harassment."

"You play a major role in Jasper's decisions, though." I kept my tone conciliatory. "I'm sure you could persuade him to change his mind."

"When he asks for my input I give it to him—that's all a responsible board member can do."

"Such as whether to offer Lamia a shot at rehabbing a Home Free project. What was your view of that?" The words popped out from nowhere, surprising me as much as him.

"You'll have to forgive me, Ms. Warshawski: I'm not as good a director as I try to be. I have to confess I can't remember which specific rehab project you're discussing."

"Even though Phoebe Quirk explained it to you at your meeting yesterday morning?"

He smiled. "If Phoebe told you that was what we were discussing it was probably because she was too polite to tell you to mind your own business."

I laughed. "You don't know Phoebe very well if you think she's that restrained."

He looked ostentatiously at his desk clock. "Well, neither am I. How Home Free selects contractors has nothing to do with you. Not only that, I fail to see what your questions have to do with Deirdre Messenger's murder. Assuming that a police investigation *is* your business, which I doubt.''

''I'm trying to figure out why you let me come in on you uninvited. Is it because of Deirdre, or because of Home Free? Or could it even be because of JAD Holdings?'' I had picked the question carefully, hoping that if he knew who the holding company was I might surprise him into a revelation.

He was too practiced a poker player; he responded smoothly, without missing a beat. ''I know about Home Free, of course, and about Deirdre Messenger. But I'm ignorant about . . . what was the third name?''

''So your papa keeps some things secret from you? I've seen the letter he wrote Fabian about the Boland Amendment. In a file marked JAD HOLDINGS.''

His reaction showed that he knew, all right: he spun around in his chair to face the smoky glass. The neon lights gave him a ghostly reflection, turning his square good looks into a lantern jaw, his mouth a knife gash across it. In the window I could see the gash move sideways, a giant splayed wound, as he spoke.

''You take an extraordinary interest in affairs that don't concern you, Ms. Warshawski—even our experimental fields. I have to question your true motives in coming out here.''

I laughed again. ''You think I'm really a spy for Pioneer or one of the other big agricultural outfits? You must have some mighty powerful DNA in those fields to photograph anyone who stops to look at them.''

''Even so, I think I'd like my security force to search your pockets before you go. Just in case.''

He called Bart, my twangy-voiced escort, and asked him to send up a couple of women security officers. While we waited I tried probing further about Home Free, about Deirdre, Lamia, and JAD Holdings and Century Bank, but he'd decided on a course of action: I'd been there to spy on his uncle's corn plants and I needed to be given the boot. Despite my frustration I had to applaud his ingenuity—it made a perfect cover.

After five minutes—of my relentless questions and his stonewalling—two women in tan uniforms arrived, wearing armbands that sported the ubiquitous Gant-Ag logo in gold. They escorted me to an empty office and looked through my pockets and socks. I offered to show them my bra and panties, but they demurred. When I'd retied my shoes they led me—politely but firmly—to my car and drove with me past the guard station.

Near the experimental cornfield I pulled over again. Reaching through the fence I pulled up a couple of stalks. I stood for several minutes, ostentatiously studying them, lifting them up to the dull April sky to inspect them against the light, pulling off individual blades. Holding them aloft I made a show of carrying them back to my car.

Maybe Gantner was more concerned about his corn plants than anything else, but no helicopter stopped to bomb me. All during the long drive back to Chicago I tried to decide why Gantner had agreed to see me. Was it because of Deirdre? Or Home Free? And what was JAD Holdings, to generate such a startling response? I longed to disguise myself as a load of fertilizer and infiltrate the corn company.

□32
A Needle in a Corncrib

When I left the remote exurban reaches at First Avenue I saw the city for a moment as an outsider. Compared to the outsize malls and massive roads I'd left behind, Chicago looked decrepit, even useless. I wondered if my beloved briar patch was as tired as I was, and what would keep either of us going.

I wanted to round out my day by talking to Donald Blakely, the third musketeer, but it was five-thirty when I drove under the post office. I stopped hopefully at the Gateway Bank building. The guard in the lobby told me both Mr. Blakely and Ms. Guziak had gone for the day—even hardworking execs leave on time on Fridays. I managed to get back to my car just before a meter maid reached me. Hot dog—my luck was turning.

I wished Tish wasn't such a prickly pear—I'd love to know how Home Free's decision to drop out of direct placement had been reached. And whether Home Free really was more effective now that they only built housing.

The building they did was the crux of the matter. It was the one thing about Home Free that smelled funny. Their projects couldn't be such a secret. Even in Chicago they'd have to pull construction permits.

I stopped in front of the Pulteney. Maybe that was what

Cyrus Lavalle, my City Hall gopher, had found out: that the three musketeers had bribed enough aldermen to keep from having to pull permits. That would certainly make Home Free's affairs hush-hush around City Hall.

I smacked the steering wheel. It was before Lamia got involved with Home Free that Cyrus had finked on me. Century Bank was what he hadn't wanted to talk about. And it was my mentioning Lamia, not Home Free, that had made Eleanor roar off to use her phone in private.

Heccomb was up to something that Blakely and Gantner knew about. And Phoebe, I supposed. But what could it possibly have to do with Deirdre? On the other hand, if it didn't, why was Gantner using his powerful daddy to pull strings to track the investigation? Or was that coming from Fabian?

Gantner was right about one thing: it was hard to see any connection among Home Free, Century Bank, and Deirdre's murder. So why was I wasting time asking questions about them? Certainly not solely out of concern toward Camilla or spite against Phoebe. Some of it was curiosity, but a big chunk came from my old street fighter's resentment of rich, powerful people who tried to spin me around.

Last week I'd told Phoebe I didn't have time to undertake an investigation without a fee. That was still true this week—how much resentment could I afford? Maybe enough to track down JAD Holdings.

I climbed out of the car. An old man in a shapeless overcoat was rummaging through a trash can out front. I went into the coffee shop. Melba greeted me with the ease of old friendship but said she hadn't seen any trace of Emily.

"I asked around, too, girl—this town ain't no place for young people to be out in, not on their own without any money or sense. But no one's seen a sign of them this end of the street."

I went around the Pulteney one more time, looking along the alley as well as the front, but saw no trace, either of Emily or Tamar Hawkings. No way in. How had Tamar

managed it? Could she have slid inside when I had the door
unlocked on one of my forays to the electrical box? I tried a
grating in the alley but it was firmly fastened in place.

Out front I inspected the flaps in the sidewalk that
opened for deliveries. They hadn't been used in years, not
since the last of the big retailers had moved out of the
Pulteney. They didn't budge, even when I got my jack out
of the trunk and tried to pry them loose.

The man in the shapeless coat watched me with interest.
"You drop something down there, girlie?"

"An old friend," I said absently. "You see her? She had
a couple of children in tow."

He came over to peer through the cracks in the flaps with
me, as if hoping to see his fortune in the dark beyond.
When I repeated my question he shuffled back to the garbage can mumbling that he minded his own business and he
expected other people to do the same.

I tried to pry at the plywood with my jack. Rensselaer
Siding had done a great job—there wasn't a chink or loose
flap anywhere. I could break through the boarding with
enough time and the right tools, but this part of the city has
too many cops patrolling it, trying to keep it safe for tour-
ists.

I looked up as the el rattled past overhead. Ten years ago
I might have shinnied up a girder and made the ten-foot
jump to a window ledge. Now I was almost forty and leaps
like that were beyond me.

"I'm getting smarter, not older," I said aloud.

The old man looked up from his trash can. "That's the
spirit, girlie. You keep getting smarter and pretty soon
you'll be back in kindergarten."

He chuckled to himself and repeated my remark.
"Smarter, not older. Yeah, you keep getting smarter you
start getting younger."

I fished in my jeans for a dollar bill. "A good thought.
Keep working on it. And have a cup of coffee on me." As I
climbed back into the car I could hear him repeating the
comment and laughing idiotically.

MacKenzie Graham's Spider was parked out front when I got home. I didn't know whether to be touched or annoyed. He climbed out and tried to take my bag of groceries from me.

"I've been looking at your computer. The files are retrievable, but it's hot, dull work. I thought you could show your gratitude by coming out to dinner with me."

"My boyfriend's coming to dinner. And I'll take the bag." I felt a spurt of irritation at his casual invasion of my evening. "You know, you'd have a community service placement by now if you'd put the energy into looking for one that you're devoting to me. And you'd be back in college for the summer term—you could graduate with your class."

"You only date college grads? What's your boyfriend do —is he some kind of hotshot lawyer?"

"He's in the law, that's for sure. Your dad gave me until five today to find a placement for you. Do you want me to tell him you're working for me instead?"

He gave a saucy grin. "It might get his goat, which would be worth something, but maybe you'd better say I'll have to go to jail instead. So what would I have to do before you'd go out to dinner with me—kill the guys who are following you?"

"Get a job. Narrow the gap between us from twenty years to ten."

Mr. Contreras had apparently been watching the melodrama from his living room, because his door was open and the dogs bounding out when I went into the foyer. Ken followed me inside. When I saw how happy the old man was some of my irritation evaporated. Mr. Contreras's life has been a little dreary since the death of one of his old friends last year. Now he told me how much he enjoyed talking to a young kid with a real mind.

"Great." I pumped enthusiasm into my tired voice. "You two have a good time. Ken could even run the dogs— that might count as an hour of community service."

I went upstairs on Mr. Contreras's protests that Ken was

a nice young man, why couldn't I show a little kindness for a change. When I finished unpacking my groceries and checked in with my answering service I found Ken's father had indeed phoned. Promptly at five, my operator said, just as he'd threatened. Although it was close to seven now, Darraugh was still in the office when I called back.

"I haven't had any luck," I said, before he could speak. "I've been to all the charities I know and they don't want a hacker. They feel he might violate their confidential records."

"What'd you tell them for?" Darraugh snapped.

"Because when it's court-mandated community service work they have a right to be told the truth. I can't lie in such a situation."

I held my breath, wondering if I would get the ax and what I'd do for my mortgage payments then. Darraugh was a little inhuman, but he wasn't unreasonable. He grudgingly accepted my explanation and asked me to keep looking.

"Anything so I can get him back to school. He's a pain in the ass."

"No quarrel here," I said drily. "Meanwhile I've got him working on a project for me. I don't know whether we could persuade the probation officer that that counted for something: in my current state you could easily prove I was a not-for-profit outfit."

Darraugh's infrequent laugh came out as a rusty wheeze. Adjuring me not to let MacKenzie distract me from my own work he hung up. Conrad phoned a few minutes later to tell me a late meeting with a witness would delay him. He didn't think he'd get to my place before eight-thirty at the earliest. My heart sank; I was so exhausted I wanted to put him off altogether, but our life together had been through too much strain lately. At least with some time to myself I could bathe and take a nap.

I started the bath water running and looked up Cyrus Lavalle in my Rolodex. He lived on Buckingham Street, but, in keeping with his ideas of how the rich and famous live, had an unlisted number. I'd acquired it once during a meeting with him when he'd scribbled it on a napkin to give to a waiter he'd been eyeing.

He was not pleased to hear from me. "I keep my phone unlisted just so people like you won't bother me. Go away, Warshawski. I'm getting ready for dinner."

"So the sooner you tell me what I want to know the sooner you can finish primping. Was it Alec Gantner or Donald Blakely who made Century and Lamia off-limits at City Hall?"

"I don't know what you're talking about." He dropped his voice to a whisper.

"Let me ask the question a little differently. Century is obviously doing something funny with their community loans, or they wouldn't have made Lamia a hot potato. It would be worth a lot to me, Cyrus, a real lot, to know what." If he took me up on it, could I get a real lot of money together to pay him?

He was tempted—he took a long minute to answer. "You're poison around town these days, Warshawski. You know that? If people found out I was even thinking of talking to you, I'd be dead. Now go away and don't bother me."

When he'd hung up I climbed into the tub. I leaned back in the water, wondering how I could find out what they were doing. It couldn't be anything as simple as violating the community lending act. They wouldn't be bribing aldermen over that, anyway—that was a federal offense. Although it might explain how young Gantner tied into the picture, I couldn't come up with a plausible scenario for the whole story.

I finally gave up on it and let myself relax, drifting into a light sleep. I woke up shivering in the cold water. Hoping to get a real nap in before Conrad came I dried off and climbed into bed. As soon as I lay down, though, my mind refused to relax. I began a relentless churning through the same muddy paths I'd been following since leaving Morris.

If only I could see one of Home Free's buildings maybe I'd understand what was so sacred about them. Shoddy materials, most likely, for which they were paying off the building inspectors. But no, I reminded myself fretfully, it was Century Bank, not the charity, that had caused the *omertà* at City Hall. So maybe I could go to City Hall or to Dodge Reports and see whether Home Free had pulled a permit recently.

Tomorrow was Saturday; I wouldn't be able to get at the records until Monday. And anyway, they were filed by contractor, not developer. And I didn't have a contractor. As I tossed irritably from my right side to left I remembered the beefy man who'd been so upset the first day I'd gone to Home Free. Gary somebody. Camilla might know.

I reached her as she was changing for a night on the town. She was in high spirits—a week of hard work was over, she'd recently met a guy she liked, and Phoebe had given Lamia the go-ahead to start ordering materials. She was willing to forget our last strained conversation, and talk to me on the fly.

"So you start work in ten days—great," I said. "Conrad and I'll have some champagne to toast you. . . . You met any of Home Free's other contractors? I saw a guy there once, Gary somebody, who looked like he might tear sides of beef with his bare hands."

"That'd be Gary Charpentier. He does look like an angry kind of guy, at that. I think he was hoping to get our job and didn't take it kindly that Jasper gave it to us. Now, there's a smoothie, that Jasper Heccomb. I could almost go for him, but I figure his office manager would slice my breasts up for Easter dinner if I made a move."

I laughed. "She might if she knows the thought even crossed your mind. She was ready to murder me just for suggesting he was getting together with Phoebe Quirk."

"You think he is? With Phoebe? I've never seen her with a guy—I always wondered if she liked women better."

"I think it's putting together deals—that she likes better than guys, I mean."

Camilla laughed and hung up. Phoebe had always been relentlessly single-minded in all her pursuits. If she took on a lover, of any sex, she would wear the other person out in a week.

I switched on the bedside light and looked up Charpentier under general contractors in the yellow pages. There he was, with a business address in Des Plaines. On Monday I could go to City Hall to see what permits he'd pulled lately.

I put on jeans and a T-shirt and began boiling water for pasta. By the time Conrad pressed the bell I had dinner ready. A proper little housewife, welcoming her man home from a hard day in the crime mines.

"You got me pinned now, babe," Conrad said by way of greeting. "The old guy inspects me every time I come in the front door and now you have a sprout guarding the sidewalk. Where'd you pick him up? Kindergarten?"

I made a sour face. "More like nursery school. His father's my only reliable customer these days. I'm supposed to find a 501-c(3) for the kid to do some community service in. Maybe your African American Police Benevolent Fund could use a volunteer."

Conrad wiggled his eyebrows. "I'd love a chance to put a puppy like that through his paces. He bugging you, or you enjoying being the object of puppy love? Ah, ah, the girl is blushing. Maybe I ought to bust the kid again—what's he need to do community service work for? Selling dope in his nursery?"

"Working in West Englewood is making you trite. There's lots of crime besides drugs and murder—you just don't see any of it."

"You've got that right, white sugar. This has been a day and a half. I am almighty thankful to see its end. Did I leave any beer here?"

Conrad stocks his own, since I don't drink it. I pulled a Moosehead out of the refrigerator for him and moved the conversation on to the Cubs—just as dismal as the mayhem on Chicago's streets, but not as life-threatening.

□33
Knock Before Picking

Conrad's beeper went off at two-thirty. He stumbled to the living room to use the phone, trying to be quiet about it. A few minutes later he moved stealthily back to the bedroom. I could hear him fumbling in the dark for his clothes. I switched on the light and sat up.

"Sorry, babe. Didn't think both of us had to be roused by the city's punks. One of my informers was just killed. Could be a simple drive-by, or it could be a warning to other stooges. I've got to go listen to some statements. If we finish before dawn maybe I'll come back here?" He finished it as a question.

I put on a T-shirt and went to the kitchen for my spare keys. "You wearing your vest?"

He ran a hand through my hair. "I'm just going to be at the station listening to lies."

"You don't know where the night will take you. You can't afford to move around without it these days, you know that, and the super would tell you the same."

"Call Fabian and get him to put in a word to the chief of detectives for me," he gibed, but he went back to the bedroom and took his vest from the chair.

I locked the door behind him and went to the living room window to watch him leave. When he'd unlocked his car he looked up and waved at me. After he'd driven off I continued to watch the street, focusing on nothing in particular, depressed by the amount of pointless violence in the city. I stood there for some minutes, until I realized that Ken Graham's Spider was parked down the street.

I didn't know whether I felt more angry or amused. Did he think he was protecting me? Or was he just filling in time? I wished fervently I'd been able to find a placement for him so that he'd have a legitimate piece of work to look after, instead of trailing around after me. Although it would be a boon if he could rebuild my files, his hovering presence was a worse nuisance than Mr. Contreras's.

Somewhere between dreaming and waking I'd decided to become aggressive in my search for Home Free's secrets. It would be difficult to break into the Gant-Ag complex in search of information about JAD, but if the musketeers were all for one and one for all, Jasper might have some data. And at the very least I might find out why their construction projects were so secret.

I trotted to the bedroom to put on jeans and a jacket. I thought for a minute about what I needed. My picklocks. My Smith & Wesson. A couple of pairs of surgical gloves, donated by Lotty in a friendly mood. I had a flashlight in the car. A stepladder? I didn't think I could get one from the basement without rousing Mr. Contreras. If I needed something more than the portable stool I kept in my trunk I'd have to improvise. A note for Conrad taped to the front door telling him I'd gone out on an errand.

If Ken saw me leaving and decided to follow he would be a nuisance on this particular trip. I started to undo the bolts to the back door when I remembered the electronic alarm system—I hadn't had time to take a class on bypassing phone lines. What I needed—of course, what I needed was a hacker.

I ran lightly down the front stairs. Mercifully the dogs slept through my exit—it would have been hard to exclude Mr. Contreras from my expedition and impossible to take him along.

I jogged down Racine to the Spider. The sodium lamps allowed an excellent view inside the car. Young Ken was asleep behind the wheel. I pounded sharply on the window with my picklocks and was perversely pleased to watch him jerk upright in alarm. The car was small; he banged his knee against the steering wheel.

When he opened the door his face was still soft with sleep. "You felt my pull like Jupiter on an asteroid. I knew if I waited here long enough you'd ditch the cop and come to me."

"And how right you were. I want to ask you to do something Sergeant Rawlings will kill me for if he finds out. So if you tell him I'll kill you."

"You can't commit adultery if you're not married."

He grabbed my wrist and tried to pull me onto his lap and looked aggrieved when I twisted his arm away. "Get your mind above your belt for a minute, sonny. I want your help with something that's dangerous and illegal, and I want you to think about it seriously before you agree."

He rubbed his forearm where I'd twisted it and scowled at the ground. "Are you always this bossy? How does your cop friend stand it?"

"He loves it. He's got a thing for women in black leather with whips. Anyway, I thought you liked bossy women— that they reminded you of your old governess. . . . Can you bypass a phone alarm system?"

The prospect of adventure appealed more to him than romance. He stopped rubbing his arm and looked up. "You mean one that goes to the police via a security firm? Sure. If I had the right equipment. And also—is it a continuous feedback system?"

I shook my head. "I don't know. I don't even know what that is."

"One where you have to program in a code word to respond to the security phone every few minutes. If it is I can't bypass it until I've been inside and studied the specs."

"Can we assume it isn't—and be ready to run like hell if the cops pull up?"

He flashed a smile. "That's what I like about you—life on the edge. I *knew* you were too radical for Darraugh or a cop. We'll need to go out to Niles and find one of those big hardware stores that's open all night. I can't do this without equipment."

"You need to think for a minute, Ken. If we get caught you could go to jail. You already have one criminal offense on your record."

"And what about you?" He gave a cocky smile. "We could use one of those his and hers jails—don't they have some in Texas?"

"I'd probably sweet-talk my way out of an arrest," I said brutally. "Of course I'd feel racked by remorse at your sentence, but it would pass with time."

He shrugged. "Okay. We'll just have to avoid getting caught. Hop in. I'll drive you to Niles."

"I'll follow you. I want to make sure someone isn't behind us. If I pass you, hang back and look to see what else is behind us. And make sure you stay within the speed limit. It's a fundamental rule for a life of crime. More punks give themselves away because they're stopped for moving violations than for leaving prints at the scene. And speaking as a sports car driver, you're a favorite target in this thing."

He flashed a grin. "I know. I spent my whole first-quarter allowance on traffic tickets. Darraugh was not happy. But what else do you expect from a man who drives a Lincoln?"

He waited for me to cross the street to the Trans Am. Just to prove he couldn't be bossed he took the turn onto Belmont at forty. He quickly gained a couple of blocks on me. I pulled over to the side, forcing him to turn around and come back for me. After that he went across town to the expressway at a sedate pace. A couple of times I pulled in front of him. Occasionally I moved to the shoulder for a brief halt. We seemed to be clear.

Once we got to the suburbs I stayed closer to Ken's tail-lights. A slow rain had begun to fall, making it harder to keep track of traffic. The drizzle turned the streets to a black gloss that broke and spilled the lights a thousand different ways.

Ken led me to one of those shopping zones that dot the suburbs—mile on mile of malls, with discount stores the size of football fields, each identical to the next. The strip looked like a mammoth theme park—all the rides you want through America's wasteland.

I admired the nonchalance with which Ken, suburban born and bred, found his way through the anonymous megaplex. He turned left on Route 43, idled impatiently through two slow lights, and shot left again in front of a semi to pull up under the shadow of a giant billboard proclaiming the mall was open twenty-four hours a day. I waited in the Trans Am while Ken went into the hardware store, not wanting to give him more occasion for flirting, and also to make sure no one was watching.

He was gone about half an hour. When he returned, his arms laden with parcels, he was walking fast, with the excited, self-satisfied air I remembered from the young punks in my PD days.

My arms prickled with embarrassment. Inviting Ken to help do illegal work was morally indefensible. I could tell him I'd changed my mind. He didn't know where we were going—he couldn't possibly carry out the operation alone.

I got out to ask him if he had everything, and gave him Home Free's address, adjuring him to park around the corner from the office, near the mouth of the alley running behind the building.

When we arrived I sent Ken to the front door to make sure no one was in the office. Primed with a story about needing emergency shelter, he rang the bell and pounded on the glass. I played lookout at the corner. When no one answered, we went to the alley to scout the alarm.

While I shone the new flash over the wires Ken located the phone lines into Home Free. It was four in the morning.

The sky was still black behind its thicket of drizzle, but I was beginning to be nervous about time: people on early-morning errands would be leaving home in an hour.

"Okay, Vic, here's what we'll do." Ken spoke low, near my ear. "We're going to splice the line and attach it to a jumper box so it thinks the connection is being maintained. I want you to hold these by the tips and hand them to me as soon as I ask for them."

"These" were a pair of needle-nosed clips—alligator clips, Ken explained—which would attach the phone line to the jumper box to complete the circuit. He turned over a garbage can and hoisted himself on top of it. It brought him within working distance of the line. I held the end from the phone pole while he cut it, stripped the sheath away, and attached the clip. I handed him the other end of the line and he repeated the operation. Once he had the line clipped to the jumper box he laid the box against the side of the building so that its weight wouldn't drag down the line. The whole procedure took less than three minutes.

He was grinning like a fool when he climbed down from the can. "I knew the theory, but it's interesting to see it in practice. Now what do we do?"

"Move to the mouth of the alley and wait to see if all hell breaks loose."

We sat for fifteen minutes in the dark shadows. Ken put an arm around me and kissed me. I twisted his arm down to his side.

"What's that hard thing next to your breast? A gun? You ever use it?"

"Yep. But I'd just break your arm for you if I thought you were getting out of hand."

"Think you could?" He made fighting sound like an exciting form of foreplay.

"I know I could," I said in a voice like chalk.

He was quiet for a minute. "You don't think I seriously like you, do you?"

"I think you don't know if you're playing a game or if you like me. And either way it doesn't matter. I'm old enough to be your mama and I'm not Cher—I don't need perpetual youth to keep me from feeling my age.''

Maybe I needed to keep breaking and entering to stay young at heart. I kept that thought to myself, though, and let Ken beguile the rest of the wait by telling me of his hope to join the Peace Corps in Eastern Europe, and Darraugh's conviction that if he didn't get a job or go to graduate school straight out of college no employer would take him seriously. I tried not to think about time passing, or—worse —what Conrad would say if he knew what I was doing.

When we'd waited long enough for an army to arrive, I went around to the front and used my picklocks on the door. Ken kept watch, but the streets were empty in the hour before dawn. The locks were solid but nothing special —Jasper relied too much on his alarm system. Even having to fumble in the dark it only took five minutes to get inside. I relocked them behind us and turned on the lights.

□34
A Few Bucks in Petty Cash

I sent Ken to Tish's computer. "I want to know what her files say about five things: Century Bank, Gateway, Lamia, Home Free's construction projects, and JAD Holdings. The best place to start is the accounting files. I'm going to look in Jasper's private office."

Ken switched on Tish's machine, but grumbled that it was no challenge to break into a system like hers: all the files were neatly labeled and accessible. "It would be better if you'd let me use your picklocks: I've never actually broken in through a door. I could show you how to look at the computer while I practiced with the door."

"We don't have time to screw around," I snapped at him. "Even though it's Saturday, Tish or Jasper may come into the office."

The wood veneer on Jasper's door covered a steel plate and a couple of sophisticated locks. I squatted in the narrow space and set carefully to work while Ken began studying files. Working with gloves on slows you down because you lose some of the sensitivity in your fingertips, but I wanted to make sure I left no prints behind. At the end of half an hour I managed to get both locks undone.

Before going inside I went to see what Ken was finding. He had Home Free's payables on the screen for March. I scanned it. They had paid payroll taxes, insurance for Tish and Jasper and the premises in Chicago and Springfield, and had made various payments to what I presumed were construction firms, since Charpentier's name figured several times in the list. Poor Tish got only thirty thousand a year—not much for all the work she did. Jasper didn't treat himself much more royally: he earned fifty thousand. Their travel budget seemed large, but Jasper said he went to Springfield a great deal.

Total payables for the month came to a little more than a million dollars. Since their state filing last year had shown them with ten million in funds, that seemed like a reasonable monthly payout. I asked Ken to print out last year's accounts and to keep hunting for the names I'd mentioned.

Inside Jasper's office I moved gingerly among the electronic equipment—I didn't want to trip off some ancillary alarm. I poked around the room hunting for a back exit, just in case, and found it finally in the small bathroom that had been carved out of the far corner. It seemed kind of funny to have a shower with a bolted steel door for a back, but it was an efficient use of space.

I glanced nervously at the clock built into the desk console: almost five now. I went back to the front room for Ken and saw with annoyance that he'd shed his gloves.

"You fool! You can't leave prints in here. You're on file, you know. If we mess something up or have to run for it they may be suspicious enough to print the place!"

"I can't work with them. I thought you saw me take them off when I spliced the phone line."

"Put them on or go home."

He looked at my face and decided against argument. When he'd pulled them from his jeans pocket and put them on again I asked him to come into Jasper's office with me.

"I'm getting nervous now that day has arrived. I want to switch on his street monitor. I'm afraid if I hit a wrong switch I'll trip some secondary alarm."

Ken inspected the controls on the left side of the desk, then knelt to look underneath. "I can't tell what all these are, but this one seems to be attached to the wire that goes out to the camera on the front door.''

He turned on the screen and hit a switch. The Korean restaurant across from Home Free came into focus, followed by a picture of a car coming up the street. I thanked him and began looking through drawers, briefly scanning paper files.

A rosewood cabinet underneath the desk had a lock built into it, and not a trivial one. In the interests of time I was tempted to let it go, but was too curious about what had to be secured inside a locked office. When I had it undone I glanced nervously at the clock: it was five-thirty. I checked the monitor. Someone was getting into a car in front of Home Free; more cars were starting to pass the building. I was thankful for the thick shielding Jasper had placed on the front windows.

I pulled open the cabinet. My jaw dropped. The drawer was packed with neatly wrapped packets of bills. The top layer showed hundreds except for a corner sectioned off with cardboard that held twenties. I lifted a few packs. Hundred dollar bills as far as the eye could see. I did some quick calculations, trying to estimate the hoard. As near as I could reckon it would be close to five million dollars. No wonder the building was so secure.

In such large quantities the money didn't look real. The only context I had for that kind of cache was television news pictures of drug stashes. Was Jasper dealing on the side? I remembered my words to Conrad earlier—drugs were trite. What else could generate that much cash—and why else would it be in cash? Maybe it was counterfeit—maybe Jasper was funneling funny money into the system. That would explain why he needed both an acquiescent bank and to put the lid on City Hall.

''Hey, Vic—come here a minute. I've found something that might interest you.'' Ken called from the front room.

I shot a quick look at the monitor as I stood up, and nearly froze. Jasper Heccomb was climbing out of a car in front of the building.

"Ken!" I screamed. "Come in here *now*!"

I ran to the door. He was gaping at me, bewildered.

"Now!" I hissed, "Jasper's here. Move!"

As he stared, immobilized, we could hear Jasper's key scrabbling in the lock. Running to Tish's desk, I grabbed Ken's arm. Yanked him in my wake into the inner office. Slammed Jasper's door shut, turned the dead bolt, hustled Ken into the bathroom with me. I took an extra second to shove that lock home. It was a flimsy one, but probably didn't open from the outside.

I climbed into the shower. "Stand behind me while I move these bolts. There isn't room in here for two."

The hair was standing up on my head. Sweat poured down my neck. My fingers were clumsy with fear but I finally slid the bolt free. I pushed the door open into the alley just as Jasper started pounding on the bathroom door, demanding that we come out with our arms above our heads.

As we loped down the alley I heard a shot—Jasper breaking the door down. "Come with me. Don't worry about your car—you can pick it up later."

I opened the Trans Am and was in with the motor running while he was still fumbling with the door, looking worriedly at his own car. At last he climbed in beside me. I roared down the street.

Lawrence Avenue was coming alive in the thin gray morning. It was after six now—I'd goggled at the money longer than I thought. The Korean and Arab merchants who dotted the area were starting to arrive at restaurants and bakeries. Traffic was still thin enough that I could keep an eye on the road behind me. I didn't think Jasper was after us. I wasn't sure what he drove—when I saw him on the monitor I'd been too shocked to pay much attention to the vehicle. A little sports coupe, I thought, trying to remember the image. Maybe a Miata.

At Burton I turned north, drove up to Foster, and made a giant U on the side streets to the Kennedy. I thought we were clear. I took the expressway to Belmont but parked several blocks from my apartment. If Jasper had alerted my watchers I wanted to come at them on foot.

"Go down to my building and see whether you can spot anyone—either hanging around the entrance or sitting in a car. I'll wait up here by the diner."

How had Jasper known we were there? Maybe one of those wires on his desk console fed an alarm in the rosewood cabinet, something that went off in his house. He wouldn't want the cops, or the alarm company, to come in on that wad.

The image of Deirdre floated to my mind, her brains and blood forming a sticky mass on my desk top. Had she found the money in the course of her volunteer work and taxed Jasper with it? Was he the man who was meeting her in my office that Friday night?

Jasper could easily guess I was behind this morning's break-in—I'd been asking questions with the subtlety of an elephant in musth. Maybe he assumed I knew something was amiss at Home Free—he probably thought I was trying to goad him. No wonder he had been so scornful when I asked if he could find a placement for Ken.

I felt the skin on the back of my head tingle and tighten, in the spot where they'd hit Deirdre. Why was I still walking around? Why hadn't my followers taken advantage of any number of opportunities to assault me? Maybe they were waiting to find out how much I knew. After this morning they wouldn't wait much longer.

As soon as Ken returned with an all clear I took him into the diner, stopping at the counter to snag orange juice from the cooler. I forced Ken to drink a glass. His green-gray pallor eased slightly.

I took him to a booth. Barbara, the waitress who usually looks after me, came over with the coffeepot. She wanted to check out my date, teasing Ken until someone at a neighboring table asked for her. For once he let sexual innuendos roll past him without a response.

"Eggs for me this morning, Barb—poached with hash browns," I called after her.

"How can you eat?" Ken muttered. "I feel like I might throw up. Do you think he'll check my fingerprints?"

"You feel sick because you've been up all night and you've had too much excitement on an empty stomach. Believe me, food is what you need." I flagged Barbara and got Ken to order something. "As for your prints—you probably rubbed them out when you put the gloves on. Even so, he's sitting on something so volatile I doubt he would call the cops in. Unless he's got exceptionally cool nerves. What did you see down the street?"

"There's no one in front of your place, but your cop pal's car is there. How did you shake him off when you left last night?"

"He'd gone out after a murderer. What had you seen in the files—you called to me just before we ran away."

"Oh, that." He swallowed coffee and rubbed his head, trying to make himself behave with my own coolness. "I'd found a couple of interesting things. The first was a contributors' list. Someone had given a huge amount of money to Home Free last year—a good quarter million dollars."

"Do you remember the name?"

He squeezed his eyes shut, thinking, then gave an embarrassed smile. "Running away chased it out of my head."

"I'm going to write out a list of names. You tell me if you recognize any of them. Do you have a pen on you?"

He fumbled in his pocket and came up with a grimy ballpoint. I took one of the napkins and listed a dozen names, including Fabian, Gantner, and Blakely along with nine others that I made up at random. Ken studied the list, squinting at the fuzzy writing on the napkin.

"Gantner. I'm pretty sure. I think Blakely was a donor—big, but not as huge as Gantner. Bill Buckner sounds familiar too."

"He should." I took the napkin and shredded it. "He used to play first base for the Cubs. Back when you were in kindergarten."

"You think I'm a baby because I got scared this morning," he muttered.

"I'm delighted you got scared. I've been feeling a hundred brands of guilt for encouraging you to break the law with me. It's a relief to see you have normal feelings underneath your punk exterior."

Barbara dumped our eggs in front of us. "You two look like you've been up all night. Doing something fun, I trust. What's Conrad got to say about it?"

"I'll find out soon enough. Nothing very happy, I fear."

I wolfed down my eggs and buttered my toast with a lavish hand. Ken ate a tentative bite of an omelet, realized how hungry he was, and began eating as greedily as I.

"I also saw Century Bank's name. That was what I was looking at just before we took off," Ken said through a mouthful of potatoes. "I found some secured accounts—you needed a special password to get at them. Century is running a fifty-million-dollar line of credit for Home Free."

My jaw dropped. "What ever for?"

His cocky smile appeared briefly. "You figure that one out, Sherlock—I'm just the hacker."

35

Promises, Promises

Mr. Contreras was divided between pleasure at helping out and annoyance that I'd gone burgling without him. After doing penance for ten minutes I finally was able to leave Ken to give him the play-by-play and stagger wearily up to my own place.

I slipped into the apartment as quietly as possible, but Conrad was sitting in the living room with a cup of coffee and the *Herald-Star*. He had on jeans but he was barefoot and bare-chested. The scar from his old knife wound showed faintly pink against his copper skin. He looked at me soberly.

"What've you been up to, babe? What kind of errand takes you out for four hours in the middle of the night?"

"Oh." I sat down on the piano bench and slumped against the piano, suddenly too tired to hold myself upright. "I was inspecting the Home Free premises."

"You had to do that in the dark?"

"You think I took the chicken's route not trying to pick a lock in full view of the street?"

He set his cup down so hard, coffee splashed over him and onto the couch. "You broke into the place? For Christ sake, Vic! I spend my life arresting people for that kind of shit. What'd you want to do it for—to prove how cool you are?''

"Jasper Heccomb keeps about five million dollars in hundreds in a drawer in his office. Don't you think that's interesting?''

"I don't want you treating this as a joke. You can't go around breaking the law like you're above it.''

"It's not a joke. He really does. Makes you wonder.''

"The only thing I wonder about is how far you'll go to prove a point.'' He finally became aware of the trickle of coffee on his abdomen and fished in his pocket for a handkerchief to mop it up. "I remember last year someone broke into this place and trashed it pretty good. That seem reasonable to you? Or is it only a good idea when you're doing it to someone else?''

"I didn't like it, but I didn't come squealing to you, either, if I recall. How else could I have gotten that kind of information?''

He put the paper down and came over to sit next to me. "Look, Vic, it's why we have laws and give jobs to people like me to enforce them—so everyone doesn't go buzzing through the streets defining justice however it suits them that morning. It's bad enough we got a million guns in this town so every second jerk can play Shane if he wants to. You think someone's hurting you, go to court and swear out a complaint. You think Heccomb's sitting on vital information, go to the Finch and he'll get a warrant.''

I eyed him thoughtfully. "You think he would? Or just tell me to run away and play? For that matter, just because the guy was stiff-arming me would a judge have granted a warrant?''

"Either way, girl, you can't keep doing this stuff.''

I didn't say anything. I was too tired to argue. Anyway, he was right. No one should set herself above the law. Worse still, I'd encouraged a kid on probation to commit a felony. And even worse yet, I would do it again, even knowing I was wrong. Maybe I was a latent psychopath.

Conrad, relenting, put his arm around me and pulled me

next to him. I leaned into his shoulder and asked what kind of night he'd had.

"Oh, the usual ugly residue of the kind of street justice you like to practice. I'm fed up to my eyeballs with it. I'm going to the park this afternoon, play a little ball with some of the guys. My old team is having a reunion, trying to show those young sprouts what we can do. Terry and I may go out for a beer afterward. I'll probably spend the night with my mother. Tomorrow's Palm Sunday; she likes her chickens to gather round for the occasion. What are you up to?"

"I'm going to lie down for a bit."

"And then what?"

"Depends on how long I sleep. I need to figure out where all that money came from."

He gripped my shoulder and pushed me away, far enough to be able to look at me sternly. "Not by breaking in someplace. Promise, Vic?"

I held up three fingers. "Scout's honor, Sarge." I leaned against his shoulder again and started to drift to sleep.

"Bed for you, Ms. W." He got up and pulled me to my feet.

In the bedroom I kicked off my shoes and socks and lay down in my jeans, too tired to finish undressing. Conrad unbuckled my holster and put it on the bedside table. He gave me a long, sweet kiss, but I couldn't tell if it meant absolution or withdrawal. I was asleep before he'd left the room.

I woke at noon so thickheaded I couldn't remember at first the events of the previous night. The dogs were barking out back—that's what had roused me. I stumbled to the kitchen to look, but they'd found nothing more exciting than a passing cat, now perched on the fence and yawning delicately at their frenzy.

I went back to bed but couldn't get back to sleep. With the edge off my exhaustion I kept churning around questions about Jasper's money. Maybe Deirdre had stumbled on the stash and confronted him with it. But where did that leave Fabian? Her violent bludgeoning looked like the work of an angry man, letting slip the last threads of control. I'd seen Fabian like that, but not Jasper.

Maybe Fabian was somehow involved in whatever project had generated the stash—maybe his advising Senator Gantner extended far beyond implications of the Boland Amendment. To what? I didn't have enough information to speculate on a scenario.

But say Deirdre did know about the money. And that she'd arranged to meet Jasper in my office the night she died. So she's talking to him and Fabian walks in, sees her in her taunting, gloating mood, and blows his mind. Then Jasper really would stay quiet because he couldn't afford to lead the cops to his stash.

I sat up suddenly, a cold chill down my spine. If *Jasper* had killed Deirdre over his cache, my life wasn't worth a plugged nickel about now. I needed to get moving, to find out something concrete enough that Finchley would get a warrant. What I needed to do was come in on the other end of the story. What was he doing with all that cash? And the only place I knew to look were those construction projects he guarded so tightly.

I lumbered down the hall to the bathroom, where I stood under a cold shower until my teeth were chattering. Looking through my closet I tried to pick something that would make me a mistress of disguise in case Charpentier remembered seeing me at Home Free. In the end I put on a navy blazer over jeans with an outsize straw hat that would effectively hide my face. Suburban maps, the newspaper, and my gun completed my portfolio.

Before I left the building I peeked through the blinds at the street. No one was lounging on the walks, but I couldn't see into the cars. I went out the back way just to be safe. You can see the whole yard and most of the stairwell from my tiny square of porch, but going down the front you can be blindsided at almost any point.

My car was still safely parked at the corner of Belmont

and Morgan. I got in and drove to the Kennedy in a long, looping route. No one was behind me.

Charpentier's office was in Des Plaines, a long trek out to the land beyond O'Hare. He operated from a low-slung brick building, the kind of small office most contractors use. No one was inside. It would have been child's play to break in, but I'd promised Conrad I wouldn't burgle. I sighed and looked up Charpentier's home address. He lived on down the pike a few miles in Arlington Heights.

Charpentier's house was a brick two-story, a neo-Colonial or fake Georgian, or whatever the real estate jargon for those phony pillars is. It was large but not outlandish. The plot was only of average size, but meticulously attended. Early though the season was, the grass was already green, covering the ground like spun silk—or Alec Gantner's experimental corn.

A late-model Nissan stood in the drive. As I watched from up the street a boy came out with a skateboard, followed by a woman who drove off in the Nissan. Driving back to the main road I found a filling station with a phone. After getting Charpentier's voice on an answering machine I bought some coffee and a doughnut and returned to Charpentier's street. Waiting around the corner—to avoid scrutiny by the neighbors—I ate my doughnut, studied the map, and listened to Jessye Norman singing Tchaikovsky lieder.

A little before two Mrs. Charpentier's Nissan returned. I waited another twenty minutes, to give her time to settle in with whatever shopping she'd done. Fishing in the backseat for something to give me authenticity, I found a stack of flyers for an Arcadia House benefit. As a board member I'd been supposed to sell twenty tickets.

The kid who'd been skateboarding came to the door. He was a slender, freckled boy, perhaps ten, who bore no resemblance to the beefy man I'd seen at Jasper Heccomb's. I frowned portentously and demanded to speak to Gary Charpentier.

"He's not here." His voice hadn't changed yet; he had a husky contralto that was rather appealing.

"Where can I find him? It's important that I speak with him today."

The kid bit his lip, then announced he would get his mother. He disappeared into the back of the house, yelling, "Mom! Mo-o-om!"

Mrs. Charpentier hurried to the door. A woman about my own age whose blond hair had turned a muddy gray, she was pretty beneath a layer of harassment. Early though it was, she had apparently been starting supper: she was drying her hands on a dish towel and smelt strongly of onion.

"Mrs. Charpentier? I'm from Alec Gantner's office. He wanted me to get some materials to Gary Charpentier."

"Oh." She looked at her son hovering behind her. "It's all right, Gary—just business for Dad. I can take it—he's out now but he'll be back around five."

I drew the folder holding the Arcadia House flyers away from her outstretched hand. "I'm afraid that will be too late: it's important that he sign some documents in time for the last FedEx pickup. That's five on Saturdays, you know. Mr. Gantner will be really upset that I didn't get to him in time."

She bit her lip, much as her son had done. "I guess if you want . . . If it's from Mr. Gantner he ought . . . He doesn't like it if—"

"I'll be happy to go to him. Is he in his office? I did try there first."

"No. No, he went into Chicago. And he doesn't like people to go on job sites when he's working. But I guess— let me try to reach him on his car phone. What's your name?"

"Gabriella Sestieri." My mother's name was the first that popped into my head. "If you'll just give me the address it'll be easy for me to stop there—I have to go back to the Loop with the forms when they're signed, anyway."

"It's better if I check. He won't be so angry that way."

She hurried into the interior. I was sweating—with impatience, annoyance, and an unwelcome twinge of fear. At the same time I wondered if I should leave one of the Arcadia emergency service cards with her. How seriously annoyed did Gary Charpentier get? With Jasper Heccomb he'd been red-faced and irritable, but with his wife he might be less restrained.

She came back a minute or two later to say she hadn't been able to reach him—he must not be in his car. After I commiserated on how hard it was to know how to keep a man from getting angry, reminded her how important Alec Gantner was, how his ties to Jasper Heccomb made it unwise for her husband to leave the great man hanging, she gave me the address of a construction site. It was on Elston, just north of where Pulaski cut in.

36

She Who Fights and Runs Away—Gets Mugged

Elston Avenue cuts a diagonal swath through the Northwest Side. A busy road during rush hour—it parallels the Kennedy Expressway—at other times it's a no-man's-land. Bleak stretches where warehouses and factories once stood dot its route. Few shops or restaurants have filled the gaps, so people from the surrounding neighborhoods don't frequent the street.

Charpentier's construction site was hidden behind the tall grass and broken walls of one of those desolate patches. I drove by it twice without seeing anything, searching for a street number that would let me know I was in the vicinity. I finally parked on Cullom and started hunting on foot.

It wasn't until I'd picked my way across chunks of asphalt—the remains of a parking lot—that I saw where building was taking place. No signs blazoned the Charpentier name to the world or warned of construction in progress. Supplies and workers must come in through the alley, instead of down Elston. Unless you knew what to look for you wouldn't know anything was going on. If this was indeed a Home Free project they believed in hiding their light under a bushel.

I walked through the dead prairie grass to look more closely at the site. Concrete had been poured for the foundation. Furring for the first story stood about waist high. Some eight or ten men were working, nailing cradles across the furring for pouring concrete. They were calling out in a language I didn't recognize—it might have been some regional form of Italian, or a bastardized Spanish.

Lumber was piled along the edge of the alley. Beyond it a cement truck was churning, its giant snout sticking out like an impatient elephant waiting for food. The big panel truck Gary Charpentier drove away from Home Free last week was parked on the edge of the alley.

The men were dressed in a hobo's assortment of jeans and ragged shirts. Several, despite the cool gray day, were stripped to the waist. One of them caught sight of me as I climbed over a nest of rusted reinforcing bars. He stopped hammering and called to his fellows. A couple of them let out catcalls and encouraging shouts, which I could translate without a dictionary.

In response to the outcry a huge man in a cowboy hat emerged from the far side of the cement truck. He glanced at me before turning to swear at the crew. The lookout picked up his hammer and started pounding again, but slowly; the whole crew slowed down to watch. The swearer —presumably the foreman—moved across the weedy ground to me. He was formidable, almost a foot taller than me with an impressive girth.

"Private construction, miss. Hard-hat area." A rich accent, reminiscent of my mother's, seemed incongruous with his cowboy boots and Stetson.

I gestured at the crew. "Then why aren't they wearing them? Or you, for that matter?"

He eyed me narrowly and spat, just missing my left toe. "Their heads already plenty hard. You go on to your shopping or whatever lady thing you do today. These men working."

"This one of the Home Free sites?"

He moved closer to me, so that his gut was almost level with the bottom of my shoulder holster. "Who wants to know?"

"I do." It cost an effort not to take a step backward.

"Then you leave not knowing, lady. This is private, this work, this nothing to do with you."

"But they've invited me to invest. How can I possibly do so without seeing the kind of work they do?"

He frowned, weighing my story, but decided he didn't like it. "You take their word. You coming with one of the bosses, we let you look. Otherwise, go do your own business."

I frowned in turn, assessing my choices. Not only wasn't I big enough to take him on, there was no point to it. Except to show I wasn't scared. Sometimes there's an advantage in people thinking you're scared—they don't keep an eye on you. I could come back anytime, now that I knew where they were.

I spread my hands and smiled. "Fine. I'll get one of the bosses. You recognize Eleanor Guziak by sight, or would it have to be Jasper Heccomb himself?"

His scowl deepened. "They coming with you, I let you look. Now you go."

I backed up a few steps to make sure he wasn't going to follow me, then turned to pick my way through the rubble toward Elston. I took my time, trying to appear nonchalant. As I left, the crew let out a few more raggedy catcalls. I turned and waved, to show I appreciated the spirit, and saw a late-model Bronco pull up next to the cement truck.

The foreman saw it too. He hurried over to it as Gary Charpentier climbed out. The contractor bellowed something at him. I was too far away to make out the words, but it must have been an order to come and get me, since the foreman started after me on the run.

Charpentier followed him, moving so fast he didn't bother to shut his car door. The time for nonchalance was past. I leapt over chunks of concrete, heading for the level grass nearer Elston. A few steps from the sidewalk I heard a whine and a thunderclap.

I hit the ground almost before I realized the bastards were shooting. I landed on a brick that knocked the wind out of me. Gasping painfully I wrenched myself onto my side and fumbled inside my jacket for the Smith & Wesson. I slipped off the safety and pointed it at the foreman, then realized I had a good chance of hitting the crew if I fired. As the cowboy fired again I rolled over until I found a piece of concrete big enough to provide a minimal barricade.

Charpentier caught up with the cowboy and wrenched his gun arm down. I pushed myself to a sitting position, holding my gun out prominently. Charpentier lumbered over to me, the cowboy following.

"Just what the fuck do you think you're doing?" He was leaning so far over that flecks of spit sprayed my face.

I staggered upright and made a great display of rubbing a tissue over my cheeks before I spoke. "My very question. Where does this great ape get off firing guns at people?"

"You were trespassing on a private work site." He was so angry his cheeks looked like slabs of raw beef.

"It isn't posted. And even if it was, what earthly justification does that give this hyena to fire at me?"

"I telling her to leave," the cowboy said. "She wanting to know if this is a Home Free site. I telling her to mind her own business."

"And I was leaving. You should have been pleased instead of trying to mow me down."

"I told him to go after you," Charpentier said. "I called my wife as I was heading to the Kennedy and she said Alec Gantner had sent a girl around with some papers for me to sign. So I called Gantner—to apologize for missing her. And he said he hadn't sent anyone. I want to know what you thought you were doing, worming the site location out of my wife. I'm within my rights."

A couple of the crew had come up behind him, still holding their tools. I wondered what would happen if the cowboy gave them the order to jump me.

"I'm a Chicago taxpayer. I have a right to walk on Chicago streets and alleys without justifying myself to you."

Charpentier raised a hand to hit me, saw the men watching him, and thought better of it. "You don't have any right to harass my wife. And this is private property. Even in Chicago that must still have some meaning.''

''What are you trying to hide here? If it's so private, why isn't it posted?''

''She saying she want to invest,'' the cowboy informed Charpentier. ''I telling her she bring one of the bosses, she look all she want.''

Charpentier stared at me closely. ''Haven't I seen you? . . . Oh, yes. You're the detective who's been bothering Jasper Heccomb over at Home Free. My, my.''

He turned to the cowboy. ''She's precious, Anton. Treat her like gold.''

''This is Warshawska?'' Anton gave me a full Polish pronunciation. ''Why not . . .'' He made a suggestive gesture with his gun.

Charpentier's full lips curved in an unpleasant smile. ''Because now isn't the right time. You be on your way, detective. But I'll tell Jasper you stopped by.''

I turned around and slowly made my way to the street. Under the circumstances I didn't see I had any other choice. When I crossed Elston I turned around to look. Charpentier and Anton were watching me, arms akimbo. The workmen let out some more catcalls. The tone seemed friendly; I turned to wave.

During the short drive home I turned Charpentier's final words over in my mind a dozen times. The only sense I could make of them was that he and Anton were the two men tailing me, and that they were waiting for something specific to happen before they assaulted me. But what?

I was startled to find how angry I was with both Charpentier and his cowboy-foreman. They had insulted me in a mean, ugly way. I don't like being called a girl or told I'll be assaulted to teach me a lesson. As I checked the entrance to the alley behind my building I wondered who'd thought up that idiotic saying about ''sticks and stones.'' It was Charpentier's ugly talk that rankled me more than my bruises.

At least I'd found a Home Free construction site. It

would be interesting to go see if Charpentier had pulled a permit for the job. And more interesting would be to look at Charpentier's books, to see if Home Free was paying him on schedule. He'd been unhappy with Jasper last week, but it couldn't have been over money. A guy like Charpentier wouldn't keep coming back if he wasn't getting paid.

Presumably Heccomb hadn't talked to Charpentier today. If he had told them I was snuffling close to the truffles they might well have killed me. I tried not to dwell on the picture of my dead body buried in cement.

MacKenzie Graham had told me my tail was in a sedan, maybe brown. That certainly would include Charpentier's wife's Nissan. But in case it was someone else—or in case Jasper had reserves—I parked again on Morgan and walked the two blocks home.

I kept my hand on the Smith & Wesson as I unlocked the inside door. No one was lurking in the entryway. My keys in my left hand, I trotted up the stairs, my mind more on a bath than on Anton.

I heard them an instant before I saw them, an instant that got the Smith & Wesson into my hand, safety off. Three hooded shadows rose at the top landing. I fired and ran down the stairs, bent double.

"Fucking bitch! Stop her!"

I careened around the corner of the landing. One of the shadows launched itself down the stairs. I fired at it, missed and heard an answering shot. Spinning on my toe I started down the next flight when the shadow flung itself on top of me. We rolled down the stairs together. My gun went off, searing my hand.

At the half landing I couldn't wrench myself free. Drawing my knees inside his dark embrace I pushed into his gut. He grunted and grabbed my hair. I bucked hard. My legs came free and I swiveled under his grip. Just as I pulled my gun up some other hand sliced the back of my head. I felt an instant of pain so exquisite I seemed to be dancing on the edge of the world, and then a merciful darkness enshrouded me.

□37
Bird of Prey

The sun was a bright light in the far distance. A falcon sat on a hooded man's arm, eyeing me coldly, wanting to carry me into the center of the sun.

"No!" I screamed. I struggled to sit up but the falconer stuck out an arm and pinned me to the earth. The bird bit my hand.

When I woke up the sun had diminished into a fluorescent light in a stained ceiling. The bird beak was an IV running into my left wrist. Shabby curtains surrounded me on two sides. A cart holding medical instruments stood on my left. A woman in a T-shirt and jeans, but wearing a stethoscope, materialized next to me.

"Oh, good. You're awake. Do you know your name?"

"Where am I?" I croaked.

"This is the emergency room at Beth Israel Hospital."

"How did I get here?"

"The police brought you. They want to talk to you, to see what you remember, but before I let them in here I need to make sure you're up to it. So why don't you tell me your name?"

"I've hurt my head, haven't I?" I frowned, trying to remember what had happened. "That's what they always ask when you've hurt your head, but I don't know how it

happened. I keep thinking it had something to do with falcons, but that was because of the eyes.''

I became aware of an ice pack wedged against the side of
my head. I put up a tentative finger to feel what lay beneath
the coolness: a tender lump, perhaps the size of a cantaloupe. My arm ached where I'd landed on it.

The nurse patiently agreed that I'd hurt my head, and
once more asked for my name. I told her that, and the date,
and who the president was. If he got hit on the head they'd
have to keep him for observation because he wouldn't know
who I was. When I suggested this to the nurse she smiled
and said she was going to find the resident, and to tell the
police they could ask me a few questions.

The light still hurt my eyes. I shut them and let sleep lap
at me until a voice spoke near my head.

''Ms. Warshawski . . . the nurse said you were awake.
How are you feeling?''

I knew the voice but couldn't place the speaker. When I
turned my head to look at her a jagged arc of pain swept
through me, a flash of lightning that discharged and left me
breathless. The copper hair that fit her head like a shield,
the stony mask of a face—but a mask that had slipped to
show compassion—I knew who she was, but I couldn't
summon her name.

''I know you. You work with Terry Finchley.'' Tears of
frustration pricked my eyes.

''Don't try so hard,'' the nurse said from my other side.
''You'll remember things better if you let yourself relax.''

''I'm Mary Louise Neely. Officer Calley is here to take
notes.'' She indicated a man in uniform hovering between
the opening in the curtains that led to the hall. ''Are you up
to talking?''

''I don't remember what happened,'' I said. ''I thought
they were falcons. Now I see it was the hoods they were
wearing. Their eyes were glittering behind their hoods.''

Neely frowned at the nurse. ''Are you sure she's all
right? Should we get a doctor to look at her?''

''They were thugs. Hoods. Hoods in hoods.'' I giggled at

the thought and suddenly found myself wrenched by sobs. "Hoods. They jumped me. I thought I was being so careful and they were waiting on my own landing."

I fought back the gusher of tears; crying only made the pounding in my head more severe. The nurse brought me some water. Swallowing set off a stab of pain in my rib cage. Maybe I'd broken something when I fell down—was it stairs or was it in the yard? I tried to assemble my splintered memory. I'd fallen twice today, that was it: once at the construction site, and then down the stairs? No, someone had landed on me: that was why my joints felt like they'd been through a cement mixer.

"I fired my gun," I suddenly recalled. "Did Mr. Contreras—"

"He came out with the dogs to see what was happening. One of the punks rammed a gun at his head and told him to call off the dogs and go back into his own apartment. That one kept your neighbor covered while the other two searched your apartment. That was what they came for, not to kill you, but to put you out so they could go through your place. When they finished they took off. Mr. Contreras called us and went to help you out, but you'd regained consciousness and were sitting in your living room. The uniforms didn't know what to make of it at first, but fortunately the old man had summoned an ambulance."

I shook my head, a tiny gesture that made my stomach heave. I found the ice pack and pushed it more securely against my swollen cantaloupe. I didn't remember the ambulance, or sitting in my living room. I couldn't remember anything except the moment I'd fired my gun.

"I have an alarm. If they opened my door and didn't turn it off the police should have gotten a signal right away. Why didn't your friends come sooner?"

Neely's face twisted in annoyance. "They get so many false alarms they don't send a detail out first thing when the buzzer goes off. Your thugs—falcons—had about eight minutes and they made every one of them count. What did they want so badly?"

"I don't know." I couldn't think, or didn't want to think —it meant facing the idea of my home in ruins.

"We got the message down on State Street because of the Messenger children: every station is looking for them, since he's such a high-profile citizen. So the Town Hall watch commander was alert enough to remember your name as part of the bulletin. I know Mr. Messenger is irritated with you, but I don't think this has anything to do with him—unless you came on some evidence about his children that we don't know about?"

I moved restlessly on the gurney. "No. Nothing."

I thought of Anton and Gary Charpentier, shooting at me from the Home Free construction site. But they would have had to move faster than the speed of light to beat me back to my apartment. Jasper Heccomb: I'd broken into his office last night. He probably guessed it was me, because I'd been asking unwelcome questions. But I hadn't taken anything, not even out of his packed cash drawer. Fabian's image spun through my mind, but I couldn't think why. Of course, I thought he'd killed Deirdre, I could remember that, but what was the connection to Heccomb?

"Does Conrad know I'm here?"

"We've been trying to reach him. He and Terry were playing ball in Grant Park, but they'd left by the time we sent someone over there. They don't seem to be answering their beepers, but we've left messages around town for them. Can you remember anything you might have that someone else wants?"

The resident on call arrived, summoned by reports of my resurrection. A grave young man with bloodshot eyes, he shooed Mary Louise and her attendant scribe from the room while he checked my reflexes. They wanted to do a CAT scan to make sure my brain waves were okay, but after that I could leave. The radiologist would examine the CAT scan in the morning and call me if there were any abnormalities they didn't detect this afternoon.

"You shouldn't be alone tonight," he warned me. "You

mustn't sleep too much—you need to be with someone who can wake you up.''

Conrad, if I could find him. Otherwise I'd have to impose on Mr. Contreras. He'd be delighted to cluck over me, but it was too much of a burden for an old man, especially if some punks thought I had a dangerous secret.

When the attendants wheeled me back from the X-ray department Lotty and Max were in the cubicle. They were dressed up, Max in evening clothes, Lotty in severely tailored black wool. Her frown matched the severity of the suit.

"The Aeolus Quintet." I remembered they were going to a concert and spoke the name aloud.

Lotty's face relaxed. "Your memory *is* functioning. The resident told me, but you never believe it until you see it yourself. I'm taking you home with me. You need to be awakened every few hours and I want to make sure that happens.''

I leaned back on the gurney and let well-being wash over me. Lotty wanted to look after me, not to beat on me for running into trouble. She had finally forgiven me for last year's assault. At that memory I sat up again, so fast that the pain thudded through me and spun the room around.

"No, Lotty, I can't. They may come after me again and I don't want you to be with me if that happens. Officer Neely is trying to find Conrad. And anyway, you have a concert to attend.''

"We've heard the Aeolus music before and we'll no doubt have the opportunity to listen to it again." Lotty put a hand on my pulse. "I know what's in your mind, Vic, but this time I'm choosing to be with you in a time of danger, not letting you thrust me willy-nilly into its path.''

"But everyone knows we're friends. If they know I'm staying with you they'll assume you're holding whatever it is they're looking for. Even Terry Finchley wanted to search your home for Emily Messenger as well as my missing computer software.''

We argued the point for a minute or two, until Max interrupted. "Why don't the two of you come home with me. That way Lotty can keep an eye on you and both of you will be out of the danger zone."

"But Conrad—" I started.

"Conrad will be welcome to join you as soon as Officer Neely locates him." He called Neely back into the cubicle and gave her a business card with his home number on it. "And we need to explain things to your Cerberus: he's fretting in the waiting room right now."

At my insistence the nurse brought in Mr. Contreras. He was voluble with relief and explanations. I apologized for putting him through such a terrible ordeal.

"Don't worry about me, doll, I've been through worse. It ain't like it was Anzio, where they was firing real rounds at us, you know, but when I saw you lying on the landing there, and then this thug pulls a gun on me—I should have let him shoot me instead of being such a crybaby."

I took his hand and pulled him closer to the gurney. "You did exactly the right thing. What if he'd shot you and I'd been badly hurt? Who would have looked after the dogs?"

"Oh, doll, don't try to make a joke out of it. I know I let you down, not checking who was coming into the building, and then letting them get the best of me. They rang the Lees' bell, see, and their English not being so hot—the kids wasn't in—the Lees just buzzed them on in. I should of gone out to look, instead of planting myself in front of the tube watching the races. No wonder you never tell me what you're up to."

I finally got him to calm down. He didn't like the news I was going off with Lotty and Max instead of letting him look after me, but he agreed in the end that Lotty could take better care of me than he could.

Before we left, Officer Neely tried again to get me to remember what material someone might have been hunting, but I couldn't think past the thud in my head. Jasper—but I hadn't taken anything from his office. If he wanted to kill me for looking at his stash I'd be dead now.

Neely wanted to come with me while I picked up a tooth-brush, to see if the sight of my place jogged a memory. Lotty objected vigorously.

"Dr. Herschel, if we don't know what they were looking for, we don't know if Vic—Ms. Warshawski—is still in danger. If they found something and took it away, we don't need to worry so much about trying to intercept someone before they find her at Mr. Loewenthal's."

Put like that, Lotty had to agree. With my arm around Mr. Contreras's shoulders, I walked slowly from the emergency ward. The scorching bursts of pain had subsided; even the cantaloupe seemed smaller to my touch—perhaps it was only a grapefruit now. The resident had taped my ribs—one had cracked, but not broken. Really, I was in good shape for the punishment I'd taken.

Fortunately Max had driven Lotty in his own car: I didn't think my head would have survived a trip with Lotty at the wheel. Mr. Contreras and I climbed into the backseat of Max's Buick. Officer Neely's blue-and-white escorted us, with a nice display of flashing lights.

□38
Safe House

I slept on the drive up to Max's house in Evanston. Seeing the shambles in my apartment had been an ordeal I couldn't handle with my battered body. The disarray hadn't jolted my memory—it only made me want to withdraw. Officer Neely had summoned a forensic team in the hopes my hoodlums had been careless enough in their haste to leave prints, but I left her to the supervision of Mr. Contreras and the dogs.

Before leaving my place I tried Conrad's number again. He still wasn't home. He might have gone early to his mother's, but I couldn't remember her unlisted number and I couldn't find my address book: it was either buried in the heap of books and papers in my living room, or the falcons had taken it. Neely agreed to get Mrs. Rawlings's number from Terry Finchley and to try to reach Conrad there.

The tidy elegance of Max's home eased my spirits. Sipping fruit juice in the kitchen while he made up a bed for me, I could feel the pain unknit itself from my head. My arms and left side were sore; tomorrow they would be stiff. But with the easing of my knotted brain I could return to some semblance of action in the morning.

Lotty examined my eyes and my reflexes. Finally satisfied that I was recovering well, she asked me if I knew something about the assault I hadn't wanted to tell the police.

"I've been chugging around between Jasper Heccomb and Fabian Messenger trying to figure out Deirdre's death. And hoping for some ideas on Emily. Someone shot at me this afternoon at a construction site, but I don't think that guy could have beaten me back to my apartment. What I don't understand is why I'm still alive." I tried to speak casually but my hands betrayed me, shaking badly enough to spill juice on the kitchen counter.

"Shot at you?" Lotty shivered. "Have you told Conrad? Or that Officer—Neely, is it?—who was at the hospital?"

I shook my head—slowly, to keep my brain from splintering. "Being knocked out made me forget it—it happened just before I came home. Who besides a contractor has muscle to spare for that kind of ambush?"

Lotty forced a smile. "I begin to understand your methods, Victoria: if you are purely clinical about damage to your body it puts fear at a distance. I'll try to join in. Surely Home Free is not implicated in Deirdre's murder: why would a homeless rights advocate murder one of their own volunteers?"

I hunched a shoulder. "Two days ago I would have agreed. But Jasper Heccomb keeps a lot of money in cash in his office—my estimate is five million. Maybe Deirdre saw it and threatened to report him to the IRS."

"Five million in cash?" Max had come back into the kitchen. "Perhaps he pays his work force in cash to avoid payroll taxes. But maybe you should take a nap instead of worrying about it right now."

"He doesn't have a work force, at least only an assistant and a lobbyist . . ." A lobbyist. Maybe all that cash went to bribe elected officials to . . . to do what on behalf of the homeless?

Lotty urged me to my feet. My vertigo returned; I held a chair to steady myself. Of course, Jasper also had to pay the people who built Home Free projects—they could be off-book employees too. Especially if they didn't speak English and didn't have any way of questioning what was going on. As Max escorted me down the hall, past Ming pots and Tang statues, I asked him what language might sound like a bastardized form of Spanish or Italian.

"Sardinian," he suggested. "Or Romanian."

Romanian, of course. Workers from the old Warsaw Pact countries were flooding American construction sites. I should have known it was Romanian.

"You don't happen to speak it, do you?" I asked him.

"A smattering. My father's mother came from the town of Satu-Mare, and I used to speak it with her as a boy. Why?"

I explained what I'd seen at the Home Free work site. "I'd like to go when I could be sure Anton wasn't going to descend on me, to see if the guys would talk about what they're doing. I don't understand why the site should be so secret, but Jasper Heccomb has certainly done his best to keep me from looking at his work in progress."

Lotty, standing behind us, gave me a smart poke between the shoulder blades. "Vic, get into bed. I'm willing to believe you didn't choose to get knocked on the head, but a wise person would turn the whole situation over to Conrad at this point."

"If I can find him," I murmured, allowing her to lead me to the bed.

She helped me undress, putting my clothes into a marquetry wardrobe. "Do you want to save this jacket? The left sleeve is badly torn."

I studied the rent fabric mournfully. I must have ripped it when I fell across the rocks at the construction site. The jacket had been one of my favorites, with little stainless steel rods and eyelets instead of buttons. Maybe the clever tailor who used to make Gabriella's clothes in exchange for his daughter's piano lessons could put it back together. He was almost seventy now, but he sometimes sewed for me when I hungered for a special outfit.

Before climbing into bed I used the mirror set in the wardrobe to examine my own rents. The diamond panes refracted my bruises, making them seem larger than they were. I squirmed around sideways but couldn't see the lump on my head. The spot was still tender, but felt only plum-sized now. I buttoned one of Max's pajama shirts around my taped ribs and climbed into bed.

"It's hardly noticeable," Lotty assured me, pulling a sheet up to my chin. "I don't think you'll even have a black eye from it—they didn't hit you hard enough. It's six o'clock. I'll wake you at ten, just to be safe, but I think you're fine."

At ten-thirty she made me walk on my stiff legs down to the kitchen for more apple juice and a little toast and jam. Conrad had phoned at eight. He'd taken his nieces to a movie, which is why no one could find him earlier.

"He wanted to drive up here, but I didn't see the point, since you need to rest and there's nothing he can do for you. I told him you'd call when I woke you."

I used the kitchen phone. Conrad answered on the first ring. His concern alleviated by Lotty, he was more worried about what I was sitting on than my health.

"The doc tells me you gonna live this time, Ms. W., but she isn't saying for how long. What did they want so bad they tossed the joint? Level with me: this isn't a game anymore, if it ever was one."

When I didn't speak Conrad said, "Come on, Ms. W. You busted into Jasper Heccomb's place last night. What did you walk away with that he'd want bad enough to pull a dangerous trick like this one?"

"I told you I saw a drawerful of cash, but I didn't take any. Did you go look?"

"We couldn't—dude never called us. What else did you see?"

"Nothing. Honestly. Unless I'm blocking it out—but I don't have amnesia, except for the part of my life between when I was jumped and when I woke up in the hospital." I probably never would remember coming to and walking up the stairs to my own place, Lotty had warned me.

"Well, who else you been burgling lately?"

"No . . . oh." Like a turning kaleidoscope the memory of Fabian's letter from Senator Gantner dropped into my mind. I'd left it on my bedside table. Neely had commented at the time that they must have been looking for paper—they'd pulled all my books and papers in the living room. But the bedroom had been left tidy. They'd gone in, spotted it, and fled.

"What are you remembering?" Conrad demanded. "Do you do so much B & E that individual episodes slip your mind?"

I told him about the letter. "I mentioned it to Alec Gantner when I was out at the plant yesterday afternoon. He's got a pet security force out at Gant-Ag. They probably do whatever he asks, even knocking out strangers in their own stairwells."

Conrad howled. "Why did you go through Messenger's files in the first place? Don't you see we're in an impossible spot now? What if Gantner did come looking for it? What can I—what can the Finch do? Go to Clive Landseer and say, excuse me, we'd like a warrant to search the Gant-Ag premises, also Alec Gantner's home, because a private eye stole a letter from the home of one of our leading citizens, and she thinks it's possible Gant-Ag's security guards jumped her to retrieve it?"

My head started to throb again. "I don't expect you to do anything. When have I ever asked you to help me out of a mess?"

"Never, girl. And that's what pisses me off. If you'd talk to me before you got into a mess, we might be able to work out a way to get what you want to know without going through forced entry, theft, and then grievous bodily harm."

The painted flowers on the sink backsplash began to bend and nod in a breeze only they could feel. "If I talked to you ahead of time you'd try to talk me out of it. And then I wouldn't know."

"What? You wouldn't know what?"

"That there was a connection between Gantner and

Fabian, for one thing. Or that Jasper keeps all that cash lying around. I may solve Deirdre's murder while you guys are still trying to finger her poor runaway daughter.''

"Vic, listen. If I solved Deirdre's murder by getting evidence without a properly issued and executed warrant, the guy would go scot-free. The evidence wouldn't be admissible. Didn't you ever study the fucking bill of rights in law school?''

My face got hot. It shouldn't be happening this way—a cop lecturing me on illegal search and seizure. I was a progressive.

"You still there?''

"Struck dumb. All I can say is—you're right. So I can't argue with you, even if my head were up to it, which it isn't. I'm going back to bed. You have a good time in church tomorrow.''

"Believe me, babe, I'll be saying a prayer for you, asking the angels to persuade you not to hug your cards so close to your chest. It makes it hard for anyone else to get in a game with you.''

◻39
Bus to Romania

A little after five-thirty Lotty's fingers on my wrist wrenched me out of sleep, interrupting a dream I'm prone to in times of stress: I'm trying to reach my mother behind the maze of equipment in which her final illness wrapped her, but the tubes keep sprouting and spreading like plant roots, knitting a plastic thicket that keeps her from me.

"Sorry, *Liebchen*. I have to go into Chicago—there's an emergency at the hospital. But since you're awake let's take a quick look at you." She prodded me, lifted my eyelids, and listened to my heart. "You'll do. I'll check on your CAT scan with the radiologist, but—as long as you don't take on any hooligans—you should be able to get up today. Remember to drink plenty of fluids, and no alcohol: that's most important."

A few minutes later I heard Max's Buick pull out of the drive. I got up and fumbled my stiff arms into the dressing gown Max had laid out for me. In the guest bathroom down the hall I stood under a hot shower, slowly moving my arms until I could raise them above my head, then massaging the taut muscles in my neck. After fifteen minutes of home-brewed hydrotherapy I went back to the guest room and went through a longer stretching routine. It's hard to make yourself do exercises when you're sore, but you heal much faster if you get the blood flowing vigorously.

When I got down to the kitchen I found Max drinking coffee over the *New York Times*. He had driven Lotty into the city—she didn't have her own car with her and he'd seen Lotty at the wheel too many times to lend her his own.

"You look well this morning, Victoria. A happy recovery. Coffee?"

I drank a cup in scalding drafts while Max toasted a bagel for me. Max offered me part of the paper, but I wasn't interested in New York or Yugoslavian news this morning and the *Times* has lousy sports coverage. After watching him read for a few minutes I asked when he was going back for Lotty.

"I'm not. We drove by her apartment for her car. Was there something you needed?"

"My own car. I have some errands to run."

Max put the paper back down. "You must not drive, Victoria. Not after the beating you took yesterday. Why not see if Conrad will take you where you need to go?"

"I can't rouse him this early in the morning—especially not when he's staying with his mother." And especially not after last night's conversation.

"And this is something that can't wait?"

Fiddling with a glass of orange juice, I told him I wanted to go back to the construction site, now, while it was early enough that no one would be there. "If I wait until tomorrow, or even this afternoon when Conrad might drive me, I run the risk of finding Anton or Charpentier."

The light on his glasses hid his eyes from me, keeping his thoughts secret. "You know Lotty would absolutely forbid such an excursion."

"I know: that's what keeps our relationship so strained all the time. Maybe after this case I'll resign and go into real estate or teach Italian."

"And somehow be the only Italian instructor embroiled on the wrong side of P-2 or the Banco Ambrosiano. . . .

If you feel an urgent need to go to this construction site I'll drive you there.''

"Which Lotty would also absolutely forbid. I can't put you in danger, not when she's finally forgiven me for doing it to her.''

"Not out of concern for my personal safety, I'm happy to hear.'' Max's snort of laughter interrupted my blushing disclaimer. "If it's likely to be dangerous, you mustn't go. If it's not, I'll drive you.''

I bit on my thumbnail. If Anton or Charpentier was there it could be quite ugly, and I was in no shape to take them on. But my bet was we would avoid them. I finally asked Max if he could scout the site from the alley while I waited on Montrose. If anyone was there he'd pick me up and we'd come back to Evanston.

"I don't suppose they'll shoot at a strange car just for passing by their work zone,'' he agreed.

Leaving a message for Lotty, in case she finished earlier than she expected, he solicitously took my elbow and helped me into the front seat of the Buick. "Lake Shore Drive?''

"Edens—the Cicero exit will decant us almost on top of the construction site.'' The interior of his car was as immaculate as his house; I saw some crumbs on my T-shirt and tossed them out the window.

I leaned back in the seat. Max didn't speak for several minutes, but as we turned onto Dempster, the road that led to the expressway, he asked if I was carrying my gun.

"Yes. I found it in the stairwell when we went to my apartment yesterday. Does that trouble you?''

He made a face. "I don't like the world of guns, but if your hoodlum is going to shoot at you again I suppose it's good for you to have one. You know how to use it correctly, I'm sure.''

"Oh, yes. My dad saw too many shooting injuries from kids getting hold of guns. He started taking me to the range with him when I was ten. My mother hated it—he wanted her to learn, also, but she wouldn't acknowledge that he even carried a weapon.''

Those Saturday mornings come back to me whenever I go to the range, Gabriella's back rigid with anger as she settled some child at the piano for a lesson. "If you would work on your breathing as you do on those ghastly toys we could make a singer out of you, Victoria—a creator of life, not of death,'' she said when I returned in guilty triumph from hitting a bull's-eye.

We moved fast through the empty streets. In the city someone is always about doing something, but in the suburbs people must sleep later: for long stretches of westbound Dempster we were the only car around. It wasn't even seven-fifteen when we exited the expressway and turned onto Elston. When we reached Montrose I showed Max the entrance to the alley that ran down behind the construction site.

He left me at the corner of Montrose and Elston, where I could feign waiting for a bus to account for my solitary presence. A pay phone stood nearby. If Max didn't return in ten minutes I would call Conrad. Some missing chunks of memory had returned in the night, including Mrs. Rawlings's phone number, but in case excitement fragmented my mind I'd scrawled the number on my wrist.

I paced the sidewalk to loosen my muscles and sang Italian folk songs under my breath to distract my mind. A cop car slowed to take a closer look at me. I frowned at my watch and looked up the street, miming impatience for the bus. The car drove on. The ten minutes stretched to fourteen. My hand was hovering over the number pad when Max returned.

''I couldn't see anyone, but a large truck was standing there. I drove by twice, but there didn't seem to be anyone about. Do you want to risk it?''

I couldn't imagine why Gary would leave his truck at the site. It made me uneasy—it might mean he'd be showing up at any moment. We finally decided to drive down the alley and park south of the site. That way we could get to the car if anyone came in—the pattern of one-way streets made the north end the entrance to the alley. I tried to get Max to agree to wait in the car where he could call Conrad from his cellular phone, but he vehemently refused.

We stopped for several minutes just beyond the truck, where we could see the whole site. When no one appeared Max pulled forward to a spot where the remnants of a garage hid the Buick from the mouth of the alley.

We picked our way across the rubble. We couldn't see the Elston traffic but we could hear it; every passing car made us jump nervously. My head was starting to ache again. I realized it had been foolish to insist on this pilgrimage.

As I was starting to inspect the piles of materials, jotting down names of suppliers, Max called to me in a loud whisper. I turned and froze. The back of the truck was opening. I gestured to Max to kneel down behind a stack of lumber and pulled my gun from its holster.

One of the work crew stumbled over to the high grass beyond the site and urinated. He moved over to a large metal container and fiddled with it. A motor came to life— it apparently was some kind of portable generator. As he returned to the truck he spotted me, gave a wide grin and called out something. Two more of the crew came to the back of the truck and peered at me.

"Bay-bee!" one of them crowed, jumping down.

He made an explicit suggestion, using his hands, but lost some of his zest when Max rose up from behind the pile of lumber. Max walked over to the trio and began speaking, not fluently, but apparently making himself understood. The man who'd called out to me clapped Max on the back, and gestured to the truck. A few more crew members stumbled from the truck, shouting out questions, or perhaps greetings.

I stood idly by, my hand on my holster, although the mood seemed more festive than dangerous. The relation of the language to Italian meant I could pick out words here and there, but not the overall sense. Anton's name cropped up several times.

After a few minutes Max turned to me. "They are from Romania, as we thought. And they don't wish you any harm, but no one is supposed to come onto the site without Anton's permission. He broke someone's face—jaw, I guess—for wandering around, and they think you should leave in case he shows up."

"Agreed. Could you ask them a couple of questions first? See what they know about the project they're working on?"

I watched the crew's faces while Max fumbled through some questions. They started talking in excited gusts, gesticulating wildly. Max got them to slow down. A wiry man with an outsize black mustache silenced his fellows and spoke slowly, in the loud, simple sentences one uses with foreigners.

"Someone brought them over here about two months ago," Max reported. "I didn't understand the word for the kind of person who did it, but I suppose it might be a labor contractor. They're working long hours . . ." He turned back to them and asked them something, holding up his fingers to make sure he was understanding them.

"Yes. They work six days a week, ten hours a day. They're living in this panel truck." He peered inside. "It looks like the hold of an old ship—just rows of bunks nailed into the wall."

I made a gesture to the men, asking if I could look inside. Letting out more ribald shouts they welcomed me on board. When I hoisted myself up they cheered, with more cries of "Bay-bee." The main speaker put down a crate for Max, then gave him a hand to help him onto the tailgate. Inside they turned on a flex lamp, throwing a harsh light onto their home.

Bunks for twelve men were attached to the walls. Eight were occupied. Along the back their clothes dangled from a series of rough hooks. Between the bunks they had hung pictures torn from magazines. Some were frankly pornographic, others scenic posters of home. A few had put up photographs of their families.

A board across two short sawhorses served as a table. It was crammed with empty beer bottles and cigarette stubs. Another sawhorse table held a hot plate and a small black-and-white TV.

Two men were still sleeping when we entered. Roused by their comrades' outbursts they sat up, naked and surly. I turned and swung my legs over the tailgate, sliding off to stand on the crate underneath. My shoulders and head were too sore for me to leap on and off the truck like a goat, but the men deserved a modicum of privacy, they had so little else. It seemed a ghastly way to acquire hard currency.

A minute or two later Max sat down next to me. He shook his head in dismay, muttering about sights he didn't think existed in America.

The spokesman came back out and bent down to ask Max something. He translated for me. "They want to know who you are—if you're looking for a lover, or if you're a government official. What should I tell them?"

"Oh. They think I may be with INS. Tell them I have friends who've agreed to do some work for Anton's boss, and I'm worried about whether they'll be paid properly—that I wanted to talk to someone who was already working for him to find out their experience."

"I'll do the best I can with that—remember, my Romanian's pretty rudimentary."

They roared with laughter at this question and went into a wild exposé. Max kept interrupting, unable to follow what they were saying. At one point he tried German, but they didn't understand, any more than they did my Italian or schoolgirl French.

As far as Max could interpret, Anton was an overseer. A Romanian who had been in America for fifteen years, he had a green card. He had met the crew at O'Hare when they arrived two months ago on tourist visas. He told Immigration they were students he was showing around America, and immediately chauffeured them to the truck, where they'd been living ever since. When they first arrived they finished work on a building. They had been here on Elston about two weeks.

Before they ever collected their pay some money was deducted for the jobber who'd brought them over, and some sent directly to their relatives in Romania. They were charged for their room and board, even though they were living in an old bread truck. Their net pay amounted to about thirty dollars a week.

"That's outrageous—it's like the agricultural exploitation in the South," I cried. "We need to report this to someone."

"The problem is, they're here illegally," Max said. "Anton holds the threat of deportation over their heads. They all have families back home they're trying to help out. Some are married, others have parents they're supporting. Obviously they're exploited, but they need the money."

I frowned. I knew a lawyer, a woman named Ana Campos, who did advocacy work for low-income immigrants. I didn't know what choices the men had, but surely something better than this unsanitary cattle car could be provided them. I told Max about Ana.

"I'm going to have to give her a call—I can't walk away and leave this situation as it is. How many different crews do you suppose Charpentier has stashed around the city like this?"

Before Max could answer, one of the crew grabbed me and cried out, "Anton!"

The urban cowboy was driving down the track in a pickup truck. He hadn't seen us yet, but if we tried to flee up the alley we'd be easy targets. Anyway, neither Max nor I was fit enough to run for it.

I scrambled to my feet and stretched a hand down to Max. "Come on. Ask the guys if we can crawl into an empty bunk for a bit."

Max followed me, gasping out a few words. The spokesman smiled, said okay, and hollered to his companions in the back. We were hustled handily under some bedding,

Max in a lower berth, me in an upper one. One of our new pals stuck his hand inside my shirt and—purely autonomically—I brought my knee up to his stomach. He hastily pulled a blanket over my head and jumped down.

The back of the truck opened. I could hear Anton but neither see nor understand him. It was terrifying to lie like that, not knowing what the men were saying. I clutched the Smith & Wesson tightly, but my palms were so sweaty it kept slipping in my grip.

After a sharp exchange between Anton and the men he seemed to be taking roll. My heart started pounding painfully—had he noticed the extra lumps in the bunks? Below me I could hear a faint wheezing from Max, and prayed the sound wouldn't betray us.

Anton barked out something ominous. The men mumbled, and then there was silence. I lay still, breathing as shallowly as I could. When someone pulled the blanket away from me a minute or two later I had my gun out, pointing it at his head. It was our spokesman. He blenched and jumped quickly away.

"It's okay, Vic," Max said quietly. "Anton has taken off. He seemed only to be checking that everyone is here—he told them they were going to move to a different job later today, so to stick around."

"Oh." I pocketed the gun, feeling foolish. "Tell the guy I'm sorry I scared him."

When Max finished translating—a long flourish that made me wonder how I was being described—the spokesman blinked and nodded, but didn't look very happy. I had a feeling our welcome was long outworn. My head was pounding in earnest; Max seemed exhausted. I touched his arm and told him I would get the car.

"I'm fine, Vic, really. But maybe I will wait here for you."

My arms and legs were as weary as though I'd done ten hours' hard labor. I sat on the tailgate like an old woman, and slowly slid my legs over the edge. I had just made the ground when a car drove up, an old blue Dodge carrying four men.

I stumbled back into the truck as they ran toward it. Before I could cry out, or offer any kind of warning, they had jumped up on the tailgate. One of them held a gun; another flashed a badge.

"Immigration, boys. Hands in front where we can see them. We're going for a nice, long ride." He repeated the command in Romanian.

40

Tops on Everyone's List

The INS agents had a van waiting at the top of the alley. They were totally uninterested in Max's and my protests and refused to look at our identification, shoving us inside so hard that my head was jolted against a seat back. For a dizzying moment I thought I might pass out again. I bit my lip hard enough to use the pain to steady myself.

The van itself could have held eight comfortably. The fourteen of us were jammed in with legs and elbows at all angles. I was wedged in a corner with one of the workmen on my lap. Garlic and the cloying sweat of fear filled the airless space.

The men were convinced that Max and I had fingered them, even though we were cuffed just as they were. They spewed invectives at us during the ride to O'Hare. Although Max refused to translate, it wasn't hard to figure out the burden of their cries.

We spent almost four hours at the airport, first in a small room with the Romanians, then in a minute room by ourselves—and a guard. They confiscated my gun at the outset. I was strip-searched to make sure I wasn't concealing other weapons. The city cops toyed with arresting me on a felony weapons charge, even though I clearly had a permit for the gun. Neither they nor the immigration officials wanted to hear that Max and I were citizens—they kept trying to claim we had stolen our driver's licenses and credit cards. They would have shipped us off to Bucharest if any planes had been leaving just then.

During the time we were together with the Romanians the man with the mustache continued his tirade. His comrades squatted on the floor, staring dejectedly at nothing. Max, gray about the mouth, gallantly tried to translate for a few minutes. He finally gave it up—he said their speech had become so colloquial he couldn't make it out.

"I could make an educated guess, but my English vocabulary wouldn't be wide-ranging enough in any event for what they're trying to say," he added.

"Mine is," I said sourly. "And I can live without hearing it again."

It was noon when INS finally let me call Freeman Carter. That was not due to any eloquence on my part, but because they'd fingerprinted us. A check through AFIS, the automated print system, had given them a perfect match with a private eye using my name and address. Somehow this didn't convince them that I was who I claimed to be—or more likely they were so furious at being proved wrong they wouldn't release us without putting us through legal hoops.

I was reeling by then, my head a giant hammer pounding the anvil of my body, but concern for Max kept me from keeling over. I was alarmed by his pallor and the beads of sweat on his forehead. I told the officer in charge that if Max had a heart attack I would use my connections with Senator Gantner's office to make sure none of them ever worked again. Grumpy, but not sure whether I might have such contacts, they let me call my lawyer.

When I found Freeman—by portable phone on the Kemper Golf Course—he wanted me to wait while he finished a round. He thought being held at O'Hare as an illegal alien a rather exquisite joke, but agreed Max's character didn't need developing through punishment the way mine did. He would finish the hole he was playing and come on over to the airport. While we waited for Freeman I tried to get the cops to let me call Ana Campos as well—I thought the Romanians deserved some kind of legal counsel before being thrown onto a plane home, but I couldn't persuade the law.

When Freeman finally showed up he was laughing a little, but at the sight of Max's gray face his lightness evaporated. He wanted to call an ambulance, but Max said all he needed was to get out in the air. Freeman took down the names of the arresting officers, said they would hear from him, and ushered us to his waiting Maserati—he'd managed to persuade the cop on duty to let him park right in front of the terminal.

"Vic is the one you should be worrying about," Max said as we sped away from the airport. "She was badly injured yesterday—knocked out, in fact. I was afraid she might swoon in that stuffy room."

His words released the string with which I'd tethered myself to consciousness. I tried to speak, to pay attention to Freeman's response, but I fell into a well of darkness. I remembered nothing—not even how I made it from the car inside—until Freeman was shaking me awake in Max's living room. He handed me a cup of coffee and stood over me while I drank it.

When he judged I was aware enough to respond, he said, "I know you're dead to the world, Vic, but I'd like a thumbnail sketch of what this was about before I leave. You can give me a more complete report tomorrow."

When I told him he was not supportive. "You're not getting much sympathy from me on that one. In the first place, finding Deirdre's murderer is a job for your friend Conrad, and in the second, why should any business open its books to you? Just because you want to know something they don't want to tell you does not constitute prima facie grounds of wrongdoing."

He held up a hand to forestall my outburst. "I agree that bringing in a planeload of illegal immigrants and exploiting them is shameful behavior. Charpentier has a lot of explain-

ing to do to the immigration authorities. And maybe Home
Free's backers ought to know about it—but that isn't your
problem. Your problem, as I see it, is to find enough clients
to make a dent in the two thousand dollars you still owe me.
Not to mention what today's little junket will cost. Fortunately for you I don't charge overtime for Sunday rescues."

Maybe if I hadn't been so tired I would have thought of
an equally sharp rebuttal, but the idea of his bill made me
remember my taxes, due on Wednesday. Not to mention all
my other obligations. I crawled wearily from the living
room to the spare room without bothering to tell him good-
bye.

Lotty had been tending Max, but she came in to give me
a brusque, not to say unsympathetic, exam. As she once
again pulled the sheet up to my chin, she told me that for
two cents she'd sew it into a shroud and bury me with it.

"I love you, too, Lotty. Good night."

"And what am I supposed to tell Conrad and Mr. Contreras?" she demanded.

"That I love them, too, and I'll call them in the morning."

"No. You sleep for a while, and then you use the telephone. They are seriously worried about you, although why
anyone would go to that much bother I don't know. After
what you went through yesterday, to do this—and then to
put Max at risk also—is absolutely unconscionable."

Max's name pulled me briefly back from the edge of
sleep. "Is Max okay? I was afraid he might be having a
heart attack, but I couldn't get those idiots to pay any attention."

Lotty's twisted smile came. "Not his heart. Maybe his
soul. Max fled Europe for his life when he was thirteen.
The thought of a forcible return was a terrible nightmare. It
would be for me, I know. I've given him a mild sedative; he
should be fine in the morning."

"I didn't mean it to happen," I pleaded. "We took every
precaution. How was I to know they were warehousing illegal immigrants in an old bread truck on the site?"

Lotty sat down next to me. "You should have known. And you know why? Because no matter what you set out to do the most disastrous possible outcome takes place. If you go to the corner to buy milk, that is a guarantee that the store will be held up at precisely that second."

"When I was born Mars and Venus were both ascending, or whatever planets do. They can't make up their minds which one is going to dominate me. Is that my fault?"

I struggled to sit up. "Why do you think INS descended at that precise moment? Not because I was there today. But because I'd been there yesterday. One of the musketeers must have called and reported the van so that the crew would be scooped up and out of the country before I came back. If they knocked me out yesterday afternoon they'd think they had today clear."

"I don't know what you're talking about. You're proving, though, that it was your presence that caused disaster to strike. Now go to sleep." Lotty pushed me back against the pillow, but her touch was gentler than her words.

It was nine o'clock when she roused me again, to tell me Conrad was on the phone. I pulled my jeans on and stumbled along the hall to the phone, disoriented in the strange house, and by having slept at such a strange time of day.

"How come you get arrested and I learn about it first from my mama?" Conrad greeted me.

"Is this twenty questions? How did your mother hear about it?"

"On the news, same as everyone else in Chicago. Everyone but me, I mean. On top of that, how come you get shot at yesterday and I hear about it from that self-satisfied creep Ryerson?"

I sat on the spindle-legged chair by the phone and rubbed my eyes. "I haven't talked to Murray at all since Thursday. So I don't know how he knew."

"Well, I got most of the story from him—when he had the fucking nerve to call me to ask for corroborating details."

"He picked it up on the wires, then, and acted as though

we'd spoken, as a reporting ploy. Or to cause trouble between you and me—which certainly worked. Please, Conrad—don't call up rapping out accusations.''

Conrad was too angry, or hurt, to pay attention. ''Why the hell didn't you tell the cops out at O'Hare to call me? I could have gotten you out of that jam a lot faster and a lot cheaper than your high-priced lawyer.''

I rubbed the sore spot on the side of my head. ''I was shoved into an overcrowded van and carted off to O'Hare, where they strip-searched me. Have you ever had that special pleasure? It's disorienting.''

''You'd rather have flown to Bucharest and figured out how to hitchhike home than ask for my help. That's what it boils down to, doesn't it?'' His voice was like the bitter edge of an aloe leaf.

''Of course I'd rather call you. I'd rather call you when I'm afraid to walk up my front stairwell. Can't you see why I don't? It's so fundamental, Conrad.''

As I spoke I wondered whether my pride was so fierce that I would have let them bundle me onto a plane than involve my lover. It was something I preferred not to know.

''When were you going to let me know about this particular mangle?'' he demanded.

''Tonight. When I woke up. I would have called before if I'd known we rated the four o'clock news. Come to think of it, I'd better get in touch with Mr. Contreras before he goes into outer space.''

''He already has. Believe it or not the old guy called me —a sign of true desperation. But going back to what's fundamental, Vic, it seems to me you guard everything you do like you were protecting baby Moses from the Pharaoh, and when I learn of it by accident you grudgingly hand me a bulrush or two.''

''Conrad, if you knew I had planned this morning's outing you would have protested mightily. Was it so wrong of me to want to protect myself against that kind of reaction?''

''I object to you breaking the law, not to you exercising a healthy curiosity about your investigations. Can't you tell the difference? And can't you respect my feelings as your lover when it has to be a reporter who tells me you've been shot at?''

''Maybe if you hadn't been so fierce about the Fourth Amendment last night I would have. But you were chewing me out, after I'd sustained a head injury, and it made me forget the earlier fracas.''

''I think the truth is you like to fly solo, girl. If someone's in your wing, even if it's a friendly plane, you'll shoot it down.'' He hung up before I could think of anything to say.

I started shivering in the dimly lit hall. Lotty appeared, ghostlike, with a cup of fresh coffee. I sipped it gratefully, then rested it on my leg so I wouldn't leave a stain on the piecrust table Max used for the hall phone.

''Max still asleep?'' I asked.

''He'll sleep until morning. Is Conrad coming for you?''

''He's so angry with me I don't know if he'll ever speak to me again. And don't tell me I deserve it: I don't need that kind of comfort tonight.''

She leaned a hand across me to push the switch on the small lamp next to the phone; her eyes were shiny in the golden light. ''Does it ever occur to you, Vic, that I don't want you to make the same mistakes I've made? Using anger or fear to put up walls between you and other people is an uncomfortable way to live.''

I clasped her hand briefly. When I talked to Conrad was I acting out of fear or anger? Some of both, I concluded uneasily. I released her fingers to dial Mr. Contreras's number.

As I spoke to my neighbor I wonder why I could treat his frantic questions more gently than I did Conrad's. I patiently explained how Max had come to be involved, how that didn't mean I preferred Max to him, how sorry I was that he'd had to deal alone with the television crews who'd arrived around three—knowing he secretly must have relished the encounter.

''How long you planning on camping out? The dogs

need a good run. And what are you doing to Conrad? I called him to find out what you was up to, and learned the hard way he didn't know. You can't treat men the way you do and expect them to hang around forever. And it's not like I'm a fan of you dating Conrad Rawlings, because I'm not. But he ain't a bad guy for a colored fellow; he's always been real polite to you. To me too. But what are you, pushing forty? And living by yourself without even any proper furniture? What's your life going to be like when you're my age?''

"I give up. I can't think that far ahead. I don't even know what it's going to be like tonight. So don't push on me, okay? I can't take any more of it right now.''

"Okay, cookie, okay,'' he said gruffly. "But try to think about other people's feelings every now and then—that's all I'm asking. You go back to bed now, though. And don't forget to call me in the morning.''

When he'd hung up I studied the table lamp Lotty had switched on. Like everything in Max's house it was a carefully chosen piece, two clear bells with flowers etched in them attached to a small brass post. Sometimes his exquisite taste makes me come to his house as to an oasis of goodwill, but tonight I wanted to smash the lamp against the Chinese vases lining the stairwell.

41

The Quid Pro Quo

Lotty was curled up in the breakfast nook with a novel, something in German by Inge Bachman. She'd slept for several hours after putting Max to bed and was wide awake now. I made a broccoli frittata to share with her, then sat at the cooking island with a yellow pad she'd dug up in Max's study, trying to marshal the facts I had about Home Free, Deirdre, and Century Bank.

The five million or so in Jasper's cash drawer was the most significant item I had. Presumably he paid off contractors like Charpentier in cash. If all the work force was exploited like the crew I'd spent the morning with, payroll outlay would be pretty small. Supplies add up, but how many suppliers would take payment in cash? Some outlays must run to tens of thousands of dollars. And even if all his suppliers were crooked, Jasper couldn't possibly use up the amount of money in his drawer paying them off.

Suppose Deirdre had found the stash and confronted Jasper with it. Could he have murdered her after all, instead of Fabian? I was passionately committed to Fabian as the murderer. It wasn't just my dislike of him that made me think he killed his wife, but the ferocity with which she'd been beaten—it argued a personal rage.

Still, Deirdre had a difficult personality. She might have

inspired a personal rage in someone else, as well. She could well have found out about the exploitation of immigrant workers—since she was in the office a lot she could have found out anything. Maybe she'd confronted Jasper about it and had her brains beaten in for her trouble.

Tamar Hawkings might have seen who came to the Pulteney the night Deirdre was killed. If I could find her before the cops did, maybe she'd talk to me. I added her name to the to-do list I was compiling under Deirdre's square.

Then there was Tish, the Home Free office manager. How much was she a participant—witting or unwitting—in Jasper's crimes? What would horrify her enough about Jasper to make her talk to me? I didn't have any ideas, so I drew another neat square next to her name and filled it with question marks.

I drew a line underneath that section and wrote down Lamia in block letters. Century Bank had withdrawn their loan approval. As soon as I started investigating that action, Home Free had given Lamia a rehab project and the tradeswomen, spurred on by Phoebe, had accepted the job, accepted the loss of funding, and booted me off the case. Century Bank was running a fifty-million-dollar line of credit for Home Free—an unbelievable amount for a small not-for-profit. Why?

There was some tight connection among Phoebe, Gantner, and Jasper: I'd found them all meeting together right after the deal was struck. JAD Holdings—that was the name that connected all these people. JAD was buying Century. Fabian's advice on the Boland Amendment had been filed under that name, and the words had acted powerfully on Alec Gantner on Friday. I wrote JAD in block capitals at the top of the page.

Why wasn't I dead? The question slipped unprompted onto the paper. They could have killed me so easily instead of leaving me unconscious long enough to trash the apartment. I didn't think it was compassion, or a fear of the death penalty, that had stayed my assailants. If the same people had killed Deirdre, those kinds of concerns didn't trouble them. They must have thought I knew something, or had something, that they wanted, and they wanted me alive until they got it from me.

I couldn't imagine any possibilities. Finally I slapped the pencil down in frustration.

Lotty looked up. "Bed for you, *Liebchen.* It's midnight. Drink some more juice and I'll tuck you in."

I awoke at ten to an empty house. When I finished a careful stretching of my stiff muscles and wandered down to the kitchen I found a note on the table in Lotty's tidy hand.

8:00 A.M.

Max is fine and has gone in to work, as I am about to do myself. Please, Victoria, try to spend a quiet day. I know it goes against all your DNA to sit still, but you need the rest. Maybe you could take a long walk by the lake. A set of keys is in the drawer with the silverware.

Love,
Lotty

Her affectionate words filled me with a peaceful glow that lasted while I cut up an apple and some cheese for my breakfast. Putting on water to boil for coffee, I flipped idly through the papers on the breakfast table, not really reading, just passing time.

The name caught the corner of my eye as I flicked the pages of the business section: Cellular Enhancement Technology. I dropped the rest of the paper on the floor and spread the business pages open on the table. The article was on the bottom of page three, just ahead of last week's futures trading. If it had been placed higher I probably wouldn't even have seen it.

CELLULAR ENHANCEMENT TECHNOLOGY GAINS TEST APPROVAL

Chicago. The FDA will announce approval this morning for preliminary trials to test a drug touted as a T-cell enhancer. IG-65, the name of a lipoprotein that purportedly helps fortify the T-cell membrane, has the potential for boosting immune systems of people who've tested HIV-positive. The drug, in early development stages, is the product of a small Skokie company, Cellular Enhancement Technology. Announcing the FDA's decision on Friday afternoon, Senator Alexander Gantner (R-Illinois) said that where so many lives are at stake it was of vital importance to bring drugs like IG-65 to maturity as fast as possible.

I searched the paper feverishly but could find no other mention of the company. I shoved the paper aside and stared sightlessly out the window. So that was Phoebe's quid pro quo. Draw the Lamia women away from their project and Alec Gantner will get the FDA to approve preliminary trials. But why had she done it?

As anger started to build inside me the back of my head began to pound. Easy does it, I admonished myself. Getting angry only made you careless Saturday afternoon and got you this headache.

I went to the phone to call Phoebe. Because I didn't have my address book I had to call Capital Concerns's main switchboard instead of using Phoebe's direct line. I dialed and got a recorded message.

"Due to the emergency evacuation of the building none of our staff can answer your call personally. If you will leave your name, the name of the person you're trying to reach, and a number, we will return your call as soon as possible."

Emergency evacuation of the building? I held the receiver in one hand, my jaw slack with incomprehension, until a beep on the other end roused me. I replaced the receiver without leaving a message and went down the hall to the small sitting room where Max kept his television.

Channel 13's Mary Sherrod was standing in the backyard

of a clapboard building next to the Chicago River. As I watched, the camera moved from her to the river where a pickup truck was dumping gravel.

"That small whirlpool you can see shows where the breach is. Right now city trucks are dumping gravel on the site, hoping to fill the opening from above. It's too soon to tell how big the hole is or how extensive the damage will be. It may be a disaster for the city, but newlyweds John and Kathy Beamish are enjoying a front-row view of the activity of the city's terrified engineers."

The camera switched to a couple in a hot tub. The man grinned and raised a glass of white wine at the camera. I switched channels.

After a while the story became clear. Water was pouring from the Chicago River into a series of tunnels that ran deep beneath the Loop. The barrier that shut the river off from the tunnels had been breached, perhaps when pilings along the bank had been repaired earlier in the spring. Water had begun flooding the tunnels early this morning.

I had never heard of these tunnels. According to one reporter they'd been built at the turn of the last century. Originally designed to carry the first underground cable for a phone company, the network had grown so large that businesses could haul coal and other supplies from barges to their offices. The tunnels hadn't been used for transport for decades, but the space had been ideal for modern skyscrapers to house their electrical lines.

Channel 5 showed frenzied activity at the Board of Trade as a private engineering firm tried to pump water out of the deep basement that had been built into the tunnel. The computers had been shut down because of damage to the electrical plant; no one knew when trading might resume.

"You and I aren't aware of these subbasements," the reporter pointed out. "They lie three levels below what we consider the basement of the building. Those of you who've been in Marshall Fields's 'Down Under Store' will be surprised to know there are three more basements below that subterranean shoppers' haven. One is used for storing inventory; managers are grimly aware that they can do nothing but pray while water continues to rise.''

Not all buildings were affected as severely, Channel 13's Beth Blacksin assured us, but the Loop was being evacuated until the city could determine which ones were safe to use. In any event power was out downtown; no one could work there today anyway. The next shot showed the Loop as a ghost town. Traffic lights and streetlights were dead. The el wasn't running. Skyscrapers were dark. I watched, fascinated, my quarrel with Phoebe briefly forgotten.

Beth Blacksin went on to describe the tunnels themselves. ''No one at City Hall can agree on how extensive the network is—I've heard estimates ranging from forty to eighty miles. And no one knows how many of those miles are underwater right now—especially not at City Hall, where workers are feverishly trying to move sensitive records from the basement to high ground and beating back rats in the process.''

I shuddered involuntarily at the thought of fighting off rats, as Blacksin showed stills of the tunnels. Some looked like ancient caves, covered with lime deposits and waist high in sludge. Others, though, appeared ready for immediate use. The tracks for the mule-drawn trains were as tidy as if they were a model railroad laid out for Christmas.

The camera switched back to Blacksin, who was standing in poor light in front of a brick wall. ''A number of Loop buildings boarded up their entrances to the tunnels years ago. Older buildings with small plants didn't make use of the deep tunnels, or they shared power with a giant neighbor.''

Something about the brickwork behind her seemed familiar. I studied the wall as best I could for the brief time it stayed in the shot. When they went back to Mary Sherrod at the Chicago River I turned off the set and shut my eyes.

The wall behind the Pulteney's boiler—that false inner wall I'd shied away from because the rats came and went through it with ease. No wonder that was their main nesting place. They were coming and going through holes in the brickwork to the tunnels underneath. And so were Tamar Hawkings and her children.

That was how she entered the Pulteney without anyone noticing her. How did she get into the tunnel to begin with? Through a ventilator shaft? By somehow gaining access to Marshall Fields's—or some other business's—inventory basement? I cut off my speculations mid-thought: Tamar and her children had no way of knowing the danger they were in. If the Board of Trade basement was already underwater, what state was the tunnel beneath the Pulteney in?

I hurried to the hall phone and called Mr. Contreras. "I need to go downtown and break into my old office building. And I need help. Are you up for it? It's going to be risky, because the Loop is crawling with cops."

He was thrilled to be called into action. Not the young punk, nor the cop lover, nor even yet the smart-ass Ryerson, but Old Reliable himself. He hadn't seen the news. I told him to turn on the TV and get caught up, that I didn't want to take time to explain things now.

"We'll need a crowbar, some rope, maybe a pickax. Work gloves. Waders. See what you can dig up. I'll be home as soon as I can find a cab in this bucolic fastness."

I hung up on his enthusiastic assurances and looked up the number for a local cab company. While I waited for the cab I stuffed my few belongings into my backpack, checked the clip on the Smith & Wesson, and got the spare keys from the silverware drawer in the kitchen. I was about to leave the house when my conscience pricked me.

I went back to the kitchen phone to call Lotty. She was with a patient, her receptionist, Mrs. Coltrain, told me, and couldn't be disturbed.

"Tell her I'm on the trail of our missing homeless family," I said. "If I'm lucky I'll be bringing them into the clinic later on today."

I started for the door again, then returned to the phone: my conscience was doing double overtime with its pricking. Conrad wasn't at his own place, his mother's, or at the station. I heard the cab honk out front. Hurriedly leaving word with the dispatcher at the precinct, to tell him I was going to try to get into the tunnels at the Pulteney, I jogged down Max's sidewalk to the cab.

42

Dead Loop

The unlit Loop looked like the abandoned city of a science fiction horror. The loss of electricity turned the buildings to dark towers. The sky itself was the color of tired lead, with a white sheen of ozone reflected onto a dull cloud cover. Normally on such a day the streetlights would turn on. People moved silently through the dark streets, as if the blackout imposed quiet.

All downtown parking had been abruptly banned. A phalanx of blue tow trucks swept the streets to scoop up those unfortunates who had parked ahead of the hastily posted notices. Police barricades shut off a number of streets. Traffic crawled along those that remained open. At various intersections we could see jury-rigged pumping stations, with fire hoses stretched into sewer outlets.

I dropped Mr. Contreras at the corner of Wabash and Monroe with our equipment and went off to find parking outside the tow zone. When I'd collected him we had gone to a hardware store to fill in the gaps in our supplies—a couple of heavy-duty flashlights with spare batteries; wading boots; safety glasses; a dolly; and the kind of portable ladders that are sold as fire escapes. I shut my eyes when I signed the MasterCard receipt—I didn't want to know how much my debt had increased.

We already owned hard hats and overalls. Mr. Contreras had a wedge and a sledgehammer. In the hopes of finding the Hawkings family I brought along some blankets and clean T-shirts, a first-aid kit, and a case of fruit juices. It had taken a good hour to assemble all these accoutrements. They filled the trunk and the backseat, with the dolly sticking out the window.

During the drive south I kept listening to the news. None of the stations mentioned any homeless people turning up, but it didn't sound as though the city engineers were crawling around looking for them, either—everyone was racing away from the water.

From what I'd seen on television the tunnels formed an elaborate maze: if the water moved in slowly enough people could find other avenues and perhaps stay dry. And if Tamar Hawkings and her children were indeed camped out down under they might climb back into the Pulteney's basement. They would be boarded into the building, but at least they wouldn't drown.

I had to park almost a mile from the Pulteney. I jogged through the dark streets as fast as I could in my overalls, trying to ignore the incipient throbbing in my head. At the Pulteney I found Mr. Contreras in belligerent confrontation with a cop.

"And I'm authorized to break into this building," my neighbor was saying. "The owners want us to check whether the water's coming in on them or not."

"The place is due to come down next month. What do they care about water in the basement?" the cop demanded.

"Who knows?" the old man said. "You ever figure out what's on management's mind, you let me know. This here's my partner; she'll explain it all to you."

"Freddie Culpepper is the owner," I told the officer. "I have his car-phone number if you want to try to reach him to confirm the order—he's in Olympia Fields today checking on some of his holdings down there."

I pulled a ballpoint pen from the side pocket of my overalls and scrawled Freddie's number on one of my receipts.

Whether that made us seem authentic to the cop or whether he decided to gamble that looters wouldn't be after an abandoned building, he abruptly gave in and went back to steering cars along Monroe Street.

Knowing that we didn't have to worry about the law made the job of breaking through the boarding a lot easier: we didn't have to be subtle. I held the wedge while my neighbor thumped the sledgehammer into it. The vibration shuddered up my arm and increased the throbbing in my head. My cracked rib began to ache as well.

Mr. Contreras might be pushing seventy-eight, but he still had impressive muscles in his shoulders. The boarding splintered with a satisfying crack. A crash of falling glass followed: he'd slugged the wedge hard enough to shatter the door behind it.

Moving quickly before the cop changed his mind, or called the Culpeppers, we pried the plywood apart and dragged our equipment inside. Except for a ghostly finger of light from the hole we'd created, the lobby was black. It smelled of stale urine and mildew.

I switched on one of the flashlights. Sealing the building had accelerated its decay. The dust had caked into grime, covering the floor, the walls, even the ornate brass doors of the elevator.

If the Hawkings family had come up for air their footprints would show in the filth on the floor. Halting Mr. Contreras with a gesture, I studied the floor, skirting the lane from the basement to the stairwell, but couldn't detect any signs of disturbance.

I finally went to open the padlock on the stairwell. It was already undone. Maybe Tamar Hawkings had used the key I'd left for her. If she'd come up for air and found the building boarded over she could have moved along the tunnels to any other part of the Loop, in which case I'd never find her.

We tied the flashlights to our sides, then loaded the remaining equipment onto the dolly and rolled it to the stairs. Delivery men routinely bump that kind of load up and down stairs, but neither the old man nor I had the upper back strength for such a workout: we unloaded the dolly once again and carried the supplies piecemeal into the basement.

Near the bottom of the stairs I could hear the rats. They moved around the abandoned pipes with an insolent ease, conversing in loud, high-pitched squeaks. My palms began to tingle. I dropped the load I was carrying. Rope, hammer, and wading boots landed helter-skelter on the floor beneath me.

"You okay, cookie?" Mr. Contreras rushed down the stairs to my side.

"I'm fine—I let these oily creatures intimidate me."

I shone my flash in the eyes of a long rat who'd slithered over to investigate the rope. He stared at me contemptuously and then slowly sauntered away. He seemed to be saying, "I'm moving off because I want to, not because you scare me. I dare you to attack my lair."

"Can't let them bother you," my neighbor grunted. "Sewer workers are around 'em all day and never get hurt. As long as they don't think they're trapped they won't attack you."

People always say that about rats, but I don't believe it. I think they wait until the odds are in their favor. Why else do they bite babies left alone in slum beds?

My fingers thick with nervousness I reassembled the equipment I'd dropped, put it on the bottom stair, and ran back up for another load. I pulled my waders on in the lobby. It made going down the stairs awkward, but they gave me a greater sense of protection.

When we'd reassembled everything on the dolly I led Mr. Contreras to the wall behind the boiler. The squeaking increased as we reached it. I took a deep breath and moved behind the furnace, kicking aside two red-eyes who were blocking my way. They retreated a few steps, then turned to watch me. I shone the light directly at them with unsteady fingers. When they wouldn't move I picked a piece of metal tubing out of the rubble and poked them. They seemed to snarl, then retreated a few more paces. The old man picked up another pole and helped beat a clear path for me.

"I'll go first, doll," he offered.

I shook my head but didn't answer. I couldn't let myself give in to fear at this point; we had a lot of enemy territory still to cover. If Tamar Hawkings, clad only in rags, had negotiated these beasts with her three children, I could do it also. I gritted my teeth and stepped forward aggressively. The rats stared at me a long moment and then squeezed past my boots and strolled into the basement.

The gap between the boiler and the wall was just wide enough for my shoulders. As I scraped the metal with my left arm I tried not to think what might be moving above it, but the hair beneath my hard hat grew wet. A trickle of sweat ran down my nose. Mr. Contreras was close behind me, giving little chirrups of encouragement.

When I moved clear of the boiler the space widened enough that we could stand side by side. I shone the flash around, but didn't see an opening in the brickwork. The old man grunted and got down on his knees. A couple of rats suddenly appeared and launched themselves at him. He yelped and fell backward, scrabbling at his face. I grabbed one by the tail, wrenched it free of him, and slammed it into the furnace. The other one ran down his arm and disappeared.

I was trembling as I shone the light on his face. The flesh below his left eye was torn and bleeding.

"I'm okay, doll." The old man was working hard to make his breathing sound natural. "Stupid of me. They thought I was heading for their nest, of course."

"Right. They only attack if they think they're cornered."

Shaking, I backed slowly past the boiler to our equipment dolly. I rummaged for the peroxide in my first-aid kit, then decided to bring the whole load. There was just room to roll the dolly in front of me. I kept stopping to cover my face every time I heard one of the beasts near me. The one I'd slammed against the furnace was starting to limp back toward Mr. Contreras. In a sudden access of fear and fury I rushed at it with the dolly, running the wheels over its fat body with every ounce of strength I owned. It gave a horrible cry. I was demented enough with fright to be pleased at the sound.

The old man sprang up at the noise. "Oh. You killed one of them. I thought it was you, doll. Gave me worse of a scare than when the beast jumped me. I think I found your hole for you."

In a corner behind the boiler he'd located a gap in the brickwork. A chunk of masonry from the foundation had broken off, leaving an opening just big enough for a slender person to slide through. I hadn't noticed it on my earlier foray. Even if the rats had kept me from penetrating this far behind the boiler, I wouldn't have found it in the poor light —if you didn't know about the caverns below you wouldn't search for an entrance to them. Mr. Contreras had found it by feeling along the wall while he waited for me.

I took off my gloves and cleaned his wound. "You should see a doctor for this. Do you think you could catch a cab out on Michigan?"

"I think I could give you another crack over the head for even thinking I'd run out on you, Warshawski, is what I think. You clean it up good. It's bleeding and that's a good sign. We can worry afterward about rabies or bubonic plague or whatever these vermin carry."

I bathed the wound over and over, far more than it needed, until I realized the old man was flinching, that I was scraping the raw flesh against the bone. I put some salve on it. Worrying that the rats might be attracted to the smell of salve, I tried to cover the wound as completely as possible. They wandered around us as I worked on him but didn't try to avenge their fallen comrade's death.

Back on his feet, Mr. Contreras picked up the sledge and rapidly enlarged the opening behind the brickwork. More rats poured out as he worked. My arms were wet inside my coveralls. I began to shiver in the clammy air.

When he'd finished he needed a few minutes to catch his breath. I peered through the hole he'd made. The opening led directly to a set of stairs. I could see the top two or three in the light from my flash.

I picked up the rope, the ladder, the spare flashlight batteries, and a blanket from the dolly. I looped one end of the rope around my waist, then tied the other to my neighbor. As a final preparation I took the Smith & Wesson out from my armpit holster and stuck it in one of my side pockets. It was absurd—I couldn't possibly shoot all the vermin milling around the space—but it made me feel better.

My neighbor nodded to show he had recovered his wind. "Ready, doll? Take it easy going down. You don't know what kind of repair the place is in, or if you'll be landing in water, or what."

"Right. Heigh-ho, heigh-ho, it's off to work we go." Taking my metal tube in one hand for a walking stick, I climbed through the hole in the wall.

□43
Tunnel Vision

Damp had mixed with coal dust to form a black glaze over the stairs. The flashlight glinted on it like moonlight on black ice. We tried looking down the stairwell to see how far we had to go, but could make out nothing beyond the circle of light. We started gingerly down, using our poles for balance.

Beyond the flashlight the darkness was absolute. It was as though a giant hand had squeezed all the light from the air. We seemed to move not through dark air but the essence of darkness itself, a physical presence that squashed and flattened our puny light. We moved quietly, oppressed by the weight of the air, and of the earth above us. Only the twittering of the rats, taunting our slow movements by the speed and ease with which they ran past us, broke the silence.

For a moment I panicked, confusing the lack of light with lack of oxygen. Dizzy, I reached out for the iron bar someone had bolted to the stairwell. It came away in my hand and I landed with a smart thump on my rear end. Mr. Contreras hovered over me anxiously, but my coveralls provided a good padding. I got up again with nothing more than a twinge of pain in my tailbone. The jolt cleared my mind.

The air stank of mold and rat droppings, but it was not stale. I lit a match to prove it to myself. The flame burned bright. To overcome the weight of the atmosphere I started to sing Figaro's jaunty farewell to Cherubino. Mr. Contreras and I were like a couple of butterflies ourselves, floating downward into the bowels of the earth instead of off to battle.

My singing released the spell holding back Mr. Contreras's speech. He began to regale me with his own battle stories. I had heard most of them before, from how he'd stolen Clara away from Mitch Krueger to the piece of shrapnel he'd taken at Anzio, but his vibrant voice, echoing from the walls, filled the shaft with life.

At the bottom of the second flight the light caught on a lump. I stopped to pick it up. It was cloth of some kind, with shreds of a lining hanging from it. The synthetic outer shell still had enough shape to show me what it had been: a child's ski mitten, originally a vivid aqua. I had no idea how fast mold and grime work on fabric, but it looked as though it had lain here for years. I put it back down—it would protect no child's hand at this point. At least it confirmed that we were on the trail, if not of Tamar Hawkings, of some human life.

We continued downward, sobered into silence again by the frail relic. The stairs seemed to stretch endlessly away past the pale rim of light to the center of the earth. I lost my sense of time. I thought we had been moving senselessly downward for an hour, but when I looked at my watch at the third landing I saw we'd spent only seven minutes on the stairs.

At the end of the fourth flight we came to a closed door. Water had spilled around it and was lapping at the bottom step. We sloshed through it to the door. A couple of rats were climbing through a grate at its top. While Mr. Contreras grabbed the handle and pulled I used my pole to try to keep the rats away from him.

He had trouble shifting the door against the water. I finally abandoned my battle with the rats to help. Sticking a hand through the gap at the jamb, I yanked while he pulled. Panting, we managed to heave it open.

On the other side lay the tunnels. We waded past the threshold and stood ankle-deep in water to look around. We had used only one flashlight coming down the stairs so as to conserve our batteries. Now we turned on both to get a better look.

Our flashlights danced on the greasy surface of the water. A few rats were swimming toward us. They moved to the open door and disappeared up the stairs. Trying to ignore them I looked up and down the tunnel. Moving slowly, kicking through the water, I found rails in the middle of the floor. The walls, made of set stones, rose about five feet above our heads to form a vaulted ceiling.

"Now what? You reckon they've gone on to safety someplace?" Mr. Contreras's voice echoed dully against the stone like the clanging of an ancient bell.

"I don't reckon anything. I don't even know if they're down here. That mitten we found shows some kid was here, but how long ago?" I stuck a nervous hand into the fetid water to feel the current; water was rising from the right of the door. "If they got surprised by the water they'd have moved away from it. We don't think they went into the building. Why don't we go up the tunnel a ways? If the water gets to our knees we'll come back."

I wiped my hand over and over on a tissue before putting my work glove back on. Mr. Contreras surveyed me and then the water, then grunted agreement.

"We'd better figure out some way to tell when we're back, in case the place is littered with identical doors," he added.

We didn't have paint or any kind of marking. Finally I tore a strip from the blanket and tied it around the grating of the open door. The rats should be too busy climbing to safety to stop to eat a scrap of cloth.

Using our poles to steady ourselves we waded up the tunnel. Mr. Contreras turned off his flashlight. Every now and then we checked the water level. It wasn't rising fast, but I couldn't suppress a sense of panic. What if we got trapped down here? We could drown and never be discovered.

"You know, cookie, I've had a good life," Mr. Contreras announced, his thoughts apparently running on the same track as mine. "I had a good marriage—Clara was the best, she really was. I'm sorry you never met her—you two would really've hit it off. But I don't think I was ever as happy in my young days as since you moved into our building. What's it been—six years now? The things you get up to—if any of the guys in my local is doing something half this interesting this morning—breaking into a building—looking for a runaway family—I'll eat a pipe wrench, threads and all."

I had to laugh. "You're having a good time and I'm scared out of my wits worrying about drowning."

"Yeah, you get scared—you ain't no robot without feelings—but you don't let fear stop you. That's why I admire you so much. I sure am going to hate it if one or the other of us has to move away from Racine Avenue. Specially if it's me and I end up with Ruthie out in Elk Grove Village."

We came to a bend in the passage. On the other side of it the water was swirling in tiny whirlpools and starting to rise faster around our ankles, reaching midway to our calves. I hesitated, then plunged onward. Mr. Contreras looked at the water, shrugged, and followed.

After fifty feet or so we came to an intersection with another tunnel. Water was pouring from the right-hand shaft into our shaft. That explained the whirlpools—that flow was meeting the tide rising behind us. I had no sense of direction down here, no idea where we were in relation to the breached wall or how water was flowing, so I didn't know if we were walking to or from the main source.

"Can you stay here a minute?" I said. "I want to see what this left-hand fork looks like."

He turned his flashlight on again. "When you're ready to come back, turn off your light. You'll see mine. Just head for it. And holler every thirty seconds or so, so I know you're okay."

I turned in to the left fork, dutifully shouting out every ten paces. After thirty steps the water seemed to be lower. Another fifty and I was standing in sludge. Shining my light ahead I could see dry ground as the tunnel curved away from me.

I tried calling out to the old man to join me, but the bouncing of sound from the walls made me doubt whether he would hear me. I made my way back to him.

The water was halfway up our calves by the time I reached him. "You want to try this? If we don't find anyone in ten minutes we can call it quits."

"Sure, cookie. We've come this far with a whole lot of trouble and nothing to show for it. We might as well go a bit more just to see."

I tied another strip of blanket to a bracket that hung at the intersection. As I looked back I could see a row of similar hooks—perhaps they'd been used to hang lanterns when the tunnel was in regular use. Above the hook I could see faint lettering. I stood on tiptoe to look: Dearborn and Adams, I deciphered. We'd gone two blocks west and one block south in the twenty minutes we'd been down here.

My flashlight was beginning to dim. I switched it off and let Mr. Contreras lead the way with his. The water had moved a bit farther up the left fork, but once we were on dry ground we moved fast. On the other side of the bend a shadowy mass suddenly started moving away from us. I couldn't make it out, but the motion was definitely human.

"Hey, wait up!" I called. "Mrs. Hawkings? Jessie? It's V. I. Warshawski. I've come to help get you away from the water."

The figures continued to scuttle away from us. They weren't moving very fast, but I wasn't going to make much headway in my waders. I wrenched them off and started jogging down the middle of the tunnel between the tracks. Mr. Contreras followed as fast as he could but I was soon beyond the rim of light. I switched on my own flashlight again. It was almost dead, but in its feeble glow I could avoid tripping on the tracks.

In another minute I had caught up with the scrambling group. I grabbed the nearest figure, a small child. He struggled briefly, then stood still and began to wail softly. The rest of them stopped. There were more than four, but how many I couldn't tell in the light of my failing flashlight. Above the smell of mold and coal and rats the stench of urine and fear rose to smite me. I swallowed a gag.

"Let him go. You have no business holding him."

One of the larger figures tried to pry my hand from his arm but her fingers were weak and she couldn't free the child. His own arm underneath my hand felt frail. Mr. Contreras arrived, panting a little.

"These them, doll?"

In the stronger light of his flashlight I made out Tamar Hawkings, backing soundlessly up the tunnel with her children clustered around her. The woman who'd been trying to pry my fingers loose stayed near me. She was carrying a toddler who started to wail in a thin, helpless thread of a voice.

"It's okay, Natie, it's okay. Don't cry; I'll take care of you."

"Emily?" Her name exploded on my lips so loudly that she backed away from me. I stared at her astounded. If she hadn't started to talk I would not have known her. Her frizzy hair was matted to her head, her face pinched and gray with hunger and filth. Her blue jeans and shirt hung on her shrunken body.

She backed away from me. I put a hand on her arm.

"I need to get you and your brothers to safety. You must come with me. Do you understand?"

Too much white was showing in her eyes. She looked feverish, her breath fast and rasping. I wasn't sure she could follow anything I said. I turned to Mr. Contreras.

"These are the Messenger children. Can you hold Joshua while I get Mrs. Hawkings?"

He picked the older boy up like a negligible load and

cradled him against his chest. As I trotted farther up the tunnel Mr. Contreras began crooning to the child in the soothing tone you usually hear only from women.

When I reached Tamar Hawkings I didn't try to argue with her—I scooped up the youngest of her children and headed back toward Mr. Contreras. Hawkings followed, clawing at me and whispering invectives. Her two older children staggered after her. When I had the group reassembled I spoke briefly.

"The Chicago River is pouring in here. The wall between the river and the tunnels broke last night. If you don't get out now you may all drown. You certainly will starve: it will soon become impossible to get aboveground to find food. You must come with me. We're going to have to go back through the water. We'll be able to get into the Pulteney and then we'll get you medical care. You must come with me. If you don't, you will all die."

Emily tugged wildly on my arm. "We can't go back. We can't go back! Tamar, don't let them take me back!"

"You don't have to go back to Fabian, Emily. But you must come with me now."

Mr. Contreras held both Joshua and the older Hawkings girl while I struggled back into my waders. I fished the spare batteries for my flashlight out of a side pocket and changed them. With Mr. Contreras in the lead bearing Joshua, we turned back down the fork in the tunnel and headed for the water. I continued to carry the younger Hawkings girl, holding the boy by the hand. All the children except Emily were whimpering and Jessie's asthma began racking her slight body.

By the time we got to the intersection with our tunnel, water was swirling above Emily's knees. Mrs. Hawkings, even smaller than Emily, was swaying against the current. None of them had waders to protect them, and all of them were too weak to hike back through the flood.

"We're going to have to do this in relays," I said to Mr. Contreras. "Can you carry Joshua and leave him on the stairs? I'll stay here with these folks. If you can make two trips alone we can manage the rest of the children between us in a final run.''

His face grim in the half-light he nodded agreement. ''Okay, son, you and me is going for a quick ride. No need for you to cry—we'll have your sister to you in no time flat. You just leave it to your uncle Sal: I'll get you out of here shipshape, you'll see.''

His voice, uttering these soothing words, mingled with Joshua's faint cries for Emily. The two sounds echoed and reechoed down the tunnel after his flashlight had disappeared around the bend. Next to me Emily was trembling, tears cutting ribbons through the muck on her face. Nathan clung to her, wailing in a soft monotone.

The two older Hawkings children were in water now up to their waists. I tucked the toddler into the bib of my overall—she was so small from malnutrition that she fit inside without difficulty—and picked up the boy. He clung to my neck like a small monkey, his arms trembling with fatigue.

Jessie was gasping so violently for air I was afraid she would suffocate. There was nothing I could do for her; I was so breathless from exertion myself I could scarcely summon the strength to speak.

I took my piece of rope and looped it around Tamar Hawkings's waist, planning to attach her to Emily. It was a battle: they were resisting me, fighting to return to the dry ground we'd left behind.

Tamar suddenly slipped in my grasp and fell into the water. I yanked her to her feet, pounding water from her, struggling to maintain my hold on her children.

''Damn you,'' I panted. ''You're going to drown your children as well as yourself. Stop fighting with me.''

She stood sullenly, coughing the sooty water from her throat, and let me tie the end of the rope around her. When Emily saw Tamar had stopped struggling, she let me tie the rope around her waist as well. I held the end, leaning against the wall to catch my breath and to spread some of the load the two children were putting on my body. The blow on the back of my head was beginning to throb. My cracked rib pushed against my lungs with exquisite agony.

While I leaned there, panting, Mr. Contreras finally returned. He was staggering a little in the water, holding on to the wall for support.

"We'd better try to get everyone out now," I said. "The water's rising faster and I don't think you have the stamina for two more trips."

He nodded, gulping down mouthfuls of fetid air. "It's . . . up . . . to the fourth stair . . . on that bottom flight now. I took . . . the little boy . . . up to the landing. He'll be okay there. The rats ain't coming so fast—I only saw two—and I gave the kid a stick just in case."

We waited while he caught his breath. I tied one end of the rope to him and the other to myself. After a minute he scooped up Jessie, whose whoops had subsided to a shallow wheezing. Her eyes were rolling sightlessly.

I fished the toddler out of my overalls and handed her to her mother—I couldn't walk and carry two children. Our little train started in motion down the middle of the tracks, Mr. Contreras in the lead, followed by Tamar, then Emily holding Nathan, with me bringing up the rear.

It was a slow, difficult journey. Emily had only been underground a week but was already weakened from malnutrition. Mrs. Hawkings, who'd been living down here for months, was so feeble she had to struggle hard to make headway against the water. She fell more than once. The third time she went down she dragged Emily with her. Hampered by the children we were carrying, Mr. Contreras and I had a hard time righting them. I was scared that we would lose Jessie and both toddlers.

The water was almost level now with the tops of my waders. If it rose any more I'd have to take them off so as not to get bogged down by its weight inside the boots.

"Stop a minute," I gasped to Mr. Contreras. "I want to tie the rope to one of these brackets and haul Mrs. Hawkings along."

As soon as he understood what I intended he took her

son from my arms. I untied everyone from the rope. He held one end while I sloshed down the tunnel as far as the rope would stretch. Standing on tiptoe I tied it to the bracket and pulled hard. It held. Mr. Contreras rapidly tied Emily to the rope and I started reeling her in, hand over hand. It was relatively easy work: as soon as I started pulling she lost her footing, which meant the water was working for me.

Ordering her to stay put, I sloshed back to the old man with the end of the rope. We tied up Tamar and I slogged my way back to Emily and the bracket and hauled in Tamar. Mr. Contreras followed behind her.

We had to repeat the operation three times. By the end I'd given up the fight with my waders, yanking them off so that I could swim between the bracket and the fugitives. By the time we got to the Pulteney stairwell Tamar seemed barely conscious. I myself was in a state beyond exhaustion, where my throbbing head and sore arms seemed as remote from me as the surface of the earth itself. Mr. Contreras's deep, rasping breaths came from some distant spot, reminding me of life, of the need to keep moving. Only Emily seemed to have some reserve of energy: when we got to the stairwell she gave a little cry of ''Josh'' and stumbled up the stairs to hug her brother.

I don't remember how we climbed the four flights up to the Pulteney basement—some combination of carrying children, shoving children, hoisting children, bullying Tamar and Emily—a routine that began to seem like the regimen of a lifetime. I had forgotten sun and air—they were just dreams handed down from ancient literature. It wasn't the desire for light that impelled us upward, but the stultifying routine of motion. So numb had I become that when the feeble glimmer of my flashlight showed us the hole behind the Pulteney's boiler I stared at it a long, stupid moment, trying to understand what it was.

Once inside the basement I sent Mr. Contreras to the surface for help. I moved our little band past the boiler to the crates where I'd kept my electrical tools. With my last bit of energy I pulled some of the crates into a semicircle and leaned against one of them. I cradled the two youngest children against my breast. Joshua, clinging to Emily, lay against my left side. Near me I could hear Jessie's labored breathing. The rats were swarming around us but I was too exhausted to try to keep them at bay. I was asleep when Mr. Contreras returned with a cop.

□44

For Mules, There Are No Rules

Jessie didn't make it through the night. The pediatric staff at Northwestern, where we'd all been sent, worked heroically, but malnutrition and damp had done too much damage to her lungs. Lotty brought me the news when she stopped to see me before going off to make her own rounds at Beth Israel.

Despite my incoherent protests the hospital had kept me overnight for observation. When they called Lotty—whom I listed as my physician on the emergency-room form—she infuriated me by telling them about my recent head injury and reinforcing their decision.

"In fact, give her a complete neurological workup while you're at it," she had told them.

"What about your belief that patients should take an active role in deciding on their care?" I had demanded when I forced the attendant to give me the phone.

"That doesn't apply to mules, my dear, only to those with enough sense not to climb Mt. Everest with a broken leg."

I knew as soon as she hung up that she was right. I was too exhausted to move, let alone cope with protecting myself from anyone who might be gunning for me. I pulled myself together long enough to leave another message for

Conrad, telling the precinct dispatcher to make sure he
knew I was at Northwestern's hospital, before letting the
staff load me onto a gurney.

I came to periodically as people bathed me and took
blood from me, but for most of the evening I lay in a sleep
so deep that neither the intermittent pages nor the hospital
routine of blood pressure and temperature taking could
rouse me. Conrad came by around seven in the evening—I
found a note from him attached to a bunch of daisies when
I woke up—but I hadn't stirred.

I finally emerged from my stupor around four in the
morning. After some initial confusion about where I was
the events of the last few weeks flooded my brain. I
thrashed uselessly in the bed, worrying about Mr. Contreras
and the children, Deirdre's death, the immigrant workers,
wondering what to do next, until Lotty arrived a little after
six.

"So you were right." I turned away from her when she
told me about Jessie. "I should never have left the Hawkingses in the basement that first night I found them. If I'd
called Conrad as you urged me the girl might still be
alive."

Lotty sat down next to me on the bed, her dark eyes large
in her vivid face. "You can't know that, Vic. I spoke that
evening in the heat of the moment, and I shouldn't have—
after all, we didn't do such a good job hanging on to them
when you got them to the hospital the next night. Also, I
gathered from Conrad that the passage between the tunnels
and the basement was almost impossible to find if you
weren't looking for it."

When he couldn't wake me Conrad had called Lotty to
make sure I was all right—since we weren't married, the
hospital refused to give him any information. He told Lotty
that he and Finchley had stopped by the Pulteney to figure
out why Finchley's search team had missed the entrance to
the tunnels when they went hunting Tamar the morning
after Deirdre died. When they found the space behind the

boiler they were amazed that Mr. Contreras and I had been able to discover it at all.

"We lost one child, Vic," Lotty went on, "but six other people are alive who would be dead now if not for you and your cowboy neighbor. Who seems in fighting fettle this morning, by the way. They want to start a course of rabies shots because of the rat bites, so they're checking his heart to make sure he's got the stamina to tolerate the series. I told them it would take a large truck to stop him."

I nodded. "I wouldn't have survived yesterday without him. How's Tamar Hawkings doing?"

Lotty knit her brows. "She's being given IV fluids—all of them are. But there's some concern about her mental state. And that of the girl, Emily Messenger. Mr. Messenger came by yesterday afternoon as soon as he knew the children had been found. Emily apparently screamed and made them take him away. Now no one can get a straight story out of her. They want a psych resident to talk to her, but first she has to recover her physical strength—her emotional trauma can easily be at least partly from delirium. The little boys, her brothers, will recover soon, at least physically, and the staff are hopeful about the other two Hawkings children."

Leon Hawkings had been around to demand custody of the children, she added. He had alternated between threatening the hospital with legal action over Jessie's death, demanding that his wife be returned to him, and threatening her with jail for endangering the children's lives. Lotty had called Marilyn Lieberman at Arcadia House. She was sending Eva Kuhn over to see if there was anything that could be done to help Tamar.

"The city is also squawking about child neglect, so she's got a lot to cope with when she's strong enough physically to face all these people," Lotty added.

"The police haven't arrested Emily yet?" I asked.

Lotty gave a sardonic smile. "For Deirdre's death? Given Fabian's standing they're moving very gingerly. Also, one of your police friends is proving an unexpected ally—the red-haired woman who questioned you in ER on Saturday . . . yes, Officer Neely, that was her name. . . . Vic, I've asked them to give you an NMR scan and check your brain function before they let you out of here.''

''On the grounds that anyone who went into those tunnels must be out of her mind?''

Lotty got up from the bed. ''On the grounds you've sustained your third serious head injury in the past seven years and I want to make sure that thick Polish skull of yours is holding up under the bludgeoning.''

I sat up, flushing with anger. ''I can't afford that kind of exam. I don't have insurance, you know. And I've debts reaching from here to Skokie. They did a CAT scan at Beth Israel on Saturday. Besides, I need to get moving. There's too much unsettled business around me, and finding Emily makes matters more urgent, not less.''

She put her fingers around my wrist, part caress, part checking my pulse. ''Our equipment and our technicians at Beth Israel aren't as good as the facility here. The radiologist told me yesterday that your CAT scan was not of good enough quality for him to rule out a subtle subdural insult. I'll work something out with Northwestern about the billing. You can't afford to be careless with head injuries.''

When she left I got out of bed, determined to put on my clothes and leave. I couldn't hang around a hospital waiting on the medical establishment's pleasure just to have thousands of dollars' worth of useless tests done.

My muscles refused to respond with the immediate suppleness I demanded of them. I moved stiffly to the clothes cupboard. Someone had put my things in a plastic bag labeled WARSHAWSKI—402-B. I opened the bag and recoiled—the smell was appalling. Oily water left in a sealed bag overnight should be bottled to use as a self-defense spray. It would take more stomach than I had right now to step into those things.

When I shut the bag I realized some of the smell was clinging to me: they'd given me a sponge bath yesterday, but my hair remained matted with sweat and dried bilge.

The room had a private shower. I stood under it for a glorious half hour, feeling the heat soak into my sore muscles while the muck flowed away from my head.

A clean gown and hospital robe were hanging in the bathroom. I put them on and went back to the bed to call Conrad.

"I know Lotty said you were okay, but you had me worried there, girl. I don't like it when you're sleeping too deep for a rub on the shoulder to get you even to twitch."

"When I was seven a fortune-teller on Maxwell Street assured me I had nine lives. I figure I've still got five or six left to me."

"Way you've been running through 'em lately I'm worried you're on borrowed time now. Can I come by to see you?"

"Please." I asked him to stop at my apartment for some clean clothes. "If you can find any in the mess my attackers created on Saturday. I need everything—shoes, socks—my Nikes are going to have to be fumigated before I can put them on my feet again."

Conrad agreed, but said he wouldn't arrive before noon. Lotty had already been on to him, getting him to promise he wouldn't help spring me before I'd had my brain scan.

"And anyway, Ms. W., it's time you gave that ravaged body of yours a break. Spend the day with a book. Take the dogs over to the lake and hang out. You've earned it. Hell, you need it."

I temporized, torn between pleasure at his concern and annoyance at his conniving at hog-tying me. Fasting had cured my headache; underneath my worries and sore muscles I felt a surge of euphoria. For the first time in three days I felt clearheaded enough to think. If I couldn't leave here until noon, at least I could get my body loose enough to move easily when the time came.

As I stretched I watched the early morning news. City engineers had been unsuccessful in blocking the hole between the river and the tunnels; water continued to pour in.

I shuddered as I pulled my neck gently to one side: Mr. Contreras and I had been exceedingly lucky.

The Board of Trade was still closed—an unprecedented event. Marshall Field was looking at tens, possibly hundreds of millions in damage. Rain was forecast, which would further hamper crews pumping out flooded basements. The Loop el lines were shut because of flooding at Dearborn Street—people were being bused from remote sites.

"And at Northwestern Hospital doctors were unable to save one of the children heroically rescued by Chicago private detective V. I. Warshawski and her neighbor yesterday." I watched Beth Blacksin talking to a fatigued pediatrician in front of the very building I was standing in. "Ms. Warshawski, who recently sustained a head injury, is being held for observation. Our reporters were not allowed to talk to her."

I switched off the set at the commercial break. Pressing my lips together, I tried to concentrate on my exercises instead of my guilt over failing Jessie Hawkings.

The solemn-eyed train of interns and residents arrived as I was in the middle of a sequence of leg raises. I had spent five minutes stretching my sore hamstrings by resting one leg on the bed and using the hand controls to raise it. Now I was lying on the floor using a piece of IV-tubing to pull my legs up higher. The doctors thought at first I'd collapsed from my head injuries and raced over to me in great agitation. When I explained what I was doing the neurology resident escorted me back to bed.

"That can wait until Dr. Herschel says you're fit enough to work out again. I want to test your reflexes."

Breakfast arrived while he was sticking safety pins into my feet. It was an eclectic collection, ranging from a box of cereal to a sweet roll, with something approximating scrambled eggs in between. On an ordinary day I wouldn't have wanted any of it, but I couldn't keep my eyes from it while the exam progressed—both yesterday and Sunday I had put in strenuous days on short rations.

The neurology resident told me the NMR scan was scheduled for ten-thirty; someone would be along with a wheelchair to take me to the facility. When I protested that I could walk there on my own steam he smiled gently.

"I'm sure you can, Ms. Warshawski. But while you're a guest here I'm asking you to do us a favor and follow our house rules. It's just a precaution—probably unnecessary—but we have had people who thought they were fine collapse from blood clots. So why don't you rest. Someone will be around with a newspaper. Before you know it you'll be out of here."

I tried to smile acquiescently, but I haven't had much practice—I don't know how convincing I made it. As soon as they left I dove at the food tray and devoured everything, including the sweet roll, which was quite stale. When I'd finished I strolled down the hall to find Mr. Contreras. Someone at the nursing station waiting for her shift to end was happy to look up his room number for me. She got me Emily Messenger's as well.

My neighbor's pleasure at seeing me was tempered by embarrassment at his skimpy hospital gown. In the years we'd known each other the old man wouldn't even open his door to me if he'd stripped down to an undershirt and trousers.

His usual good spirits had been dampened by a phone call from his daughter. Roused to righteous action by last night's news reports on our heroic rescue work she was coming at noon with a set of clothes and a van to haul him and the dogs back to Elk Grove Village.

"My only hope is that Mitch will bite her when she tries opening the door to the apartment," he said gloomily. "Although then she'd have him put to sleep."

"Don't go. No reason you have to."

"She'll have the dogs," he explained. "I made the mistake of saying I couldn't go with her on their account. You'll come pick us up, won't you, cookie? Although, if I can't come up with that tax money I may end up staying out there."

"First thing Thursday," I promised rashly, having no idea what tomorrow might bring. I wrote down his daughter's address and gave him a consoling hug. "And we'll think of something about the taxes."

I wish I felt as optimistic as I made myself sound. If I had to sell my little apartment, where could I afford to live next? I tried not to think about it as I wandered the halls looking for Emily's room—I had enough on my mind right now without adding tax woes to the general brew.

I finally discovered that Emily had been put in the children's wing, perhaps the first time in years anyone had thought of her as a child. I had to cross the street to get to the building. I looked down at my paper hospital slippers and flimsy gown.

"Who wills the end wills the means," I muttered, striding outside.

Under the sullen sky I joined the throng of hospital workers moving among the buildings of Northwestern's vast complex. As I crossed the street I saw the NMR building. I could get there so easily on my own, assuming I wanted to go. I ground my teeth and entered the pediatric wing.

When I got to Emily's room I came upon an altercation. A tall, bearded man was arguing with a nurse outside her door. He broke off at the sight of me.

"Warshawski! What a break. Explain to this woman why I need to talk to Emily Messenger."

"Not a chance, Ryerson. The only thing that surprises me is that I wasn't expecting to find you here."

□45
The Mouse Between Two Cats

"You can help me, Warshawski," Murray said. "The kid's the key to the whole Messenger murder, but they won't let me see her."

"You've got a hell of a nerve," I said, my tone light but my eyes murderous. "You told Conrad on Sunday that I talked to you when I hadn't. You think now I'm going to help you torment a child who's coming off a stint in hell? No way. And if"—I squinted at the nurse's badge—"if Ms. Higgins feels squeamish about getting hospital security to boot you, I'll call the city. Conrad would love an excuse to run you in for a few hours."

Murray put an arm around me. "You turn me on when you threaten me with hobnailed boots, Vic. If you're going in to see the kid I'll just sit and listen."

I twisted away from his grip. "She's not 'the kid.' She's a person, and one who needs help, not interrogation."

"That's what I've been trying to tell him," the nurse said. "Dr. Morrison said no reporters, no distress."

"Murray, when women say 'no,' they mean 'no.' Stop bugging a hard-working nurse and get out of her hair."

"Then how about an exclusive with you, Warshawski? After all, you went and pulled the female person and her brothers out of the tunnel. Come with me for a cup of coffee and tell me all about it. I'd love a shot of you in that robe: that V neck recalls some fine evenings."

"Great." I started for the elevator. "Come on, big guy."

Murray gulped—he hadn't expected me to call his bluff. He followed me perforce, asking me questions all the way down the hall. When the elevator came we climbed on together, followed by a lab tech wheeling a loaded cart. I waited until the doors were starting to close, then wriggled out past the cart. His protesting yelp followed me as the doors shut.

Ellen Higgins, emerging from a patient's room, stopped to thank me when I came back up the hall. "We've had reporters around here all night. Why, one man tried going into her room at three this morning. And when the night ward head, Lila Dantry, stopped him he had the nerve to pretend he was a friend of Mr. Messenger's come to help out his daughter."

"At three in the morning?" I felt a chill in my stomach. I couldn't imagine a reporter doing that, but one of Fabian's friends might, if Fabian sent him to harass Emily on his behalf.

"They should post a guard," I said.

"That's the family's decision," Higgins told me. "But I think we can protect her from journalists—they usually cooperate with hospital personnel."

I didn't like the idea of strange men dropping in on Emily. A hospital is too easy a place to get in and out of. I thought I might call the Streeter brothers, some friends of mine with a bodyguard service, when I got back to my room.

When the nurse realized I was the person who had helped rescue the children yesterday, she took me over to see Joshua and Nathan—Sam and Miriam, the two Hawkings children, were still in intensive care. The two Messengers still had IV's in their arms for fluids, but normal color had returned to their faces. Joshua was studiously playing with some kind of handheld game, ignoring me, Ellen Higgins, and the nurse adjusting his IV, but Nathan was restless. The ward nurse said he was crying for his sister.

Back in the hall Higgins debated letting me visit Emily. "She's so withdrawn, we were worried initially that she might have sustained some brain damage, but the EEG looks normal."

I nodded. "She retreats behind a mask that looks almost retarded when she feels threatened. Have the cops been to see her?"

"They told me a very nice woman officer tried talking to Emily about her mother's death, but she became so agitated, we had to ask the officer to leave. What do the police think she knows about her mother?"

I shook my head. "They don't confide in me. They may think she knows something about the murder weapon."

"Oh." Higgins eyes grew round. "We had a psychiatric resident in because we wanted to make sure she hadn't been too traumatized by her time in the tunnel. When he asked her her name she said she didn't have one, that she was a mouse between two cats. She wouldn't say anything else. He thinks maybe she's had a psychotic breakdown."

"She could just be too angry to want to talk to any more adults at this point," I suggested. "When she ran away from home last week she was on her way to see me. She may trust me more than a strange man."

Higgins compromised by trying to page Dr. Morrison to ask her permission. When the pediatrician hadn't answered after five minutes, Higgins decided to let me into the room. Although most of the children were in rooms with four or even six beds, Emily had been put by herself, Higgins explained, after her hysterical outcry against Fabian. Dr. Morrison, the pediatrician, had worried about the effect on other sick children if Emily had further outbursts.

When I came into the room Emily was lying with her eyes closed, but the tension in her neck and arms made me believe she was awake. Seven days underneath Chicago had leached the roundness from her arms and face. An IV was stuck into one thin wrist. Her frizzy hair lay bunched on the pillow like a badly wrung dish mop.

I pulled up a chair next to the bed. "It's Vic Warshawski, Emily. You were looking for me the day you ran away from home, but your dad wouldn't let the school call me. I'm sorry. Sorry you couldn't find me, and sorry you've had such a terrible time of it."

The muscles in her jaw moved, but she gave no other sign of having heard me.

"I hear you told the psychiatrist you didn't have a name, that you were the mouse between two cats. That kind of statement gets doctors all excited—they start imagining the papers they can write about you in medical journals. Maybe you should go back to being Emily while you're here so they don't exploit you."

At that she gave a snort that was half giggle, half sob. She didn't open her eyes to look at me, but spoke in a tight, defiant voice.

"I'm *not* Emily. I *am* a mouse between two cats."

I licked my lips as I tried to think of how to talk to her. "I read your poem about the mouse. You write in a very powerful way—it's a gift that you should nurture. But the poem also sounds as though you were tormented by your parents. When did you write it? After the dinner party your dad gave for Manfred Yeo? He treated you in a very mean way that night. You know I thought so at the time."

I waited a long few minutes to see if she would speak further, but she remained silent, her body taut, the tendons standing out on her neck and arms like strings that would snap if pulled any further. I felt the back of my own neck tense up in response. The tension reminded me to keep my voice calm. I shut my eyes, trying to conjure up the events that ultimately drove Emily underground.

"You wrote the poem after the dinner party. After I saw you, while Fabian and Deirdre were in their bedroom fighting. It must have seemed as though they were fighting over you, you poor little mouse."

She shuddered along the length of her body but still

didn't speak. I could feel the intensity with which she was listening. If I could work out what happened, work it out right, she might trust me enough to speak to me.

When I looked back at the house as I drove away that night I'd seen a light turn on in a side room. I'd thought at the time that Emily might have gotten up to do something. The party had been on Wednesday. It was Friday when Deirdre died, but something about her murder had made Emily want to bring the poem to Alice Cottingham, to use it as a cry for help. I pinched my nose, as if that would help focus my imagination.

"Your mother left a note saying that she was going out, and that you were to fix leftover salmon since the housekeeper had the night off." That much was true, or at least that much Fabian had said—the police had never actually seen Deirdre's note.

"She said in the note that she was going to my office. Your father blew up at the idea of her going off without getting his permission and tore up the note."

That part I was making up, but it had to be true, at least the business about Deirdre informing them where she was heading. I didn't know what had become of the note, but Fabian or Emily or both of them had to have gone down to the Pulteney: how else had the bat reappeared in the Messenger house? I couldn't ask Emily—she wouldn't answer a direct question right now.

She started to shiver. One chance to get things right—it was like crossing the Grand Canyon on a tightrope. Heads, Emily went down to the Pulteney alone. Tails, Fabian went down to the Pulteney, killed Deirdre, and planted the bat in his daughter's room. Surely not even Fabian was that demented. I took a deep breath.

"You wanted your mother. Even though she was one of the cats who tormented you, she was also the only person who might protect you from your father. So you went downtown to find her. And she was dead. When you saw the baseball bat you recognized it—it was your dad's signed Nellie Fox that stood in your front hallway. You were afraid he had killed your mother. You wanted to protect him, so you took the bat home and hid it in your bedroom.''

Her chest heaved with dry sobs, and then suddenly, on a gulped whisper I could barely hear, she said, ''I saw him.''

I longed to put a hand on her but didn't know what that would mean to her in her present state, so I knelt down with my head near hers. ''Whom did you see?''

''My—my . . . Fabian. He was there in—in your office.'' She was gasping with the effort not to cry. ''I thought he was home in bed. I didn't know—know how he beat me downtown. I thought . . . I could . . . escape from him. Now I never will.''

''Emily, when you took Joshua and Nathan last Monday you came down to my office building again looking for me. You knew I would help you out then. And you were right. I would, and I will. If you need to escape from your father I can help make that happen for you.'' I hoped my voice sounded authoritative. ''But if we're going to get you away from him, I need you to tell me as clearly as you can what you remember from that night.''

I looked up to see Ellen Higgins and two other people in medical coats—a woman my age and a younger man— standing in the doorway. They were anxiously watching the drama at the bed and looked ready to spring into the room. I had no idea how long they'd been standing there. I shook my head slightly, hoping they would stay away, and turned back to Emily.

She was gasping for air and heaving so badly that her back was arching with the strain. I fumbled on the table for water and a straw.

''Drink this,'' I said brusquely.

She took the cup from me, but her hands were shaking so badly she spilled it on herself. She cried out in rage—with herself, or me, or the cup itself—and threw it across the room. At that she began to cry in earnest.

The medical trio surged into the room.

"I think you'd better leave now," the strange woman said. "She needs to calm down."

I stayed in the room, hoping Emily would feel I was keeping myself in connection with her. I thought Emily's hurling of the cup was an expression of the helplessness she felt, compounded by spilling water on herself, and that it would be a mistake to treat her like a baby now. It would only make her feel more helpless. She was sobbing now into her hands.

I spoke to her directly, in a slow, loud voice. "Emily, you have to make a choice right now. There are four people in this room who want you to be well and happy. Do you want to go on talking to me now about the night your mother died? Or do you want me to leave so that you can get some more rest? Whatever you decide to do, all four of us will respect your decision. No one will be angry or feel that you did something we didn't want you to do. But you must tell us what you want."

The medical trio, who'd been advancing on me, stopped in the middle of my speech. They could hardly throw me out under the circumstances. Only Ellen Higgins went directly to Emily's side, where she started wiping her face with tissues and pouring her a fresh cup of water. Ignoring the rest of us she put an arm around Emily and coaxed her to drink. Gradually Emily's sobs subsided to a faint hiccup.

"Do you want to try to sleep now, honey?" Higgins asked.

Emily hugged her knees, rocking slightly. Finally she whispered, "I want to talk to Vic."

"Are you sure that's what you want to do?" the strange woman asked. "You know you don't have to talk to anyone."

"I'm not as stupid as that," Emily screeched, starting to cry again. "You don't have to keep repeating it."

The man and woman gave me a strange glance, compounded of resentment and admiration, but they left the room. Ellen Higgins stayed on the bed holding Emily. I moved back to my chair.

"That Dr. Morrison?" I asked.

Higgins nodded. "With Michael Golding, the psych resident . . . You want me to leave, too, honey?"

Emily shook her head and leaned against her. In a tiny voice, with a lot of pauses, she told us what happened the night Deirdre died.

▫46

A Night to Remember

Deirdre often went to meetings at Home Free or Arcadia House, but every Sunday she pinned a weekly schedule to the kitchen bulletin board so Fabian would know which nights she planned to be away. And she was careful not to be gone on Mrs. Sliwa's nights off. Although Fabian often had evening meetings himself, he expected Deirdre or the housekeeper to take care of dinner on the nights he was home. Before the Friday of Deirdre's murder Emily couldn't remember another time when her mother had made an unscheduled departure like that.

"It got Daddy angry. He likes everything to be planned in advance," she said in a soft, hiccupy voice.

"How did he show you he was angry?"

"He yelled a lot and got us all scared. Joshua hid in his room and wouldn't come down to dinner and then he said that since Daddy was always telling us to be self-controlled he should learn to control himself. Daddy said I wasn't managing him properly, that if Josh talked back I should make him mind. Then—then Joshua came down and we had dinner and I put him and Natie to bed. That part was okay. I usually read them their stories even if Mrs. Sliwa gives them their baths. Then I went to my room to do my homework."

Here she started to cry again, silently, without moving, as though tears were air covering her with a glossy sheen. Finally I prodded her gently.

"When did you decide to go down to my office? When you finished your homework?"

She shook her head. "I got into bed and—and Daddy came into my room. He often does. To talk, you know. He likes to talk to me in the dark."

"Does he like to touch you too?" Ellen Higgins asked quietly.

"No. Just to talk." Lying against Ellen Higgins's arms she stared ahead, looking at neither of us. "He says I'm the only one who understands him, that we need to be patient with Mom because—because of her drinking, and that I help him be patient with her."

She broke off, remembering that Deirdre was dead now. "I mean, that we needed to be patient."

"Is that all he talks to you about?" I asked after another long silence.

"Oh, he tells me about what's going on at work, the people who are frustrating him on the job, how good people always suffer and their work goes unrewarded." She was speaking in a monotone, quickly but so softly that I had to strain to hear her. "I know he needs my help but it's kind of hard, too, hard to . . . I don't know, it's just hard. I try not to go to bed until . . . you know, he and Mom, but that night she wasn't home, it got later and later, I couldn't stay up. And he came in. He was still mad, he couldn't stop talking about how awful . . . Vic was."

She looked at me for the first time, a timid glance to see if I might react violently to this criticism. I smiled in reassurance and she looked away again.

"What he thought—what he said—first you tried to corrupt me, and now Mom. How it was all Vic's fault Josh was talking back to him, Mom was traipsing off to her—Vic's —office. How none of us cared about his career, that he was slaving away to make a good life for us and all we wanted to do was humiliate him. And then he—he got really angry and started . . . at first I didn't know what he was doing . . . you know . . . he—he—''

She started to retch. I fumbled on the bedstand and found a tray. Ellen Higgins tucked it under Emily's chin and helped her cough up bile. I went into the bathroom for a wet washcloth, which I handed to the nurse. My bones were aching with Emily's torment. Ellen Higgins had tears glinting at the corners of her eyes as she gently cleaned Emily's face.

"You don't have to explain," I said. "But you decided you needed Deirdre. Your mother."

She nodded and gulped. "He—he told me what a bad girl I was and left my room. I got dressed and snuck out the back door and caught the bus downtown. I don't know what time it was, probably midnight or something. It was horrible downtown. No one was on the street except one drunk man who tried to touch me. I ran away and found your office building. I—I looked it up on a map after you gave me your card. And I went upstairs to your office. I saw Tamar in the hall, only then I didn't know that was her name. Only later she told me, when she helped me get into the tunnel. She said don't go in there; and I said it's my mother, I need to see her, so I opened the door. The light was on and I could see Mom lying on the desk.''

She gave a hysterical little giggle. "At first I thought it was just Mom drunk again and I got really mad. I started to shake her and yell at her, something like, 'Wake up. Can't you do anything for me, ever?' Only then I saw—it was her head split open. I still didn't get it; I thought she'd passed out and hurt her head. And then suddenly the door opened. It was Tamar hissing at me to get out, to hide, someone was coming. By then I could see Mom was dead, her brains—'' She had to stop again for a minute.

"I was too stupid to move. All I could do was stare at Tamar and then she disappeared and I heard footsteps, men's footsteps, so I crawled under the desk. And I saw him come over to the desk. I thought, he'll find me here, now he'll really beat me up. I thought he'd come looking for me.''

"You thought it was your dad," I prompted. "Are you sure? Did you see his face?''

"I couldn't. I was under the desk.''

"His shoes? Did you recognize his shoes?'' I persisted. She fell silent. "I don't know. I guess—who else could it be? What other man would be so mad that he'd hurt Mom like she was hurt?''

"What did he do? Could you tell?''

"I was scared if I moved he'd hear me. I held my breath and heard this clicking noise. First I didn't understand. Then I thought he was doing something to the computer, it was that kind of sound. And then he left. I waited. I thought Tamar would come and maybe help me; like I said, I didn't know it was her, but you know, the woman who warned me, maybe she would help me, but no one came. So finally I crawled out. I was so scared. The building made so many noises and then when I got outside I thought I saw him standing on the corner. I ran. All the way home from downtown, running and walking, and being so scared of him finding me outside I wasn't even scared to be alone on the lakefront.''

"Was your dad home when you got there?''

"I didn't want to find out," she whispered. "Then he'd know for sure I'd seen—seen him and—everything. I pushed my desk in front of my door to—to barricade it and got into bed and just lay there until it got light and I heard Nathan trying to come and find me.

"And all day long Daddy acted like nothing weird had happened, like it was life as usual, yelling at me to get Joshua to drink his milk and not spoil him, where was Mom, like he never hurt her or—or anything. I didn't say anything. He's like that. He gets mad, he hits Mom or—or does something, then he acts like it never happened.''

I wanted to let her rest, let her move away from her misery, but I had to ask one more question, about the bat. Where had she found it?

"When I got off the floor from under the desk." She was still whispering. "Suddenly I saw it lying there, covered with—with—you know. That's why I knew for sure Daddy had been there. I took it home with me and hid it behind my radiator. I was thinking—I don't know what I was thinking. If he came in in the night again I would yell at him that I'd tell the police about the bat and how he killed her."

She started giggling again, not with mirth but with agony. "Of course I didn't. He just came on in when he felt like it and I just lay there like—like a mouse."

Higgins rocked Emily against her chest, crooning softly to her. I squeezed my eyes tightly to keep the tears inside. I didn't want my voice to shake when I spoke.

"You were very brave, Emily. You tried to get help, you tried to look after your brothers. We're going to let you get some rest now, but I'm not going to abandon you. When you're strong enough to leave the hospital we'll find some safe place for you to go."

"See if Dr. Morrison is on the floor," Ellen Higgins said to me. "It would be a good thing if we got her a sedative and let her sleep this off for a while."

When I stood up my muscles had frozen again. I moved to the door with a slow shuffle, as if the water from the tunnels had poured into my feet, weighting them down too much to lift. I found Dr. Morrison and Dr. Golding in the hallway outside the door. They'd clearly been listening in, but I don't know how much of Emily's whispered words they might have heard. Dr. Morrison gave me a quizzical look, started to speak, then moved quickly into Emily's room.

By the time I found my own bed again I was shaking so badly I thought I might fall before I reached it. When the attendant came half an hour later with the wheelchair I couldn't imagine what she wanted me to do. I looked at her blankly while she kept telling me they were going to wheel me over to the other building to take a picture of my brain.

She must have decided I had some kind of brain damage —she went off to get a nurse to help her lift me into the wheelchair. As we made our way to the NMR building I tried to imagine what a picture of my brain would show. How the technician would recoil in horror, faint, leave me pinned in the machine at the sight of my thoughts: Emily's agony printed over and over again on X-ray paper, like a shredded flower.

Brain Scan

It was while I was trapped in the metal tube of the NMR scanner that a frightening insight came to me. The machine made an ear-shattering clanking noise; the space was about big enough for a cigar. To keep from having a claustrophic freak-out I tried to turn my mind to something pleasant—the dogs at the beach, an evening with Conrad—but I kept coming back to Emily's story.

In her overwrought state it must have seemed wholly believable that her father could have gone downtown, killed Deirdre, returned to the house to attack his daughter and returned once more to the Loop to do something to the computer. In her terror Fabian seemed omnipresent, trapping her wherever she turned. In reality Fabian must have been home as he'd been claiming all along.

The thought that he really hadn't killed his wife was so disappointing that I lay flinching from the racket of the scanner for some minutes before the rest of the story dawned on me. Someone else had killed Deirdre. And maybe when Emily thought she'd seen her father standing on the corner as she left the Pulteney it had in fact been the murderer.

Say that was so. The murderer was waiting for—who knows? A cab? A confederate? Anyway, he sees Emily leave the building. And he debates—is this a witness to his killing? He doesn't think so—he's been careful, he would have noticed anyone in the halls or office. She must just be a tenant leaving late at night. He doesn't try to accost her. Only after the bat was discovered in her bedroom does he realize Emily must have been in my office, and now he needs to find her—desperately—to see whether she can finger him.

That's why I wasn't killed on Saturday. They thought I was sitting on her and could lead them to her. Which meant Jasper definitely knew who killed Deirdre. It was him or one of the other musketeers. Maybe the contractor, Charpentier. The man who'd come to Emily's hospital room in the middle of the night, that was neither a reporter nor a friend of Fabian's. It had been the murderer.

Sweat oozed down my neck into the hospital gown. I was trapped in a steel cigar tube with noise pounding into my head. Panic rose in me, choking me.

"You have to lie still in there," a voice said over a loudspeaker. "If you move you ruin the image and we'll have to start all over again."

My brain was roaring, almost splintering from the clanking of the machine. "I have to get out of here."

"We're almost done." The metallic voice was Olympian in its assurance. "Try to relax and not think about the exam. It will be much easier for you if you take some deep breaths and remain calm."

The smooth sides of the chamber were a coffin burying me alive, the racketing sound an exquisite torture. My fingers dug into my palms hard enough to draw blood. I felt an overwhelming fury with Lotty for subjecting me to this at such a moment. It was the rage of helplessness, what Emily must have felt the moment she hurled the plastic cup of water across the room.

My mind had stopped working in my urgency to be gone, to get moving before anyone else got to Emily. In the infinity of five minutes that I lay helpless I tried to marshal all the figures I'd encountered in the last two weeks, from

Phoebe Quirk to Gary Charpentier, in an orderly procession through my mind. As a distraction the exercise worked, but the faces and facts lay jumbled in my brain.

The clangor finally stopped. The pallet slid free of the tube. I sat up and swung my feet over the side of the table. When the technician came in with a glass of water and a cheery, "That wasn't so bad, now, was it?" I wanted to paste him, but I merely smiled grimly and climbed down from the table.

"We want you to sit out here for a few minutes while the doctor reviews the pictures to make sure we have everything we need. You drink this water and you'll feel better. We'll call transport to get a wheelchair for you."

I took the water and followed him to the waiting area. My muscles were still stiff, but I was most emphatically not going to hang around while they fetched first a radiologist to look at my brain and then a wheelchair. I collected my skimpy hospital robe from the changing room. As soon as the technician left the waiting area I shuffled outside.

My paper slippers were only slowing me down. I kicked them off and jogged across the rough asphalt in my bare feet. I was panting, with a stitch in my side, when I got back to my room.

I opened the plastic bag full of fetid clothes and dumped it on the bed. The stench made me fight back a gag. I held my breath while I pulled my jeans and T-shirt free of the overalls, then rummaged in the overall pockets for my keys and the Smith & Wesson. My wallet was still in my jeans pocket. I had one leg inside the foul pants when Conrad came in.

"Ms. W.! What are you doing? I thought you were taking it easy today."

"Conrad! Thank goodness. Did you bring my clothes?" I thankfully took the jeans off again.

"It's good to see you upright and lively, girl. You had me good and scared last night." Conrad hugged me close, then backed away, wrinkling his nose. "What have you got here? The CID landfill?"

Despite my sense of urgency I couldn't help smiling. "Worse: city sewage. These are the clothes I was wearing yesterday. Only desperation made me want to put them back on."

Conrad tied the plastic bag shut and led me to the bed. "What are you so desperate about? You got seven people out of a tunnel yesterday. You're a hero. You even tried to let me know before you went underground, so you're a hero I can feel good about. Rest easy, girl. Take some time off."

"There is no time," I said impatiently. "Emily saw her mother's murderer. He thinks she can finger him. We've got to get some protection for her."

"Damn it, Vic, I don't understand a word you're saying. Pretend you're glad to see me and take it from there."

I almost screamed with frustration. "I *am* glad to see you. But I can't take time to worry about personal things right now. Someone went into Emily's room in the middle of the night. It was a fluke that the night nurse saw him. I don't want to leave her alone."

He gave a twisted smile. "You ought to be a marine sergeant, Ms. W.—with you the job is first, last, and foremost. I still don't know what you're talking about, though. Who went into the girl's room in the middle of the night, and why is that something to worry about?"

"Oh." I realized I hadn't been very coherent. Taking a minute to marshal my thoughts I led him through my conversation with Emily. When I finished her story I explained the train of thought that had panicked me as I lay in the scanning tube.

"And you believe her?" he asked when I finished.

"About what in particular? I believe she went downtown that night, in a state of considerable distress. I believe she saw her mother's dead body sprawled across my desk. I believe she hid under my desk while a man came in and fiddled with my computer. I don't think the man was Fabian, although I wish it were—that would be the only surefire way I can think of to keep the guy from getting custody of her again."

He clasped his hands in his lap. "She won't talk to us. Terry sent Mary Louise in, thinking a woman might have better luck, but she couldn't pry a word out of the girl."

"I'll be happy to tell Officer Neely what I just told you. Don't you see, Conrad—if I'm right in my interpretation of who's been tailing me, and why, Emily's in considerable danger right now."

He looked unhappily at his hands. "Her story made a deep impression on you. But we have to consider the possibility that she did kill her mother—that the rest of her remarks were . . . not necessarily—"

"No!" I felt color flame up in my cheeks and tried to make myself speak temperately. "If you had heard her—heard the anguish—you wouldn't doubt her. A nurse sat in on the interview, Ellen Higgins. She can corroborate everything I've just told you."

"I'm not saying Emily's deliberately trying to dupe you, Vic, but she could be putting up a hysterical defense between herself and her acts that evening. She's at an age where she would naturally be resenting her mother, and I gather the kid had to do her share of housework. If she was pushed hard enough to crack, she could have forgotten what she did and be displacing it onto her father."

I felt as though the bed beneath my body had turned to quicksand, sucking me in so fast that I would suffocate in another minute. I took a series of diaphragm breaths, holding them, exhaling slowly, trying to think.

"Fabian," I said suddenly. "You've been talking to Fabian about her."

"Yeah. Guy's her father. He's got a right to be worried about her, to talk to us. She screams when he comes into the room. He's going off his head. He says he's been worried about her for some time—that she had to carry a lot of the load in their house for Deirdre—Mrs. Messenger—because his wife had an alcohol problem. Drunk, we say on the South Side, but the got-rocks have alcohol problems. Anyway, little Emily was doing so much around the house that she started having fantasies about supplanting—"

"Spare me," I interrupted. "Fabian's using the crudest trick in the book, one started by good old Dr. Freud himself. We can't believe a respected man rapes his daughter, so we'll say she's having a fantasy about having sex with him. So not only does she get violated physically, we deny her her story and she gets violated emotionally."

"Calm down, Vic. The first thing you have to learn as a cop is not to be a partisan. Everyone wants to put their story out there for you. You got to weigh the probabilities. Maybe you should talk to the Finch, see what he knows about the father, before you jump in foursquare for the daughter."

He took my hands between his own and looked me full in the eyes. His own were dark pools, in whose depths lay compassion, not cynicism. To dig a channel between us would be like cutting off a piece of my heart. But to abandon Emily to salvage my life with Conrad would mean cutting off a chunk of my soul.

"I will try to keep an open mind about Messenger," I said slowly, "if you will get a guard outside Emily's door before we take off."

Conrad looked unhappy. "I can't authorize that just on your say-so, Vic."

"Someone did try to go into Emily's room in the middle of the night last night—claiming to be a friend of Fabian's. The night nurse saw him."

"The night nurse thought it was an enterprising reporter," Conrad pointed out. "She could be right."

"She could be at that." I don't know when I've ever felt so bleak. "Did you bring some clothes for me? Why don't you let me wash up and change. I'll meet you outside in a few minutes."

Conrad studied my face, then said he'd bring the car around to the Huron Street entrance. He handed me his canvas gym bag and left the room. As soon as he'd gone I phoned the Streeter Brothers, a collective that does furniture moving as well as bodyguarding. We've worked a lot together. I got Tim and explained Emily's situation.

"As soon as she's fit to move I'm going to get her out of here. But that may not be for a few days. When you get here talk to a nurse named Ellen Higgins. I'll try to reach her before I leave, but she's the one person who will go to bat for Emily right now."

"If I get booted, where do I reach you?" Tim asked.

"Leave a message with my answering service. And if you do get booted, can you figure out a way to hang around, make sure no one goes injecting strychnine into her IV tube?"

When he'd agreed, with the laconic good humor that was the Streeter brothers' hallmark, I climbed into the clean jeans Conrad had found for me. He'd stuck a single rosebud into the pocket of the T-shirt. I felt my heart twist in my chest. I took an extra minute to comb my hair and place the rose over my ear with an IV clip I found behind the bed.

Before leaving the room I paged Ellen Higgins, to let her know the Streeters would be around. Emily was sleeping, the nurse told me, from a sedative that would probably keep her knocked out for the rest of the afternoon. Higgins didn't know if Fabian or Dr. Morrison would allow me to keep a guard there, but she would accept Tim for the time being.

Ken Graham came in as I was hanging up, clutching a bunch of tulips. "I thought I was going to have to plant these on you, but you can carry them instead. How come you get to gondola through the tunnels of Chicago while I have to sit on my ass in Kenilworth persuading Darraugh I'm not a psychopath?"

"Is your dad home? The flood knock out his building?"

"Yeah, they don't have power, but he's directing operations from an emergency bunker. Being Darraugh, he was smart enough to bag space in a Gold Coast Hotel yesterday morning while everyone else was wringing their hands. Except for people like you hogging the fun stuff down under, I mean. This episode may finally unwind the last screw in Darraugh's brain: they can send people into his building to get papers, but for some kind of screwy safety reason they can only go one at a time. So the physically fit are going one at a time to fetch vital papers. On foot, up forty flights, because there's no power. I did one load for him and he still thinks I'm a psychopath. So I came to see if you would marry me.''

"And you brought a bridal bouquet. How truly thought-ful. You put any energy into my accounts lately? Taxes are due tomorrow.'' I picked up my bag of filthy clothes with one hand and took his proffered flowers with the other.

"The IRS is giving everyone in the Loop a filing exten-sion—it was on the news this morning.'' He put his arms around me. ''If I reconstruct your files in time, will you marry me?''

I dropped the flowers and the bag and extricated myself from his clasp. ''If you reconstruct my files I'll see that a 501-c(3) counts it as community service. You need that much more than you do a wife. . . . I want to write a note for a pediatric patient. Will you take it over to one of the nurses, please?''

I tore a blank page from my chart and wrote a careful message to Emily, in care of Nurse Higgins, telling her who the Streeter brothers were. With an exaggerated sigh Ken tucked it next to his heart. He had to return to his father's hotel to act as a messenger boy, but he'd get back to my accounts tonight, he promised.

"I don't think my calves are up to scaling Darraugh's building again. Why do you have to leave so soon? We could rest in this cozy little bed together.''

I picked up the bag and left the room without answering.

□48

The Three Musketeers

My fatigue pushed me into a deep sleep, but it was filled with tormented dreams. Sometimes I could hear Emily crying but couldn't see her. I would follow her voice through the unlit water-laden tunnels without finding her. At other times, I was trapped in a steel coffin through whose walls I could see Fabian torturing his daughter while Conrad and Terry Finchley laughed at my immobility.

When I finally came to, my mouth was thick and my arms felt as though someone had systematically pounded them with bricks. I gasped when I looked around, unable to recognize my surroundings, thinking for a moment I had plunged into the kind of nightmare where you think you're awake but you're not. After a few seconds my heart rate returned to normal: the scrupulously tidy room was Conrad's. I laughed a little to myself—I'd have to tell him that when I wake up to clean surroundings I think I'm having a nightmare.

His bedside clock read a little after five. I'd been out almost four hours. I could hear Conrad moving around in the living room. Wrapping myself in his terry-cloth bathrobe I went to join him. It turned out to be Camilla, settling herself in front of the television with a plate of chips and dip. When she saw me she switched off the sound.

"If it isn't Lady Lazarus herself," she said. "When my big brother said he had to go to work I offered to come baby-sit. I wanted to see you walking and talking with my own eyes."

I went over to hug her. "Lady Zombie is more like it. Why'd Conrad have to go to work? I thought he was on days until summer."

"He traded shifts with one of the brothers so he could look over you today. He'll be off at midnight. Now tell me all. Everything that the TV people didn't cover in your sixty seconds of fame and glory."

I scooped up a handful of chips and gave her the highlights of my search through the tunnels. Although she didn't want to hear it, I also told her about Gary Charpentier's immigrant scam.

She was quiet when I finished. Over her head I watched the frenzied crews trying to pump water from Chicago's belly. The Loop was crawling with cops, sanitation workers, and engineering teams.

"You know what really sucks about that?" Camilla suddenly burst out. "Outfits like ours that are scrambling to get a toehold don't pay union scale so we can compete. But we can't make a living because creeps like Charpentier are willing to use sharecropper labor."

"Home Free did give you the rehab job," I pointed out.

"Yeah, but we wanted new construction. Of course, that building we wanted to put up didn't have anything to do with Home Free, but at the same time you don't see them opening up jobs like the one you looked at to outfits like ours."

She followed me to Conrad's kitchen while I made some coffee. I wanted to rest for a week, but somehow I had to find the reserves to keep going. Caffeine wasn't the answer, but it might provide the illusion of energy.

While I drank, Camilla rummaged in the refrigerator. "Ever since Conrad got that bad cholesterol report there's been nothing to eat here. I want a ham sandwich after my hard day on the job, not low-fat yogurt."

"Tell me something, Zu-Zu. What city ordinance would Charpentier have been violating out at the worksite?"

She shook her head. "Beats me. Feds deal with immigrants. Of course, far as the job itself goes, you name it, the city has an inspector. Plumbing's the worst—their guys are like the hounds of hell."

I couldn't imagine a problem with plumbing inspectors that would have made Cyrus Lavalle, my little City Hall spout, so nervous. I tried to imagine what other kinds of things the city might worry about.

Camilla found a can of tuna fish and divided her attention between me and making a plate of sandwiches. "There's Wage and Hour sheets." She licked low-fat mayonnaise from a spoon and made a face. "You know, they come around to see if you're paying prevailing wage. Of course, they don't do a site audit—say you're paying out five thousand a week in payroll. At prevailing wage that would mean you might have six people working full-time. But maybe you have twelve and you're paying them half the scale—the city wouldn't come around to check how many were there. If you told them six they'd believe you."

I thought about it. Wages aren't the limit of payroll expense. There are taxes. Workers' compensation, which must cost a bundle in construction. Health insurance, if you're a union shop.

Eight men had been at the site I'd stumbled on. If Charpentier was paying them prevailing wage that would be sixty-four hundred in wages. Plus maybe another thirty-six in benefits, insurance, and payroll taxes. Ten thousand a week. But since all these guys were here illegally Charpentier wasn't paying taxes. Clearly the men weren't getting union wages. Charpentier—and Heccomb—were probably shaving six or seven thousand off the cost of the job. No wonder Home Free fulfilled the liberal dream of building affordable housing.

Were they bribing the inspectors to stay away—at a sufficiently high level that Lavalle would be warned off for asking questions? I needed to call my informant, but his unlisted home number was in my address book. Which was either buried in the rubble of my apartment or stolen by my assailants on Saturday in an effort to track Emily.

I ate one of Camilla's tuna sandwiches, ignoring her protest. She'd made four, and even a hardworking carpenter could survive on three. If I couldn't find Cyrus until tomorrow—oh, no. Not even at work. City Hall was closed indefinitely because of the flood. For the same reason I couldn't try to find him at the Golden Glow.

"Phoebe," I said out loud. "Do you have Phoebe's home number on you?"

"Maybe." Camilla ate the last sandwich. "Not if you're going to call to harangue her about Lamia. Jasper may be a scumbag, using illegal workers to take bread out of American mouths, but I don't want to jeopardize our first real contract."

I cocked my head. "I think I can talk to Phoebe without getting into your affairs."

"Promise? In writing?"

I took Conrad's shopping list from the refrigerator and scribbled a promise on the back. Camilla laughed and went to the living room to dig out her address book. I called Phoebe from the kitchen, while Camilla watched me from the doorway.

"Phoebe!" I cried heartily. "Good work! I saw it in yesterday's paper but couldn't reach you sooner. I got tied up—you might have seen the story on last night's news."

"What do you want, Vic?" She did not sound as if I were her long-lost sister.

"To congratulate you on getting FDA approval for clinical trials for Mr. T—your T-cell enhancer, I mean. I've always admired your moves, but this one was something special."

"It was bound to happen sooner or later. We were delighted, of course, that it happened sooner." Her voice was cautious.

"And what did you give Senator Gantner in return? Not

a hundred thousand for his war chest. It must have been something else. Can I have three guesses?''

"You can mind your own damned business." She was angry but she didn't hang up.

"Camilla's standing here watching me. I promised not to mention Lamia or the tradeswomen. So I won't. But what was it about Century Bank that Gantner and Heccomb wanted to protect—bad enough that young Alec got his daddy to pressure the FDA for you?''

"You know, in all the years we were in school together I didn't realize you had such a vivid imagination." Phoebe had mastered her temper, at least on the surface, and spoke with light mockery. "There's nothing wrong with Century. They were in a squeeze. They couldn't afford Lamia's bid, so they went to Jasper—"

"And got him to dress up as the Easter bunny," I cut in. "Jasper and Alec Gantner used Mr. T to persuade you to take a hike—Alec promised you his daddy would put in some Republican muscle at the FDA, and he came through. I suppose you could've cut Big Alec in on Cellular Enhancement, but I can't see the owner of Gant-Ag needing a venture capital concern as a revenue enhancer. You must have smelled a rat. You may be the most arrogant woman I've ever worked with, but you've never been stupid. Or even, as far as I know, dishonest.''

Camilla started to move around the kitchen in her nervousness, opening cupboard doors, straightening Conrad's already neatly aligned dish towels. She dropped a pot, which clanged loudly against the linoleum.

"You throwing furniture now?" Phoebe asked at the noise. "It's a red-letter day when a woman like you thinks she can call someone else arrogant. All right—I don't think it's a crime to admit I asked Alec for help. Mr. T—Cellular Enhancement—is a good little company. They just needed some high-level attention. So Alec got Jasper to give Lamia a Home Free rehab job. There's nothing sinister about that.''

Camilla put the pot back on the stove. She frowned at me anxiously and left the kitchen.

"You got *two* big favors. My, my. And they didn't ask for anything back. They are both Easter bunnies, I guess. Did Jasper talk to you about who they were buying off at City Hall on their construction sites? And don't pretend you don't know what I'm talking about—the story of my arrest at a Home Free site made all the networks Saturday."

I heard a click. "Are they messing around with their Wage and Hour reports, Quirk?" Camilla had picked up the extension in the bedroom.

"Hi, Zu-Zu," Phoebe said. "If they are they didn't confide in me."

We batted it around another futile minute. Phoebe was an experienced high-stakes poker player; she wasn't about to fold during this phone conversation. Even Camilla's nervous desire for information about Home Free's legal standing couldn't budge Phoebe. Finally, in exasperation, I told her I was going to talk it over with Murray.

"Maybe I'll never know who's so spooked down at City Hall. But if the *Herald-Star* runs a story on the Wage and Hour scam, Murray can at least put a temporary spotlight on the other Home Free job sites. It'll be a while before they start flying Romanians in again. Maybe it'll give some American workers a crack at getting jobs. And Senator Gantner will enjoy the publicity on how he comes through for his constituents."

"Just don't shine so bright a spotlight on them that we lose the rehab job," Camilla adjured me sharply from the extension.

"It's what they got in exchange for giving you the job that I want to know about. The tie-in is through Century Bank."

"But Home Free didn't have anything to do with that deal," Camilla reminded me.

"That's what I'd like to know. Eleanor Guziak sits on the Century board. She's Donald Blakely's right-hand woman, so he must know what's going on there, and if he does, so do the other two musketeers, Jasper and Alec—'' I broke myself off. "JAD Holdings. What an imbecile I am. Jasper, Alec, and Donald. One for all, all for one. Right, Phoebe?"

"I'm sure you know what you're talking about, Vic," Phoebe said. "I don't. Go to Murray if you want. But if you screw up the Lamia deal you'd better have some back-up project up your sleeve for the tradeswomen."

She hung up. Camilla came back to the kitchen, troubled by the conversation. I couldn't reassure her that the Lamia project was safe—if my investigations pulled a major rug out from under Home Free, they probably wouldn't be able to fund even Lamia's rehab work.

"What are the guys up to?" I demanded. "They're buying Century and it's supposed to be a deep, dark secret. If I've guessed right about who makes up JAD Holdings, that means Jasper pulled back on your original project, then threw you the rehab job as a crumb. Don't you want to know why?"

"Aren't our jobs more important than whether Jasper's working a fiddle with City Hall or some banks? It's hard for women to get this kind of work," Camilla pleaded.

"Someone killed Deirdre," I told her. "If it was these guys, do you really want to take their money?"

Camilla came over to me and made a great pretense of staring into my ear. "Just like I thought," she announced at last. "They didn't put compromise in your head. Look it up in the dictionary. Study it. It's a useful concept. I'm going home. You don't need a baby-sitter, you need a strait-jacket."

I didn't like her leaving angry, but nothing I said could calm her down—unless I agreed to let go of Jasper Heccomb. She even suggested I put my investigation on hold until the end of the summer, when Lamia expected to be done with their job. I shook my head miserably and watched her storm out the door.

I felt the ache between my shoulder blades that I get from fighting with the people I like. I shuffled back to the kitchen to call my answering service. I had a message from Eva Kuhn, the Arcadia House therapist.

She wanted to tell me what she'd learned from Tamar Hawkings. It had been difficult, but in the end she'd managed to get Hawkings to talk. Eva had also persuaded Tamar to let her speak with Sam and Miriam, the surviving children. Tamar's mistrust of the social welfare system was apparently rooted in the history of her sister Leah.

Leah, married to an abusive man, did all the right things: after getting out of prison, when he continued to batter her, she went to a shelter, she found her own apartment, got an order of protection, went through a jobs program, and landed a position as a data-entry clerk. And then was murdered. Tamar was convinced the same fate awaited her if she went through the shelter route. Her daughter's death couldn't persuade her that she wasn't better off foraging on the streets than putting herself in the hands of the social welfare system.

"I'm working on it, but it won't be easy. Just thought you'd want to be kept posted on what we're doing," Eva finished. "I did check up on the sister, by the way—she was murdered by an angry husband who stalked her for months beforehand. Even beat her up at work one day. She was in the hospital for three weeks that time."

When I hung up, my bleak mood only deepened. I wanted to crawl back to bed. When I thought about all the men beating on women, beating on their daughters, beating on each other, I couldn't imagine my own efforts to intervene as anything but futile.

"But if you don't act there may be one more dead child," I said out loud. "And then you really had better crawl under a rock."

I drummed my fingers on the kitchen counter. I would need help if I was going to put the squeeze on Cyrus. I phoned Murray Ryerson at the *Herald-Star*.

"Warshawski!" His voice dripped sarcasm. "The queen herself condescends to speak to the common folk."

"You're about as common as they get, that's for sure.

You want to talk business, or trade love songs? I'm ready to tell you everything I know.''

"And in exchange?"

"And in exchange, if you decide any of it's a story, maybe it'll goad people into showing their hands. Also, you can buy me dinner. At the Filigree. In which case I may overlook you smearing me with Conrad on Sunday.''

"O Queen, your wish makes me tremble and hasten to obey. Filigree in half an hour.''

I looked at the clock: seven-thirty. Conrad lives in Chatham, almost half an hour south of the Loop, and I needed to make another call. Murray agreed to give me an hour.

I reached Sal Barthele at home. She was depressed about having to shut the Golden Glow indefinitely—in these hard economic times it was her main source of cash flow. Fortunately she wasn't directly affected by the water in the tunnels—the Glow sat on a shallow basement.

"I've been following you around Chicago on the tube,'' she said. "One day arrested and almost deported, the next a mighty heroine hauling the homeless out by the scruffs of their necks. I tried the hospital but they told me you'd already left. Where are you now, girlfriend?''

"Down at Conrad's. Someone tossed my place on Saturday and I didn't have the stamina to do cleanup.''

"You don't lack stamina for that, Vic—you lack desire. Me, when something goes wrong, I scrub. You, when something goes wrong, you shoot. You moving in with Conrad as a way to solve your housing problems?''

For some reason that option had never occurred to me. I said No so emphatically that Sal laughed.

"Why I really called was to see if you know how to get in touch with Cyrus Lavalle,'' I said.

"What do you want with that ridiculous clotheshorse?'' she asked. "If you need a dress, isn't he thinner than you? . . . Someone told me when he doesn't drink at the Glow he hangs out at the Grand Guignol. That's up on Broadway, at Cornelia or Brompton, something like that. If you really need him he'll probably show up there.''

When she'd hung up I called Murray. He grumpily agreed to the Grand Guignol instead of the Filigree—it was a long trek north of the newspaper and we probably wouldn't be able to eat there. I scribbled a note to Conrad and scrambled into the jeans he'd brought to the hospital for me. I was about to leave when I had a second thought. I took an extra half hour to clean and oil the Smith & Wesson and load a new clip.

▫49

The Price of a Bottle

As soon as I entered the Grand Guignol I knew I was out of place. The inside of the massive door was lined with beaten bronze. The walls, as nearly as I could tell in the dim light, were covered in matching leather. The customers, perching thickly at tables and along the bar in the narrow entrance hall, were all men. Men in leather, men in silk, men in shredded cutoffs with holes to expose tattooed buttocks, men in makeup and high heels, and even a few in business suits. At the rear of the bar the only other woman was crooning throatily into a mike. Her sequined dress just covered the essentials.

As I passed along the bar the men on the stools eyed me narrowly, then fidgeted uneasily in their seats. I felt like Gary Cooper making that solitary walk down Main Street. I tried to stand tall in my loafers, saying, "Easy, boys, and none of us will get hurt," but kept the remark under my breath.

Cyrus wasn't in the room, but Murray had arrived ahead of me and bagged a small table in a corner. A young man with olive skin and bleached blond hair, wearing a pink silk jumpsuit open to the navel, was leaning across the table in the facing seat. When I came up to the table he glanced at

me, made a face, and went back to cooing something at
Murray.

I smiled nicely. "I'm afraid he's my date, but I've only
paid for the first hour. When I leave you can claim him."

The youth got up, languidly, picked up Murray's hand to
plant a kiss in the palm, and strolled to the bar. Murray
looked venomous. I couldn't help laughing, and once I'd
started I couldn't stop. The other patrons turned around to
frown.

"You wanted revenge, Warshawski, you got revenge, I'll
give you that," Murray said in a savage undertone.

"I didn't know it was a queer bar," I gasped in between
hiccups of laughter. "But if you could have seen your face
when the guy kissed your hand . . ." I sat down and
clutched my sides. "I'll cherish that till the grave."

"Which will greet you soon if you don't shut up that
cackling," Murray hissed.

When I kept howling he grabbed my shoulder and
pointed out a bouncer about the size of a refrigerator,
watching me with the gaze of a junkyard dog who's spied
dinner. A waiter was frowning at us as well. I pulled myself
together as best I could and ordered a whisky in a gasping
voice. Murray was drinking Holstein's, his favorite beer.

The waiter told me that people wanted to hear the music
and he'd appreciate it if I didn't crash a place where I
wasn't welcome if I was going to laugh at it. In the middle
of my apology the sequined woman finished her set and
exited to massive applause. As she sashayed through a back
curtain I realized it was a man. I don't think I could ever
look that good, even if I could afford a dress like hers. His?

Under cover of the applause and renewed conversations I
told Murray why we were in the bar. "Cyrus is my source. I
don't mind you meeting him, but you put him in print and
he's a dried-up source. Dig?"

"Go teach your grandmother to suck eggs," he said irritably. "Why are we going through this charade? What's
your source got?"

"I used to watch my granny take old sweaters apart so

she could use the yarn on something new. She'd start with a shapeless wad, tugging at it here and there until suddenly she'd find the thread that would turn the wad into a long string. I'm hoping Cyrus has the thread.''

I pulled a pad of paper from my shoulder bag and started drawing blocks: one for Century, one for Gateway, one for Lamia, one for Home Free. Above the blocks I listed the people who were connected to each block.

''All these guys come together, but I don't see how. If I could find that out I'd probably know why Deirdre died. Even though I'm pretty sure it was Jasper Heccomb or one of his pals who killed her, I'm not a hundred percent certain. And until I can see why, I can't see who.''

Bad temper wasn't one of Murray's vices. Before I was halfway through my story about Century, Phoebe, and Lamia, about Jasper's stash and my encounter with Anton at the Home Free site, he had pulled out his own pad and was writing furiously.

''You think JAD Holdings is your three musketeers. I ought to be able to find that out.''

I grinned. ''Spoken like a true coconspirator.''

''Where's Jasper's cash coming from?''

''I don't know. I also don't know where the cash is going. Some of it's used to pay the contractors off the books so they don't have to file taxes, but you don't need five million for that.''

''And Emily Messenger?''

I shook my head. ''I'd like to get part of her story out. I think whoever killed her mother is gunning for her because he thinks she can ID him. If he knows she didn't see anything but a pair of shoes maybe she'll get some breathing room. But she's been mauled around pretty badly. She doesn't need the media groping at her too.''

Murray drained a bottle and signaled for another. ''My sources say your pals think she killed her mother. That they may apply for a warrant in the next day or two—it's a question of which way they think Fabian will jump.''

I tried not to let my face or voice show my shock at the

news, but I couldn't keep aside a twist of anger with Conrad and Finchley. Conrad must have known that this morning, but he couldn't tell me. The applause heralding the sequined performer's return gave me room to collect myself —I didn't want to denigrate Conrad to Murray.

Halfway through the first number Cyrus came in. He'd dressed to be noticed: in a room filled with gaudily or shockingly clothed men his white silk shirt and soft black trousers pulled the eye. The shirt alone, with the epaulettes and notched collar that proclaimed Thierry Mugler, must have set Cyrus back a grand. He kissed one man, waved at a few others, and settled himself on a bar stool like a lion willing to be courted. I edged my chair deep in the shadows to keep him from spotting me.

"We need to get him apart from the crowd before he gets too attached to anyone," I muttered to Murray.

"Don't expect me to use my charms to compete with the talent in here," Murray muttered back.

"Spoilsport." I scribbled a note on my pad. "Give him this, and use your body to block his view of the room. If I'm lucky, when he reads it he'll be ready to go out the back way with you."

As soon as Murray's bulk was between me and Cyrus I put a twenty on our table and moved casually through the curtain at the back of the room. On the other side were the toilets, phones, and the cubicles the owners used for offices and storage. Couples were groping each other in the narrow hall; here and there used condoms dotted the floor. The smell of sweat and semen was intense.

I breathed through my mouth while I tried the door to an office. It was locked, but not very seriously. The people around me were absorbed by their own affairs. I took a credit card from my wallet and pried the lock open just as Murray and Cyrus came through the curtain. Cyrus was looking nervously over his shoulder as they came—he still hadn't seen me. Before he did I grabbed his arm and hustled him into the cubicle, with Murray pushing from behind. I switched on a light, found a chair, and sat in it with my back against the door.

"Cyrus, this *is* a pleasure."

In the fluorescent light his skin looked pasty. "Warshawski! What . . . ? How . . . ?"

"Sal told me you come here. Don't worry about the enforcers—it was me who sent the note. A lucky guess."

I'd written—anonymously—that someone demanding payment had come looking for him, armed with a tire iron, but that my friend would help him escape out the back. Given his expensive habits it seemed like a good possibility that he owed more than one person money.

"What do you want? I could start screaming. Gee-Gee would hear me and throw you out."

"Nah. My friend here would just say he'd gotten carried away—like some of the guys in the hall. Gee-Gee might resent his using the office but I bet he wouldn't throw him out. We're going to talk. You're going to tell us what's happening at City Hall."

"What if I don't?" He was sulky but no longer frightened—he knew me well enough to know that whatever threat I might pose it wouldn't be physical.

"Oh, Murray here is with the *Herald-Star*—show him your press pass so he knows I'm not lying—and if you don't talk he'll run a big story on you as a City Hall mole. That would probably get a whole lot of people peeved. Might even cost you your job."

Murray perched on the corner of the paper-laden desk, which filled most of the cubicle. He pulled out his wallet and showed Cyrus his pass, then asked me for the correct spelling of Cyrus's last name.

Cyrus looked from Murray to my chair blocking the door. "You wouldn't dare. Libel laws—"

"Only apply to lies. This would be the truth. Of course, if you felt like giving me a few simple facts, Murray would forget he ever met you. He's got plenty of City Hall sources. No one would think about you in connection with anything he writes."

As Cyrus licked his lips, hesitating, Murray pulled the phone over. "I can call the news desk and tell them to reserve space in the late edition."

Of course he couldn't, really—only on television do stories about corruption go directly into the paper without a hundred editors, fact checkers, and lawyers deciding whether the article will offend an important advertiser. But Cyrus didn't know that. His shoulders sagged and his face crumpled.

"Century Bank, City Hall, Home Free, Lamia." I ticked them off on my fingers. "We'll cover those and you're free. I know that Home Free is fudging their Wage and Hour reports in a major way. Who are they paying not to investigate?"

His face cleared—he was so relieved, the Wage and Hour sheets couldn't be the main problem. He talked his way glibly through the characters in the city building and labor departments who were on the dole. I recognized some of the names but Murray knew all of them—local politics are his meat and drink.

Cyrus rattled off names for about five minutes, including two more contractors besides Charpentier that Home Free worked with. "That's all I know. So you can get away from the door."

"That's all you know about the Wage and Hour inspection," I corrected. "But that isn't what got everyone downtown excited about the Lamia project. Lamia had a building permit, and suddenly, overnight, that got canceled. Why? Was it the aldermen or the mayor? The aldermen own zoning and building in their wards, so I know it wasn't the building department."

It took another five minutes of prodding. It wasn't fun: I don't like myself in the role of bully and Cyrus wasn't attractive as a scared rabbit. Finally, when Murray actually got connected to the *Herald-Star*'s city desk, Cyrus started to talk—and then only after repeated pledges of absolute silence on his name.

"It was the bank, see. Century had always been a small

bank, and most of their investment was in their own community. Then they suddenly started changing their lending policies. Apparently some big management group bought the bank or was trying to buy the bank—I don't know that part.''

He licked his lips nervously, worried that I might doubt him on this point and blow his cover. I told him not to worry, I knew who Century's new owners were.

''We heard about it because people complained to the city's Fair Housing Department. Loans were being turned down that Century always used to approve—minority businesses, women's stuff, minority home mortgages. All that kind of thing. Of course, the U.S. government regulates banks, not City Hall, but people complain, they talk to the alderman, maybe their particular alderman has an in with someone in Congress who can help, maybe the alderman just passes a note to the Fair Housing Department.

''When you called up and started asking questions about Lamia I thought that was the story. I'd ask a few questions, see if the alderman could be approached, and you could take it from there. So I talked to a few people. In housing and in finance. And I heard rumors, nothing specific, but all kinds of reasons why no one was supposed to ask questions about Century Bank. One guy said the president—of the United States, I mean—had told the mayor it was off-limits. A woman in the treasurer's office said no, it was someone in Congress. Someone else said it was the U.S. Housing Department—that they would cut off all Chicago's public housing money if we questioned anything Century did.''

He licked his lips again and pulled a packet of cigarettes from pants so tight I wouldn't have thought the pockets could hold anything. I hate the smell of smoke, but his need was greater than mine. I didn't say anything while he lit up and sucked in a mouthful of smoke.

''If the rumors were that high-level I knew someone important was involved. So I didn't want to push on it. I'm just a clerk in the zoning department. I was going to call and tell you it was more than I could take on. And then I got the phone call.''

He toyed nervously with the cigarette, until he suddenly jumped as it burned his fingers. He looked around for an ashtray. Murray silently handed him a coffee cup. Cyrus dropped the butt into it and rubbed his fingers together.

''They told me—I can't tell you what they told me. Then they said no one was supposed to ask questions about Century Bank or Lamia, and why was I. Vic—you got to believe they threatened me in a—a dreadful way.'' For a moment I thought he might cry, but he fought it back. ''I—they were so specific. I told them it was you. That you were a friend of mine and you'd wondered because the Lamia women were friends of yours. So they told me you were poison, and anyone who talked to you was poison, and they'd know, they had ways of knowing, if I talked to you. I didn't mean to betray you, Vic, but I couldn't help myself.''

The three of us were silent for a moment. I rubbed the side of my head where I'd been hit on Saturday. They were a mean bunch of guys. I looked at Murray and he nodded fractionally: that was all Cyrus knew.

''We'll go out the back way,'' I told Cyrus. ''I doubt anyone is paying attention to you—it's been two weeks. They must know you haven't been in touch with me, but let's not run any risks.

''I'm flat,'' I added to Murray. ''Cyrus ought to be able to buy a bottle of the Widow to celebrate getting me off his back. I saw it on the menu for eighty bucks.''

Murray made a face at me but pulled four twenties from his wallet. We gave Cyrus a couple of minutes to get back into the room, then picked our way past the athletes in the hall and went out through the alley.

Night Watch

Murray and I wandered down Broadway without speaking. It was close to ten, but on Belmont we found a storefront pasta place willing to feed us. The waiter was sitting at a table with the only other customers, a group of five arguing about the rival merits of Eagle River and Spring Green, Wisconsin, for vacation homes. As soon as he'd taken our order he rejoined the argument. The waiter preferred Eagle River.

"So Century's new owners are violating the Community Lending Act. Does that mean they have to break Cyrus's legs for asking?" I said when I was sure no one was paying attention to us.

"Maybe the sale isn't complete and they're afraid a whiff will get back to the feds, who'll block it. Or maybe Cyrus is right and you're poison—they're afraid that you looking into it will put the kind of spotlight on the situation they can't afford. As long as people are only grumbling to their aldermen, JAD Holdings isn't in much trouble. Especially if the rumors Cyrus heard are right and someone high up in Washington is pressuring the city not to act. I personally liked theory number two, that pressure was coming from Congress, 'cause maybe that's our pal Alec Gantner."

"It doesn't matter." I paused while the waiter dumped

spinach tortellini in front of me. "I mean it doesn't matter if it's Gantner, the president, or the housing secretary—they're all Republicans singing from the same score. What I have trouble with is why the White House, or even a senator, would go out of their way to cover up violations of the banking act."

Murray snorted. "It's when you act naive that you're unbearable, Warshawski. Look at Iraqgate. Look at BCCI—children of the high and mighty in both parties making out like bandits, knowing their daddies will keep the FBI or IRS from ever digging too deep."

"Maybe JAD is doing something else with Century besides cutting back on minority lending." The pasta was soggy from having sat in hot water all night; I ate enough to take the edge off my hunger, then pushed the plate aside.

"You think they're laundering money." Murray finished his lasagna in one large forkful and spoke thickly through a mouthful of cheese.

"It stands out a country mile. They're giving Home Free a fifty-million-dollar line of credit. No storefront not-for-profit needs money on that grand a scale. But the real question is—where's it going? If we knew what JAD Holdings was up to— How soon can you start getting a line on them?"

Murray leaned across the table to start on my tortellini. "Depends on what's available through Lexis. Or if one of my Washington sources is willing to squeal. If I have to do a manual search—I don't know when I can get into the government offices downtown. They're all closed indefinitely, you know."

"I could have guessed." I smacked the table in frustration. "If I don't get some hard information soon, either Emily or I—or maybe both of us—are going to be fish food."

The restaurant had a pay phone by the entrance. While Murray tried getting the waiter to disgorge a bill I called my answering service. They told me to check in with the Streeter brothers as soon as possible.

I got Tim Streeter out of bed. "V.I. No, no—I'm glad you woke me up. We got bounced from the hospital."

"What happened?" I demanded sharply. "I thought Ellen Higgins had agreed Emily needed some protection."

"A combination of Fabian and the night shift. During the day I was cool because Nurse Higgins let me park a chair in the hall. When Emily woke up in the late afternoon I went in and introduced myself, brought her brothers in to see her, and got a rap going. Your note helped, by the way: she was wary, but figured if I was with you I was cool.

"Anyway, when the night staff came on duty they made me retreat to the waiting area. Higgins explained the story to them but they didn't totally buy. And after Fabian showed up everything unraveled anyway.

"See, he shows up at six-thirty with this older dude—white hair, black eyebrows, suit. They confer with the charge nurse, who calls a doctor. And pretty soon all four of them go into Emily's room. One of the other nurses says the guy with the eyebrows is a private headshrinker Fabian's dug up—Mort Zeitner." He spelled it for me. "So I go in to make sure the kid knows she's got the right to refuse medication or whatever else they want to do to her."

Murray and the waiter showed up next to me making signs that the restaurant was closing and I should get off the phone. I turned my back on them and hunched into the receiver.

"And then what?" I asked. "Fabian blew sky-high?"

"Yeah," Tim said. "Maybe I should have waited in the hall, but it looked like four against one. Fabian is in there saying she has to talk to Zeitner about her mother's death and I tell her she has the right to remain silent, and Fabian wants to know who the fuck I am, and Emily starts howling and demands to see you, and then Fabian really goes totally around the bend. And the next thing I know three hospital security guards are showing me the gate."

"Shit!" My stomach churned with worry. "She's been alone since six-thirty?"

"Not quite that bad. It was after seven by the time they

booted me. I got Tom, who managed to hang out in the waiting room until eight-thirty, at which point the charge nurse got suspicious. We thought about covering the entrances, but for one thing there are too many, and for another, we didn't know who we were looking for. Fabian and Zeitner left around eight. If you have any ideas, Tom and I will go back down there. We feel terrible letting you down like this.''

My shoulders sagged. ''I'm fresh out of ideas. I'm north now, heading south. I'll stop at the hospital and have a word with the night ward head. Lila Dantry, is it?''

''Yeah, but don't expect a parade and flowers when you introduce yourself.''

I hung up and plunged outside, completely oblivious of Murray, who caught up with me at the corner of Broadway.

''Where are you off to so fast?'' he demanded, panting. ''You trying to stiff me? You owe me eight bucks for dinner.''

As the light changed I pulled some singles from my pocket and handed them to him. ''You ate most of my food. You can have four.''

He hurried into the intersection after me, grabbing my shoulder. ''If you've come up with an idea you'd better share it—you owe me something for that routine at the Grand Guignol tonight.''

''Right now I'm more worried about Emily Messenger. I posted a guard at her room, but Fabian busted it up. Maybe it would be better if Finchley did arrest her: at least that way I'd know she was safe from the real murderer.''

''You're taking for granted that she didn't kill her mother.''

We had reached the Grand Guignol, where we'd left our cars. I paused with my hand on my door to look him in the eye. ''I believe her story, yes. It had a sort of authentic ring to it. If—unlike the cops—you'd try to believe that I'm a reliable judge of what I hear, I'd forgive you all your recent transgressions. I might even give you the other four bucks for my food.''

The noise of my engine turning over drowned out most of Murray's sarcastic response. I made a dramatic U, flaring exhaust across him.

It was almost midnight on my dashboard clock. Conrad would be off duty soon; maybe he could talk Terry into posting a police guard at Emily's room.

I didn't like the possibilities for her, near term. If Terry arrested her it might protect her from the murderer: he might feel his best defense was having someone else stand trial. But the trauma of arrest was something she didn't need, poor little mouse. And whether they arrested her or not, in a day or two she would be released back to Fabian's custody.

I swooped around a double-parked newspaper van and made the turn onto Lake Shore Drive. So even if I could look after her tonight it wouldn't solve the problem of protecting her from Fabian, which I had promised.

The thought of that promise reminded me of another I'd made recently—to pick up Mr. Contreras from his daughter's in Elk Grove Village Thursday morning. As I waited for the light at Lake Shore Drive I punched the steering wheel in irritation. He needed to go in daily for rabies shots. If I brought him home would I have time to look after him?

I exited at Chicago and found a parking place on the street. Anxiety made me sprint the two blocks to the hospital. Waiting for the elevator I drummed my fingers on a nearby planter. When it came I shared the ride with a mother whose child was having emergency surgery on a heart valve.

I followed her to a waiting area halfway down the hall where other parents of critically ill children were keeping an anxious vigil. I could just make out the door to Emily's room from a pay phone on one wall. I called Conrad to explain where I'd been and why I'd be late getting back.

Conrad couldn't totally believe that I only met Murray for business, but he roared with laughter at the description of the man in the pink silk jumpsuit propositioning him.

"Thanks, babe. That did me more good than a beer. How long you think you'll stay up there?"

"Until I feel it's safe to leave. You don't think you could talk Terry into posting a guard here, do you?"

"I think I'd rather walk down South Morgan without a vest than get between you and the Finch on this case. I have roll call again at eight, so I'm not going to wait up. You be careful driving down here in those fancy wheels, okay?"

"Yes, Papa." I hung up on his exasperated snort.

I thought about checking in with the nursing staff, but I didn't want a fight. The halls were empty; I slipped into Emily's room.

She seemed to be sleeping. I moved quietly to an arm-chair in the corner. After a while the stillness of the room and the stresses of the last four days combined to make me doze off.

I was startled awake at two by a light being switched on: a nurse had come in to check on Emily's vital signs. When she caught sight of me she beckoned me into the hall to demand who I was.

"V. I. Warshawski. I was told that she was calling for me earlier tonight. I wanted to stay with her in case she woke up looking for me."

"Are you related to her?" the nurse asked.

I shook my head. "She doesn't have any female relatives in town that I know of. You know her story, right? She's been through too much lately for anyone to cope with, let alone a child. I'm here to help her feel safer."

Whatever Lila Dantry had told the owl shift about the Streeters and Fabian had apparently not included an inter-dict on me. Other than telling me to stay in the waiting room, since I wasn't Emily's mother, but that they would call me if Emily asked for me, she didn't try to kick me out.

"We do ask people to check in at the nurses' station," she said. "We try to make our children as comfortable as possible, but we can't have strangers moving in with them. You do understand that, I hope."

I understood it, all right. I hoped that the musketeers, or

whoever killed Deirdre, would be similarly circumspect before visiting Emily. The nurse escorted me to the waiting area. By moving a chair to the edge of the enclosure I could just make out Emily's door. No more dozing on duty now: I'd have to strain to keep an eye on the hall.

The woman whose child was having valve surgery was sharing a nervous vigil with three other parents of critically ill children. We exchanged anxious, fragmented conversation. At two-thirty one of the men offered to fetch coffee— he was a habitué of the hospital and knew the fast routes to and from the all-night vending stand.

At three the heart surgeon came to talk to the mother. They stood outside the waiting area, blocking my view of the hall. I got up so I could see around them. After a few minutes they headed for the elevators. It was three-twenty when Anton walked swiftly past the nurses' station and opened the door to Emily's room.

"Call the police," I said to the man who'd brought coffee. "Someone just went into my kid's room— a guy I know." I was down the hall on the run, my hand on my gun, before he could ask any questions.

Anton was leaning over Emily with a pillow. I brought my gun down on his head. He didn't fall, but the blow rocked him enough that he lost his hold on the pillow. I kicked him in the small of the back. At that he turned around, aiming a punch for my head. I ducked under his arm and hurled myself against his legs. I shoved hard. The momentum of his punch made him stumble forward over me. Behind me in the bed Emily started to scream.

Anton righted himself as he fell and grabbed my head. I twisted in his grasp but couldn't free myself. I bucked as he tried to suffocate me, brought my legs over my head and managed to hook my right toe under his chin. His fingers loosened. I pushed hard against his windpipe.

In the next instant the room was full of light, of people. Anton let go of me. He knocked a nurse and a security guard out of the way and crashed through the door.

□51
Droit du Père

"I don't get it. I stopped the guy as he was smothering Emily, and you want to arrest her. Don't you see—Anton must have killed Deirdre. Emily was hiding under my desk. She only saw his feet, but he thinks she can ID him, because he knows she was in my office—he knows because she brought the bat home. So why in God's name are you punishing *her*?"

I was in a conference room at Eleventh Street with Terry and Officer Neely. And Fabian. And Mortimer Zeitner, M.D. Conrad had traded shifts again when he learned about the meeting, but he was sitting on the far side of the table from me, near Finchley. It was ten-thirty Wednesday morning and I felt like a building that someone was sandblasting.

After knocking over the nurse and the guard Anton had no trouble leaving the hospital: the security staff were too bewildered to give chase quickly enough. As soon as they'd dragged me away, gotten my story, and conferred with the nurses about whether they could question Emily, they'd called the city cops—but that had not, in fact, been very soon.

I had staggered into Conrad's apartment at five, where I'd managed three hours of sleep between giving him my saga and returning downtown for the conference. As far as Terry knew, Anton was still at large.

"We talked to Gary Charpentier, as you suggested," Terry told me. "He says that Anton was after you, not the girl. He couldn't have known about the bat because we never released that to the press."

"Emily!" I snapped, too tired to care about tact. "She is not 'the girl,' or 'the kid.' She has a name. Please use it. And *you* must know that Alec Gantner has a pipeline to the investigation—you felt the gusher when he got onto Kajmowicz last week. Of course they know all about the bat."

"We're not going to agree on Alec Gantner being a party to this, Vic. Let's stick to what we know right now. Gary Charpentier was very helpful and quite upset. He says Anton went berserk over the deportation of the Romanian work crew and felt it was due to your meddling. Charpentier says he didn't realize Anton was skimming their paychecks—"

When I started a passionate interjection Terry held up a hand to silence me. "I know, I know—he's bailing out and leaving his foreman to carry the can. But Charpentier does say he was worried that Anton might be stalking you. He gave us the guy's address and a couple of leads on where to find him. And, Vic, the gir—Emily saw him attack you. But she doesn't have any recollection of him attacking her."

I almost screamed. "She was asleep. Are you saying that in the absence of a witness you'll believe I made up seeing him smother her?"

"I'm saying Charpentier told a plausible story. Until we can find Anton we don't have any way to question it. Dr. Zeitner here is convinced that Emily is suffering from hysterical amnesia that is causing her to block out killing her mother. There's evidence to support that, which you cannot ignore. The murder weapon was in Emily's room. With her prints on it."

"Terry, I've told you what Emily says about that. She

was convinced her father had killed her mother. She was hiding the evidence.''

Fabian winced—the thoughtful, worried father in anguish over his daughter's emotional instability. He then treated us to his own version of events the night Deirdre was murdered: hard at work on an important lecture; believing he must have forgotten his wife mentioning she had a meeting downtown; glad that Emily stepped in to help with her brothers; not surprised when Deirdre didn't come home —she did a lot of volunteer work that often kept her out late, especially when it involved homeless shelters; totally unaware of Emily leaving the house in the middle of the night.

The three men listened sympathetically. I was so tired I had trouble sitting up, let alone responding on the level of make-believe all us grown-ups were playing.

"Vic, you can't imagine how grateful I am to you for finding my children," Fabian concluded. "I wish you'd never given Emily encouragement to come looking for you —it's what put the idea into her head of running away to your office—but I know your intentions were a sincere effort to help a troubled child. And I wish I'd been more alert the night Deirdre . . . died . . . to how upset Emily was."

He glanced ruefully at Terry. "When your own little girl becomes a teenager you'll appreciate that adolescent storms are a part of daily life. You don't pay as much attention to the individual gales as you probably should."

Before we began Fabian had established that he and Terry were the only ones in the group with children. His smile now established a special communication with Finchley. Terry, not immune to Fabian's public charm, gave him back a small, intimate smile of his own.

"Why do you think Emily was especially upset that night, Fabian?" I broke into their communion.

"In retrospect we—her mother and I—may have put too much responsibility on her shoulders. Emily always seemed so mature for her years that we forgot she was a teenager.

When Deirdre had that unexpected meeting I asked Emily to step in so I could concentrate on my lecture." He grimaced. "At the time my work took on perhaps an excessive importance. Perhaps Emily felt I was unjust. I can't ask her, because she won't talk to me."

He made a deprecatory gesture. "She's blocking out some painful memories that the sight of me may well rouse. At least, Dr. Zeitner, I don't want to put words into your mouth, but isn't that your impression?"

Zeitner cleared his throat. "Emily is an imaginative child, very sensitive, and lonely. We all know that her mother had . . . certain problems. It's understandable that Emily began to imagine herself supplanting the mother in all ways, sexual as well as otherwise. We can't be certain what made her snap that particular night—she is finding it hard to talk about it right now. But I'm convinced when she's in an appropriate setting and has the right kind of support she'll recover enough to be able to speak."

"Why do you think she went downtown, alone, in the middle of the night?" I asked. "Don't you think it took some major impetus to drive her into a dangerous city in the dark?"

Zeitner said, "We'll know that better when Emily starts trusting us enough to speak."

"Maybe if you trusted her enough to listen to her she would trust you enough to talk to you," I said.

Zeitner raised his eyebrows in a way that managed to convey polite contempt. I wanted to strangle him. Instead I turned to Fabian.

"Emily has told me how you like to come into her room after she's gone to bed, and that you did so the night Deirdre was killed. Do you remember what you said, and what you did, that night?"

Out of the corner of my eye I saw Officer Neely flinch and shift uneasily in her chair. Zeitner smiled smugly, as though I'd just confirmed his diagnosis.

Fabian leaned forward across the conference table in his earnestness. "Vic, to be honest with you, so much has happened since then that I can't recall that specific incident. If you'd ever had children of your own you'd know that you do often go into their rooms at night to check up on them. I may have wanted to make sure Emily wasn't too angry—with Deirdre's leaving her in the lurch—to be able to sleep, but I honestly can't recall.''

"So you don't remember having sex with her that night.'' I forced myself to look at him, at his gray eyes almost black with sincerity, a tiny pucker between his brows betokening nothing more than gracious attention.

He put his hand to his brow, as though unable to bear the thought of so disturbed a child. He turned to Zeitner, who patted his arm consolingly.

"If Emily is claiming that, then it's clear corroboration of what I've been saying,'' the psychiatrist said. "Except that her fantasies are more pronounced than I realized. That information will be helpful, though, in the recommendations we make to the court.''

He looked at me over the edges of his glasses, his eyes stern. "And Ms. Warchassi, you may be well-intentioned, but I must urge, in the strongest language possible, that you not go near Emily again. You have a very disturbing effect on her. The setback she sustained after last night's events, for instance—your kind of rough work does not belong in a pediatric ward.''

"Dr. Zit, without my rough work Emily Messenger would be dead. I would be very grateful if everyone in this room could abandon their fantasies about Emily's fantasies and pay serious attention to what she said. She is not crazy, nor hysterical, nor amnesiac. She has a clear and most painful memory of the events around her mother's death.''

"And you are a trained psychiatrist, Ms. . . . uh?'' Dr. Zeitner demanded.

"I'm a trained observer. I hear a lot of stories. I know how to sift the authentic from the imaginary.''

He shook his head. "You are a feminist, right? And you probably subscribe to the current feminist dogma that many girls are sexually abused. In your sympathy and the ardency of your beliefs you could easily have given Emily unconscious cues that made her believe a story of incest would be acceptable to you. I'm not saying you deliberately encouraged her to imagine that her father raped her, but that in ways you wouldn't consciously be aware of, you encouraged her to present that version of events.

"After killing her mother and then spending a week almost starving underground, Emily would be disoriented enough to imagine anything. We need to get her properly medicated and ready to reclaim her own memories. She needs *professional* support for that, not amateur—however well-meaning the amateur is."

Fabian nodded. "Vic, I can only endorse what Dr. Zeitner said. As Emily's father I must insist that you stay away from her from now on. I've left strict orders with the hospital that they cannot allow you in her room. Or your friends—those no doubt well-intentioned thugs I found around her yesterday. Detective Finchley, you can understand I have a lot to do right now. If there's nothing further . . . ?"

"I do have one question, Mr. Messenger." That was Conrad. "When was the last time you remember seeing your Nellie Fox bat in the front hallway?"

Fabian's graciousness became tinged with hauteur. "Under the circumstances most courts would forgive me for not remembering that detail, Sergeant. I hope you'll keep me posted on your progress, Detective Finchley."

He and Zeitner left. Finchley leaned over and switched off the recorder.

"They're very plausible, Vic."

"I know, Terry. A doctor and a lawyer—what a reputable double whammy. Emily was very plausible too. I hope you'll talk to Nurse Higgins before you do anything scary, like charge Emily."

Terry tightened his lips in a thin line. "Get out of your seventies cop-equals-pig mentality, Vic. It's wearing thin with me."

"Why is it that we give the man's story four times the

weight we do the daughter's?'' Officer Neely burst out. ''Is it because he's a male and she's a female? Or he's an adult who makes a lot of money? If this was a black family on welfare would you two guys pay more attention to Emily or less?''

We all jumped at her voice. She'd been so quiet throughout the meeting we'd forgotten her as a presence.

''There's been an awful lot written these days about how easy it is to manipulate children's memories of abuse,'' Terry said to her. ''I've been reading up on it the last few days. Emily Messenger spent a week underground with a woman who herself claims to be fleeing a domestic abuse situation. Emily could easily have had her mind affected by this.''

''That's Zeitner's line,'' Neely said. ''But do you believe it? Do you think Vic—Ms. Warshawski—made up what she saw last night?''

Terry shifted uneasily. ''I don't think Vic is lying. But she's been under a lot of stress herself. I'd like to talk to Anton before drawing any conclusions.''

I felt my own face grow hot with anger, but before I could speak Neely said, in a voice shaking with emotion, ''I will not have any role in arresting Emily Messenger, Terry. If you want to report me for insubordination, or send me off to do street patrol in Wentworth, I don't care.''

She swept from the room, banging the door behind her. Terry and Conrad stood on the far side of the table like carved images.

''Don't blame me, Terry—I haven't put subliminal suggestions about Fabian Messenger into her head.'' I spoke more bitterly than I'd intended.

''Can't you consider the possibility you're wrong?'' Conrad said.

''I may be wrong. I could be wrong. I often am. But I'm not wrong about what happened at that hospital last night. I'm not wrong about what Emily told me yesterday morning. And I'm not wrong about Deirdre Messenger, come to that: she was expecting someone in my office the night she was killed. Another point you refuse to credit me with knowing.

"While the two of you weigh whether to arrest Emily, there's a man roaming around town who tried to kill her, very likely under orders from Gary Charpentier, and maybe Alec Gantner or Jasper Heccomb."

My words brought back the first time I'd seen Gary Charpentier. "In fact I heard Jasper Heccomb talking it over with him! Subcontracting the job. It was Deirdre's murder they were talking about."

They didn't understand me. When I explained that encounter at Home Free two weeks ago, where Charpentier had come out of Jasper's office and been disconcerted at my mentioning Deirdre's name, Finchley didn't think it proved my point at all.

Conrad shook his head, frowning heavily. "You're putting too much emotion into this, Vic. I feel like you're trying to rush me headlong down a hill that you shouldn't be running on yourself."

"Whenever you or Terry have seen Fabian he's been the suave law professor. But I've been with him in private on three different occasions when I saw him behave very differently. I *heard* him hit his wife. I *heard* him annihilate his daughter. And I heard the girl's account of that night. The details were too . . . too . . . well, detailed—for someone having hysterical amnesia. I am not being hyperemotional—I'm a credible witness."

"I trust your judgment." Conrad spoke with the strained sincerity of someone who doesn't really. "Can't you put the same trust in Terry's and my judgment as police officers? With better than fifteen years experience each?"

I nodded warily. "You are good officers, both of you. I've seen that many times."

"Then don't ride me—him—us for disagreeing with you and Mary Louise on this."

It was my turn to frown. "It's not just a question of whether Emily is hysterical, but whose feet she saw in my office the night Deirdre was killed. And who Anton was after in the pediatric ward last night.''

Finchley made a frustrated gesture. ''That's the crux of the problem. Nothing connects him to your office the night of Deirdre's death, but everything, including her own story, puts Emily there. Dr. Zeitner could be right: if she killed her mother she's too overwhelmed to be able to admit it, so she has to create other villains to blame.''

He went to the door, then stopped to look at me. ''I'll make one compromise with you, Vic: we won't execute the warrant until we track down Anton and hear his story. But by the same token, you *must* stay away from the girl. From Emily. Her father is her legal guardian and he has forbidden you to have any contact with her. I'm going to talk to the hospital security staff about this one.''

His eyes held mine sternly. I nodded fractionally—in acknowledgment of his hostility.

When he'd gone Conrad put a tentative arm around me. ''What next, Ms. W.?''

''For you and me? I think I'd better move back to my own pad, however ramshackle it is these days. We . . . there's too much . . .'' My voice quavered and I fought to regain control. ''I don't want to break up with you. But we'll be better off if we're apart for a few days.''

Conrad withdrew his arm and put his hands in his pockets. ''And if this guy Charpentier is right, and Anton is stalking you, not the kid—Emily?''

''Then he'll find me no matter where I am.''

My slow shuffle down the hall had nothing to do with muscle fatigue. I had my hands stuffed in my pockets, my head hunched down, ignoring the world around me. When Officer Neely tapped my arm as I was unlocking my car I spun around in terror.

Her face was blotchy, as though she had been crying, and when she spoke her voice came out in a husky squawk. She was too wound up in her own miseries to notice mine.

''I need to talk to you.''

I gestured to the front seat. The Trans Am is too noisy

for private conversation. I drove north to Montrose, where the lakefront is deserted this time of year. At the tip of the spit of landfill I turned off the motor and leaned back in the driver's seat. Neely stared straight ahead.

"I have a father like Fabian Messenger. You could probably guess that, couldn't you?" she burst out.

She seemed to want some kind of response from me. "I could tell something about this case was affecting you personally," I said.

"I don't know how old I was when my father started coming to my room at night. Maybe seven. My mother—" She stopped, her voice trembling too much for speech.

After a minute or two she continued, in a hoarse monotone that made my bones ache. "I told my mother he was hurting me in the night. She washed my mouth out with soap for talking dirty. When I was in high school I ran with a bad crowd and then I just ran away, to Chicago, to the haven at Clark and Division where bad kids run to. I had sex and drugs, but no rock-and-roll."

She laughed derisively. "I was pregnant three times before I was eighteen. The third time, the abortion clinic I went to sent me to a counselor. I stopped doing drugs. I started working. I went to night school and graduated from high school. And then I took the exam and joined the force. I haven't been to my parents' house in thirteen years.

"My father's a minister. A saint in the community. At Wednesday night prayer circles the faithful beg that God will help him through the grief of having a daughter who never calls or comes to visit."

A solitary runner pounded past the car. I watched his legs until shorts and flesh merged into a blurry gray.

"It took a lot of courage for you to break away from a home like that."

She looked at me for the first time, her eyes fierce. "I didn't tell you my story to get your sympathy. I joined the force because I wanted to arrest creeps like my father. Don't you understand? But now, instead of arresting the creep, I'm supposed to arrest the kid. It's like they want me to send myself to jail. Or worse, to a mental hospital where a girl like Emily will have one chance in a thousand of coming out with her head straight.''

I thought over the years I'd known Neely—always holding herself parade-ground stiff, working harder than any other cop I knew, even Conrad. ''The police have been your family, haven't they? What are you going to do now?''

''I don't know,'' she whispered. ''If I have to resign over this I will, but—what would you do in my situation?''

I shook my head. ''I don't know. I do think letting Emily get arrested is the second-worst thing that could happen to her right now. Next to getting killed, I mean. Maybe the third worst—I don't know if letting Fabian take her home would be more damaging than incarceration or not.''

''If it's Fabian instead of jail she'll end up at Clark and Division.'' Neely spat out the words. ''She needs some place safe, and a counselor like mine. Only she—my counselor—moved to Kansas to go to graduate school.''

''I know a good counselor,'' I said slowly. ''And a safe house. But I don't know if I can get to Emily's room. Terry's asking the hospital to post a guard.''

Mouse on the Loose

It was almost one when I got back to my apartment. I was too tired to care whether Anton or Gantner or even the Fourth Army was camped on my doorstep. I parked the Trans Am out front and walked up the walk and stairs without trying to scout the street. Inside I dumped my backpack in the foyer, set the electronic alarm, and fell into bed without undressing.

When I woke again it was dark outside. I lay in bed watching the evening sky through my window. Why couldn't Terry and Conrad listen to me? Was Finchley caught in such a vise between Kajmowicz and Fabian that he was taking the easiest out, going for Emily and ignoring things like the attack on me Saturday—not to mention last night's fracas?

I was tired of taking arms against a sea of opposition. All it got me was knocks on the head, my home trashed, and accusations from smug cretins like Zeitner.

I climbed out of bed and imitated the roar of a jet engine. "The femikaze squad is coming. Watch out, boys! Hang on to your crotches and duck!"

Yelling at top volume made me feel a little better. I went into my living room and started picking up papers. If I was going to see any of the musketeers arrested I would have to dig up proof of the complete trail of money through Home Free. Although that still wouldn't prove Deirdre knew about it. I kicked the piano bench in frustration.

I had organized the books and papers in the living room and had started on the big closet in the hall when Fabian and Finchley arrived, with an officer I didn't recognize in tow. I shut my door and greeted them on the landing.

"Terry, Fabian, what a surprise. What do you want tonight?"

"Emily," Finchley said tersely.

"It's déjà vu all over again." I looked at my watch. "Is the Loop still flooded, or have we turned the whole city back a week?"

"Warshawski, *please*!" Fabian's voice broke. "Don't torment me. Just tell me where my daughter is."

"Terry, I'm beat." I couldn't stomach Fabian's histrionics tonight. "You know what I've been through the last few days. I don't need this. Has the strain turned Messenger's brain, or has he genuinely misplaced his daughter again?"

Biting off his words, Terry told me that Emily had disappeared from the hospital. "As you know. We told you to stay away from her. I can arrest you, you know, under Messenger's peace bond. But he's willing to let it slide if you produce his daughter."

"Like a conjurer from a hat." I spat out the words. "I do not have his daughter. Since saving her life early this morning I have not seen, talked to, or been near Emily Messenger. Now get the *hell* out of my apartment and put out an APB for her."

"Cut the crap," Finchley snapped. "One of the nurses told us that a detective who'd been in with the girl several times left with her around noon today. A woman. With short hair. I could make you come downtown for a lineup. Instead we'll search your apartment."

"You damned well better have a warrant, then. And you'd better tell Lieutenant Mallory to warn the city about a suit for harassment that I'll be filing at the start of tomorrow's business day."

"I have a warrant." Terry's voice was case-hardened steel. "This is Officer Galatea. He will conduct the search."

I took the paper from Galatea and studied it. My lips tight with anger, I let them into my apartment, where I planted myself in front of the television. While they went through closets, beds, searched my basement storeroom and the attic crawl space, I watched the Cubs commit two errors in one inning.

Finchley wanted to search Mr. Contreras's home as well. When I told him my neighbor was recuperating at his daughter's house he was sure he had me cornered. I refused to give him Ruthie's number in Elk Grove Village, forcing him to call in to the precinct to find someone who could get her last name from the hospital.

While we waited for the station to get the information, Terry said, "In case you're wondering, someone's already been to the doc's and to Mr. Loewenthal's. You do know that kidnapping is a federal offense, don't you, Vic? And harboring a fugitive from justice is a serious state crime."

My eyes felt like hot coals; I hoped my gaze could scorch. "Make up your mind, Finchley: is Emily the victim of a crime or a dangerous perpetrator? Why do you really want her—to protect her or to torment her? But more to the point, we had this identical conversation eight days ago. All the time you were hassling me, Emily was in terrible trouble. Now I'm telling you someone is on her tail, that she may present a personal danger to the man who murdered her mother, that that man may have snatched her in order to do her real harm—and you insult me and invade my friends' privacy. I found her for you before. You are going to look like a hundred kinds of fool in the papers, not to mention to Kajmowicz, if I do it again. But you'd better pray I find her alive."

Finchley narrowed his eyes at me. "Thanks for being so helpful to an overworked police force. I know you, Vic, that's the trouble. Heisting the kid could be your idea of a noble gesture."

"Thank you, Terry. I'm honored that you think that of me." I swept him an ironic bow and returned to the Cubs.

The station called back with Ruthie's home number. Before Terry could dial it I suggested he let me talk to Mr. Contreras.

"He won't let you into his place without a warrant, but he may if I talk to him. And the sooner you realize Emily isn't here the faster you can start trying to figure out where she really is."

Fabian objected to giving me the chance to pass signals to my accomplice; I invited him to listen in on the bedroom extension. Terry, who had experience of my neighbor, agreed with me. Fabian, in a fretful impatience, got to hear Mr. Contreras's detailed account of life in the suburbs, of the physical state of the dogs—who his grandsons were running, so not to worry, doll—of how agonizing his rabies shots were—but nothing like the shell he took at Anzio, so again not to worry—and then distress at Emily's disappearance.

Fabian kept trying to interrupt, but Mr. Contreras turned on him in indignation. "How come you're harassing Vic instead of looking after your kids? She and I had to take care of them for you on Monday. If you paid attention to Vic to begin with you would've put a guard on Emily's room, like she told you to. Now you've got one hell of a nerve—'scuse me, cookie, slipped up there, but this jackass needs to learn some manners."

"So can they go through your apartment?" I asked. "The sooner they realize she's not here the faster they may try to find out where she really is."

After another spate of volubility he agreed. He was anxious to return home, but when I asked if he could stay with Ruthie until Saturday he accepted the extension with a wistful farewell.

"You ain't gonna leave me out here forever, are you?"

"Just until I calm down enough to manage the drive without running over anyone," I promised.

When he'd hung up I dug his spare keys out of the back

of my toolbox and gave them to Officer Galatea. It was clear to everyone by now that Emily was not in the building, but Galatea and Fabian went through Mr. Contreras's apartment. I stayed with them to make sure they didn't damage anything—Fabian was unstable enough that he might break furniture to vent his frustrations.

Terry did not apologize for his suspicions. "Just so you know, Vic, I'm having a team stick to you like fleas on a dog. If you've stashed that girl someplace, we'll find her. And your future will not be pretty. Remember that."

"And the same to the horse you rode in on, Finchley. Now get out."

As soon as I saw his car pull away I stormed up to the Belmont Diner for supper and a phone. For all I knew they might have put a tap on mine.

I called Lotty while waiting for an order of roast chicken. "I'm sorry you had to have the police in your home."

"That doesn't matter, Vic: it's that poor girl. What can possibly have happened to her? Do you think—"

I interrupted her. "I'm not a hundred percent certain, but I think she's okay."

Lotty digested this, then said, "You haven't left her someplace alone, have you? or tucked away with your neighbor and the dogs?"

"I haven't done anything with her. As far as you and I are concerned, we never heard of her. I'm only telling you because you're the one person in the world I can't stand to deceive."

"I see," Lotty said, at her driest. "Are you all right yourself? Or would you like to come here for the night?"

"I think I'll sleep in my own bed for a change. I need my home around me. But thank you, Lotty."

When my supper came I ate it hungrily, but not happily. I liked Conrad. But I didn't like anyone enough to put up with this kind of treatment. I certainly didn't feel any qualms about wasting the time of an overworked police force.

"They could have listened to me," I said out loud. "It's what they get for not believing women's stories."

"You said it, honey." I hadn't realized the waitress was close enough to hear me. "This whole damned world would be better off if they ever listened to us."

□53

The Thirty-nine Stories

In the morning I packed a briefcase with essential supplies and walked to Clark Street for a Loop-bound bus. It decanted me on Madison, a brisk half-mile walk from the Gateway building.

Some Loop businesses had managed to reopen, but even those skyscrapers that hadn't lost power had to wait for the tunnels to drain, and for city engineers to declare their foundations safe. The city had closed a number of downtown streets where the pumping efforts were most concentrated. Logjams of traffic built up on those streets that were open. The snarling mess was made worse by the fact that traffic signals still were not functioning. Furious cops tried to force some semblance of order, or even manners, on the melee.

Some of the buildings west of the river were alive with lights and workers, but to my relief the Gateway building was not one of them. Its unlit windows were black against the dull sky.

The guard in the lobby let me in when I pounded on the door. I produced an old badge I'd found in my closet the night before, one that proclaimed me to be on official business for Cook County.

"I'm supposed to look for rodent evidence on all the

floors where food is prepared. Can you tell me where to start? Or maybe you'd like to come along? We've been getting reports about rats the size of beavers in some of these buildings.''

The guard hastily disclaimed any interest in rats. The executive dining room was on thirty-six, he said, and the employee cafeteria in the basement. As I'd hoped, the idea of giant rats kept him from studying my badge too closely: it was signed by a man who hadn't been in county politics for three years.

''You'll have to take the stairs to thirty-six,'' he warned me. ''We don't have any electricity in here.''

I groaned suitably. ''The executive dining room on the same floor as the executive offices? I want to be able to talk to Donald Blakely or Eleanor Guziak as fast as possible if I find anything serious.''

''People can't come to work here, miss: it's not safe. Mr. Blakely and his officers picked up their vital documents on Tuesday. And you should have seen him lead them on a race. Thirty-nine floors. Some of the kids in their twenties had to quit halfway up, but not Mr. Blakely. He stays in tip-top shape.''

''I hope to do as well.'' I smiled and followed his directions to the stairwell door.

I kept to a slow, steady pace, with frequent breaks to stretch out my calf muscles. Emergency lights burned on every second floor, providing a ghostly glow in which to read the floor numbers on the doors.

Around the fifteenth floor I abandoned my briefcase, stuffing my picklocks and rubber gloves in my pockets. Around the twenty-second my legs felt as though they were on fire. By the time I got to the thirties I was having to stop and sit for a minute after each flight. When I finally reached the door marked thirty-nine my legs felt like rubber bands. I lay down on the hall floor for ten minutes, resting my ankles against the stairwell doorjamb until the fire in my calves had subsided to a dull glow. Finally I got back up and wobbled along the corridors to Blakely's office.

I found myself tiptoeing past the empty offices. A place whose only purpose was to be stuffed with human bodies in the frenzied dance of modern business seems not just forlorn, but ludicrous when abandoned. I felt a foolish impulse to pat the walls in comfort, to make sure the building knew I was sympathetic so that it would be my ally in my search.

When I got to Blakely's suite I pulled on my latex gloves. The outer door was locked. For some reason it hadn't occurred to me to bring a flashlight; kneeling in the dark to fumble with my picklocks took longer than I wanted to spend. I didn't think the guard would hike up the stairs after me, but he might have an elevator on an emergency generator not available to people like me.

The door opened to the typical executive suite: secretary's office with waiting area for guests, a conference room, which stood open, and the door to the holy of holies, also locked. I ignored Blakely's secretary's desk and file cabinets, assuming he didn't share dangerous secrets with her. His office door yielded to the same combination of picks as the antechamber.

Once inside the ghost-room I worked fast. Blakely had a desk with one center drawer and a filing cabinet made of matching mahogany. Both were locked but opened easily. I started to pull out files, squinting at labels in the half-light. Fortunately he had a corner office, so I got two walls of windows.

Whistling softly through my teeth I flipped through executive reports on loans, profits, expansion, overseas clients, executive-suite clients—those with assets of a hundred million or more, according to a memo in the front of the file— there were only eleven, including Gant-Ag—the pros and cons of offshore banking, small banks that might make acquisition targets, personnel files of staff reporting directly to him.

The details of confidential personnel reports weren't any of my business; I returned them immediately to the desk drawer. I skimmed the acquisitions file, but found no mention of Century Bank. Overseas clients included an impressive assortment in the Middle East. I thumbed through the pages quickly, and was about to return it, too, to the drawer, when the Gant-Ag name jumped out at me.

Rolling a plush armchair over to the window, where I could read better, I went back through the file until I found the Gant-Ag name again. It was in a letter from a man named Manzoor Khalil, whose letterhead identified him as an exporter with offices in Karachi and Amman. He thanked Blakely for the opportunity to do business with Gateway and with Gant-Ag, and assured him that Gant-Ag's Agricultural Products—capitalized in the letter—had safely reached their final destination.

> My client is extremely satisfied with Gant-Ag's per-
> formance, and has, as requested, deposited payment in
> his own bank in the Caymans. I await your instructions
> on how to transfer money from this account to your
> own client.

Manzoor Khalil considered himself, in conclusion, Donald Blakely's most esteemed and obliged colleague. I read the letter through three times, then held it sideways, as though that might shed further light on it.

If Gant-Ag was doing business in the Middle East, why couldn't money simply be paid straight into their own account? Presumably they had transfer agents all over the world. Even if it was a country where civil unrest made business risky, they could still get paid, in dollars, in a bank of their choosing. Why this rigmarole of getting the customer to put money into his own offshore account?

Suddenly I remembered the letter I'd filched from Fabian Messenger's desk. Senator Gantner was thanking him for advice on the Boland Amendment. It hadn't occurred to me at the time, but the senator must have dozens or more lawyers on his staff to give him all kinds of advice on federal law. He'd turned to Fabian because he didn't want to alert anyone in Washington to the possibility that his family's company was breaking the law.

I didn't know much about the Boland Amendment. I thought it only applied to sending arms to the Nicaraguan contras. But maybe it forbade any financial deals with terrorist organizations? I wondered what Fabian would do if I called up and asked him for an opinion.

Come to think of it, a whiff of Gant-Ag's dealings must have surfaced somewhere in Congress: in the stack of documents Murray had pulled for me young Alec and the senator's brother Craig had both testified before a Senate select committee that Gant-Ag was not violating the embargo. Grain companies had been hard hit by the embargo. If Gant-Ag had felt they wanted to sidestep it, then they would have to work through a third party like Khalil.

And the fifty-million-dollar line of credit that Century Bank ran through Home Free, which Ken Graham had found in Tish's files: Was that the money from the Caymans being cycled through a not-for-profit for Gant-Ag?

If Century and Home Free were laundering money for Gantner, no wonder Blakely and Heccomb didn't want me poking around in Century's affairs. The musketeers had canceled the Lamia loan because when JAD bought Century they started to cut back on minority and women-owned enterprises. Then, according to Cyrus, they had put an effective *omertà* in place in City Hall.

Everything was fine until I started asking questions about why Lamia'd lost their zoning permit and their loan. Gantner talked to Phoebe, asking her to put my investigation into the deep freeze. In exchange, his daddy would get FDA approval for her T-cell enhancer. And to sweeten the blow to Lamia, they got Heccomb to scrounge around and come up with a rehab project for the women.

Small surprise: Home Free had gotten out of the business of direct placement of the homeless. If they were indeed serving as the point for bringing Gant-Ag's money into the country, they wouldn't have time or energy to work as a social services agency. They certainly wouldn't want the state, or even the city, to come around on the tours of inspection service providers have to go through.

At the same time, they were awash in cash. So why not funnel some of it into construction? By working with the Romanians, paying them almost nothing, they could pad their payrolls and make it look as though a lot more money was going into construction than in fact they were spending.

How much of this had Deirdre known? She might have stumbled onto the padded payrolls in her volunteer work. She might even have known about the line of credit. Since she was married to Fabian, she could have learned without too much difficulty that Gant-Ag was trying to violate the Boland Amendment.

A chill hand squeezed my stomach. Had Deirdre taken her knowledge to the three musketeers? Hoping for—I couldn't imagine. Maybe she wasn't trying to gain anything tangible—maybe she just thought if she held their secrets they would have to respect her. If fifty million dollars was at stake they might well have decided she was an expendable irritant.

The memory of Deirdre at her dinner party swam before my brain. Drunk, hostile, making innuendos—about Jasper Heccomb and how pleased Blakely and Gantner must be with him. It must have become clear to them that night that their secrets would not survive longer than it took her to drink a bottle of burgundy.

If. If all my suppositions were correct. I grabbed a piece of paper from Blakely's desk and scribbled down Khalil's name, address, and the date of the letter. Returning the FOREIGN CLIENT file to his desk, I pulled out the Gant-Ag papers. This was the biggest collection Blakely had—about six inches of documents.

I looked at my watch: I'd been up here for over an hour now. Would the guard become suspicious? And if so, what would he do? Without electricity in the building I couldn't photocopy anything. I had to study the papers here, and today was probably my only chance.

Nervous about time I flipped through the pages, not sure what to look for. Finally I pulled out sections that related to

Gant-Ag's debt. Near the end of the stack was a section on taxes. Ah, yes, the other half of Gantner's letter to Fabian, wanting an expert on tax loans from offshore banks.

I had settled back into the plush armchair with my load of documents when I became aware of a whirring in the background. The office had been utterly soundless, but at first the noise didn't rouse me because it was the commonplace hum of office life—an elevator.

I swore savagely. As I'd feared, the guard had become suspicious. And as I'd also feared, he had a machine at his disposal.

□54
Down the Shaft

I shoved the desk drawers shut, stuffed the papers I was carrying down the back of my jeans, took a quick look around to make sure I wasn't leaving anything personal behind, and scampered out of the office as fast as my sore legs would carry me. I slammed the doors behind me and went up the hallway in a shuffling run. My hamstrings protested, but I overruled them. "Move now or you can rest all you want in jail," I muttered out loud.

When I got to the elevators I couldn't hear them running. Maybe I'd been mistaken. Or maybe there was a service elevator in another part of the building. If I went back to the stairwell I could be intercepted on any floor, but at least I would hear my pursuer.

I had turned back to the hall when the motor started up again. I put my ear to each set of doors in turn: it was the left one on the far end. I looked around for cover. The elevator bank opened onto the executive reception area. A high mahogany counter separated the hall from the desk where the receptionist held court. That would have to do. As the motor behind me whined to a halt I ran to the counter, put a hand on the top, and vaulted over.

I landed with a clatter on a set of phone buttons built into the desk top. Biting off an expletive, I held my breath. The doors were rolling open. With any luck my crash landing wouldn't be noticed. As I waited I heard static from a walkie-talkie, and the grunt of someone stooping. I slid quietly from the phone buttons and crouched underneath the desk. A few seconds later a flashlight played over the rug behind me. My left leg cramped up. I stuffed my fist into my mouth to beat back a gasp of agony.

The light disappeared. Footsteps were almost inaudible in the thick carpeting, but with no sounds from lights or machines to mask them I could hear the guard rustling off in the direction of Blakely's office, the static from his walkie-talkie giving an occasional belch. When I heard his key scrabble in the lock I straightened out my cramped leg and crawled from my hiding place. I took a quick minute to massage the knotted muscle, then peered around the edge of the receptionist's cave. In the murk I couldn't make out the end of the hall to see whether Blakely's door was open, or where the guard was, but he wouldn't be able to see me either.

Staying on my hands and knees, I slithered across the open space to the elevator. He had wedged it open with a block of wood—the automatic call buttons wouldn't work, so he'd have to keep the car with him. I climbed into the car. Without a flashlight I wouldn't be able to see inside—it was hard enough to do so in the pale green of the emergency bulb in the hall.

Squinting, I saw the guard had removed a panel over a manual control that had to be key activated. My hands clammy with nerves, I fumbled with my picklocks in the dark. The slender shafts buckled at first and in the distance I heard Blakely's door slam shut.

"Patience, Victoria," I whispered. "The lock is an extension of your fingers. Feel your way into it."

The light of the guard's flash flicked in front of the door as two wards locked in place. I turned the lever two thirds of the way to the left and kicked the wedge away. The guard's outraged bellow followed me down the shaft.

The car stopped at eleven. Good guess: I wanted to go

back to fifteen to retrieve my briefcase. Aside from the fact that the case was covered with my prints, it also had my name written prominently on the inside. Reward if found and returned, or some such nonsense.

I took the Gantner files from the small of my back and removed the contents, which I tucked inside my shirt. Working the manila folders into a square, I stuck it carefully between the elevator doors.

When I got to the stairwell I expected to hear the guard running after me. The shaft was quiet. Sweat began running down the nape of my neck again. Of course. He was summoning help on his walkie-talkie.

They would assume at first that I was taking the elevator to the ground floor and wait for me there. I hoped. I started to calculate how much time I had, then decided it didn't matter: I had to retrieve my briefcase.

Going up the four flights of stairs was a punishment on my sore legs. I couldn't afford to sing or make any noise to deflect my mind. At least I wasn't going into the tunnels again. Away from the depths and toward the light, I thought, remembering a night when I was eight or nine, when a snowstorm had blown into a blizzard as I was halfway home from school.

Gabriella always put a lamp in the living room for my father on stormy nights. I knew she would set it out for me. As the balloon of snow encased me I peered up at the shadowy bulks of buildings, looking for the light. My legs right now felt as they had then, my little-girl legs in the red tights Gabriella insisted on for winter, pumping one step after the other, looking for my mother's beacon. She had been waiting on the front sidewalk for me, wrapped in a shawl. At nine my head already came to her shoulder, but she picked me up as if I were an infant and carried me into the house. She put me to bed with a treat reserved for special times: hot milk with cocoa and a dash of her strong Italian coffee.

I came to the emergency light at fourteen and found my case only half a flight above me. I paused before starting my downward journey, straining to listen. I didn't think I was being approached from either direction.

On the downward journey I found a reservoir of strength I wouldn't have imagined. Perhaps it was my mother's spirit enveloping me, but I found myself able to sprint down the four flights to the eleventh floor. Retrieving the elevator, I turned the lever all the way to the left. In normal operation it would have stopped on the ground floor, but in its manual emergency mode it took me to the service basement. Not so far from the tunnels after all.

I had my gun in my hand as I exited, but if my guard had summoned allies they were waiting in the lobby. In the dark I saw the red light of an exit sign. Moving with caution in the blackness I made my way to a door that opened on the garage. In another five minutes I was on Canal Street.

With a reckless disregard for my finances I flagged a cab at the corner of Washington and rode to my front door. I was so beat I didn't even try to keep a lookout for Anton. I kept the Smith & Wesson in my hand with the safety off as I staggered up the three flights: if he jumped me I would simply shoot him on the spot.

I reached my own door without incident. Maybe Terry's threat of a police watch had been more than bravado. Maybe the cops would help me out for a change.

Stopping only to set the alarm and do up all my bolts, I sank into a hot bath. I soaked for an hour, emptying and refilling the tub, flexing and stretching my legs against the wall. While I lay there I read the Gantner files.

The papers I'd taken away with me did not mention any Cayman Island banks. They did give a high-level summary of Gant-Ag's and Gantohol's debt position in the bank, repayment figures, and a reference to the buying of Gant-Ag debt from Century Bank.

When I finally climbed out of the tub I moved slowly to the living room to call Murray. Halfway through punching his number I thought again about Terry's threats. Maybe he'd tapped my phone too. I slowly climbed back into my jeans and went out to my car. I drove along Diversey until I found a strip mall with a pay phone.

I managed to reach Murray at his desk. "I have a hypothesis, but I need to test it. Can you meet me on the North Side this afternoon?"

"This anything to do with young Messenger?" Murray rumbled at me. "We heard a rumor she'd disappeared again, but the cops, the hospital, and Papa are all sitting mum. I should have known that my best source was you."

"The cops and Papa weren't so discreet with me—they brought search warrants to inspect mine and my friends' homes last night. Come to think of it, I'm surprised they left you alone."

"Maybe they know you're not very friendly with me. No, no, I take it back. You're wonderful. Sorry, I momentarily forgot. Are you sitting on the kid?"

"I don't know where she is. I told Finchley to look at the Home Free construction sites, but they're not paying much attention to me these days. My hypothesis, though, has to do with Gantner and Heccomb, and probably Deirdre's murder."

He was so excited by the prospect of nailing one of the Gantners that he didn't try to push me on Emily's whereabouts. He was busy until two-thirty, he told me, but would be outside my front door at three.

"The cops are on my ass. I'll go down to Illinois Center —you can enter on Michigan and leave almost anywhere. Pick me up at the Fairmont Hotel—you know the valet entrance on lower Wacker?"

"Yes, *ma'am*. The code is: John has a long mustache."

I was only half a block from the el. Just to keep Terry's crew on their toes I left my car in the mall lot and walked down Diversey to Sheffield, where I hiked up the ancient stairs to the train. At Chicago Avenue I caught a cab to Wacker and Michigan.

Illinois Center connects to a complex of a dozen or so buildings, including three hotels, through a series of underground passages. The floods had shut them for a couple of days, but they were open again now. The long passages and steep escalators made it easy to see I was alone. I emerged from the Fairmont's underground entrance precisely at three.

Murray held his car door open for me with a flourish. "Heccomb isn't in. He's not expected until five. I called on my car phone while you were hobbling downstairs. What are we going to do?"

"Imitate the Bears in their glory years. Fencik and Singletary hitting high and low. If she isn't a criminal, she'll crack."

Murray gave a mock salute. "Did they leave *scruple* out of your brain when you were born, O She-who-must-be-obeyed?"

"Never heard the word. And now I've forgotten it."

▫55
Coming Up to Bat

When we burst in on Tish she was hunched over her computer, still wearing the shapeless khaki sweater in which I'd last seen her.

"Hi," I said in my heartiest voice. "This is Murray Ryerson with the *Herald-Star*. He's doing a story on Home Free. He wants to interview you."

Her muddy skin turned mahogany with annoyance. "You can't barge in here any time you feel like it. And you can't do an interview with me. Jasper handles all press inquiries."

"And there's a good reason for that."

I pulled out my picklocks. As she gasped in fury I unlocked Jasper's office. She reached out a hand for the phone, but Murray, with an apology, unplugged it and put it on the floor.

I brought a couple of chairs from Jasper's office. "We're going to have a long talk. Murray and I want to be comfortable. As I said, there's a reason Jasper has forbidden you to talk to the press: he's sitting on some ugly secrets, about himself and his pals. He's afraid in your naïveté you might blurt out something incriminating."

She was on her feet, pummeling Murray's unmoving

arms. "You can't do this," she panted. "I'm getting the police."

"You are welcome to call them," I said, picking the phone up from the floor and reattaching it to the cord. "I'll dial the number for you so we know we're getting the law, not Gary Charpentier or Anton."

She stopped pounding on Murray to scowl at me. With his arms free Murray set up his tape recorder and tested the mike. I waited for him to finish his setup before continuing.

"We'll start by showing the cops the cash Jasper keeps in that locked drawer in his office. You know—the stuff he uses for off-the-books payments to his contractors. So that people like Charpentier can throw spare change at illegal immigrants from Eastern Europe while he pockets hundred-dollar bills."

She smiled in a contemptuous way but said nothing.

"She knew about the illegal aliens," I said instructively to Murray. "I bet her mother will enjoy reading that."

"We weren't hurting anyone," Tish snapped. "They got more money than they would have made at home. And if they lived a little rough for a few months it wasn't like they had to do it forever, like they were homeless or sharecroppers or something."

"That sounds like Jasper Heccomb speaking. Are you sure you believe that yourself, Tish?" Murray asked her, his blue eyes large and sincere. "Let alone the question of whether American workers could have had decent jobs instead of having to live on the streets, did you approve of this policy?"

When Tish kneaded her hands without speaking I added, "You knew they were being paid off the books. Did you know Jasper kept five million in that drawer in his office?"

She looked up at that, startled enough to blurt, "You're wrong: he showed it to me himself, on Monday. It was only fifteen thousand."

I nodded. "Jasper needed to show it to you because I'd broken in here Friday night and seen the drawer when it was stuffed to the brim with hundreds. He figured if he got his story to you first you'd believe it: you've looked the other way many times because you *need* to believe him. He's counting on you to do it again.

"But listen carefully while I explain something to you. Jasper and his friends are likely going to jail, possibly for a very long time. You have to decide whether you want to go with them. If the going gets rough it wouldn't surprise me if Jasper tried to set you up to take the fall for him. He may suggest that financial high jinks here began when you were interim director, for instance. I know for a fact that they're framing Anton—you do know Anton, don't you?"

She was pretending to stare out the window in boredom, but all her emotions registered on her surface with painful intensity. Despite her pose she was trembling.

"You can avoid a lot of grief by speaking frankly now. Or you can decide the crumbs of attention Jasper throws you will carry you through five years in a federal pen."

"You're the one who's going to jail," she said, her eyes full of fire. "You just admitted breaking in here."

"Yeah. I broke the law. I agree. The cops know about it" —at least, Conrad knew about it—"and they're not happy, but they haven't applied for a warrant. It'll be the FBI, anyway, not the city police, who'll look into Jasper's story. That should make for a fascinating investigation, because we'll get to see whether Senator Gantner has enough influence to shut down the Justice Department."

Tish's lower jaw jutted out. "I knew Jasper was paying people off the books, but that isn't such a big crime. The worst that can happen is we'd pay a fine. Everyone wants affordable housing for the homeless, but no one wants to pay the bill. If we had to pay union scale a lot of those people would still be—"

"Out on the streets; I know," I cut in. "But that isn't what I'm talking about. A few million over the years to contractors is peanuts compared to their main game.

"Jasper, together with Alec Gantner and Donald Blakely, formed a holding company called JAD, which they used to buy Century Bank here in Uptown. They then used

Century to funnel money from the Cayman Islands to the Gant-Ag account at Gateway Bank. Now why, you are asking yourself, did Gant-Ag need to bring money into the country in such a secretive way? And the answer is: They were violating the embargo against Iraq. They were working through a man named Manzoor Khalil in Jordan—which sat on the fence during the Gulf brouhaha. I can't prove it, but I'm betting Gant-Ag shipped corn to Saddam which meant they had to be paid surreptitiously.''

Murray's jaw dropped, then he sprang up, knocking over his mike, and shook my shoulder. "Fact, Warshawski, or fiction? Damn you, how much of this is true? And how do you know?"

"She's got some of it in her computer." I cocked my head at Tish. "Your fifty-million-dollar line of credit from Century. Didn't it ever occur to you that that was a whole lot more than a little not-for-profit like Home Free needed? Even if you'd stopped being a direct service provider and were building affordable housing instead?"

The color had receded from Tish's cheeks, leaving them a faint beige. Her lips mouthed the word *no,* but no sound came out.

"I want to see it." Murray's baritone was cracking with desire; he sounded like Mitch trying to get a squirrel on the other side of the fence.

"He did it as a favor to Senator Gantner, didn't he—really, to the whole Gantner family." I ignored him, speaking directly to Tish. "The money came through Gateway as part of the Gant-Ag line of credit. So not only did they get the money, but they got it in the form of a loan. That meant they could deduct the loan interest from their income tax while they repaid—using cash from Jasper's magic drawer. The loan repayment, in turn, financed JAD's acquisition of Century. The whole deal made a tight loop, very symmetrical.''

"No," Tish whispered. "It couldn't be that. Jasper did set up the line of credit as a favor to Senator Gantner. But in return the senator gave us almost a hundred thousand dollars. It was so much—we could do so much good with that kind of money.''

I held out the Gant-Ag papers I'd taken from Blakely's office. ''It's all in here, Tish: the Gateway money, the summary of the reports the bank sent to the IRS. Senator Gantner took legal advice on the tax code and offshore banks eighteen months ago. At the same time, by the way, that he was inquiring into the Boland Amendment.''

Murray snatched the papers from me and started going through them so fast that they fell on the floor. He dropped to his knees to grab them up again, but Tish was sitting motionless with shock. Her skin was pulled so tight across her face that I thought the bones might poke through it.

''Then Deirdre stumbled on it,'' I went on. ''She was doing all that volunteer work, and she found the accounting records.''

''I had the flu,'' Tish whispered. ''She should never have seen those files. But Jasper was out of the office and she was being a good soldier, entering cash receipts.''

''And she confronted Heccomb with what she'd seen,'' I prodded when her voice trailed away.

''He told her—what I just said. How much good we were doing, and not to get everyone in trouble when the law itself was a bad one. He said Senator Gantner would appreciate it, appreciate her support—he knew Mr. Messenger was hoping for a federal judgeship.''

''You sat in on the conversation?'' Murray asked.

She turned a deep red; her gaze flicked at the intercom box on her desk. She wasn't going to admit it, but jealous love of Jasper made her want to hear what he said to a woman alone in his office with him.

''Was that why Blakely got Gateway to make a donation to Arcadia House?'' I asked.

''I guess so,'' she whispered, looking at her hands. ''I didn't know about the money—the Century line of credit, I mean—until Deirdre stumbled onto those accounts. Jasper always kept the corporate donor files himself. I don't even know where Deirdre found the diskette. Snooping around, I suppose. Then she couldn't let it alone. Every time she came in the last few weeks she liked to try to get me to discuss it.''

We sat silent for a minute. Street noises floated faintly through the Thermopane windows—children shrieking on their way home from school, the occasional car on a short-cut to Montrose.

''When Deirdre died, you didn't think Jasper or his friends were trying to shut her up, did you?''

''No!'' The word came out as an explosion that startled her as much as it did Murray and me. ''They'd given twenty-five thousand to one of her pet charities. They were going to make her husband a judge. What else did she need?''

A list of Deirdre's needs flitted through my mind, but I said aloud, ''Did you see a baseball bat in here anytime recently?''

Surprised by the change of subject, Tish answered without thinking. ''Yes. Donald Blakely brought one in—I don't know, three weeks ago maybe. He and Jasper were laughing about it, then Jasper said something about going to bat for Gantner one more time. Why do you ask?'' she added belatedly.

The police had kept the discovery of Fabian's bat from the press, but the juxtaposition of Deirdre's death with my question made the connection for Murray. His eyes blazing, he started to say something, cut himself short in the nick of time, and instead tried to get Tish to pin down the day. She couldn't be specific, and she couldn't remember, when I asked her, if it had been a signed bat. She wasn't interested in baseball; she didn't know what a signed bat was.

Murray had the whole interchange on tape. Surely that would make Finchley reconsider his warrant for Emily's arrest. Tish's testimony definitely ruled Fabian out as well. A pity, really. But maybe he'd been an accessory.

No, that wasn't possible either. Blakely or Gantner must have taken the bat with precisely the aim of implicating Fabian in his wife's murder. Neither of them would have expected Emily to snatch the weapon away. They must have been on tenterhooks ever since, wondering why Fabian hadn't been arrested.

"So what do you want to do now?" Murray asked me. "Take all this to the state's attorney, or to the federal prosecutor? Or should I just run an exclusive?"

"What do you want us to do, Tish?" I said.

"Go to hell," she snapped.

"Understood. But since that isn't among your options?"

"You have to give me time to think. You can't print anything anyway. You only have allegations. No proof."

Her face was furrowed in agony. I did feel sorry for her. She was bright; she was dedicated to a difficult social cause. Her only crime was in falling in love with Jasper Heccomb. And he was whistling happily around the city, while she would spend the night tossing in torment.

"We have enough that proof will follow." Murray spoke with unwonted gentleness—her naked misery was affecting him too. "Can she have forty-eight hours, Nancy Drew?"

"Not on the baseball bat. But on the money? That stash isn't going anywhere very fast."

Murray moved the phone next to her. He patted her shoulder in a sympathetic way. She drew away from him with a sharp cry. Before the door shut behind us her shoulders were heaving with sobs.

□56
The Dead Speak

"I feel sorry for her," Murray said as we stood outside his car. "You were pretty rough on her."

"I feel sorry for her too. Sorry enough to give her a jolt that may keep her from washing Heccomb's dirty clothes one last time."

"Speaking of laundry—these papers are suggestive, but they don't prove a damned thing. Gateway bought some Gant-Ag debt from Century, but it doesn't say word one about the Caymans."

I grinned at him. "Here's where you get to prove you're still the boy reporter who can scoop all the kids hungry for your job. One of those stories you printed out for me mentioned Craig Gantner testifying in front of a Senate select committee that Gant-Ag didn't break the embargo. Go to Washington and find out who knew enough to get a subpoena for the senator's brother. Talk to Messenger: he did some legal work for Gantner on the Boland Amendment. Fabian won't talk to me, but he might confide to you what slant the senator wanted on the amendment."

Murray planted a wet kiss on my nose. "This could be a very big story, Warshawski. I'll take you to dinner at the Ritz if I win a Pulitzer."

"Be still, my waiting heart. How about walking me to

my front door instead? A big ugly goon is on my tail and I'm not up to fighting him solo.''

Murray responded with appropriate mockery, but when I told him about Anton's assault on Emily yesterday, and my scampering around the Gateway stairwells this morning, he agreed I had earned some support.

"Although, I don't know, Warshawski. When did Nancy Drew ever ask Ned to watch her back?'' he said when we'd reached my apartment without incident. "You're going to have to bring Anton to me in your teeth to restore your credibility.''

"Only if he's wrapped in latex—I don't want to catch rabies or worse from touching him.''

We parted on that light vein, but I wondered how long I would be left in peace by the musketeers. Perhaps, through their pipeline to the city, they knew I'd gone to Conrad's from the hospital. But at any moment they would learn I had returned to my own home.

I surveyed the street from my front window. My car was sitting there like a bright red beacon, saying "Come and get me.'' It was too late to move it—it had been there for more than a day. I couldn't worry about that now.

My legs were aching. I went to the kitchen and made up some ice packs out of bags of frozen peas. Using a couple of Ace bandages I attached them to my legs and lay down on the couch. It was supposed to be a half-hour nap, but the phone woke me a little after six.

"Don't you ever check your messages?'' It was Ken Graham. "I've called four times in the last day.''

"Excuse me, your highness, for not leaping to attention at the first intimation of your wishes. Before you execute me can I have five minutes to say farewell to my dogs?''

"Oh. You think I'm being pushy. Sorry. But I found something really amazing in your old computer. A letter to you from Deirdre.''

He laughed when I could only sputter out half-questions. "I thought you'd be amazed. I got a lot of your accounting numbers pieced together and printed out. Then I thought maybe I should take a look at your word-processing documents, see if there was anything with a recent date that you might need, and there was this message from beyond the grave.''

''What does it say? How do you know Deirdre wrote it?'' I sat up and turned on a lamp.

''She did it like a memo: To Vic from Deirdre. With the date and everything. She said—well, I'll read you exactly what she said: 'I made Fabian tell me how they bring the money in. Just ask him.' ''

''You really found this on my machine? You wouldn't shit an old hand, would you?''

''Why would I do that? I don't know what she's talking about,'' he said plaintively.

''You saw all that cash in the Home Free office.''

''What cash?'' he demanded.

I remembered that Jasper had arrived as I was going through the drawer. Maybe I'd never mentioned it to Ken. I apologized for suspecting him of making a monkey of me in order to get me to pay attention to him.

If the message was authentic, why on earth had she written it? Was she going to leave it flashing on my computer screen to greet me in the morning? Because in the normal course of things that would be the only way I'd see a file I didn't know existed. Did she know she was about to die, and was hoping to grab my attention in a way that would make me investigate her murder?

I could see Deirdre, as plainly as if she were in front of me, that little gloating smile of triumph. She thought she had Fabian? Gantner? Heccomb? all the musketeers, I suppose, on a string. This wasn't a message typed in desperation, but one she'd written out while she waited for her murderer. She'd shown it to him, and he'd bashed her brains out. Maybe he'd deleted the file after he killed her. Then, halfway home, he wondered if she'd left other messages in the machine. He decided the safe thing would be to come back and erase the whole disk.

I sat without speaking for so long that Ken demanded to know if I'd hung up.

"Sorry." I pulled myself together to thank him effusively. "You've earned your reward—within reason. I'll see you get your community service. I'll make sure you don't have to go back to Harvard. I'll get Darraugh to support you in your own apartment."

"Spend the night with me."

"No, sonny. At least, not in bed with you."

"Then dinner. The Filigree. And dancing afterward."

I couldn't help being touched. I promised him we would go out as soon as I'd stopped running for my life. Although I wondered when that would be.

"What about your accounts? You still have to file your taxes by next Wednesday," he cried as I started to hang up.

I picked the receiver up again. "Did you get my accounts out too? Well done. Let's meet on Sunday, unless you hear from me otherwise."

Or see my body in pieces on the ten o'clock news, I added to myself, hanging up. I should call Conrad, or Terry, to tell them about Tish's testimony on the baseball bat. But they would probably say it didn't count as evidence since she hadn't noticed the Nellie Fox signature. And they would deny Deirdre's message on the grounds Ken could easily have planted it in my hard drive. Jerks could have read the disk themselves while they had my machine in their evidence room all those days.

The truth was, I was so bitter at the way they'd treated Anton's assault on Emily that I didn't care if I ever saw Conrad again. I certainly wasn't going to go out of my way to help them find Deirdre's murderer. If I could keep one step ahead of the musketeers I ought to be able to get the whole story public in a few days.

I got up on legs that felt like ill-attached prostheses and staggered from my apartment, using the back stairs, taking plenty of time to shine a flashlight on each landing before proceeding, keeping my gun leveled in front of me. To my chagrin I realized I missed Mr. Contreras and the dogs.

Without them on the first floor I felt small and very exposed as I crept my way around the side of the building to my car.

No one tried to mug me as I opened the door. No one had tied dynamite to the engine. It started with its usual satisfying rumble, giving me the sense that I was queen of the road as I made a U-turn and headed for the South Side.

Fabian's house presented a black, shuttered front to the street. The night air was chilly and I'd come without a coat. Shivering, I followed the walk around to the north side of the house. A chink of light showed through his study windows. I returned to the front porch and rang the bell, rubbing my arms and clenching my teeth to keep them from chattering.

Several minutes passed. I rang again, with a longer push. As I was debating going to the study and throwing a stone at the window I heard the dead bolt scrape back.

"Oh." Fabian blinked at me from the doorway. "I couldn't believe someone was really ringing the bell at this hour."

"And now you know. How are Josh and Nathan—back to normal?" I moved forward and he stepped aside without protest so I could enter.

"Did you want to see them? Dr. Zeitner thinks they're very traumatized. He's suggested a course of therapy for them. I suppose being underground for a week could be extremely unsettling for such young boys. Emily is a very disturbed young lady, very disturbed. What she thought taking them into the tunnels would accomplish, besides giving them terrible nightmares, I don't know. I only hope we can get her some help before it's too late."

"Right." I wasn't surprised that Fabian was talking to me like this, even after yesterday's outburst in my apartment. His changeability made me edgy, but it no longer astonished me.

I shut the door and went into the hall. "Shall we go into your study to talk? Or will you be more comfortable in the living room?"

"Talk? What's there to talk about? Unless you've come

to apologize for your role in leading Emily to think running away was the correct solution to her problems. I'm considering legal action, but on the whole, if we can find Emily and get her to a psychiatrist, I'll probably let the matter drop."

"We're going to talk about Alec Gantner tonight, not Emily. About the money he and the senator are bringing in from the Caymans. Today I found a memo that Deirdre left for me the night she was murdered: 'I made Fabian tell me how they bring the money in,' she wrote. 'Just ask him.' So I'm asking you."

His mouth agape, he stared without speaking for a moment, then said, "I thought at least death would put a halt to her ability to embarrass me, but I see I was wrong."

"People are always treating you thoughtlessly, aren't they, Fabian," I said. "Your daughter, your wife, me. And I'm afraid Alec Gantner and Jasper Heccomb will prove similarly unkind. They took your Nellie Fox bat away, you see, after your party for Manfred Yeo, and used it to kill your wife. They hoped you would be arrested for the crime."

"You're wrong about that. Emily killed her mother. The police found the bat in her bedroom. I thought you knew that."

"I've seen the letter Senator Gantner wrote you after you advised him on the Boland Amendment. He also wanted advice on the tax implications of offshore money, didn't he? Did you find him someone, or did you advise him yourself to ask for it as a loan? It would certainly be the easiest way to launder so much cash, because the IRS wouldn't know—"

"You *saw* that letter?" he thundered. "After promising to be discreet, Deirdre *showed* it to you?"

"I don't think she meant to betray you," I said. "But sometimes when she had too much to drink she could forget what she could and couldn't say. Did she find the letter in your files?"

"He thought he should write me at my home—he knew

how inquisitive secretaries and students would be if they saw personal correspondence from a United States senator. He didn't realize a wife might be just as intrusive. She was always here when the mail came, and she saw the letter. She actually came into my study and snatched it from my hands while I was reading it.''

His face took on the bitter nobility of a tragic hero. ''She was like Lady Macbeth: she gave me no peace until I found out why he wanted to know. She thought if I was doing him such a large favor he would be certain to get me a judgeship. I don't know why she set so much store on my being a federal judge, but the prestige seemed to matter to her. Maybe she thought it would give her a superior position in the Hyde Park coffee klatches.''

''You had no ambition of your own, of course,'' I said smoothly. ''You didn't wonder when she was killed if it had something to do with all this laundered money? By the way, how did they bring it in?''

''Deirdre didn't tell you that?''

''Oh, I know about the big stuff, the wire transfer to Century from the Caymans, and why the three mus—Gantner and his pals made such a secret of their acquisition. But the five million that Jasper kept in his desk drawer—they couldn't have been drawing that out in nine-thousand-dollar increments.''

His lips curved in a contemptuous smile. ''If Deirdre had the grace to keep quiet on even a small fraction of what she knew, I'm not going to give my secrets over to another woman's keeping.''

''Fabian, you don't seem to realize that you are a very fragile person right now. In another few days the news about Gant-Ag's illegal sales to the Iraqis is going to be front-page news. And you know what Gantner and Blakely will do? They will decide to make you their fall guy. 'Fabian Messenger advised us to do it,' they will say. 'A University of Chicago law professor gave us full assurances that we were not violating any sections of the tax code, let alone the Boland Amendment.' They were good and ready to let you take the rap for your wife's murder. That's why they stole—''

When Fabian interrupted me with his litany about Emily and Oedipus, I overspoke him. ''No, you listen to me for once, Messenger. I have a witness who has made a tape-recorded statement. Donald Blakely brought your bat into Jasper Heccomb's office the Thursday morning after your dinner party. I suppose he picked it up and wrapped his coat around it as he left. By questioning all the guests we might even find one who saw him do it but didn't say anything on the assumption you knew about it.

''Be that as it may, Blakely stole your bat. Heccomb, or probably one of his construction foremen, a guy named Anton, used it the next night to kill Deirdre. Blakely assumed you would be arrested. All their problems would be solved in one fell swoop. Deirdre, who was giving cute hints at the dinner about what she knew, would be dead before she could squeal on them. You might be tempted to betray them, but you'd be in jail for your wife's murder. The whole thing was worked neatly. Except you raped Emily, and she ran downtown in the middle of the night to find her mother. When she was in—''

''How dare you?'' Fabian screamed, his face white. ''How dare you make such a filthy accusation about me? Emily is a very disturbed child—''

''Maybe she is,'' I snapped. ''But she did not kill her mother. Now I'm going to work out a little deal with you, Messenger. It makes me puke to deal with you, but I'll swallow it. You tell me what you told Deirdre: how they brought in the cash. And I will not tell the federal prosecutor about your correspondence with Gant-Ag.''

He controlled himself with an effort that left him panting. ''Deirdre was a sick woman. *If* she wrote you a note, and I stress the *if,* I wouldn't put much reliance on it. But it does seem strangely convenient for a note from her to surface just at the moment you need it.''

I folded my arms and leaned against the stairwell wall. ''Murray Ryerson from the *Herald-Star* is working on the

Gant-Ag story right now. He has a source in Senator Gantner's office who will find out about your correspondence with the senator if I point them in that direction.''

Fabian looked at me with loathing, his lips pulled into a thin line. ''I'll think about it and get back to you.''

First Tish, now Fabian. I was getting tired of everyone in Chicago needing so much time to think—it was like we were running a California meditation room or something.

''By noon tomorrow, Messenger. Or I'm going to Murray Ryerson and then the federal prosecutor for Chicago. Give me a number where I can reach you about that time; I'm going to be moving around.''

He wanted to fight about it some more, but finally, in the sulky voice of a boy forced to make peace with a much-hated sister, he told me I could call him at his office. Children's footsteps above us made us both look up. Nathan appeared in the stairwell, crowing with delight.

''Emee? Emee home?'' He suddenly saw it was not his sister, but a stranger, and began to cry, a wail of utter bereavement. ''I want Emee.''

Fabian turned to me bitterly. ''Now see what you've done. We'll have a terrible time getting him to quiet down again.''

He moved past me to pick up his son. ''Emily can't come home. She's a very sick girl. She needs to get well before she sees you again. . . . Sheila! Sheila! Nathan needs to be put back to bed.''

A young woman in jeans and a sweater came running down the stairs and removed Nathan from his father's arms. The nurse he'd hired to look after the boys, I presumed. No one paid any attention to me as I undid the dead bolts and left.

Your Full-Service Senator

In the morning I decided I couldn't take my lonely apartment any longer. I called Mr. Contreras in Elk Grove Village and—over the angry objections of his daughter—arranged to pick him up as soon as he returned from his rabies shot. When I thought of all the times I had cursed his intrusiveness in my life I was ashamed.

I went down to his apartment to tidy up and change his bed. I threw out the old milk, watered his plants, and laid out the morning paper with the track results showing. I seemed to be spending an inordinate amount of time cleaning these days. If my detective business crashed completely I could start a new career as a housekeeper.

I was on my way upstairs to my own place when I heard the faint trill of my doorbell echo in the stairwell. I came down and went back into Mr. Contreras's apartment to look outside. A navy blue sedan was double-parked in front of the apartment. Would a hit man be so obvious?

I wasn't moving from my doorstep these days without my gun. Putting it in my pocket where I could get at it easily I went out the back door and came up behind the man at the bell. He was wearing a navy pinstripe that matched the car and had the well-tended hair of the upscale professional.

"Can I help you?" I said.

He jumped slightly. "I'm looking for Victoria Warchaski."

It was close enough. "And you are?"

He surveyed me with cold pale eyes. "Are you Victoria?"

"I'm Ms. Warshawski. And you are?"

"We'll be more comfortable talking in the car."

I smiled thinly. "*You'll* be more comfortable in your sedan. I, however, am perfectly comfortable here in the hallway. Now why don't you tell me your name and your business."

He pouted as he tried to make up his mind—his instructions hadn't included what to do if I didn't cooperate. "This is private, you understand."

"No problem. Unless the UPS man shows up no one's likely to walk through the foyer this time of day. Spit it out—you'll find it easier than you imagine. You've come to ask me to tail your daughter's boyfriend? To find out who's selling your company's secrets overseas? To shoot me on Donald Blakely's orders? Or to give me a warning about the Gantner investigation?"

He was almost snorting in exasperation. "We need to talk seriously. I'm from Senator Gantner's office."

"And you have a name."

"It's immaterial."

"Not to me—I need to call the office and make sure you really work there. Any con artist can put on expensive threads and claim to work for a U.S. senator."

Before he could react I had a hand inside his left breast pocket. I pulled out his wallet, a thin brown thing that felt like a lover's skin in the night. Keeping one hand on my Smith & Wesson I shook the wallet open, then fished out a driver's license with my teeth. He started shouting—this was an outrage, who did I think I was—that kind of thing. I brought out my gun and waved him into a corner. The driver's license identified him as Eric Bendel.

I handed the wallet back. "I don't know, Bendel, if you

are Bendel—that picture looks like an escapee from the mental hospital in Elgin. You sure you want to claim it?''

''I have a message for you from a United States senator,'' he said through clenched teeth. ''That is something you should take more seriously than you seem prepared to do.''

''Hey, I'm a voter and a taxpayer. If he can say the same, we're equals. But lay it on me—I know you and he think it must be something special.''

''The senator called me an hour ago from Washington.'' The pale eyes had moved from cold to permafrost. ''He said to suggest that your energies would be better spent on other work—that you would know what he was referring to. He also said that if you persisted in an investigation that threatened the well-being of his constituents he would see whether the laws you have broken in the last two weeks constitute grounds for revoking your investigator's license. The state bar will also be interested.''

''My, my. And you learned all that by heart too. No wonder he likes you on his staff. Good-bye, Eric. Have a nice day.'' I opened the door and waved him out with my pistol hand.

''What am I supposed to tell the senator?'' he said in a voice like ground glass.

''That as a constituent I'm honored he takes a close interest in my affairs and I'll do my best to reciprocate. Good-bye, Mr. Bendel.''

Pushing his lips together in frustration he said, ''The senator is used to people taking him seriously.''

''He and I will have to talk face-to-face sometime. We have so much in common—first our interest in each other's business, and now our liking to be taken seriously. I hope you've learned my response by heart. Good-bye.''

He left, almost flouncing his jacket skirts. I waited for him to get into the car before unlocking the hall door. Maybe this was why they hadn't tried beating me up lately —they were hoping I might respond to senatorial persuasions. Revoke my investigator's license, huh? I laughed sardonically. The shape my business was in these days it would hardly matter.

I took extra precautions on my ride out to fetch Mr. Contreras. All the way south to Fabian's last night, and back, I'd had the sense of someone on my tail. If it was Terry's minions, that was a relief, but if not—well, if not, I needed to be wide awake at all times.

When I got to Elk Grove Village I had a difficult conversation with Mr. Contreras's daughter. Ruthie Marcano was understandably jealous of her father's affection for me. She didn't want me to bring him home. I was a bad influence on him. This was the third time he'd needed to be hospitalized in six years because I'd dragged him into danger. Two gunshot wounds and now a rat bite. Did I think I was God? If I thought she was going to let him come back into Chicago with me for any coked-up gang-banger to shoot at, I was out of my mind.

She was very like her father in one respect: words gushed out of her in an unstoppable torrent. I murmured ''no'' and ''yes'' at appropriate intervals—after all, she was right. I had given the old man a good run for his Medicaid taxes. Before I could come up with any way of stanching the flow, her father appeared on the doorstep.

''Listen.'' I interrupted his jubilant greeting without ceremony. ''Your daughter's been reminding me of all the danger I've put you in over the years. I think maybe you should stay in Elk Grove Village until we get shut of—well, whoever's been taking aim at me lately.''

He was indignant. If I thought he wanted to pack up and die he sure as hell wouldn't want to do it out here in the suburbs. He'd move into a retirement community—his local owned one in Edgewater. But he wasn't going to sit and listen to me try to wrap him up like he was dead and I was a winding sheet.

Ruthie turned on him for his ingratitude. ''Didn't I drop everything as soon as I got the news you was in the hospital? Didn't I? And all for what—for you to tell me this—

this floozy who got you in trouble to begin with is more important to you than your own flesh and blood!''

''And didn't your ma wash your mouth out a dozen times for language like that?'' her father shouted. ''Now you apologize to Vic here.''

''No need, no need,'' I said hastily.

This was a family fight—they paid no attention to me. They started in on each other's past wrongdoings at such a pitch that Mitch and Peppy roared around the corner of the house to see what was happening.

The dogs were hysterical with delight at seeing me. It had been five days, after all. While they raced up and down the sidewalk a dozen times to show their pleasure, Ruthie's younger son, a gangly fourteen-year-old, came out of the house with Mr. Contreras's suitcase. He hovered behind the old man in the manner of teenagers—wanting to say good-bye, not knowing what to do with his body.

As we finally shepherded the dogs into the car, Ruthie said, ''I can't keep running into Chicago every time this detective gets you bitten or shot.''

''Good,'' my neighbor said truculently. ''I keep telling you to leave me alone. Bye, Ben.'' He clapped his grandson roughly on the shoulder and got into the car.

On the way into town I found myself reiterating some of Ruthie's warnings. ''Too many people want my head on a platter these days. I just had a visit from one of Senator Gantner's aides, with a soft threat from the senator himself.''

''We already been through this, doll. I ain't gonna argue about it anymore. Tell me about the kids we brung out Monday morning. How are they?''

I had called Eva Kuhn before leaving the apartment. I gave Mr. Contreras her report on the two surviving Hawkings children.

''The biggest problem is the custody fight Leon Hawkings is mounting. The kids are recovering fast physically, but Tamar seems to have disintegrated emotionally. Eva says as long as she had to cope with the real-life problems of survival she was okay, but faced with the threat of losing her children she's getting withdrawn and morose.''

''Well, it ain't like she's in contention for mother-of-the-year prizes, but we oughtta think about helping her. 'Cause if the guy did mistreat her, and the daughter, the poor girl that died, he's got no business getting the other two kids back.''

''You take on that assignment—thinking of something to do to help Tamar. Maybe you could adopt the kids.''

I meant it for a joke, but his eyes lit up. ''Now, that's a definite idea, doll. We ought to get us a kid to go along with the dogs.''

''Great idea. I could run all three of them to the lake and back every morning.''

''Now, doll, you know—oh, you're pulling my leg. Okay, okay. Maybe we don't need a kid. But we could give all five of them children a better home than they've got to go to right now.''

I couldn't fight him on that one. It was one of the—many—things wearing me down these days.

It was just on noon when I had him settled into his apartment again. I left him fussing with his seedlings and went upstairs to call Fabian.

After various receptionists and secretaries switched me around the law school I was permitted to talk to the professor. His voice was so tight I could have bounced coins from it.

''Before I say anything I want you to know that my talking to you is not a sign that I agree to any of the outrageous statements you were hurling at me last night.''

''Yeah, yeah,'' I said, bored. ''You're a lawyer, you've talked to a lawyer. Now that we've read the fine print, tell me how the cash comes in.''

''By air, Warshawski. On Saturday nights.''

''By air?'' I echoed. ''Where? Surely not to O'Hare.''

''You pride yourself on being so smart, you figure it out.''

''Fabian—''

He hung up, leaving me fuming. When I called back he refused to come to the phone again, sending me a snotty message through the departmental receptionist.

By air on Saturday nights. Great. I started ticking off airports in the Chicago area. Probably not O'Hare, unless Gantner managed to pay off a whole lot of people—mechanics, controllers, customs agents. The same argument applied to Midway. There was a military runway near O'Hare—the senator might have access to that. And the naval air base in the northern suburbs. Meigs Field, the little corporate airport on the lakefront was a possibility. Gary, Indiana, had an airport. There were dozens of private landing strips in the seven-county area, but presumably the musketeers needed a jet if money was coming all the way from the Caymans.

And then I smacked my forehead. Gant-Ag had an airstrip. No customs, the mechanics all worked for the company. The elaborate security I'd encountered when I drove out there last week—that didn't have anything to do with experimental corn hybrids. Gantner needed every possible warning of visitors to the site.

"Fabian's right: I *am* so smart," I said aloud.

Or was I? Had the senator sent Eric Bendel because Fabian had called him for help? Or because young Alec had come running to Papa? Fabian might have gone to young Alec anyway. In which case this cryptic hint was a way of baiting a trap for me. But maybe, even if it was a trap, it was still true—the money did come in there on Saturday nights, but they hoped to kill me in the act of trespassing on the sacred experimental farm.

("In the dark we couldn't tell who it was," young Alec would say, more in sorrow than anger. "She'd been out here last week pulling up our sacred grass. We warned her then—how could we know she had such contempt for private property and the law?")

I called Murray. If Alec Gantner was going to unload bags of hundred-dollar bills out at the family farm this weekend, I didn't want to be the only witness. As Terry had made clear, no cops wanted to touch a U.S. senator's banker, let alone his son. I'd have to have pictures, names, and dates before I'd get anyone to listen to me.

As I'd hoped, Murray was eager to ride shotgun for me. When I'd explained the whole situation to him he agreed to come up with a camera that could take nighttime pictures. And he also promised not to nudge any of his volatile Washington sources until after the weekend.

"It's not a story yet, you know," he told me. "I played Tish's tape to my editor yesterday. He's willing to let me poke around, but he's treating me the way Finchley did you. If we get something cold and hard, like an airplane logbook and photos, I may get some real resources assigned to this."

We decided to drive out to Morris together around noon, so that we'd have enough time to scout the landscape. Murray would pick me up in the alley behind the Belmont Diner at eleven.

□58

Lover in Arms

The cold had worked its way through my windbreaker and pullover. As I lay in the damp soil next to Murray I had to clench my teeth to stop their chatter. I unfolded the blanket from my backpack and wrapped it around my shoulders. Murray grunted and grabbed a corner of it to pull across his neck.

When we reached Gant-Ag a little after one we drove the perimeter of their headquarters. On the southwest edge of the vast holdings of buildings and experimental farms we found a thicket where a stream crossed the property. Gant-Ag had left four or five acres of brush and trees as a small wilderness.

We knew we were at risk of being spotted by surveillance equipment anywhere we crossed the property line, but we thought we would be least likely to face detection here. The tangled growth bordered an unpaved side road, so slippery with mud from the spring rains that Murray's Cobra spun out of control several times.

We whiled away the rest of the afternoon in the town of Morris. After a late lunch we went into the public library, where Murray used an empty conference room to test his video equipment. Some pal in the public relations office at Ft. Sheridan had come up with a night-vision video camera for him as well as a lightweight set of field glasses. Lugging these, together with an extra battery, extra film cassettes, a blanket, a thermos, his tape recorder, and such supplies as my gun, picklocks, and a flashlight, through muddy cornfields in the dark had left both of us panting. My legs, still sore from Thursday's hike up the Gateway stairwell, turned rubbery with fatigue by the time we got close enough to the airstrip to set up camp.

The blanket was Mr. Contreras's idea. He and I had a major fight over my going off without him. The idea that I would go on an adventure with any man except him cut him to the quick, but that it should be Murray, whom he thinks of as an arrogant boor, was especially upsetting.

"We may be at this all night," I warned, "so don't panic if I'm not back in the morning. But if you don't hear from me by noon make sure Conrad gets all the details."

"You going off without telling *him*? Now, that really takes the cake," the old man fumed.

It was knowing that I hadn't told Conrad, though, that finally got him to stop arguing. He even relented enough to pack me up a blanket, some chocolate, a ham sandwich—pointedly not including one for Murray—and a thermos of coffee laced with grappa. That I'd dumped in favor of plain coffee at the diner where we had lunch. Now I was glad of all the provisions. Murray ate the sandwich while I drank coffee and nibbled on a piece of chocolate.

We kept our voices down. Although the buildings around the airstrip were dark, the main office block showed a few lights. In the distance we could hear the occasional truck rumble in through the front gate.

"You don't think your pal Fabian made this up to laugh at you spending a night in the mud, do you?" he rumbled in my ear around ten.

"My pal Fabian is capable of anything. We've been here for an hour and haven't heard anything. Let's go see what's in the hangar."

"You are the original action woman, aren't you? If someone is waiting in there to jump us, I'm awfully exposed if I carry this camera.''

"Hit 'em with it. I'll cover you anyway. In fact, when we get there you let me go around to the entrance. If someone jumps me I'll holler and you can come video us." Murray was as cold as I was. He was only objecting because he hated not being in charge of all the ideas. We carefully packed up our belongings: we'd never find this exact spot again in the dark and we didn't want to leave anything that could be traced to either of us.

The last hundred yards to the hangar we did on our hands and knees between the hills of corn. We didn't want some trucker to pick us up in his headlights as he made the turn toward the warehouses. As we crawled, a fine rain started to fall. Our knees became heavy with mud.

Near the building we found ourselves in a drainage ditch, almost deep enough that we could stand upright. Taking the burden from our weary knees we crept to the back of the hangar, where we stood up fully and rubbed our sore limbs.

Murray took a swig of coffee. We stood for a few minutes, straining to hear, but the concrete blocks would shut out any voices. I pulled Murray's head next to my ear and told him I would go to the front to reconnoiter.

"If I'm not back in fifteen minutes ease yourself off the site and go find some cops." Assuming Grundy County or city deputies would mess with Gant-Ag.

I slipped around the edge of the building and followed the west side, toward the blue lights of the runways. It was a long building, longer than I would have thought they needed for their helicopters and crop dusters. In the dark it seemed interminable.

When I reached the apron at the front I paused again, squinting up the landing strip with the field glasses. I swiveled and watched a truck move down the side road to the warehouses. Finally I slipped around the corner to the entrance. Heavy doors of corrugated metal closed the front. They were locked shut. I could probably pick them, but the noise of their opening would be horrendous. I hunted around and found an ordinary entrance on the east side, the side that faced the main office block. It also had an ordinary lock. I worked it open, then returned along the west edge of the hangar to fetch Murray.

"It took you long enough, Warshawski. I was just about to come looking for you."

"I think we're clear," I muttered back. "But let's stick to the cornfield side just in case."

When we reached the apron we waited for a truck to turn up the track toward the warehouses, then slipped past the corrugated doors to the side entrance. When Murray had followed me in I locked the door behind us.

In the dark I could smell engines. I switched on the flash, shielding it under the blanket in case there were windows up high that would show light to someone in the office block. In this restricted glow we explored the hangar.

Up front, next to a small jet, stood the surveillance helicopters, looking like malevolent insects in the dim light, their rotaries giant tentacles, their feet the stingers. I shuddered and moved deeper into the building. Murray followed, filming everything around him.

Workbenches along the west wall held the wrenches and torches needed to work on aircraft. Fan belts hung from large hooks overhead; underneath the benches were spare rotors, replacement windows, and even several extra airplane doors. Parked neatly alongside the bench stood a couple of carts that airliners use for ferrying equipment to their craft.

We passed two small planes that I supposed were crop dusters. A few helicopters stood behind them. They may have been in for repairs—their doors were stacked neatly on the floor beside them.

"What we really need is a logbook," Murray said, opening drawers in the workbench. "You know—if Fabian is setting you up and there is no plane due in here tonight."

"What would it say?" I jeered. "Another load of hundred-dollar bills arrived today from the Caymans?"

I had to admit he was right. I went to the far end of the

room, where a small desk stood, and started riffling through work orders for fuel, engine parts, and the like. Murray joined me with the camera so he could film the documents for later study.

I was pawing through a pile of coffee-stained invoices when we heard a key turn in the side door. We dropped the papers and dove into one of the open helicopters. Murray slid onto a bench next to the door. I moved next to him, taking my gun from my shoulder holster and easing off the safety.

Footsteps sounded, male voices, laughter, and then the hangar was flooded with light and I made out Jasper Heccomb's voice. "Is she coming or not?"

"No one knows where she is." That was Alec Gantner. "When Messenger called me yesterday morning I told him to give her the information but not so obviously that she would smell a trap. We didn't spot her car on the surveillance cameras, but she could have come across the fields, I suppose."

"We should have thought of that sooner," Jasper snapped. "Didn't you tell me she discovered last week that you survey the traffic on the perimeter?"

"Yes," Gantner said. "But she shouldn't be able to get down here without being spotted from the road. I asked the county people to keep an eye out for her car and it hasn't been seen around here."

"She could have rented one." Donald Blakely spoke for the first time. "How long are we going to wait?"

"Oh, the plane will be here in thirty minutes to an hour," Alec said. "My guess is she'll pop up when it lands. Unless the senator succeeded in warning her off."

"You don't seriously believe she'll pay attention to your old man, do you?" Jasper said.

"We agreed we had to try it," Alec reminded him sharply. "The Chicago cops seem to be keeping an eye on her—my source in Landseer's office says they want to see if she leads them to the girl. Until they give up their surveillance we can hardly do anything."

I didn't know whether the mike on Murray's tape recorder was sensitive enough to pick up their conversation, but moving with extreme care I slid it from my backpack and turned it on. After that we waited for the plane with the musketeers.

They seemed content to stay in the front of the hangar, their spirits frothy with excitement. The conversation jumped around, from what Heccomb wanted to do next— now that the lid had blown off the contractor scam he didn't want to continue at Home Free—to the Bulls' chances for a repeat championship. But they kept coming back to what they wanted to do with me when I showed up. Their descriptions were graphic; a chill washed across my cheeks and arms and I almost dropped the Smith & Wesson.

"You're the man for the job, Jaz," Blakely said. "Didn't she used to have a thing for you in college?"

"Good thing you didn't respond back then—broad that mean could really crack your nuts," Gantner chimed in.

"Give me half a chance and I will," I muttered.

Murray clamped a hand over my mouth but they were laughing too hard to hear me.

"Anton's itching for a go at her," Jasper said. "I left him with your security boy near the plant entrance. Anton's so pumped he may rape the exhaust pipe."

They roared again. Suddenly, when I thought I couldn't take another word of it, we heard a car drive up next to the hangar. A couple of men joined the musketeers; in another minute came the rasping clatter of the corrugated doors opening. Someone started an engine—from the sound it was one of the little carts.

Murray peered around the edge of the door, then put his mouth next to my ear. "They've all gone out to look."

We looked at each other, weighing curiosity against safety. I jerked my head toward the front. Murray nodded and slid from the bench out into the hangar. I packed up the tape recorder, stuck it in my backpack, and followed him, my gun in my hand. Using the bigger machines as cover, we slipped forward toward the entrance. We stopped behind the crop duster closest to the workbenches, where we could crawl if the musketeers returned to the building.

In the light pouring from the hangar we could see the tarmac glistening with rain. Behind the shelter of the wing we watched Gantner talking with a man in yellow waterproof coveralls. They stood next to the motor cart, with Heccomb and Blakely behind them under the shelter of the hangar. The man in coveralls was gesticulating at the overcast sky; Gantner seemed to be arguing with him. It was frustrating to watch and not know what they were saying.

"If they abort the flight we still have enough on tape to go to the federal prosecutor," I said to Murray in a prison-yard mumble.

"They can't abort the flight if it's come all the way from the Caribbean. It'll have to land somewhere," Murray rumbled back.

As if on cue the man in coveralls suddenly sprang to life. He picked up a couple of wands from the cart, glowing sticks for guiding an airplane, and walked forward. The three musketeers pulled out rain gear and climbed onto the cart, which trundled to the middle of the runway. In another minute the landing lights of an airplane appeared below the clouds.

Murray and I ran past the open hangar doors to the side entrance. No one was looking our way. We quickly skirted the building and reemerged on the cornfield side, where we dropped into the drainage ditch. Murray turned the camera on again. He filmed the small jet as it screamed down the runway, then moved up the field so that he was directly opposite the plane. I watched through the binoculars.

As soon as the plane stopped, the driver hopped from the cart to put chucks under the wheels. The musketeers jumped down and waited by the door. Murray filmed the door opening, two men coming down the stairs carrying suitcases, the musketeers slapping backs and taking the suitcases from them. The man with the cart drove them all to the hangar.

The man who'd guided the plane up the runway ran up

and removed the chucks. His partner zipped back with the cart. The two of them climbed into the plane. I supposed they were servicing it.

We were about to leave when a security car drove up outside the hangar, its roof light flashing orange. I trained the field glasses on it. They were powerful enough that I could pick out the Gant-Ag logo on the side, with SECURITY written underneath in big black letters.

A man in a tan uniform got out of the front seat and went to open the back. An enormous man in a Stetson emerged, shepherding what seemed to be a prisoner. My bowels turned to water. It was Conrad. Anton was holding his arms.

□59
Fiery Finish

"What's he doing here?" Murray demanded.

I couldn't imagine. My heart twisting, I kept the glasses trained on the hangar. The man in uniform was talking to Gantner, gesturing at Conrad. Blakely and Heccomb stood by watching. Anton held Conrad's arms behind him while they searched him. I couldn't see what they came away with —maybe his badge, because the musketeers seemed both alarmed and more menacing.

"I have to find out what they're doing," I told Murray. "You go back to your car and try to raise the state police on your car phone. The local guys are apparently in Gant-Ag's pocket. If the state troopers won't listen call Bobby Mallory. In fact, call him anyway. Unless you get flushed wait in your car for an hour. If the state cops don't respond by then, or we haven't arrived, run like hell for help."

I gave him Mallory's home phone number, which I know by heart, and sent him back through the cornfield. Murray thought he should stay, in case it came to a fight, but I persuaded him that our best bet was to get help: if they caught both of us we were doomed.

The rain was falling in a steady thin curtain, turning the ditch grasses to glass. I slipped several times as I ran through the ditch, but pushed myself upright at once, ignoring my wobbly legs, the cramp over my cracked rib, retracing my route to the hangar. I crawled over to the edge of the apron but couldn't hear anything—the mechanics had just started up one of the engines and were turning the plane around. I skirted the building once more and went to the side entrance. I was uncomfortably exposed there if anyone happened to be in the office block at this point, but I managed to open the door a crack. I could hear the conversation but not see any of the speakers.

Blakely was demanding whether Conrad knew me.

"I've heard of Ms. Warshawski, yes—she's a private detective who gets in our way so often that most homicide cops know about her. Is she working for you? If you want a recommendation I'd say she was hardworking and thorough, but too pigheaded to make a good employee."

Despite my pounding heart I grinned a little. That would bear repeating—if we made it through the night together. Blakely didn't know what to make of that answer, so he asked why Conrad had been hanging around the plant entrance. From Conrad's response they'd been through that ground more than once: he had reason to believe he would find evidence of a Chicago homicide, he said, but he couldn't give more details without the permission of his watch commander. Whom he would be happy to ask if Gantner would let him use a phone.

"Mr. Rawlings, you've got to understand our position." That was Gantner, his voice calm, pleasant. "You may be a Chicago policeman, but our security force found you trespassing on our property in—well, what the police themselves might call suspicious circumstances. If Chicago thought we had murder evidence out here, they would have come through our office. So I'm going to ask Deputy Klavin here to hold you outside for a few minutes while we check your story. I know someone in your superintendent's office. This shouldn't take more than ten minutes."

I didn't hear anything for a short bit, then Blakely burst out, "I thought you had the Chicago cops covered. Is this guy legit or is he something to do with Warshawski?"

"Maybe he's really a cop, but is moonlighting," Heccomb suggested. "She's a solo operator, but he might work with her on certain projects."

"Whoever he is doesn't really matter," Gantner said. "If he is a cop—and he did have a badge, remember—we can't afford him taking the tale of the three of us here, and this midnight plane, away with him."

"You going to send him off with Klavin and Anton?" Jasper asked. "I suppose if they drop him ten miles south of here we'd be long gone by the time he made his way back on foot."

"We need a more permanent solution than that," Gantner said. "If he really is a cop he may have some kind of evidence tying you and Don to Deirdre's murder. You say your girl Tish is upset by questions Warshawski's been asking, and that she especially wanted to know about the bat Don brought in a couple of weeks ago. I don't want to be connected with that."

"Damn you, Gantner, you'd better not be trying to back-pedal now. Even if you weren't in Warshawski's office that night you're connected," Blakely said, breathing hard.

"I don't see how any of us can be tied to a maniac like Anton." Gantner, after a brief pause, was at his smoothest. "Didn't Charpentier ask him to go to Deirdre, try to persuade her she was mistaken in what she'd found in Heccomb's files? If anyone's to blame it's Charpentier, for employing such a loose cannon. Maybe Anton—or Charpentier—saw Messenger's bat. Not realizing Don had borrowed it—as a prank toward our esteemed but hypersensitive colleague—they took it away with them to try to implicate Messenger in his own wife's death.

"Jasper, I think you should come in for censure for letting such assholes onto your premises, but I don't see any other connection between us and them. Unless the girl saw Jasper when he went back to erase the disk, we're clean. And we're going to deal with her when she resurfaces anyway."

There was a moment's silence, and then Blakely burst

out laughing. "You're a cool son of a bitch, Gantner. I've got to hand it to you. So what do you want to do about this cop?"

"The fact is, we're all out here tonight, with a plane that hasn't responded to the local air controllers," Jasper put in. "That's a story we can't afford the press or the Chicago cops getting. Especially if Warshawski does show up. How would the senator explain away a dead detective on the family farm, Al?"

"My dad's been able to keep the heat off the murder investigation through his connections in the state's attorney's office. But even the senator might have trouble fixing this story," Gantner responded.

"Klavin says no one else was with this Rawlings when they picked him up. We'll get Klavin to throw up a roadblock around the property. Meanwhile he can check with the sheriff's deputies and the Morris force to see if Chicago let them know they were sending an officer in. If Rawlings does have backup in the area, no harm done. If not, he'll be found facedown in the mud with a bullet in the back of his head—ten miles from here—and Chicago can figure out what happened to him."

The blood thudded in my head. I leaned against the side of the building, dizzy and panting. Wild visions of leaping into the hangar and shooting all of them swam before me. Through the roaring in my head I heard Gantner call sharply to Klavin to come back into the hangar. I couldn't see anything, but Conrad and Anton must be on the apron. Now or never, Warshawski.

I again ran the length of the hangar and hopped into the drainage ditch on its west side. After pulling a spare clip from my backpack and sticking it in my pocket, I took a minute to use the field glasses. Anton and Conrad were on the apron. Klavin was in his squad car on the other side of the fence from the hangar, presumably ordering the roadblock for Gantner. I couldn't see the musketeers.

The plane had been turned around. As I watched, one of the mechanics took a fuel hose from the wing and coiled it back in the ground. He returned to the airplane, leaving the little baggage cart near the tail.

I clambered out of the ditch and sprinted across the wet tarmac to the cart. The men had left the motor running. I jumped into it. After fumbling around the controls I found the brake: it worked by hand. I disengaged it and pulled on the gear lever. The cart started forward. It moved clumsily, swaying from side to side, its single back wagon acting like a flapping tail.

I trundled unsteadily across the tarmac to the apron. When I pulled up next to Anton he looked at me casually, assuming I was a mechanic.

"Conrad!" I screamed. "Get in. It's Vic, get in!"

Both Conrad and Anton stared at me dumbly.

"Conrad! I heard them! They're going to kill you. Get in!"

He finally moved toward me. Anton bellowed a warning and reached for his gun. I fired the Smith & Wesson at him and he jumped back. As I turned the baggage hauler in a wide, ungainly circle Anton started toward us, waving a giant cannon. Clutching the wheel with my left hand I fired point-blank at him. He shot again, wildly, then clutched his groin.

As I headed up the runway I heard more gunfire. I risked a quick look over my shoulder and saw Blakely behind us, sprinting after us. I tried to stay between the runway lights, but I bumped into one and the cart started to turn. I slowed to keep it upright. More shots rang out behind us. Conrad cried out and fell forward.

I pulled up in front of the plane. Using it as a brief screen between me and the guns behind us, I looked at Conrad. Someone in the cockpit switched on a headlight, pinning us, but giving me a good view of my lover. He'd been hit in the right shoulder. He was bleeding, but conscious.

I couldn't take time to bind him up. "We're going to have to try to cross a cornfield in this cart. Murray's waiting in his car about a mile from here."

He nodded, gasping a little, clutching his shoulder with

his left hand. I stamped on the accelerator. The cart moved, but it was no Corvette. Clamping my hands to the wheel, I tried to keep it upright as I headed for the edge of the tarmac.

Behind us the plane engines sounded very loud. Conrad, bracing himself, turned his head. His face went ashen in the jet's headlight. I looked over my shoulder. The plane was taxiing toward us. I gunned the cart's engine but it couldn't go any faster. The jet was fifty yards behind and rapidly closing the gap.

I jerked the wheel hard to the right. The cart caught on one of the runway lights, lurched, and slowly tipped over. We were pitched onto the tarmac. I tried dragging Conrad away toward the field but the plane was almost on us. Flinging myself to the ground, I started firing wildly at its tires. The screaming engines were so loud I couldn't hear the report of the gun. I emptied the clip as the plane roared toward us.

Suddenly it began to lurch, a wounded bird, with smoke spiraling from its wheels. It flopped to the right and landed heavily on one wing. Gyrating on its side, it caromed into the cart. A burst of hot air singed my eyebrows. The turbines were so close I could make out their striations. Bits of the baggage hauler spewed across the runway.

I forced myself to my feet. My legs were shaking badly. Conrad was barely conscious. I managed to hoist him across my shoulders. Somehow I staggered to the ditch. As I collapsed into it the plane exploded.

Sirens sounded in front of us, startling me back to life. I poked my head over the edge of the ditch. The plane was burning in a great white-hot tower. A fire engine moved as close to it as possible and began spraying foam.

I removed my muddy clothes and used my T-shirt to make a pad for Conrad's shoulder. I wrapped him in my sweater and pulled my windbreaker back over my own naked body.

The ditch was wet, not the place for a wounded man, but it would protect him while I found a way to move him. I couldn't support his weight all the way back across the field. I fumbled in my backpack for Mr. Contreras's blanket. Conrad stirred awake as I swaddled him.

"The old man called me," he whispered laboriously. "He was scared. You out here with Ryerson. The goons picked me up by the side of the road. They kept calling me nigger and wouldn't believe I was a cop."

"That's all right, baby." I cradled his head on my lap. "I'm here. You'll be okay, but I need to find a way to move you. You bleed to death out here and your mama will never forgive me."

He smiled weakly but didn't speak again. I propped the backpack under his head and tried to come up with a coherent plan. Our only hope was if they thought the plane exploded when it ran into the cart, and that Conrad and I were incinerated. That might give me time to find help. But that meant I had to make the trek to the stream and hope Murray was still there. I wasn't sure whether my body would keep moving long enough to get there, but I couldn't think of anything else to do.

"I'm going to be gone for a while," I said. "I'm leaving my gun with you. But I hope these guys think we're dead, so that they won't bother to hunt us."

I changed the clip and pushed my trembling legs upright. I was just starting to crawl backward through the field when I heard a new sound. Above the roar of the fire, the noise of the fire truck, louder engines roared. Two helicopters were approaching from the north. I dove back into the ditch as they landed near the hangar. I poked my head up through the grass again and strained to look. They had insignia painted on the side.

I moved Conrad's head to get the glasses from my backpack. The helicopters had turned, so I couldn't make out the logo. Men in brown uniforms poured from them, followed by Murray with his camera photographing the scene. State troopers. I gave a glad cry and scrambled over the top.

□60
A Poet Surfaces

The rest of the night passed in a series of jerky frames. Conrad on a stretcher in the helicopter. Orderlies prying me from his side at the hospital. Me in a hospital bed, being treated for burns, Terry Finchley at my side asking the same questions over and over, telling me Conrad was fine but that he needed blood. Stupidly fighting with the nurses to give a pint—my AB negative wasn't much use to him. Mrs. Rawlings, who showed up around dawn, crying, "What did you do to get my baby shot?"

Lotty appeared at noon and life began to run smoothly again. She tried to persuade me to come home with her. My injuries were minor—a couple of missing eyebrows and a large burned patch on my right forearm—but I wouldn't leave Morris while Conrad was in the hospital, so she booked a room for me at a nearby motel.

They'd extracted the bullet, but hadn't attempted work on his shoulder: Lotty wanted the reconstruction experts at Beth Israel to do that as soon as he was strong enough to move to Chicago.

In the middle of the afternoon, freshly washed and dressed, I went to see him. He was lying so still that my heart contracted. I put my head on his chest to make sure he was still breathing.

His eyes fluttered open. "Hi, Ms. W. I came out to rescue you. Good work, huh?"

"Perfect." I kissed him softly. "You're going to be okay, you know. Lotty's here. Top surgeons are already saluting like privates."

At that he gave a shadow of his familiar grin. I held his hand until he drifted back to sleep, then went out to meet a phalanx of state, local, and Chicago cops. They would have been on me like terriers as soon as I woke up if Lotty hadn't held them at bay.

Bobby Mallory came to represent Chicago, along with Chief of Detectives Kajmowicz and an exceedingly formal Terry Finchley. The state police sent two senior officers, while the local boys provided two each from the town and the county. And the head of Gant-Ag's own security force, Klavin, came, the corn tassel on his uniform gleaming. The feds sent an observer, bringing us to an even dozen, all crammed into a badly ventilated room at the local police headquarters. The stifling air only stoked the ill will among the different jurisdictions.

The meeting was rather confused. The local law had instructions from Gant-Ag to arrest me for trespassing and destruction of private property—namely their jet. After I reported the musketeers' plans to kill Conrad the locals had to back down in the face of Bobby Mallory's fury. The county might still have insisted it was just my word against Gantner's—and whose was heavier?—if not for Murray's tapes: everyone had watched those by now.

Unfortunately the debate among the musketeers about what to do with Conrad was not on film; that had occurred while I was lurking outside the hangar and Murray was fetching help. No one, not even the state troopers, was about to arrest Alec Gantner on my say-so alone. On the other hand, Conrad had a bullet in his shoulder, and Anton had made a statement. Gant-Ag had hired him, as he put it, "to shoot that bad black man sneaking onto their land in the dark." So the locals backed off, although with enough dirty looks to make me feel I needed to wash my clothes after the meeting.

I finally got them to tell me what had happened to the men in the plane. One of the mechanics had escaped through the tail as the machine turned over. He had second-degree burns on his face and arms, but had a good prospect for recovery. Blakely and the other mechanic had died in the wreckage. Anton was in the same hospital as Conrad, recovering from a bullet in the groin. Lucky shot—it hadn't been possible to aim under the circumstances.

Chicago planned to charge Anton with assault against Conrad as soon as he could leave the hospital. They were deliberating charging him with Deirdre's murder. Anton, fighting back, was apparently implicating not just Charpentier, but Heccomb as well. To cover their butts the Gant-Ag people claimed that Conrad had been lurking around the premises for no reason. Despite my contrary testimony they claimed Anton shot him as he was sneaking into the place. The whole discussion ended in a dull stalemate: no one was going to obey Gant-Ag's command to charge me, but they didn't want to tackle Gantner without more hard evidence than Murray and I had gathered.

Bobby wanted at least to bring in Gantner and Heccomb for questioning, but Kajmowicz overruled him. Bobby had to retire in a few years, but Kajmowicz was only fifty. He didn't want the rest of his career ruined by a vengeful U.S. senator.

Two days later Conrad was strong enough to travel back to Chicago. Lotty admitted him to Beth Israel, where they had vast experience with bullet-shattered bones.

Terry waited out the operation with Mrs. Rawlings, Conrad's four sisters, and me. Even Janice, the neurology resident, was there—she flew in from Atlanta to make sure Chicago doctors treated her brother right. It was a four-hour ordeal, but at the end the surgeon brought a happy report. The main joint in the shoulder had been spared; he'd been able to rebuild the damaged clavicle.

Mrs. Rawlings was so relieved at the news that she let me

share in the first family visits to her son. Conrad took my hand in a feeble clasp but went straight back to sleep.

As Conrad's strength returned, though, he began to withdraw from me. I tried to ignore the signs, continuing my daily visits, trying to build a smoother relationship with his mother. Camilla preached optimism, but on the day of his discharge Conrad sent his mother and sisters outside so he could speak with me alone.

He sat on the edge of the bed, his dark eyes somber. "Vic, I owe my life to you. I know that. But my life would never have been in danger if you hadn't gone headlong out to Morris without talking to me about what you planned to do."

I squeezed my eyes shut. I couldn't blow my last chance by shouting out that Murray and I would have slid out of the cornfields as easily as we came in if Conrad hadn't galloped to the rescue.

"I thought if I talked to you about it you'd give me another lecture on the Fourth Amendment." I tried to speak lightly but my words sounded petulant.

"You could be right about that." Conrad took my hand with his sound one. "I think you and I need to cool things off for a while. The last month has taken a real toll on my love for you. You don't have enough room in your breast for compromise."

"But Conrad, Terry was going to arrest Emily Messenger. If I hadn't brought back that tape recording of Gantner and Blakely's conversation, the state's attorney might *never* have vacated the warrant."

"And you couldn't trust the courts to sort it out? You're a sorry excuse for a lawyer, you know that, Ms. W.?" He was trying to joke, but the words had a real sting.

When I didn't try to respond he added, "As it turned out, you were right about almost everything—except that Fabian didn't kill his wife, the way you hoped. But I can't go through another episode like this, Vic. It isn't that I resent you for being right. It's not even the bullet in my shoulder.

It's watching you plunge ahead without regard for anything or anyone except your own private version of justice.''

I was crying so hard when I left the room that I couldn't see. Camilla sprang from a chair to escort me to a bathroom. I stayed there, alone, until I was sure Conrad and his family had left the hospital.

After that it was hard for me to take great interest in the vicissitudes of the case, except as they affected Emily Messenger. While Conrad was still in Morris I had started badgering the state's attorney to vacate the warrant against her. Terry helped. He was angry with me for Conrad's injuries, as well as embarrassed at being shown up, but he was a just cop.

The day I knew Emily was clear I drove to Arcadia House. "I'm hoping Mary Louise Neely brought Emily Messenger to you," I said to Marilyn Lieberman.

She gave a crooked smile. "You know we can't reveal the identity of our residents, Vic."

"Don't spin me around, Lieberman. I didn't come near you, not even with a letter, let alone a phone call, as long as I thought there was any chance I would bring trouble to Emily. The state's attorney has vacated her arrest warrant. The guy who tried to kill her is in the Grundy County Hospital with a hole in his groin. He's never going to be the same he-man he used to be. Donald Blakely has joined that great money laundry in the sky.

"Emily can surface now. She can go back to school and figure out what she wants to do with her life. Is she here? Or do I have to dismantle this city down to the tunnels to find her?"

Marilyn grinned at me and nodded. I'd been certain, a hundred percent certain, that Neely had brought her to Marilyn. But I needed to hear it before I could relax.

"What about her old man?" Marilyn asked. "She's a minor; we aren't about to acknowledge her existence if she has to go back to him."

"Fabian? I think I can fix him. But first I'd like to know what her own desires for the future are."

Marilyn summoned Eva Kuhn. I explained the change in Emily's most-wanted status; Eva reported on Emily's emotional progress.

"This isn't Hollywood, Vic—she's only been here two weeks. She needs a structured environment, lots of support, and some long-term therapy. More than I can provide her. But she's a fundamentally healthy girl, with a lot of gifts. With the right kind of help she should make it. I'd like her to stay here for another month or so, until she feels strong enough to move out. But where she'll go then is a major question mark."

When she took me to see Emily I was amazed at the change in her. Maybe it wasn't a miracle ending, but she already looked younger than I had ever seen her. She had on jeans that fit her and a bold turquoise T-shirt that proclaimed "Our Bodies, Our Lives." Someone—one of the mothers staying there, Marilyn told me later—had braided her frizzy mop into cornrows, complete with multicolored beads.

Emily looked at me with her usual solemnity, but her face relaxed into a grin when Eva said, "Vic thinks she's tough, but she's never beaten me on a fast break. Don't let her talk you into anything you don't like, kid."

"You shooting baskets with Eva?" I asked. "Her elbows are registered weapons—don't go near 'em."

I told her the history of the last few days, who had killed her mother and why, and why she didn't need to worry that anyone else would try to hurt her.

"I saw the plane burning up on television. Was that you?" she said in her shy little voice.

"They were trying to run over me, so I shot the tires out." As she looked at me in awe I added, "I've never been so scared in my whole life, believe me."

"And you really know for sure it was that man in the hospital who killed Mother? You're not saying it to make me feel better?"

"To make you feel . . . oh. You mean that line Dr. Zeitner laid on you, that you had amnesia about killing her yourself. No, sweetie. I'm afraid my vocabulary doesn't run to telling lies just to cheer people up." Maybe I'd be better off if it did, but it was too late in the game to change that now.

"But who did I see, then? That night in your office, I mean. I saw Daddy there."

I grimaced. "Dr. Zeitner was right about one thing: our memories aren't very reliable. If we're convinced that we saw something, that's what we remember. You saw a man's feet, and you were sure they were Fabian's. But think about it logically: you know he was home that night until after you went to bed, because you were waiting up, hoping he would go to bed first. And after he attacked you he went to his own room. He was there when you left the house.

"When you got downtown your mother was already dead. Your dad physically could not have gotten downtown, killed your mother, and left my office before you got there. Even if he came by car while you went by bus."

As she thought it over the pinched look returned to her face. "So does that mean he's right, that I made up . . . made up the other stuff? That I remember—him—doing that to me because I want to?"

"Do *you* think so, Emily?" I asked.

"I don't know," she whispered. "Sometimes I think I must be crazy and that I imagined it all."

"I know you're not crazy, Emily, not after all the talking you and I have done this week, and how I've seen you behave with other people," Eva said, sounding in her assurance like the voice of God. "I don't know your father, but I've met a lot of fathers who are so ashamed of what they've done to their wives and daughters that they pretend it never happened. They get angry, they tell lies, and they try to blame their daughters for what they themselves did."

We let Emily digest that for a few minutes before I spoke. "The question, Emily, is what do you want to do next? Eva and Marilyn and I think it would be good if you stayed here another month or so. Then we'd like to find a place you could live where you'd get the respect you need.

And where you could see a good therapist—someone like Eva, but with more time. You need to think about that, about whether you want to go back to your old school in the fall, all those kinds of things.''

"I can't abandon the boys," she whispered.

"I'm not asking you to abandon them. I'm only saying you need your own life, and that we need to find a better place for you to live than with Fabian. You have rights, Emily, not just duties. You have the right to a peaceful night's sleep.''

She started to cry. "If I move out he'll never let me see them again. He'll be so angry with me. I can't—''

"You leave that to me. I will make sure that you get to see your brothers as often as you want to. Don't worry about your dad's anger. I'll take care of that too. Believe me.''

"But where would I go?'' she wailed.

"We'll work on that together,'' Eva said. "We won't ask you to leave Arcadia House until we have a good home for you to go to.''

Eva signaled to me to leave, asking me to wait in Marilyn's office for a word with her before I went home. As I got up something occurred to me.

"Are you still writing, Emily?''

She kept her head bent over her lap, but shook it so vigorously that the colored beads bounced in all directions.

"I think you should start again. Keep a journal. Write more poems. Your poems will tell you the right thing to do.''

She looked up at that, her face alert in a way I'd never seen it. That was the face that had written "A Mouse Between Two Cats.'' I found myself smiling on my way to Marilyn's office.

61

Mal du Père

Eva joined me in Marilyn's office about ten minutes later. "We have a real problem in what to do with Emily. She mustn't go back to that dreadful father. And he shouldn't keep custody of the kids, either. But if we lodge a formal complaint with DCFS, we'll only generate a host of new problems. If they believe us, they'll whisk the kids into foster care, probably separately. If they don't, we face lengthy proceedings to establish our case. Either way, given Fabian's standing in the community, the overwhelming probability is that the kids will end up back with him."

"There's a grandmother," I said. "Could they go to her? Or are there other relatives?"

Marilyn shook her head. "None that Emily knows at all well. Deirdre had one sister, about ten years older, living near Los Angeles, but she and Deirdre hadn't spoken in years. Fabian has a sister in Baltimore, but I won't trust anyone in that family sight unseen."

I whistled a little under my breath. "Say I can get Fabian to agree to let go of the kids—is it better or worse for Emily to have her brothers with her? She's been their minder for so long, would it give her a chance to grow up if she didn't have to have them around for a while?"

Marilyn and I both looked at Eva, who thought it over for

a minute before answering. "The three are pretty attached. If we could get them in the right kind of placement, with a foster parent who took over the parenting, and let the three of them learn how to be brothers and sister, I'd say keep them together. Besides, even if Fabian isn't going to rape his sons, I don't think he should be trusted with their care. But getting him to agree to let them go is a pretty big if: the guy's a control freak."

"I'll take care of Fabian. You figure out where to put the kids." I got up to go.

"What are you going to do?" Marilyn demanded. "You can't shoot him."

"You're starting to sound like Lotty," I said. "Don't ask. You'll be happier not knowing."

Mary Louise Neely got out of her car as I came down the steps. "Emily must be in good shape, from the look on your face," she said as she passed me.

"She'll do." As I climbed into my car I realized I was still whistling under my breath—"Se vuol ballare" from *The Marriage of Figaro*.

When I spoke to Fabian on Saturday, the conversation was actually more tiresome than difficult. His responses ranged from angry bluster, through denial that anything had ever gone amiss between him and Emily, to a characterization of her as a very sick girl badly in need of help.

"That's where our minds meet," I said. "We're going to get her help. Here's the deal: We will put Emily, Joshua, and Nathan in foster care together. You will support a good day-care program for your sons where they meet and play with other children. You'll pay Emily's school fees and her psychotherapy. And Tamar Hawkings—the woman who helped Emily survive for a week in the tunnels—you pay for her stay in a top-quality residential facility where she can keep her children and receive proper help. In exchange for this you get to keep your job."

"How dare you?" His cheeks quivered in fury. "How dare you interfere with my children? I'll have you arrested if you go near them again. Now get out of my house!"

I leaned back in my chair and waited for his shouts to subside. When he'd finished, after a good—or bad—twenty minutes, my ears were ringing.

"You don't get it, Fabian. My goodwill toward your children is the only thing standing between you and an ugly meeting with the state bar association, not to mention the dean of the law school."

As he started another tiresome litany I spelled it out for him. I told him I had taped evidence that he had collaborated with Alec Gantner, not only in his knowledge of the money-laundering scam, but in trying to get me murdered. Of course, that was stretching the truth—I didn't have any of his complicity on tape—but as I'd told Fabian earlier, the Marquess of Queensberry hadn't hung out in my South Side high school.

I would be willing to publish those tapes, I warned Fabian, as well as his involvement with Gant-Ag's violation of the embargo against Iraq. And, if he proved really obdurate, I would help Emily through the process of testifying against him in a child-molestation suit.

"Maybe your tenure appointment will survive all that. It could be an interesting year for you if you wanted to slug it out in court. I've put our agreement in a document for you. Actually, I got Manfred Yeo to write it up—I've never done enough contracts to know how to write all that stuff down in a cast-iron way."

"You went to Manfred?" Fabian was stricken.

I nodded, smiling seraphically, and held out a copy of a ten-page document our old professor had drafted. I'd gone to him right after leaving Arcadia House on Tuesday. It seemed appropriate that he help finish the story, since it had all begun at Fabian's farewell party for him.

Manfred had been grieved but not shocked by my recital. Of course, he'd been following the Gantner end of the tale in the press, but nothing had appeared about Fabian. Manfred agreed that it was in Emily's best interest to keep her from going through a difficult court case with her father, and promised to draw up a document.

"Fabian was one of my most brilliant students," he told me at the end of our session. "I supported his faculty appointment. But an incident occurred early in his tenure that troubled me. He tried a case—a big antitrust suit—where the legal expenses ran to twenty million dollars. The case was selected for review in the Harvard Law School journal, and they gave it to a jury of very distinguished trial lawyers —all in private practice—who criticized the conduct of the case. They didn't think he had committed misconduct, mind you, but thought sloppy work had led to the high fees involved. They held it up as a typical example of how remote academic lawyers have become from the realities of courtroom life.

"When the article was published Fabian became utterly withdrawn. I found him one day curled up on the floor of the men's room. I helped him to his feet and told him he was in urgent need of psychiatric help. Although the suggestion wounded him, it also seemed to galvanize him back to life. But since then I've wondered whether someone so mercurial was really reliable."

Naturally Manfred had not mentioned the episode to anyone. It must have been in Fabian's mind, though, when I told him I'd been to our old professor—it was the thought that Manfred was privy to his most shameful secrets that made him stop arguing with me about Emily.

"You can tell all your colleagues that you're too shattered by Deirdre's death to provide a good home for your children right now," I suggested as I got up to leave.

Fabian started to shiver behind his antique desk. His fury spent, he had dropped with surprising speed into his shrunken, withdrawn state. On my way out I told the nurse who was looking after his sons that Fabian seemed ill, and not to let the boys play around him.

That night I talked with Lotty about Fabian, struggling to understand why he'd encouraged the police to arrest Emily. "The cops and I were fighting over whether he or Emily had killed Deirdre, but I don't think Fabian saw it that way. He wasn't trying to frame his daughter to get himself off the hook—he's so self-absorbed that it never occurred to him he could be a suspect.''

"But he was trying to get himself off a very particular hook,'' Lotty said. "Not for Deirdre's murder, but for raping Emily. He isn't rational—he didn't sit down and work this out with a slide rule—but if he could convince himself that Emily killed Deirdre, for the reasons his pet psychiatrist outlined, Fabian could convince himself that he had never touched his daughter. Everything you've said about him makes me believe he's a particular kind of paranoid: he can function well in his professional life—it probably holds him together. But he isn't pretending to forget the horrible things he does—beating his wife, assaulting his daughter: he really does forget them.''

"Disgusting.'' I poured myself another whisky. "And you know, he's likely to marry again and have another family.''

"It's not a perfect world,'' Lotty agreed. "You can't get him arrested for complicity in Gant-Ag's crimes? That would solve the problem.''

I shook my head. "We need him to keep working—he has to pay for day care and school and therapy and stuff. Besides, we're having enough trouble getting the musketeers arrested for complicity in Gant-Ag's crimes. Anyway, Fabian wasn't really a coconspirator, he just provided the senator with some valuable legal advice. He only fingered me in the hopes of staying on Gantner's good side. He knew about the money coming in, but he didn't benefit from it: all he wanted was his wretched spot on the federal bench.''

I kept drinking, even after Lotty warned me that I would feel like hell in the morning. But I couldn't get drunk. Not even Black Label could wipe the taste of Fabian from my mouth.

62

Storyteller

Eva Kuhn and Officer Neely were delighted by my work with Fabian, but once I'd resolved Emily's problems I sank into a lethargy that I couldn't shake. I did give a deposition to the state's attorney on Anton's assault against Emily and me in the hospital. I talked to endless federal authorities about the illegal Romanian workers, and I wondered, listlessly, why people from the Treasury Department weren't asking me about the money scams.

Murray came around almost daily, with energetic reports of his efforts to nail the Gantners, big and small. He kept trying to goad me into joining him in his investigations. I felt as though I were being attacked by a jumbo-jet-size mosquito and started hiding out on the lakefront with the dogs.

A few days after Fabian signed my contract, I got a notice of a lawsuit from Gant-Ag, suing me for the cost of the airplane that had gone up in smoke. Depression makes a good protector—I couldn't feel the fear I might have expected. I studied the paper for a long hour, then phoned Gantner's Chicago office and asked for Eric Bendel.

"Give Senator Gantner a message from me about his lawsuit." I cut through Bendel's efforts to pretend he didn't know why I was calling. "Tell him this: If that *was* a Gant-

Ag plane, it raises some puzzling questions about what it was doing flying in all that money from the Caymans, without a flight plan or any other acknowledgment of the Chicago area air traffic. Tell him I have the records of the jets registered with the air towers at O'Hare and Aurora for that night."

That was one benefit of Murray's frenzied investigations. The morning after the plane blew up, Murray had talked to people he knew at the FAA. No one wanted to acknowledge his questions, but two days later he'd received a bootleg copy of the logs for northern Illinois. Whoever sent it had gone to great pains to keep his identity secret—the controllers were federal employees, after all: an angry senator could see that they lost their jobs.

Bendel hung up without saying anything, but a day or two later I came back from a run to find him waiting for me. His navy sedan was double-parked in front of my building, with the children from the second floor swarming around it—limos were still a rarity on our street, even as upscale as the neighborhood had become.

Bendel got out of the passenger seat when he saw me walk up the sidewalk. "Senator Gantner would like to talk to you."

I called the dogs to heel—they were far too friendly and I didn't want them to catch any terrible diseases from licking him. "He can call for an appointment. I'll see if I can fit him in."

The back door of the car opened and the well-groomed figure I knew from campaign ads stepped out. "Humor me, Ms. Warshawski. I'm in Chicago on a very brief visit."

I made an elaborate show of looking at my watch. "Oh, very well. I can give you ten minutes."

As they followed me into the house Mr. Contreras popped his head into the hall. "Come on up," I told him. "Your chance to meet a U.S. senator in the flesh. You can be a witness to any threats or bribes he tries on me."

The old man looked startled, but followed eagerly enough. When we were settled in my living room, me in my sweaty shorts, Gantner and Bendel in perfectly tailored summer worsted, Gantner came quickly to the point.

"I've heard from Eric here that you'd had some communication problems with my brother's company, with Gant-Ag. Gant-Ag is a global concern. You know it's privately held, but it's no secret that our annual sales are in excess of thirty billion. My brother, who's been running the company since I went to Congress, doesn't always have time to understand the details of the operation. Nor should a CEO bother himself about all the nuts and bolts. When I talked to him this morning he told me he'd been mistaken in thinking that the plane that you helped destroy was one of ours—it belonged to a private company in the Caribbean that isn't interested in trying to collect damages. Craig will be sending you a letter to that effect—it should go out in today's mail."

"That will be a big relief, of course, Senator," I said, reclining at my ease in the armchair. "To him, I suppose, as well as to me."

"On the other matters of concern to you, I'm afraid my son got carried away in his zeal to help out a homeless charity here in Chicago. He's been so used to a life of ease and indulgence that when two of his friends suggested he join the board he went . . . well, overboard in his efforts to help them. He's resigned from the organization and won't take any further part in its affairs.

"Alec was a little naive. He was especially confused by his lifelong friendship with Don Blakely. Blakely apparently gave a directive to one of the Home Free contractors that ended in the murder of Deirdre Messenger. It's been a source of great grief to all of us, both my family and the company, to find that the banker whom we all trusted duped us so thoroughly. Donald Blakely apparently was using both the company and his own bank, Gateway, as a front for money-laundering schemes, with Home Free as the focal point.

"When Mrs. Messenger discovered that, she should have gone to the police. Instead, she heroically tried to confront

Don on her own, with the tragic results we all have seen. I'm urging Clive Landseer to use the full power of his office to prosecute the man immediately responsible, Anton Radescu. We're having to absolve his boss, Gary Charpentier, of everything but ignorance."

"Very smart," I said. "Otherwise he might finger Heccomb, and Heccomb might squeal on naive little Alec."

Gantner hushed me with an imperious finger. "Under the circumstances, Ms. Warshawski, I think we're all better off not calling each other names. Eric?"

He was gone so fast I almost had trouble believing he'd ever been there.

When Murray learned of the audacious defense the Gantners were mounting he almost deafened me with his scream of outrage. He had joined me in the backyard with the dogs, where I was watching Mr. Contreras fiddle with his garden. My neighbor put down his trowel long enough to tell Murray about our meeting with the senator—he was relishing the fact that he'd had a front-row seat while Murray was off someplace sweating.

"It's one giant motherfucking cover-up," Murray concluded, ignoring a dirty look from Mr. Contreras. "Gantner must have the whole Justice Department by the short and curlies, because they're willing to buy into this story. And my editor is telling me my trip out to Morris was a freelance job, so he isn't interested in giving me resources to go after them."

"Uh-huh." I played with Peppy's ears.

"What are you going to do about it, Warshawski?"

"A rain dance, I guess. Bring down the waters of God to drown every Gantner cornfield in the Midwest."

"Seriously. You cannot sit on your butt while justice is reamed out."

"You mean you want me to give you free help building the story of your career for you. I'm not doing anything for anyone these days, even when they offer me cash on the barrelhead."

Murray grabbed my shoulders and shook them. "You can't, Warshawski. You can't give up."

"That's what I keep telling her," Mr. Contreras chimed in. "When have you ever let anyone coldcock you, doll?"

"I'm tired. I spent a month risking my life for some abstract concept of justice, and all that happened in the end was my lover left me. Go to one of the big firms. They work for money, so they don't get broken on the wheel of passion."

"Come on, Warshawski. You can't play Achilles—that's a role for a Greek nobleman, not a Polish gutter fighter."

I collected Peppy and went inside. I agreed the whole story was heinous, but I was wrung dry.

The ironic thing was, now that I didn't want to do any work I was turning jobs away. Even a meeting with Phoebe Quirk didn't inspire me. A week or so after my final conversation with Fabian she invited me to lunch at Filigree's. She was uncharacteristically subdued, even apologetic.

"What with one thing and another I caused a lot of trouble for you, didn't I? Maybe Conrad wouldn't have broken up with you if I hadn't gotten you involved."

"I don't know; Deirdre would still have been murdered. I would still have tried to protect Emily Messenger. What's going to happen to Lamia, by the way?"

"Home Free is being reorganized with a new board. Tish Coulomb will take over as executive director. She wants to return the organization to providing services to the homeless, but in the meantime, they do have legitimate funds available for one last building, so the Lamia women will get a chance to bid on that. We're hopeful."

Phoebe was silent for a bit, fiddling with her wineglass, then she spoke rapidly, without pausing for air. "I know I was pretty shirty the last time we spoke, but would you consider doing some work for me? I've got a hot tip on a little biotech company a couple of pharmacy profs have started, but I've never heard of them. I'd pay you six hundred a day plus expenses."

"I'm not interested."

"Vic, I've said I'm sorry." Phoebe spoke with a flash of her usual arrogance, then remembered she was here as a supplicant and smiled. "No one else we work with is as thorough as you. What would it take?"

I thought it over. "There is something you could do for me: get Tish Coulomb to take Ken Graham on to complete his community service. If she's reorganizing Home Free she'll need help. If that works out I'll think about your problem—but this is definitely not a promise to act."

The next day Phoebe called to tell me everything was in train for Ken to start work on Home Free's files. I roused myself enough to make a written presentation for Ken to take to his probation officer. Darraugh was so pleased with the result that he wrote me a check for ten thousand dollars. I tried to turn it down—it seemed excessive for the job.

He spoke with his usual curtness. "I know what you went through on this, Vic. More than you think. A couple of weeks ago some jackass from Gantner's staff, Eric Bundle or Bindle or something, came to tell me that Ken's probation would be revoked if I continued to do business with you. I took a very dim view of that threat, very dim indeed. I didn't bother you with it at the time, but a day or two later when the Gant-Ag story hit the headlines I realized what you'd been up against. You earned this. Cash it. Get a proper office. Take a holiday."

I cashed the check. I even got Mr. Contreras to accept a thousand to help with his taxes. I still couldn't summon the energy to work, but maybe I'd follow the rest of Darraugh's advice and take a holiday, too—lately I'd been studying travel brochures for Reichenbach Falls.

I was mulling it over when Officer Neely surprised me one morning as I returned from a run. She waited in the living room while I took a shower and made coffee.

We talked a little about Emily, then Neely said abruptly, "I'm resigning from the force. I can see that I'm not much good in a hierarchical organization when I don't agree with the hierarchy. I was lucky that Terry was my commanding officer—he rotated me to other assignments and put Gustavo Galatea in my place on the Messenger case, but he didn't write me up or tell anyone else that I'd blown up at him. But I can't go through a situation like that again.

"What I wanted to know . . . Why I came to you . . . There are a lot of stories going around about you, that you're quitting. I wanted to find out." Her face was flushed with embarrassment and she fiddled with her empty coffee cup.

When I told her what I'd been doing lately she took a deep breath. "I have a proposition for you. I'd like to work for you. If you want to take a vacation I could even run your operation while you're away. I've been talking to Emily about her and her brothers living with me. She's willing to do it, and Eva Kuhn thinks it would be a good fit, especially since Fabian will pay for a nanny for Nathan. Fabian would pay their school fees, too, but I need work—I can't support them if I resign from the force."

I laughed. "If you think an operation like mine provides enough income to support two people, let alone three children, you have sadly inflated ideas about it."

She flushed again but wouldn't let me mock her into silence. "If there were two of us we could take on more work, and a wider range of it. I'm very organized. You wouldn't have to worry about the details that bore you. And I wouldn't mind the dull, repetitive jobs, at least not for a while: it would mean I could keep a regular schedule. I'm twenty-nine, I'm very fit, and you know I'm experienced."

It was such an unexpected proposition that I couldn't even decide how I felt about it. I left her with the promise to think it over.

□63
It Ain't Over Till It's Over

July 27th was a blisteringly hot day. At Mr. Contreras's urging I packed the dogs into my car and drove down to the Indiana Dunes for a picnic and a swim. He stayed behind to work on his garden. I left him to a happy afternoon of mulching or mowing or whatever the plants needed.

It was six when we got back. Coming up the walk I thought I heard laughter from the rear of the apartment. The dogs and I went through the narrow passageway and found the yard full of people. When I appeared there came a great cry of "Surprise!" and "Happy Birthday!"

Someone—I later learned it was Ken Graham—had rigged my name up in lights, with the message, "Life Begins at Forty." I stood at the corner of the yard with a foolish smile on my face.

Mr. Contreras surged forward with a glass of champagne. "You thought I didn't remember it was your birthday, didn't you, doll? Have a happy one."

Lotty and Max came over to kiss me. Max handed me a Chinese vase, filled with flowers from his own garden. Much touched, I took that inside, out of harm's way, and returned to greet the rest of the party.

Sal was there, with her current love, a young actress. Mary Louise Neely brought Emily and her brothers. Neely was doing freelance work for me now—we were trying that for six months before considering a more formal arrangement. Emily, her unruly hair sticking out from her head like a giant bush, in jeans and a crimson tank top, looked alert, even young. She had written a joke-filled poem for me, copied out in a careful calligraphy.

Darraugh and Ken arrived together, in a rare display of family harmony. Ken, thinking he might fill the void in my life left by Conrad, had stayed in town to attend summer school. We'd had our promised dinner at Filigree's, and I'd gone sailing with him a couple of times—I'd even enjoyed myself. But Ken's calf love was waning—in the fall he was joining the Peace Corps in Eastern Europe. Darraugh had mastered his disappointment with more graciousness than I'd expected.

Bobby Mallory and his wife, Eileen, Phoebe Quirk, Camilla Rawlings, Marilyn Lieberman, and Eva Kuhn and the rest of my basketball squad were there. Even Manfred Yeo showed up. I arched a sardonic eyebrow at Murray when he showed up with Tish Coulomb. He smiled at me sheepishly, but they looked quite happy together.

Mr. Contreras gave me back my mother's picture of the Uffizi, the walnut frame so expertly restored that only my most anxious searching could find the nicks in it.

Darraugh, at his gruffest, handed me a round-trip ticket to Milan. "I told you to take a vacation. Go find your mother's home. And while you're at it you can visit one of my subsidiaries outside Milan. I've needed an Italian speaker to look in on them. I'll messenger over the details in the morning."

What else can I say, except that good friends are a balm to a bruised spirit? And that Mitch—aided by Nathan—got into the cake and ate most of it. And that champagne flowed like water, and we danced until the pale moon sank.